# LAST DANCE AT
# JITTERBUG LOUNGE

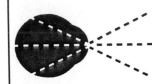

This Large Print Book carries the Seal of Approval of N.A.V.H.

# LAST DANCE AT
# JITTERBUG LOUNGE

## PAMELA MORSI

**WHEELER PUBLISHING**
*A part of Gale, Cengage Learning*

GALE
CENGAGE Learning

Detroit • New York • San Francisco • New Haven, Conn • Waterville, Maine • London

GALE
CENGAGE Learning

Wheeler Publishing Large Print Hardcover.
The text of this Large Print edition is unabridged.
Other aspects of the book may vary from the original edition.
Set in 16 pt. Plantin.
Printed on permanent paper.

**LIBRARY OF CONGRESS CATALOGING-IN-PUBLICATION DATA**

Morsi, Pamela.
    Last dance at Jitterbug Lounge / by Pamela Morsi.
        p. cm.
    ISBN-13: 978-1-59722-802-2 (hardcover : alk. paper)
    ISBN-10: 1-59722-802-8 (hardcover : alk. paper)
    1. Married people—Fiction. 2. Marital conflict—Fiction.
    3. Large type books. 4. Domestic fiction. I. Title.
    PS3563.O88135L37 2008
    813'.54—dc22                                                    2008018983

Published in 2008 by arrangement with Harlequin Books S.A.

All the heroes

# THURSDAY, JUNE 9, 8:22 A.M.

The old man shuffled out the back door of his small clapboard house and leaned heavily on the wood railing as he negotiated the two back steps. He was dressed in clean, striped overalls, a white shirt and a wide-brimmed straw hat. In his left hand, the hand not clutching the rail, he carried a small bouquet of flowers he'd cut that morning, mostly zinnias, with a few canna lilies and two long brightly colored gladiolas.

Beneath the shade of his hat brim was the face of a man marked by time. The lines bore witness to laughter and sadness, hard work and good humor.

He walked the well-worn path toward the shed. He was tall and straight, though his gait was unsteady these days. He was too proud to carry a cane, but he kept a long stick, formerly a rake handle, at the back door of the house. He leaned on it regularly as he did his chores around the yard, but today he spurned it completely.

He checked the padlock on the door to the shed. It was secure enough to keep out the honest people and the most stupid of criminals. The door hinges were on the outside and anyone with half a brain could get the door off in two minutes. To his thinking, if you were going to be robbed, it was better to lose your property to somebody who might have enough sense to make something with it.

On the side of the shed was a lean-to carport. Parked beneath its shelter was the green Oldsmobile that belonged to his wife, Geraldine. He started it up every Saturday and kept it in running condition. But it hadn't been driven anywhere in three years. His own vehicle, a 1968 Ford pickup, was left out in the weather. He didn't figure sun or rain could damage it much. Its color was now an indecipherable mix of aging primer and encroaching rust.

The metal door groaned loudly as he opened it up. He leaned in and laid the flowers gently on the far side of the seat. With one hand on the door and the other on the steering wheel he hoisted himself inside.

The key was in the ignition. He left it

there so he'd know where to find it. He joked to his friends that he hoped somebody would make off with the old clunker in the night. No one ever did. The truth was, a classic car collector had offered him good money to buy it, and he'd been torn. Frugal all his life, it was tough for him to spurn cash money for what amounted to little more than a pile of junk, but he just couldn't part with the old truck. It had seen too much of his life.

He pumped the gas pedal a few times, hesitated a few seconds and then turned the key. The rusty old truck sprang to life immediately. The man smiled. He waited a couple of minutes, ostensibly to let it warm up, but just as much for the pleasure of hearing it run. Finally he stepped on the clutch, shifted into Reverse and turned the truck around so that he wouldn't have to back out the long narrow drive.

Where his gravel driveway met up with the pothole-pocked blacktop, he went to the right, of course. There was nothing to the left but cow pastures and a few lazy oil wells. He lived in the last house on Bee Street, and for the most part, he always had.

The sun glinted in his rearview mirror as he headed west. He braked at the stop sign on the highway and while looking right and left, he gazed fondly at the old nightclub where he used to dance. These days it was church, but he'd always think of the place as Jitterbug Lounge.

With no traffic coming in either direction, he crossed the pavement and continued the blacktop climb. It was a solitary drive punctuated with occasional nodding or waving at neighbors he passed. His eyesight wasn't what it once was, but he knew this road by heart. He'd pulled a little red wagon along this way, delivering milk for two cents a quart. And he'd flown down it on his bicycle on the way home from school. He'd walked it to the bus station when he'd left for boot camp. And driven his wife and newborn son home from the hospital. He knew this road. And he knew what lay at the end of it.

Bee Street wandered through town along the near edge of Versy Creek, around by the ball field and the Pentecost church, to the edge of the business district, crossing Main Street at the fire house. Then it got straighter as it climbed higher. The houses were nicer now, newer, but that was a relative term, as well. Nothing had been new in this town since the 1980s.

At the very crest of the hill Bee Street ended abruptly. If he turned right he could connect up with a half dozen town streets. He turned left and drove across a cattle guard into Hilltop Cemetery.

His parents were buried here, by the huge oak in the southeast section. Geraldine's folks, too, nearer the back road. His best friend from high school, Les Andeel, was in the Gold Star sector, where free plots were given to WWII boys killed in action.

He didn't even think about any of those graves this morning. He headed to one more recent and more dear. He brought the truck to a stop in the far north corner of the graveyard. The door creaked open and he eased himself onto the ground. He retrieved his flowers and walked the length of the pickup, casually steadying himself with one hand. Then he stepped off into the grass, angling unerringly in exactly the right direction. He saw his son's headstone first. As he passed he patted the top of the granite lovingly as he once had the head of the boy long gone. Beyond that was a newer grave. The stone was set, but the grass had not completely filled in the area below it.

"Good morning, Crazy Girl," the man said aloud. He didn't even glance around to make sure he wasn't overheard; he was beyond caring what anybody might think. "It's your birthday, today," he said. "Or it

11

would be if you were still here." He chuckled lightly as if it were a joke. "I brought you some flowers from the garden. I've been taking care of it the best I can, though it's not nearly as nice as when you tended to it."

He squatted down and laid out the flowers, fussing with them more than necessary. He missed her more than he was willing to admit. And it wasn't just her cheerful voice around the house or the companionship of a life shared together. He realized, now that it was too late to tell her, how much he'd leaned on her all those years. Those years when he'd thought she'd been leaning on him.

"I saw that old red bird in the persimmon tree," he said. "I don't know what happened to his mate. I never see her around anymore. But there are some wrens that have made a place for themselves up in the porch eaves. They've still got eggs in the nest. I see the two taking turns with them. I guess we'll be having some little peepers in just a few days."

A gust of wind tugged at his hat. He grabbed for it, almost losing his balance. He caught himself on one knee. He was a little embarrassed, still unaccustomed to the clumsiness of his old age. Then, surprisingly, a smile slid across his face giving a fleeting glimpse of the younger, livelier man he used to be.

"Well now, Geri, you've finally brung me to my knees, haven't you?"

He chuckled aloud and shook his head. Then he lingered in that position for a long moment before reaching out to touch the letters of her name etched in granite.

"I miss you, Crazy Girl," he said. "I miss you every day."

With a sigh of resignation he braced himself on the edge of the tombstone and rose to his feet. The instant he was standing straight, he heard it. As clearly and closely as if he were in a ballroom instead of a cemetery, he could hear the music of Les Brown and his Band of Renown backing Doris Day as she sang "Sentimental Journey." He glanced around. It had to be a radio. He saw nothing and no one, but the sound was close enough that it seemed all around him. He felt a momentary light-headedness. Then the ground was coming up at him.

Jack Crabtree stood in the chaos and dust of a new home building site, looking typically relaxed and low-key. Those around him might have been melting in the heat and humidity of a hot south Texas summer, but he was cool. Wearing the clothes he considered his work uniform, khaki shorts and a brightly colored Hawaiian shirt, he was tall, dark-haired, tan and smiling, always smiling. That was part of his uniform, as well. Or maybe it was his product? He was selling good looks, fit lifestyle, social confidence and affluence. And it was all packaged together in the most eclectic and expensive custom-built swimming pools in San Antonio.

"Oh, I love it up here!" Jack's assistant, Dana, gushed. "It's like I can see forever."

Dana wasn't pure eye candy, but she certainly could behave that way if the situation called for it. The house's owner, Big Bob Butterman, was certainly a client for whom she would pull out all the stops.

"The view is good," Jack agreed, his words evenly factual.

"It is damn good!" Butterman insisted. "Worth every penny."

Jack nodded as the two of them stared off into the distance once more.

The site was high, on the edge of the hill country with the city skyline in the distance. The house itself was a mish-mash of architectural types, old-world Mediterranean meets California contemporary, palatial in scale and boasting all the latest features

14

available in the current real-estate market. It was designed for entertaining and was exactly the canvas for one of Jack's esoteric layouts.

In the back of his mind, Jack was already planning the project. He would use the natural curve of the land for shape. And Plexiclear for the bench around the hot tub. The infinity-edge pool would lead the eye outward as if going straight off the end of the world. It would be phenomenal and every person who saw it would ask about it. They'd ask who built it.

The prospect made his mouth water, but he never let it show.

"With a view like this," he told Butterman, "you could buy a pool from Wal-Mart and your guests would still be impressed."

"Hell, son, my guests will be impressed just by getting an invitation," the man said with a deep, hearty laugh over his own joke. "The person you need to worry about impressing is me."

Big Bob was exactly what his name suggested. Surprisingly tall, and broad as he was high, he'd made a name for himself in the 1960s playing football for Georgia Tech. For the past thirty years he'd been franchising appliance stores with the slogan *Big Bob's Best Deals!*

He talked like he was a regular guy, proud of his humble origins and immune to social climbing. But Jack was pretty sure that a man didn't wear five-thousand-dollar Italian suits, ostrich boots and diamond rings on every fat finger because he didn't mind being mistaken for poor.

The vibrate feature on Jack's phone distracted him. The office knew to hold all calls unless there was an emergency. His first thought was his kids, but he ignored the phone nonetheless. A half minute later, the call kicked over to Dana's cell, as he knew it would. She glanced down at it and, with a smile of apology, excused herself.

"I can give this area the poolscape it deserves," Jack told Big Bob. "I'll put a series of waterfall features on this side, to block the sight of that house on the top of the hill across from you."

He saw Butterman glance in the direction he indicated, suddenly concerned and annoyed with neighbors he'd never noticed before.

"I'll curve it around the landscaping to give it a natural brook appeal," Jack continued. "And the infinity edge will make it a flat surface that just flows off the end of yard. Aesthetically, it will have all the wow factor you can imagine, and functionally it will be absolutely top-notch."

Big Bob was nodding.

"But you'd better call down to your stores and tell them to put those refrigerators and flat screens in a deep discount," Jack warned. "To do this right, and that's the only way I'll do it, it's going to scorch the seams on your wallet."

Butterman hesitated only a minute and then emitted a giant guffaw. "Gottdamnit! I like your style, son," he said. "I do like your style."

Jack smiled, maintaining his laid-back demeanor while mentally pumping his fist in the air in triumph.

Dana returned and continued to ooh and aah about the location as Jack carefully explained the technical engineering details. Men liked to know the details. They always wanted to know how the plumbing worked even if they never intended to look at it.

Butterman asked a few simple questions. But the final one caught Jack off guard.

"Now, you're some shirttail relative of Dr. Van Brugge, right?"

If the man could have said anything likely to make Jack uncomfortable, that was it. Ernst Van Brugge was the most renowned cardiac surgeon in the city. Brilliant, wealthy, successful. He was a beloved physician, socially prominent and a generous philanthropist.

"He's my stepfather," Jack answered.

"Really! Well, I knew there was some connection," Butterman said. "I had no idea it was that close. I thought all his boys were in practice with him?"

"My half brothers," Jack said. "I leave the heart surgery to them. They leave the swimming pools to me."

Butterman chuckled, but Jack was only faking humor.

"Well, your stepdad sure did a great job on my old ticker, I'll tell you that," he said. "In my book, he's a gentleman and a scholar. And I'm more than happy to throw a little business in his stepson's direction."

Jack continued to nod and smile, though the taste in his mouth had turned surprisingly bitter.

It took another hour to completely firm up the deal and sign contract intent. Dana took care of a lot of that, but today the phone kept ringing. He got several more buzzes that forwarded over to Dana's phone. Each time she checked the caller ID, she gave Jack a reassuring glance and then allowed the calls to go to voice messaging.

By the time they were ready to leave, Jack had managed to regain his enthusiasm for the project. Maybe a lot of people thought he owed his success to his stepfather. Maybe Ernst did occasionally steer clients to him. But Swim Infinity was Jack's business. The capital had been his own, the ideas were his own and the blood, sweat and tears that had been invested in the last decade were his own, as well.

So when Butterman finalized his handshake with a slap on the back and an admonition to, "remember me to the doctor," Jack hardly had to fake his goodwill at all.

They made their way through the unfinished front yard to where Dana had parked her car at the curb. The pink Mini Cooper looked like something that Barbie would drive. Jack was sure that Dana wanted to encourage the comparison. She was a tiny person, barely five feet tall, diminutive facial features, slim thighs, little hands and feet. But her legs were longer than would be expected. And her breasts. On her very small frame, Dana's breasts were enormous. Inhumanly enormous, Jack thought, though he never voiced that opinion. Dana was very proud of her bosom and had made a point of telling him, shortly after they'd met, that they had been a significant investment for her.

"Some girls in my high school saved money to go to college," she said. "I stashed my pennies away for a boob job. And I'll bet I've gotten a lot farther in the world with these than any stupid piece of paper could have gotten me."

Jack didn't quibble with results. Scientists had proved that taller men had a better chance of rising to the highest levels in the corporate world. He wasn't sure that bigger boobs did the same for women, but if Dana thought it helped, then that was an edge in itself.

She slid into the driver's seat and turned to him with a dazzling smile on her lips.

"We did it!" she exclaimed.

Jack grinned back at her. "I think we'd better save the wahoos! until we've sedately and professionally driven far enough away that there's no possibility the client might see us."

Dana shifted into Drive and crept along the pavement at a pedestrian pace until they were around the corner. Then she raised both arms in the air and cheered with laughter.

Jack shook his head, chuckling with her. It was great. A big client, a fabulous project and a great coup for the company.

"I feel like celebrating," Dana said.

"Champagne and fireworks, that sounds like a good idea to me. Maybe we could have a party for the crew at your new house. It's time you got some use out of that place."

Jack kept smiling, but it was a little tighter. Jack was building a home in a development not far from the office. It was a grand, spacious place with all the amenities. Jack had planned every bit of the design. But months after construction was completed, it still hadn't been finished inside. That fact and the reason for it was a very sore subject.

"It sounds like fun," he said, hedging. "But I'd better get back to the office."

She pouted, but she didn't press him.

"Who were all those 'emergency' phone calls from?" he asked, deliberately changing the subject.

"Oh, just some of your cracker-barrel relatives," Dana answered. "Believe me, I read Laura the riot act for putting them through on your line. The last thing you need when trying to negotiate a deal with a man like Butterman is the entire Clampett clan distracting you with questions about their cement pond."

Jack chuckled. It was the truth that the only time he ever talked to his aunts and cousins in Oklahoma was when there was trouble with their swimming pools.

21

"My family are the Crabtrees not the Clampetts," he said. "Am I supposed to call them back?"

"I told Laura to have them call your wife," Dana said. "*Family* is really in her job description, right?"

Jack nodded tightly.

"Actually, Claire called back twice," Dana reported. "I told her that you were busy with an important client and she'd just have to deal."

Jack gave his assistant a glance, aghast. He wouldn't have wanted to be a fly on the wall for that conversation.

"Did Claire say what they wanted?" he asked.

Dana shrugged. "I'm sure it was nothing. You know how it is for those women who are trapped at home. They get piddling little concerns all out of proportion. I'm sure she can handle whatever it is on her own. I mean, she used to do my job, so she's obviously capable. She's probably just checking up on you and needed a little reassurance. Give her a call."

Jack flipped open his phone to do just that, but he hesitated. Dana refused to put her call through — Claire would be mad as hell. It was one of the unfortunate facts of his life that his wife and his assistant were not on the best of terms. There was no open warfare, but the undercurrent was unmistakable. The whole situation didn't make sense to Jack. When Claire decided to stay home with the kids, she'd hired Laura to replace her on the job. Laura did fine in the office, but was often intimidated by the clients. Then, one day Dana had shown up at his office and insisted he give her a chance at sales. She had worked out fabulously. Claire should be pleased by that, but somehow she was not.

Jack considered just bypassing his wife and calling Aunt Viv to see what she wanted. Of course, it could have been Aunt Sissy, though last he'd heard, the old woman was in a nursing home. Aunt Opal had died the same year as Jack's grandmother. And Aunt Jesse didn't have a pool. Then he realized that no matter who it was, he didn't have any of their phone numbers in the directory of his cell. He hit the speed dial for the office. It was picked up on the second ring.

"Swim Infinity, this is Laura."

"Hi, Laura, it's Jack," he said, deliberately smiling into the phone. He knew the receptionist was a little bit afraid of him. He always tried to put her at ease. "Dana and I are on our way back. And we've got good news. We made the deal."

"Oh, great!" the receptionist replied.

"Listen, do you know which of my aunts called this morning?"

"Oh, it wasn't your aunt . . . wait a minute." He could hear her shuffling through papers. "The man said he was your cousin, Bernard Halsey from Cat-a . . . Ca-ta . . ."

"Catawah," Jack finished for her.

"Yeah, that's it," she said. "There's a family emergency. I gave him Mrs. Crabtree's number like Dana told me. I told him that she would take care of it."

"Thanks."

"Mrs. Crabtree has called several times since then."

"Okay, thanks."

Jack sighed. He really needed to call Claire but didn't want to do it in the car with Dana. If they were going to have a fight, he wanted to be in the privacy of his own office.

The small pink car made the exit off Interstate 10 and onto the 1604 Loop. Immediately the traffic got worse. As they slowed to a crawl, Dana rolled down her window.

"Get your fat-butted Navigator out of my way!" she hollered to one driver. "That rusting pile of junk should be taken off the road," she screamed at another.

Jack held himself very still. Riding with Dana in a traffic jam was like taking his life in his hands. He didn't want to be shot in a road-rage incident, so he tried not to make any sudden movement. A hot-tempered cowboy might hesitate in killing a pretty girl like Dana, but he knew they'd kill him just to see if the gun worked.

"Bovine-mobiles to the slow lane, dip-shit!"

You could take the girl out of Dimmit County, he thought, but you couldn't take the Dimmit County out of the girl.

It was nearly another half hour before they made it to their exit. The showroom was just off Stone Oak Parkway. It was modest by business standards, but that's how it was intended. Jack wasn't building hundreds of cookie-cutter pools. He was willing to let other companies do that. He was building unique, high-end poolscapes. So while his offices needed to be comfortable and el-egant, he didn't need or want to sell tubs of chemicals to people passing by on the street.

Jack had designed the courtyard in front. It had a three-tier waterwall at one end that ran into a narrow river and off the infinity edge at the end of the building. A wide, Asian-inspired covered bridge connected the parking lot to the offices. It was opulent and eye-popping. When clients saw it they thought to themselves, or voiced aloud, the sentiment that if he could do this with such a small space, he could do fabulous things with their huge backyards. In truth, the narrow confines were a lot harder to get right. Jack likened it to building a ship in a bottle. It was easy to overwhelm small spaces and make an area too busy.

Beside him Dana was chattering about the Butterman deal and how quickly they could get to work on it. As soon as they stepped into the front door, they were surrounded by congratulations.

Swim Infinity had one full-time construction crew composed of Jack's handpicked laborers. If they needed more crews, they subcontracted and his people ran the show. Having your own crew was more expensive, but Jack believed it improved quality control.

All of his guys were shaking his hand and slapping him on the back.

"Laura told us you got the contract with Big Bob," Crenshaw, the crew chief said. "We thought we'd come grab you up and make you take us all to lunch."

Jack chuckled.

"How come you're not out working at the

Pershing site?" he asked. "Isn't that what I'm paying you for?"

The crew chief shrugged. "We're waiting on a delivery and you know how crazy it makes the homeowners when they see us just sitting around."

Jack nodded.

"So we thought we'd do an early lunch, and when we found out about the new job we decided to drag you along with us."

Jack grinned. He was honestly pleased to be invited. It wasn't that long ago that the job of crew chief was his. He was glad that the guys still thought he was one of them.

"Come on, boss," Miguel, a twentysomething with a baseball cap and ponytail, implored him. "My wife's put a fried egg sandwich in my lunch pail. I know you can do better than that."

Jack laughed and feigned reluctance as the guys dragged him away. He waved goodbye to a smiling Laura and a left-behind and pissed-off Dana. They headed out in the crew chief's truck to Take-a-Taco.

He completely forgot about returning his wife's call.

The way Claire saw it, she had two options. She could pace the floor for the rest of the afternoon, silently screaming at her hus-

27

band. Or she could load her kids up in the minivan and go get help. She chose the latter.

Not that it was the easier choice. Zaidi, who was nine, had shut herself off in the solitary peace of her bedroom with a new Harry Potter novel.

"Just leave me alone," her daughter insisted. "What good is a summer vacation if I can't do what I want!"

"It's time off from school, not a holiday," Claire answered. "And even if it were Christmas, your birthday and Halloween all rolled into one, you can't stay at home by yourself."

"How come I never get to do what I want to do?" she countered.

"Because you're a kid," Claire stated firmly. "When you grow up you'll get more choices than you even want."

Claire knew that was cold comfort now.

"You can bring your book, but you have to get in the car."

With a huff of disgust disguised as a sigh, the little brunette with the long French braid and her daddy's flashing eyes, stomped out to the garage.

The twins were equally troublesome. Peyton and Presley, both six, were as close as a brother and sister could be. They could hardly bear to be separated, yet they argued and bickered almost constantly.

Claire had decreed it time for the kids' bedrooms to be divided by gender instead of age. That meant that Peyton and Zaidi switched rooms. The hew and cry of all three children still reverberated on a daily basis.

That was not atypical of summers generally. Changes in routine, no matter how welcome, always caused a certain amount of upheaval. It would have been nice, Claire thought, not for the first time, to be able to complain about it. To whine and unload at the end of the day had always been one of the sweetest perks of being with Jack. He'd always been able to make her laugh at her problems. But she hadn't mentioned a word of this to him. She knew exactly what he would say.

"In the new house, all the kids will have their own bedrooms."

And then she knew what she'd say.

"I'm not moving into that house, Jack. Not now, not ever."

Claire locked up as the kids got situated in the van. By the time she took her place behind the steering wheel, a seating argument was already in progress.

"I'm not sitting on this side of the car,"

Presley insisted. "I'm sitting on the other side."

"This is my side," Peyton answered. "Mom decided last week."

"That was last week — it doesn't stay the same forever."

"Yes, it does."

"No, it doesn't!"

"MOM!" they both pleaded simultaneously.

Claire wasn't listening. The check oil light had come on two days ago. She was praying that the car would start. She'd meant to take it somewhere immediately, but she'd had to get the twins to their swim meet. And then they'd barely got out of there in time to make it to Zaidi's piano lesson. Afterward the twins were starving. By the time they'd finished dinner and Claire had cleaned up the kitchen, it was too late to find any kind of auto repair shop open. So she had put it off until yesterday, which was even worse. Then this morning she'd gotten the call from Bernard and she hadn't thought about it again until she sat down in the driver's seat.

"The sun shines in on this side," Presley complained. "I'm not sitting over here anymore."

"Dumbface, the sun shines in on both

sides. It depends upon what direction we're going," Peyton snapped back.

"Mom! Peyton called me dumbface!"

Claire turned the key and after a little sputter, the engine started. She had to go directly to Mister Auto. That had to be her first stop.

"I'm not a dumbface," Presley told her brother.

"No, I guess not," Peyton agreed snidely. "You're more like a poot breath."

"Don't you call me that!"

"Poot breath."

Presley struck her stubby little finger up her nose and then threatened Peyton with it. Her brother did likewise.

"Oh gross!" Zaidi screamed from the farthest backseat. "Mom, they are doing snot attack."

Zaidi's voice was the only one that could get Claire's attention.

"Stop it!" Claire scolded them all. "Everybody just stop it. Presley, buckle up."

"I want to sit on that side," she said.

"This is my side of the car," Peyton piped in. "You said so."

"I did say so," Claire agreed. "Presley, buckle up. And the next time I hear anything about snot attack, you're both going to timeout."

31

Neither looked particularly threatened by that. They were getting too big for time-out. Claire wasn't sure what came next in terms of disciplinary strategies. Prison? The rack? Claire didn't have a clue. By the time Zaidi was their age, she was already obedient — pouty, but obedient. The twins didn't even seem headed in that direction.

She pulled out of the driveway slowly, carefully avoiding the big crack that had opened up just inside the curb. Claire hadn't figured out how to do a repair. It was on her list of things to figure out. Like how to fix the broken garbage disposal in the kitchen. How to seal the windows in her bedroom that let in cold air. And how to deal with the leak in the bathroom lavatory beyond putting a bucket under it and emptying it regularly. Those were all things that were on her list.

So was, how to get your husband to return an emergency phone call. It was his family after all, not hers.

She glanced in the rearview mirror as she headed down the street and saw her beautiful children behind her in the seats of the minivan. It was *their* family, she reminded herself.

Claire was a great believer in family. It was something that had always been in short supply in her own life. Her father was a career diplomat, her mother brilliant and charming at his side. As their only and adored child, she got to see the world. They had lived and worked sometimes in distant provinces, sometimes in palaces. Claire had learned art and culture and history with her parents. And she learned loneliness from boarding school. She had been determined to make sure that her children grew up in an ordinary home, a simple family place that was filled with love.

That's what Jack wanted, too. They'd talked about that the summer they'd spent together as lifeguards at the pool, the summer they had fallen in love.

"I'm not like my parents," Jack had assured her. "I'm not interested in having my photo in the *AroundTown* pages. 'Dr. and Mrs. Van Brugge seen at the fabulous midtown gala, donating a fabulous check to the fabulously worthy cause of the Society for the Prevention of Hangnails.' Thank you so much, dear Dr. Van Brugge."

His gushingly theatrical pronouncement made Claire giggle so hard that she snorted.

"At least your parents are only stuck-up as a hobby," she pointed out. "For my folks, it was a career choice. 'Ambassador and Mrs. Keeding wear traditional ceremonial

33

dress at the coronation of tribal leader Katu wo Watu in the small African emirate of Bango Cheeputti.' "

Jack laughed and slung his arm around her neck pulling her closer. "I am so lucky I found you," he told her. "I was beginning to think I was the only person in the world who doesn't want to be rich and famous."

Claire shook her head. "No, rock stars are rich and famous. That's very low class. What our parents and their friends want is to be wealthy and renowned."

"You're right," Jack agreed. "That sounds so much better."

This time they laughed together.

"I'm just an ordinary working guy and that's all I ever want. And I don't need a country club membership, though they do have a very nice pool. I just want a job I like, a wife who loves me and a couple of healthy kids."

She'd already believed she was falling for him. That confession had sealed the deal.

They were seated together, as they had been so many nights after closing and cleanup, at the edge of the pool, their feet dangling in the water. There was something about those evenings together with a sky full of stars and the gleam of moonlight on the water.

Sometimes they kissed. Sometimes caressed. And as August hurried toward September they allowed themselves a sexual intimacy that even now, after twelve years of marriage, could still cause Claire to blush.

It had always seemed unbelievable that he could be hers so easily. Every female eye between thirteen and eighty-three followed him as he passed. His long, lean swimmer's body attracted attention, but it was his easy smile that made him such a favorite.

"I love you, Claire," he'd told her beneath those stars. "I need you. All I ever want in the whole world is you."

That was so long ago. Now it seemed that Jack wanted much more.

The sound of Peyton's voice snapped her out of her reverie. "I thought we were going to Toni's house," he said. "If we are going to Toni's house, the sun would be on Presley's side of the car."

"We've got to stop at Mister Auto," Claire told them.

"Noooooooooooooooo."

The groan was unanimous and in unison.

"I hate Mister Auto," Presley said.

"Do it later," Peyton begged.

"I can't do it later. I have to do it now," Claire told them. "We have to take care of the minivan. If something happens to it, we won't have any way to get you to swimming and piano and T-ball and Sunday school."

The twins continued to whine.

"Ugh." The sound Zaidi made was a blend of disgust and disbelief. "It's not like we're in love with this beat-up old minivan," she said. "You should get Daddy to buy you something new."

"We need a car like Dana's," Peyton said. "Have you seen the car that Dana has? It is so cool."

"I know," Presley agreed. "Dana has the best car in the world. Mom we should get a car like that."

Peyton snorted derisively. "Mom can't have that kind of car. It's for cool people who are young and hip. Mom's way too old and fat."

"Hey!" Claire was stung by the words. "That's a mean and hurtful thing to say to me."

"I didn't mean it like that," Peyton dodged. "I just meant you're like a mom and moms are not all hot and cool and stuff."

"Hot or cool?" Presley correctly snidely. "You should make up your mind."

Claire ignored that. "It doesn't matter how you meant it," she continued. "Hurtful things even spoken casually are still hurtful."

The children were momentarily subdued.

"It's not like you're really that old, Mom," Zaidi said, attempting to smooth the waters. "And you're not fat, you just seem fat next to Dana."

"Yeah," Peyton agreed, warming up to the subject. "It's like you're just a little bit fat and Dana is like totally not fat."

That didn't make Claire feel better, but she let it go. The truth was, these days she felt both old and fat. It was futile to argue that she wasn't.

She pulled into Mister Auto and the kids all piled out of the car. She was told it would be at least forty-five minutes, but she wasn't concerned. She knew that with her kids running wild in the waiting room, the mechanics would be encouraged to get her in and out in record time.

Zaidi sat down to read in a corner with very bad lighting. The twins quickly located the TV's remote control and were flipping through channels looking for something they wouldn't be allowed to watch at home.

Claire decided to try Jack again, though making a call was difficult. The TV was loud, but if she stepped outside, the noise level of the shop was even worse. She walked out of the room and across the parking lot where she could keep an eye on the kids through the glass and have a better chance at hearing what was being said. Even there she had to stick a finger in her other ear to drown out the traffic on the street.

"Swim Infinity, this is Laura."

The last time she'd called, they told her he was on his way back to the office. He had to be there by now.

"Hi, this is Claire Crabtree again. Is Jack in?"

"Uh, Mrs. Crabtree. He was here, but he went to lunch."

"He went to lunch?" Claire was incredulous. She was barely able to hold back her anger. "Did you give him my message? Did you say it was a family emergency?"

"Well, I . . . I . . ." The receptionist sounded decidedly shaky. "Let me transfer you to Dana."

"I don't want to talk to Dana!"

Click. Click-click.

"This is Dana."

Claire hesitated, drawing a deep calming breath.

"Hello? Who is this?" Dana was impatient.

"It's Claire," she answered evenly. "I need to talk to Jack."

"He's at lunch."

"Yes, that's what Laura told me. It's a family emergency and for some reason the receptionist won't put me through to his cell."

"Is it about the kids?" Dana asked.

Claire was tempted to answer none of your business, but she managed to restrain herself. "No," she said. "The children are fine. This is something else."

Dana hesitated as if expecting Claire to elaborate. She wasn't about to.

"Well, Jack has left strict orders not to be bothered if it's not the kids or a client."

"Just put me through to his cell phone. You won't be blamed for the interruption."

"I'm sorry, Claire, I just can't do that," Dana answered, her firm, unruffled tone was extremely patient, as if she were dealing with a willful child or a deranged person.

"Dana, am I going to have to come out there and sit in the lobby with my children?"

That shut the woman up. Claire could almost see her floundering on the other end of the line. Victory was almost within her grasp when she was suddenly distracted.

"Mom!" Zaidi called from the doorway to the waiting room. "The twins are tearing up stuff."

"Got to go," Claire said to Dana and ended the call abruptly. She hurried across the parking lot and into the building to discover that Peyton and Presley had used the seat cushions from the cheap waiting room couches and chairs for a pillow fight. The ruckus had resulted in knocking a lamp off a table. Fortunately, the lamp was mostly metal and plastic. The lampshade however, would never be quite the same.

The twins were timed-out in opposite corners while Claire righted things as best she could and apologized to the waiting room's other two occupants, an older balding man who was very nervous and skittish and a smiling guy who apparently didn't speak English but understood kids.

They were out of there fifteen minutes later, which included a five-minute lecture on regularly checking the oil level because you are *never* supposed to actually run out.

Claire considered just driving to Swim Infinity as she had threatened. The image of being there in Dana's face held a lot of allure for her. But she knew better than to try to play games with the woman. Dana was the kind of person who always won, no matter what. There were people like that in every city, in every culture. And there were people who wasted their whole lives butting up against them. Claire wasn't going to do that. She had determined that her safest course of action was not to compete.

As she drove across town to the wealthy neighborhood of oversize homes near the Medical Center, she thought about Dana. She didn't think about Jack. Thoughts of Jack haunted sleepless nights and her idle thoughts. *Maybe if I had done this. Maybe if I had said that.* The unending analysis, self-recrimination and second-guessing drove her crazy. She'd given up thinking about Jack. So she thought about Dana.

Dana was a conniving, calculating bitch and a potential home wrecker. While Claire had been home virtuously breast-feeding twins and chasing a preschooler, Dana had managed to lure Jack, Claire's Jack, into believing things, wanting things that he'd never been after before. Her husband had changed. Their marriage had changed. She wasn't sure when it happened or why it happened. But she was sure it was Dana's fault.

When she and Jack had run the business together, all he'd wanted was to design unique pools and support his family. Now he wanted money, he wanted status and he wanted social position.

Claire knew she was lucky that he still wanted to be married. And she was grateful that Jack was not the kind of guy who would have an affair. But their love had somehow worn out. And their relationship seemed as if it was headed nowhere.

How did that happen between two people who'd been so much in love?

She parked the minivan in the circular driveway in front of the lovely Shavano Creek home of Ernst and Antoinette Van Brugge, Claire's in-laws. The kids were all racing to the door before she'd even made it out of the car. Toni greeted them as if the unexpected drop-in was the highlight of her day.

Four tables of gray-haired and heavily bejeweled bridge players occupying the living room belied that fact. The twins headed immediately for the elaborately decorated punch table.

"Don't touch anything!" Claire warned them under her breath.

"Hello, hello." Claire smiled and nodded toward all the ladies, sure she had cemented forever their opinion that Toni's son, Jack, could have done better.

"You can have two cookies each," Toni told the children. "Eloise, will you set places for them at the table in the family room and get them some milk?"

The maid, uncharacteristically uniformed for the day, hustled them off in that direction, while Toni led Claire into the library nearby.

"What a surprise," Toni told Claire. Although Claire was convinced her true sentiments were more along the lines of, *What in the devil are you doing showing up here unannounced with three kids in tow?*

"I've been trying to call all morning, but it went straight to the answering machine," Claire explained.

"I had Eloise unplug it," Toni said. "We were too busy to chat."

"There's been some kind of accident up in Oklahoma," Claire continued. "Bernard called me. Old Mr. Crabtree is in the hospital in a coma or something. Jack is listed as the person to make medical decisions for him."

"Oh, my goodness." Toni's face and demeanor changed immediately. "Poor old Bud," she said. "I've worried about him since Geri died. I should have gone to her funeral. I've been beating myself up about it every day since."

Claire hadn't gone to the funeral, either. Jack hadn't even suggested it. "Somebody has to stay home with the kids," he'd said. Claire had complied without argument. They never went up to Oklahoma. The old relatives had never even seen their children.

"So I suppose Jack is going up there," her mother-in-law said to Claire.

"He doesn't know yet."

Toni's brow furrowed unpleasantly.

"I can't get through to him at work," Claire said. "His cell phone goes through their receptionist and they just keep saying that he'll return my call."

Toni walked over to the desk nearby and picked up the phone. She punched in the numbers and only had to wait a moment.

"This is Antoinette Van Brugge, Jack's mother," she said with a voice as smooth as sugar and as tight as a garrote. "I need to speak with my son immediately."

There was a half minute of silence.

"Oh, Jack, I have some terrible news," she said.

# BUD

I was in the water. It was dark and gray and cold. I was exhausted. But I was alive and I had to stay awake. To sleep was to drown. I had to stay awake. I was so sleepy, but I had to stay awake. Maybe if I could open my eyes. But my eyes wouldn't open. My arms wouldn't move. I would surely drown. I would never make it home. I'd never be with Geri again.

Wait! I couldn't be in the water. I had been with Geri. We'd had a life. I wasn't in the water. I'd been rescued.

That thought calmed me. I realized that my heart was pounding in sheer terror. The same terror that I'd felt in the water. But I wasn't in the water now. Where was I?

I did what I could to take stock of my surroundings. I couldn't open my eyes. But I could smell. It was that antiseptic scent. Medicine and rubbing alcohol and plastic all mixed together in one memorable odor.

Once you'd been in a hospital, you would recognize the smell anywhere. And there were the sounds, too. Incessant digital beeping and the unfamiliar huff that was somehow connected to my own breathing.

My eyes were closed.

What was I doing in a hospital? I couldn't remember what had happened. I'd been at the cemetery. It was Geri's birthday. And now I was here.

But I wasn't alone. Someone was murmuring on the other side of the room. As they came closer I recognized Viv's voice. My sister-in-law's voice was similar to Geri's, but it was higher and the sound carried across the room.

It was funny that I could recognize the sound, but had no sense of the words being said. It was all just noise, familiar noise, but unrecognizable.

Someone was standing closer to me now. Was it Viv? No, it was a stranger. Perhaps it was a doctor or a nurse. I couldn't tell, but I knew it was a stranger. I don't know how I knew that, but I did.

Sometimes you can know things and you don't know how. It was that way the day I first met Geri. The day I came to her rescue.

The memory swelled up life-size in my mind. I gave myself up to it. The snap of

46

cold air on an autumn morning. My scratchy wool scarf around my neck. The smooth feel of my overalls and the pinch of last year's boots on my feet.

It was 1933. The scent of fall was on the breeze. There were clouds high in the sky, like angels I suppose, so quickly passing by above us with little time to concern themselves with our petty troubles. The leaves on the trees had colored up brightly. A welcome change from the frightening summer of heat and drought. It was reassuring that nature hadn't turned against us completely.

I remember the year exactly, because it was one of those years that stood out in my life. Some years seemed the worst. And in others wonderful things happened. But there was always a little of both in every sliver of time and it's only when you view a whole life that any of it ever makes sense.

But I didn't know that in 1933. All I knew then was that my father had died in February. And after the funeral, my mother took to her bed. I don't mean she was ill, at least not in any way that was obvious. She just couldn't seem to stir herself to get up and live.

At first the pastor came repeatedly, along with two of the ladies from the church auxiliary. Several of her longtime friends, wives in the neighborhood, all pleaded with her to face her loss, to get up and get on with it.

She just couldn't.

"If you won't do it for yourself," Old Mrs. McCrary told her, "then you must do it for Buddy. The boy needs you."

I remember Mama turning to look at me, standing worried and anxious at her bedside. Her eyes were huge and ringed with dark circles of care. But she managed a small smile just for me.

"Buddy's nearly a man already," she said. "He can take care of himself."

I was ten.

In the end, though, she was right. My childhood dropped away from me right there, and I became her caretaker and her sole support.

That's what I was doing that autumn day, making a living for us. Our Guernsey cow, Becca, didn't know that there was a depression. Every morning and evening she gave me two buckets of milk, just as she had when times were good and my father was alive. I strained it into the milk can, put the can in my red wagon, a Christmas gift from better days, and delivered it to my customers all over Catawah.

Finished and on my way home, I had just

48

passed the Pentecostal church when I noticed a crowd of boys standing around the piss pit just dug for the church's outhouse. They were all guys I knew, Piggy Masterson, Orb O'Neil, Stub Williams, the McKiever brothers, Hackshaw Hurst. They were laughing and having a good time. I figured that something had fallen down in the pit and couldn't get out. The churchmen hadn't gotten around to moving the outhouse over. That's what you did back then when your pit began to fill up, you dug a new one and slid the outhouse over the top of it. Then you'd lime the old pit and use the dirt dug from the new pit to fill in what was left.

But during this process there was always a time when the new pit was just a big open hole in the ground and a squirrel or a possum might fall inside. Unable to get out, the creature would scramble frantically, which was always entertaining for boys to watch.

Although I knew Mama was home and there was plenty there that needed to be done, my curiosity got the best of me. I left my empty milk can in my little wagon at the side of the road and went to see for myself.

I heard her before I saw her, but the sight

itself was something I'd never forget. She was a wild-haired little ragamuffin with a dirty face and threadbare overalls.

"You don't scare me, Piggy Masterson," she declared adamantly from the bottom of the pit. "I'll whup your sissy lily liver and all your friends, too."

The boys found that uproarious. She was younger than us by a year or two and small even for that age. Piggy, the biggest kid in school, was twice her height and outweighed her by a hundred pounds.

"I'm not scared of any of you!"

There was truth in her words. She stood fists clenched, eyes narrow, defiant. I admit to being totally fascinated by her. She was like some strange creature I'd never seen before. Her hair, instead of being neatly bound in pigtails, was sticking out in every direction. Her stance downright pugilistic. She couldn't really be a girl, I thought. Girls would cower and cry and be helpless until someone came to their rescue. This girl was talking mean as a hornet and didn't even seem to realize that she needed help. She was a crazy girl, pure and simple. I think I must have been drawn to her that very minute.

"What's going on here?" I asked Stub. The nine-year-old had lost his right arm to a threshing machine. He was now Piggy's chief sidekick and spokesman.

"We're just trying to get rid of some junk," he said. "We figure Dirty Shirts's daughter probably is garbage and she'll feel right at home in a pit."

That's where I'd seen her before. Her, or one of her sisters, they all looked pretty much the same, riding on the junkman's garbage cart. In those days, picking up trash was a trade, just like carpentry or tailoring. Our junkman was named Darby Shertz. Kids, with our affinity for nicknames, called him Dirty Shirts, because that's pretty much what he wore.

Dirty Shirts rolled his pushcart up and down the streets of Catawah every day, picking up cast-off items, broken crockery, bent metal, rags. The citizens paid him a pittance to haul off the things they couldn't use. He made a living from repairing and reselling these items. In the best of times it was a poorly paid and unpleasant job. During the Depression, when basically every human in town was living hand to mouth, it was hardly a living at all.

Dirty Shirts and his wife, a thin, exhausted-looking woman rarely seen in town, lived in a tin-roofed, tar-paper shack at the dump. They combed through the scraps of other people's rubbish as a way of life.

They had a whole slew of daughters. One was in my class at school. She was routinely made the butt of jokes. I remembered one day in class when all the girls who sat in desks behind her put clothespins on their noses. The suggestion that she smelled bad was a great joke. I'd chuckled along with everyone else. But this girl, a bantam hen ready for battle, was somehow no laughing matter.

I squatted down to get a better look.

Beneath the dirt and the hardened expression, the girl had a heart-shaped face. Those flashing eyes were the warm brown of maple syrup. And her chin, held high in the air, had a dimple on one side.

"So you're Dirty Shirts's daughter," I said.

She gritted her teeth and her words were almost a snarl. "I sure am. And I'm proud to say so. He's the best daddy in the whole world. Better than yours. Better than all of yours." She used her arm in a gesture to include the entire motley crew.

That statement had the boys bent over with laughter. It was too ludicrous to be believed. But she obviously believed it.

That's when I decided to rescue her.

"She's a raving maniac!" I declared. "The

confinement has driven her out of her head. She doesn't know what she's saying."

She opened her mouth in her own defense. I gave her a conspiratory wink. At first she seemed almost puzzled, but then she eyed me more closely. Slowly I saw understanding dawn on her. She was quick-witted and smart as the dickens.

Suddenly she began running back and forth in the pit. Her hands in the air, yelling like a crazy person.

"My God, what's she doing?" Orb asked.

"She's lost her mind," I answered. "Quick, somebody go get a bucket of water."

"A bucket of water?"

"That's what you do when somebody's having a fit," I replied. "You throw cold water on them."

"Who's got a bucket?"

"We'll have to get one at Hackshaw's house."

"The nearest water is in Murphy's cistern."

Within seconds they were all running off just as I knew they would. I turned to the girl.

"Give me your arm, Crazy Girl," I told her.

I was able to pull her out easily. She weighed little more than a bag of feathers.

"Thanks," she said.

"You did it," I assured her. "I've never seen anyone act so much like a wild woman."

She grinned at me.

"I'm Geri," she said.

"Jerry? That's a boy's name."

"No, it's short for Geraldine," she answered. "What's your name?"

"J. D. Crabtree, but my friends call me Buddy."

When she smiled her eyes almost disappeared in the crinkles of her eyes.

"Then I'll call you Buddy," she said. " 'Cause you're the kind of friend I want to have."

I shook my head in disbelief. "I'll call you Crazy Girl, 'cause that's what you are. You'd better get out of here before they get back," I told her.

"I'm not scared of them," she said, defiant once more. "I can fight anybody I have to."

"I'm not worried about fighting," I told her. "That Piggy is so clumsy, he might trip and fall on us and we'd be squashed like bugs."

She laughed then. It was the first time I'd ever heard the sound. It was better than music, sweeter somehow.

"I like you, Buddy Crabtree," she said.

Then she jumped up and took off running. I watched her go with the strange, certain sense that she was important somehow to my life. She turned out to be the most important person I would ever know.

Just thinking about her made me feel better. I felt myself, once again, in the vacant lot beside the church that autumn morning. And from somewhere in the near silence of the place, I could hear the buzzing bees in clover and the distant barking of a dog. I began to hear music. I recognized it immediately, Count Basie's orchestra playing "Wiggle Woogie." A smile came to my face. I began tapping my foot. I glanced around. It must be playing on a jukebox somewhere.

That stopped me. There was no jukebox in town in 1933. And Count Basie wouldn't play "Wiggle Woogie" until years later.

But I wasn't in Catawah. I was in a hospital.

Was I hearing it here, in the hospital room?

# Thursday, June 9.
## Evening

In the kitchen Jack could hear the twins arguing with each other at cyclic volume levels, as Claire cooked dinner. He wasn't hungry, but he could appreciate the effort to include him in a meal. He was leaving for the airport within the hour and he didn't know how long he would be gone.

He had his suitcase open on the bed and he stared into his underwear drawer. Jack was a briefs guy, specifically ribbed knit in navy or gray. He owned a million pairs. Tonight, in the drawer, there were only boxers. And novelty boxers at that, decorated with lipstick kisses or leprechauns or reindeer. He wanted to swear, but he didn't bother. A man ought to be able to have a supply of clean underwear. But sometimes the simplest things were the most impossible.

He knew Claire was busy, but somehow she could never get around to doing his laundry. It shouldn't be a problem. He was perfectly capable of doing it himself. But that always caused a fight. If he put a load of clothes in the washer, she took it as a criticism.

To Claire it meant that she wasn't doing her job. Which meant that she was not a good wife. Which meant that he was sorry that he'd married her. Which meant that he wanted out.

Before they reached the rinse cycle the *D* word would be on the table again. It all just made his head hurt.

If he wanted a divorce, he would get one. All he wanted was clean underwear. That was just not going to happen.

He dug through the boxers until he came up with three that didn't have lights or bells. One had a giant peanut on the front flap, another looked as if it were made from candy wrappers and the final one had birthday cakes with the directive, EAT ME! The twins had gotten him that pair, thinking it was very funny. Their weird sense of humor didn't indicate any comprehension of the vulgar suggestion.

He put them in the suitcase. If he needed more, he'd just have to buy some. He wasn't sure what to pack. His typical wardrobe didn't seem exactly suited to a place like

Catawah. It always seemed to him more like a jeans and T-shirt place. Should he take dress clothes? It would probably be the smart thing to do, but if he did it would seem as if he were planning on going to a funeral. But better to carry it than to not have it, he decided and pulled his most dour dark suit from the back of the closet.

He heard a car pull up into the driveway and walked across the room to peek out through the blinds. He was surprised to see his mother's car, but was grateful, too. Maybe she could give him a ride to the airport, and Claire wouldn't have to load up the entire crew in the minivan.

When the passenger door opened his brow furrowed. Both his mother and stepfather were here. Ernst had only been to his house a couple of times and that had been years ago. Jack fought the inexplicable impulse to run out and bar the front door. The mid-century three-bedroom ranch home that they'd managed to buy the year after Zaidi was born was cute and on the far edge of a very good school district. Jack had been very proud when he and Claire had signed their names to the mortgage note. But compared to his parents' fabulous home and the million-dollar stucco fortresses of his step-brothers, it was extremely modest. The new house, near his office, would be a showplace. But, to Jack, this home looked like what a guy who didn't finish college might live in. A guy like himself.

"My parents are here," he called out to Claire from the hallway.

"Toni!" he heard the twins screech in unison.

They came racing through the living room and actually got the front door open before Jack could get there. His stepfather was standing in the living room before anything could be done to stop him. The man was tall and stiff, with a prominent jaw and a confident stance. He was far from handsome, with thinning blond hair, slightly bulging eyes and glasses. There was a reserve about him that was almost glacial. But he thawed somehow when it came to his grandchildren. To them he was Pops. For Jack, Ernst might be the only father he'd ever known, but still he called him sir.

Toni, Jack's mother, was slim and chic. She was always in the right place wearing the right clothes and saying the right things. Rigorous personal grooming, good genetics and an excellent plastic surgeon kept her as fresh and youthful as women a decade younger.

He gave her a loving, but dutiful peck on

the cheek.

"We weren't expecting you," Jack said, before realizing how unwelcoming it sounded. He doubted if his mother noticed. The kids were all talking a thousand words a minute, competing for her attention. Even Zaidi, who usually allowed herself to be overshadowed by her siblings, had urgent things to say.

Claire came in from the kitchen. She was barefoot and wearing ragged jogging shorts that had seen better days. There was no need to guess about the age of her faded blue T-shirt. Emblazoned across the front of it was KidsFair 2000. Her hair, which was actually a butterscotch blond, appeared mousy brown pulled back from her face in a ponytail.

Ernst hugged her.

"Hello, gorgeous," he said to her, as always. "You get prettier every time I see you."

It was his standard greeting for females between eighteen and eighty-nine, though it wasn't insincere. Ernst was a casually congenial guy. He was most comfortable in the company of men, but he liked women and he liked to see them smile. He'd figured out early in life that a nice compliment was the quickest way to accomplish that.

His stepfather turned his attention in Jack's direction. "What's the status with your grandfather?" he asked.

Jack knew his stepfather well enough to know this was not a polite inquiry. Dr. Van Brugge expected to be briefed on the old man's condition. Jack responded as factually as a resident giving a report.

"According to the information that I know now," he said. "And I'm getting all of that from the family. The doctors believe that his fall was actually due to a stroke. He struck his head as he went down, and that apparently complicates the assessment of how much damage has been done."

"How old is the fellow?" Ernst asked.

"Eighty-four."

Ernst shook his head. "It's not good. But it might be several days before you know anything."

"Know anything about what?" Peyton asked.

"About the prognosis for your great-grandfather," Ernst answered.

"What are prog noses? And why does our great-grandfather need one?" Presley asked.

Zaidi made a disparaging snort. "A prognosis is not something on your face," she told the twins with great superiority. "It's an idea about what's going to happen."

61

"Very good, Zaidi," Ernst said. The girl raised her chin, proud and beaming.

"Nobody knows what's going to happen," Presley piped in, clearly not pleased with her older sister's getting the attention. "You'd have to be like a witch or something to see into the future."

"Or maybe if you had a time machine," Peyton suggested. "You could go to the future and then come back and tell everybody what happened."

"Yeah, like when Jimmy Neutron was trying to save the school mascot," Presley agreed.

"So is Grandpa Crabtree going to die?"

Zaidi's question was mostly intended to impress Ernst with her toughness and lack of emotion. Jack knew it was a facade. She might not know Grandpa Crabtree very well, but she was a girl who could cry copious tears over road-kill. It was best to keep the kids out of this conversation.

"Why don't you guys go . . . ah . . . set the table or something," he suggested. "I need to talk to your grandparents privately."

"Zaidi has already set the table," Peyton informed him.

"Then find something else useful to do," Jack suggested.

"Why don't you go pack up your bags,"

his mother said. "You're going to be staying with Pops and me for a few days."

That bombshell was met with ecstatic exuberance by the children. They went racing to their bedrooms in celebration. Jack glanced incredulously at Claire. Her expression indicated as much surprise as his own.

"You're taking the children?"

His mother nodded. "Claire needs to go with you to Oklahoma."

"No, she doesn't."

"Yes, she does," his mother insisted. "You don't know what you're going to find up there. You'll be dealing with all those people that you hardly know and you'll be in a strange place all by yourself, struggling with serious family issues. A man needs his wife with him for that. I still feel badly that Claire didn't go with you to your grandmother's funeral. Bud is the last tie to your father. That's important."

Jack was caught off guard by that statement. He felt he had no ties to his father at all. His father was a faded photograph and a name on his birth certificate. His grandparents were distant strangers for whom he was forced to make a dutiful visit every few years. They had nothing to do with his life or his family.

"I'm not planning to stay up there long,"

Jack told her. "I'm thinking to get the old man stabilized. If it seems like he's getting better, I'll make arrangements for a nursing home. If not, well, I'm taking a suit for the funeral."

Toni nodded. "And that's exactly why you need Claire with you. You always think everything is either this or the other, but when it comes to people, it's always some of both. You'll need her beside you to keep your head on straight."

"I can't just leave the children with you," Claire piped in. "It's summer and they have activities."

"I know what time of year it is," Toni said. "And we have as many activities in our neighborhood as you do here. I've raised children myself. I'm sure I can manage this healthy trio."

"Mom, it's really not necessary. I —"

"I don't want to hear another word about it," his mother said. "Claire's going with you. You need her. Ernst and your brothers are all going to pitch in. That's what families do for each other. So go get your bags packed. We'll get you to the airport."

Claire felt completely un-put-together and was certain that she'd forgotten something essential. That was not particularly surprising since she'd organized her suitcase in about fifteen minutes, during which time her children were constantly interrupting her with packing concerns of their own. They'd arrived at the airport to buy tickets and were told if they could make it to the gate quickly, they'd have fail-safe connections to Tulsa. Running to security and then sprinting for the gate, they managed to get the plane that laid over in Dallas. Unfortunately, their flight to Tulsa was canceled, and they sat at Love Field for hours before being rerouted to Oklahoma City. That meant a two-hour car drive after they landed. And it was already after 10:00 p.m.

Beside her, Jack had been mostly quiet, but as he stared out the plane window, watching the sprinkling of lights on the ground, he spoke to her.

"Welcome to Oklahoma City," he said with a thoughtful sigh. "It's the only metropolis in the world with two airports each named after someone killed in a plane crash."

Claire frowned at him. "That's not good."

He took her hand and smiled at her. "Think of the upside," he teased. "If we're killed in a fiery crash, then we don't have to show up in Catawah."

She shook her head at his sarcastic humor, but she enjoyed having him hold her hand, having him smile at her. It seemed, lately, there wasn't a whole lot of time for smiling and hand-holding.

"Catawah will be fine," she assured him. "It's not so bad, really."

Jack raised a skeptical eyebrow. "The best thing I can say about the place is that when you're not there, you never feel like you're missing out on anything."

She laughed and shook her head. Claire knew that Jack didn't care much for Catawah. She'd only visited three times in ten years of marriage. Not enough to really have an opinion. But it seemed like an ordinary, rural place. The Crabtrees always appeared delighted to see him, though maybe a little ill at ease, not certain about how to behave around the grandson they hardly knew. Jack was very different from them. Not in appearance. He actually favored each of them in some way. But it was difficult to even imagine that they shared genetic material. They were so guileless and uncomplicated. And Jack . . . Jack was not.

They landed without mishap and taxied into the gate at Will Rogers International.

As they gathered their things and deplaned, Claire thought about the very first time she had been to Oklahoma. It had been just the two of them and only a few weeks after their wedding. Back then an eight-hour interstate car trip had seemed like an adventure. And it had been a relief to be away from the disapproving adults in San Antonio. She hadn't known what to expect of Jack's grandparents.

"They're just country people," Jack told her. "Not very sophisticated. They've lived their whole lives in this dinky, run-down little town and they're satisfied with that."

They had also seemed perfectly satisfied with Claire. While Jack's parents and her own had been furious about their hasty, no-nonsense nuptials at City Hall, the Crabtrees had been delighted. To this day, Claire still vividly remembered meeting the sweet couple.

"If this girl suits you, Jack," Bud said, grinning at Claire, "then she suits us just perfect."

The old man's smile was a lot like Jack's, the same handsome face with a sun-browned complexion and beautiful white teeth. The two men had a similar long, lean build, as well. Claire realized even then that looking at Bud was in some ways looking into her husband's future.

"And what about you, Miss Claire?" he

asked. "Are you going to be able to make a good provider out of this rapscallion?"

Claire smiled at the use of the ancient descriptor, but replied with complete seriousness. "He's such a hard worker," she assured him. "I don't have any worries about that."

Bud gave her a wink and a nod. "That's good," he said. "You keep him on the straight and narrow."

Geri was equally delighted. "You're just such a down-to-earth girl," she told her later as they watered the flower garden. "That's what our Jack needs."

She had been a tiny, petite woman, hardly more than five feet tall. Around her heart-shaped face, her gray hair was clipped short, but appeared to have a mind of its own rather than a style. She had a pointed chin and her makeup-free face was adorned only with an attractive dimple.

Claire was grateful for the vote of confidence. She sighed. "I wish Jack's mother felt the same about me."

"When a son marries up so quick, his mama is always going to worry," Geri told Claire. "You just have to grit your teeth and bite your tongue and live over that. Toni's a fair person. She'll come to appreciate you if you give her cause to."

"I hope so," Claire answered. "And I hope my mom and dad can do the same."

"Your parents are angry, too?"

Claire shrugged slightly and shook her head. "Not angry exactly, more disappointed, I think. But they blame Jack. They see him as the one who instigated the wedding. If he had returned to Austin like he was supposed to, we wouldn't have gotten married."

"Why didn't he go back?" Geri asked.

She shrugged. "He said that he didn't want to be up in Austin — he wanted to be with me."

Geri nodded as if she understood, then she handed Claire the garden shears. "Cut back the spent ones," she said, indicating the blooms that were past their beauty. "It gives the new ones a better chance to grow."

Claire began deadheading the flowers.

"How did the two of you meet?" Geri asked.

Without even turning to look at the older woman, Claire felt a smile drift across her face. "We were both working as lifeguards at Dellview Pool. I was . . . I mean I am a student at Trinity University."

Claire glanced over at Geri, and she was nodding.

"Over the summer, we fell in love."

"I can see how that would happen," Geri said.

"For sure neither of us meant for it to happen," Claire said. "At the end of the summer, we both planned to go back to school. I love my classes. And Jack's on the swim team at UT. We wanted to go on with our lives as they had been. Our colleges were only a hundred miles apart. We talked on the phone every night and we e-mailed constantly, but it wasn't the same as being together. The entire semester felt like torture."

Claire had tried to explain that to her parents. They'd accused her of being overly dramatic.

"It is very hard to be apart," the old woman agreed. "I do remember that."

"So, over Christmas break, Jack just decided that he wasn't going back," Claire continued. "I guess we probably should have asked our parents for advice. But we are both legal age, we don't need their consent."

"No, you're both old enough to decide for yourselves," Geri agreed.

"Thank you!" Claire said adamantly. "I wish you had been there to speak up for us at their little 'family meeting.' Toni cried as if her heart were breaking. Dr. Van Brugge talked to Jack with such disrespect. And my parents were completely off base. They swooped into town like some earth-shattering calamity had occurred, and my mother demanded that I confess to being pregnant. I am not pregnant. She couldn't even imagine any other reason for us to marry."

"Like being so in love."

"Yes, like being so in love that we couldn't be apart."

Geri reached over and took Claire's hand in her own. "Sometimes parents forget what it is like to be young."

"Well, you haven't forgotten," Claire pointed out.

Geri laughed lightly. "When you get old, you spend a lot of time remembering. And you remember the good things most of all."

Claire had been so grateful for the older woman's words at the time. Now she considered them from a different perspective. Maybe if they hadn't allowed the thrill of the moment to rush them into marriage, she would have known Jack better. She still loved her husband, but she wasn't sure anymore if loving was enough.

She and Jack collected their luggage and walked the million miles to the rental car pickup. He got a map and directions to the turnpike that would get them out of town and on the way to Tulsa. Claire acted as navigator helping him look for the signs. Traffic was minimal and they found the interstate linkup without incident.

"You can put the seat back and take a nap," Jack suggested.

Claire shook her head. "You have to stay awake, so I'll stay awake to help you."

Jack chuckled. "Well, I really don't see why both of us should have to suffer through the misery of the Oklahoma countryside."

"At this time of night, it looks as scenic as Highway 1," she pointed out.

His shrug was an agreement.

After a moment she asked him, "Why do you dislike the place so much?"

"Oh, I don't really," he answered. "I'm just ticked off at losing the time at the job. I got a big new contract today. I want to get working on it."

"I imagine you'll get more uninterrupted design time here than at your office."

"Probably so," he admitted.

"But you really don't like coming here," she continued to probe.

"No, I don't," he said. "I don't fit in very well here. I've got all these relatives, but I don't really know them and they don't really know me. I'm just not comfortable."

Claire nodded. "Of course, that would change if we came up here more often."

"And if I had any desire to change the status quo, we'd do exactly that. But I'm not interested. I don't see any reason to."

"These people are your family, your heritage."

He glanced over in her direction. Even in the dim light from the dashboard she could see the flash in his eyes.

"I'm not particularly proud of that," he said. "A lineage of ignorant, hand-to-mouth crackers is not something I'm anxious to brag about. And I'd prefer that our children define who they are based on role models from your family, or my mother, or even the Van Brugges."

"But our children are named Crabtree," Claire said. "You can't just blot that out."

"I tried once," Jack admitted. "When I was in junior high I suggested that Ernst could adopt me and I could be Jack Van Brugge."

"Really? You never told me that."

"It's not one of my favorite memories," he answered. "Mom and Ernst both turned me down flat. And they were adamant. I suppose in retrospect they were probably trying to be respectful to my dead father and my grandparents. At the time, though, it felt

73

like they didn't want me mucking up the pristine perfection of the ancient Van Brugge pedigree."

Claire scoffed. "That's just your own personal craziness, Jack. I've told you that a million times."

He acknowledged that with a nod and then changed the subject.

They talked amiably for the better part of an hour, flitting from subject to subject. Ernst and his mother taking care of the kids. The kids and their busy schedules. The kids and their future. The money they were trying to sock away into college funds. Money in general. Finally making it to the subject that they never talked about. It was frequently brought up in conversation, but it never engendered talk, only argument.

"Once we move into the new house," Jack said. "All the interest on that loan will be tax deductible."

Claire hesitated. She gave herself a long moment to think about it. She could just let the discussion go by. They didn't have to fight about it. She could just ignore it. It was late. They were tired. They were headed to the hospital where an old man lay desperately ill. It was not the right moment to redraw her line in the sand. She really should resist the urge to do so. But she didn't.

"Jack, I think I've made myself absolutely clear on this," Claire announced, firing the first volley. "I am never moving into that house."

It was the mere swirl of a red cape that he needed.

They were still arguing, snarling at each other through clenched teeth, when they pulled into the hospital parking lot twenty minutes later.

# BUD

*I have to keep swimming. I have to keep swimming. Move your legs or you'll go under. Keep kicking or you will drown.* I tried to cough. I was drowning. There was water in my lungs and I couldn't get it out. I was having trouble treading water. There was something wrong with my leg. The pain was like being stabbed by a hot poker. What was wrong with my leg? Had a shark bitten me? Had a shark chomped off my leg? The thought occurred to me that it might be better to bleed to death than to drown. Still, I didn't give up. I tried to swim. What was I tangled up in, a net?

No, that wasn't it. I tried to open my eyes but there was light, a light that was too bright. Then I remembered I wasn't in the water. It wasn't the moon. This wasn't the Pacific. I was in the hospital.

Immediately, I relaxed. The pain in my leg must be just a pain in my leg. I welcomed it now. Reality was good. I was an old man in the hospital. What I was trying to cough up wasn't sea water. And I wasn't alone.

From somewhere near my bed I could hear murmuring. I couldn't make out the words. It wasn't a conversation, just one voice, one long speech. Was that person talking to me?

It didn't seem like it.

I felt very far away, very distant. The way I used to feel as a boy when, in those late afternoons, I was looking for my old cow, Becca.

My mother and I lived on a little plot of land near the edge of Catawah. There wasn't nearly enough ground to graze a cow. So every morning, after milking, I'd turn Becca out into the open fields at the edge of town. She'd range all day, eating whatever and wherever struck her bovine fancy. This was good most of the year, except when snow was thick on the ground. Of course, every evening before dark, I'd have to go out and find her and bring her home for milking.

By the time I was in high school, I'd become an expert at doing this, and in the easiest, most efficient manner possible. I wouldn't just head off in any direction and hope to run into her. There were oil derricks all over the countryside, some of them a hundred feet high. I'd climb up and look around to see if I could spot that old cow and save myself a wild-goose chase.

I loved being up above it all. It was such freedom. As if I'd escaped from all the miserable drudgery of my life.

My mother persisted in her life as an invalid. She could hardly manage to keep herself washed and groomed. Everything else was left to me. I started my day milking before dawn. By the time the sun was on the horizon, I was delivering milk in the neighborhood. As Becca aged, the amount she gave was less and less. I needed to buy a new cow, but I was already fed up with the dairy work. Mr. Givens at the Anchor Oil let me pump gas at his filling station after school. I didn't get paid, only tips from customers. But I was fast and thorough and people in the community liked me. At six foot one inch I was one of the tallest boys in school, but I'd grown early and by junior year I was past clumsiness and had balance and control of my arms and legs. So Coach Burne picked me to play center on the basketball squad. The Catawah High School Cedars were a top team in the conference, and I was a pretty good player, I admit to that. But the team would have been nothing without Les Andeel. We won a lot of games and were a source of local pride. People remembered that when they were filling up and they remembered me. I quickly found out that I could earn as much filling gas tanks and washing windshields as I did selling milk.

But I still had Becca. And at her age, her output was worth more than she was. So I kept up my usual routine:

Milk the cow and walk her to pasture.
Make Mother's breakfast.
Pack lunches. Me for school. Her for her
    bedside.
Deliver milk.
Wash up and dress for school.
Attend classes and basketball practice.
Work at the filling station.
Bring the cow home.
Feed Becca. Wash her down and clean out
    her stall.
Shower.
Fix dinner for mother and me.
Wash the kitchen and straighten the house.
Go to bed.
Get up and do it all again.

I saw my friends only at school. The only fun time I had was the hour of shooting baskets in the high school gym. Even on weekends there was work to do. While my pals were loitering on Main Street or taking girls to the movie shows, I was patching the roof or chopping kindling or digging potatoes.

That was my life. I didn't like it. But I didn't know how to get out of it. I was angry. I was bitter. But I'd been taught respect. I'd been taught responsibility. So I kept a civil tongue in my head and never complained. There were people who had it worse. I saw evidence of that on a daily basis. But there were people who had it better, too.

The most visible example of that was Bertha Irene Melrose. Berthrene, as everyone called her, was the only daughter of Cut Melrose, who owned a small machine shop on Cherry Street. The shop was a nickel-and-dime place, but the Melroses lived better than anyone in town. Their poorly kept secret was that Cut warehoused illegal whiskey in his building for all the local bootleggers.

Of course, Berthrene didn't have anything to do with that. She may not have even known about it. Her personality was so cheerful and full of fun, it was hard to imagine that she was aware of any of the darker side of life. She was also the most vivacious and sought-after girl in high school. Only a sophomore, she looked like a lush, full-grown woman. Physically she was more developed than any of the senior girls.

"You think she's at her best coming toward you, until you look at her from behind," Piggy Masterson declared one afternoon. And I couldn't help but agree with him.

I'd had several very chaste dates with her. She may have been the daughter of a shady dealer, but her mother taught Sunday school. We walked. We talked. She was a genuine dish. And I was a little in love with her. But her mother insisted that she be home by ten o'clock on a Saturday night. So after I'd given her a peck on the cheek, I'd wander down to the Jitterbug where the night was still young.

The nightclub was not really a place for teenagers and for the most part they stayed away. Not because they weren't attracted to the place, but more because their parents wouldn't approve — and in a town like Catawah, anything you did always got back to your parents.

For me, one of the more positive advantages of being my mother's sole support was that no one thought it out of the ordinary that I'd show up for some fun on a Saturday night. I wasn't a man, but I was working like one and the men gave me respect for that.

The place was flashy and fast-paced, loud and rough. I liked it. To my eyes it was everything desirable about adulthood without any of the drudgery of it.

Of course, I didn't have anything much to say to the oil-field workers and the smelter shovelers. So it made perfect sense that I drifted in the direction of the only person near my age.

Geri Shertz worked at Jitterbug Lounge from the time she'd been about fifteen. She wasn't actually employed, but she was always there, picking up change for errands. She'd check your hat, sell you cigarettes or find you a bottle of illegal hooch. Being Dirty Shirts's daughter meant the townfolk expected nothing of her. And that lack of expectation meant a freedom that other girls her age couldn't even imagine.

She was different at the Jitterbug. At school she was mostly quiet, careful, defensive. But on Saturday nights she was happy, laughing, dancing. Whether it was the sight of her smile or the lighting of the place, it was there that I first realized that Geri was pretty.

And I didn't go unnoticed by her, either.

My first night in the place, she sidled up to me, teasing.

"My stars, it's one of those tall, dark and handsome Catawah Cedars," she said. "What will Coach Burne think of one of his players in a joint like this?"

I knew for sure that Coach wouldn't like it one bit, but I shrugged as if I was uncertain.

"Are you going to let him know?" I asked her. "I never figured you for a tattletale, Crazy Girl."

She laughed. It was not the deep, husky sound of a vamp, but sweet and natural and genuine.

"People in this town suspect me of all kinds of things," she answered. "But I haven't heard myself accused of that."

I nodded, sagely. "So I'm safe."

She raised an eyebrow at that and with a big grin answered, "Not more than you'd want to be."

Geri was right, of course. For a teenager, the hint of danger in a place like the Jitterbug was at least half the draw.

"I'll tell you what," she said. "If the coach shows up, it would be best that he sees you're here to get the exercise."

With that she pulled me out onto the dance floor.

I just stood there, on full display as an ignorant galoot.

"Sorry I . . ."

"You don't know how to dance? Well, of course you don't." She answered her own question. "You're lucky you've run into me. I can make it easy for you."

She clasped my palms in her own. "It's rock step on six," she said.

"Huh?"

She began to move, first one foot and then the other while her torso swayed in rhythm.

"Come on," she encouraged. "Just listen to the beat and start to rock back and forth. I know you can move on the basketball court. The dance floor is not that different."

She was right. Slowly I began to get the steps down and relax into the music. It was easy. It was fun. I found myself laughing.

"Hey, don't get so sure of yourself," Geri warned. "You haven't even tried a swingout or a sugarpush yet."

"I'm ready to try anything," I assured her.

Every new move was crazy and clumsy at first, but Geri was a good teacher and a great dancer. With her in my arms my mistakes felt more humorous than embarrassing. I caught on fast and found it to be a lot of fun.

For the next weeks and months, I met

Geri every Saturday night at the Jitterbug Lounge. Although I occasionally danced with other women, she was my favorite partner. And I discovered that not only did I prefer dancing with her, I did not like to see her dancing with somebody else. I wasn't angry or even annoyed. But I found I was a little jealous of any man lucky enough to get to spin her around the floor.

Dancing wasn't all that we did. Sometimes on hot starry nights or cold, crisp cloudy ones, we would sit outside in the darkness and talk. Geri was always easy to talk to. With Berthrene, I often stumbled over my words, but with Geri I just said whatever came into my head.

I talked about basketball and the guys at school and funny things that happened on my milk route.

Geri talked about the big bands on the radio and the songs she liked best and the movies she saw at the Ritz Theater.

And some nights, when the moon was full, I had no fear about speaking my heart.

"I want to go someplace, see some things," I told her. "See some things I've never seen before."

"I want a man who loves me," Geri confessed. "A tight house that keeps the wind out and a half dozen kids to call me Mama."

85

It seemed so little for a woman to ask. I felt a desire swell up inside me to see that she got it. The silence between us lingered a long moment and then Geri laughed that wonderful laugh of hers.

"So when you come home from your travels, Mr. Explorer," she teased, "stop by the house and say hello to the young'uns."

I laughed, too. And then, somehow, someway, I leaned forward and I kissed her right on the lips. It wasn't one of the chaste little pecks I'd been giving to Berthrene, it was a real kiss and it caught us both off guard.

"Uh . . . uh, sorry," I mumbled.

"It was nice," she answered.

As if to test to see if it had been a fluke, we tried it again and then again. Kissing became as much a part of our nights at the Jitterbug as the chassé and the Susie Q.

But that was on Saturday nights. Monday through Friday at school or around town, I officially didn't know that Geri Shertz existed. I never talked to her, never looked at her. Away from the garish lights of the Jitterbug, my Crazy Girl was just a skinny tadpole of a person hidden in ragged clothes. I didn't want to know her and I didn't want it known that I knew her.

What Geri thought about my weekday

amnesia, I don't know. She never said. But she wasn't the one to give us away, it was me.

One morning before school I was standing around with the guys on the steps heading to the door. Head down and clutching her books to her chest, Geri passed by.

"What do you think of her?" Piggy Masterson asked of nobody in general. "I kind of like the way she moves. They say her older sister could be had. Do you think she could be, too?"

I didn't say a word, but Les piped up in her defense.

"Aw, come on," he said. "She's just a kid."

"Yeah," Hackshaw Hurst joked. "Her tits still look too flat, but you can't tell if a gal's heels are round until you try and tip her over."

Piggy and Stub laughed.

I punched Hackshaw in the nose.

That got me a retaliatory punch from him, howls of shocked disbelief from my friends and a trip to the principal's office.

Later that day, as I perched high above on the oil derrick, looking for Becca, I tried to leave it all behind. But I couldn't. I wasn't noble enough to openly acknowledge her. But I wasn't cad enough to let a cheap remark go by. Both ways, I came up short.

I closed my eyes, felt the breeze on my face.

"Hey, Buddy!"

I startled, nearly losing my seat.

"Hey, Buddy, are you daydreaming up there?"

I glanced down to the ground below me. Geri stood there, looking up, her brow furrowed with curiosity.

"Uh . . . hello." I hollered down to her, embarrassed to be caught loafing. "I'm . . . I'm looking for my cow."

She nodded. "I saw Becca down in that draw on the near north of the ball tank," she told me. "You probably can't see her for the dad-blamed cedars."

I climbed down the rig and dropped to the ground beside her. I felt uncomfortable. She was more familiar than any girl I knew. But I'd seen her mostly at night, laughing and happy, at ease in the world. In the full light of day, she looked very young and not nearly so confident. It was almost as if I could already feel her leaning on me. I didn't like it and I didn't want it.

"I'd better go get Becca before she wanders on," I said and moved away quickly.

"I'll go with you," she answered, falling into step.

I wasn't particularly keen to that idea, but

I couldn't chase her off. So I decided to ignore her. I didn't speak. As we forged a path through waist-high milkweed and scraggly brush, I didn't look in her direction. I pretended that she wasn't even there.

Of course, my actions had no effect on hers.

"I wanted to thank you for what you did," she said.

I didn't bother to pretend not to know what she meant. Instead, I discounted it. "I've been looking for a reason to break Hackshaw's nose. It was just the first reason that showed up."

"Yeah, sure," she agreed. "Still, thanks for doing it. It was kind."

I didn't comment or even look in her direction. I just continued moving forward, stepping up the pace. Geri was practically running beside me to keep up.

"That's what I like about you," she said. "I mean, you *are* good-looking and smart, too. And you're a hard worker and a comfort to your mama. All those things catch a girl's attention. But mostly it's that you're kind to me. And you're a good dancer."

She added the last with a little laugh that made me stop and turn to face her.

"I'm not kind," I stated adamantly. "You are a sort of friend of mine, and I take up

89

for my friends. But I'm no kinder to you than I would have been to a stray cat. I don't deserve any admiration or thanks."

I watched Geri take a deep breath and straighten her shoulders; she raised her chin in that defiant, determined way that was so familiar.

"Okay then," she said. "No admiration or thanks. What about love? I am in love with you, Buddy Crabtree."

She couldn't have surprised me more if she'd suddenly sprouted wings. I had no idea what to say, so I didn't say anything. I turned to walk away, but she wouldn't let me go.

"You know they ruined my sister Cleata," she blurted out.

"What?" I turned to Geri genuinely shocked. "Who?"

"Some boys at the high school, two years ago almost," she answered.

I had, of course, heard rumors. In a town as small as Catawah, news traveled fast and gossip even faster.

"Is that why she left?" I asked. Cleata had been in my class at school. One day she just didn't show up and we never saw her again.

"Daddy sent her to live with some cousins over in Hominy," she answered. "He said if she stayed here, them boys would continue to pester her and she'd never find no one to marry."

I nodded. Old Dirty Shirts was probably right.

"Some of these guys in town, they think that if a girl is real poor, then she can't have morals. But I do," Geri stated resolutely. "And I mean to keep them. That's why I want to marry before something bad happens. I want to get married. And I want to marry you. I'm a good cook and I been taking care of my mama for years. So I know that I could take care of yours."

The instant I recognized where her conversation was headed, I looked at her in shock.

"I know I'm not the prettiest gal in school," Geri admitted. "But you like me and we have fun together. I'd be a good wife for you, Buddy. I could be a helpmate."

"No!" My answer didn't call for further discussion.

"You don't need to make up your mind right away," she assured me quickly. "You should take some time to think about it."

"I don't need to think about it," I told her. "You *are* a crazy girl. There is no reason on this earth why I'd ever want to marry you."

I remember so clearly standing there in

that field with the sun on the horizon, star-ing at her in disbelief. She wasn't upset or angry. She wasn't crying. She just continued to look hopeful.

"Nothing I can even imagine would ever cause me to want to marry you," I had told her.

But, of course, I could never have imag-ined Pearl Harbor and a world at war.

Somewhere in the distance I heard the music playing. It was the music that brought my thoughts back to the hospital. It was the music that got me to the room of blinking machines and medicine smells. I could hear the piano and the horns as clearly as if Cab Calloway himself was out in the hall. It was the "Hep Cat's Love Song" and he was playing it for me.

# FRIDAY, JUNE 10.
## JUST AFTER MIDNIGHT

The medical center was like most Jack had been in, with lots of neutral color and confusing directions that contributed to the vaguely uneasy feeling he always got inside hospitals. Because it was so late, they had to get passes from the security officer. Between him and Claire an unannounced truce had been called, but their argument still lingered and they didn't speak as they rode the elevator up to the eighth floor. The building was so quiet, so empty, that every sound seemed magnified. As they approached the nurses' station, the conversation there registered loudly against the whispered ambiance of the night.

"Hi, I'm Jack Crabtree," he announced to a large blond woman in a nursing smock festooned with cowboy motifs.

"Crabtree? Is that yours, Lucy?"

A black woman with a thousand braids twisted into an elaborate upswept hairdo glanced down at the computer screen in front of her.

"Yes, he is," she answered. "Jack Dempsey Crabtree, Sr." She chuckled as if it were funny. "Are you Jack Dempsey Crabtree, Jr.?"

"No, that was my father," he answered her coldly.

"May we see Mr. Crabtree?" Claire piped in. "We know how late it is, but we've come all the way from San Antonio. We're really exhausted, but we'd feel better if we could see him."

"Sure," Lucy said, sympathetically. "He's right down the hall and around the corner, 8417. There's a little waiting area just beyond his door. There's already some family there."

"Oh, thanks," Claire answered.

Jack felt himself being dragged away from the desk, but he allowed it to happen. He didn't come here to start a fight with the people caring for his grandfather — he just came to make sure the old man was being taken care of.

"I wonder who from the family is here?" Claire asked. "Your poor old aunts shouldn't be hanging around a hospital at night."

Jack nodded in agreement. He didn't have time to comment. As they turned the corner, a scrawny, weathered-looking woman with no makeup and a gigantic hairdo popular in 1985 came running up to him.

"Thank you, Jesus! Jackie Crabtree is here at last."

She threw her arms around Jack. He drew back, but not far enough that she didn't manage to entangle him in an effusive embrace.

Apparently she was aware of his startled response.

"It's me, Jackie. Your cousin, Theba."

From a vague place in his memory Jack recalled a pair of buck-toothed twins. Reba and Theba, Aunt Opal's daughters.

"Theba, I . . . ah . . . I'm surprised to see you."

"Oh, I understand. Your mind must be just a misery of feelings," she said turning to Claire. "Hi there, I'm Theba McKiever. My mama and Jack's grandma were sisters. You must be Claire?"

"Yes." Beside him, his wife offered her hand.

"Oh, honey, we're family," Theba said and threw her arms around Claire in a bear-hug, as well.

"How is Bud?" Claire asked Theba.

"Well, the doctor was by a few hours ago," she answered. "He said that there was still a lot of bleeding on the brain."

"Did he give you any kind of prognosis?" Jack asked.

She shrugged. "He pretty much said it was wait and see," Theba told him. "But he did ask us about what our life-support and do-not-resuscitate orders were. I told him that sort of thing would have to be your decision."

Jack nodded, though he didn't like the idea that something so serious, so personal, should be up to him. Normally, he didn't shy away from taking charge. He was willing to assume responsibility for his wife and his children, even for his mother and step-father. But he felt as if he hardly knew his grandfather. Surely someone who truly knew him, who knew what he thought, what he believed, would be a better choice to speak on his behalf. Jack didn't want to admit that. He didn't want to think about it. So he simply changed the subject.

"We didn't expect anyone to be here with Bud this late," he told Theba. "Do you live in Tulsa now?"

"Oh, no, we living in Aunt Sissy's house in Catawah," Theba answered. "We've been there ever since the dear old gal went into the nursing home. It's been like manna from heaven for us. The preacher and I are just living off the bounty of the Lord."

It sounded to Jack as if she were living off the bounty of Aunt Sissy, but he chose not to say so.

"It's good of you to stay here with the old man," Claire said to her.

"Oh, the preacher is laying a prayer cover upon your granddaddy and I'm here to support him in his work," she answered.

When both Jack and Claire stared at her without understanding, she continued.

"The preacher is my husband," she explained to Claire. "I call him 'the preacher' 'cause that's what he is. His real name is Conrad and his folks call him Con. But with ex-con and con man, well, it just don't seem a fitting name for a preacher now, does it?"

"No, I don't suppose so," Claire agreed.

"How long does it take?" Jack asked.

Theba's brow furrowed, puzzled. "How long does what take?"

"Putting this cover on him."

Theba laughed a little too loudly. "Oh, darling," she said, "it's not like a quilt or a bedspread or nothing like that. He's covering him with prayer. He's praying over him until that admonition to the Lord fills up all the eternal void around him."

Jack nodded slowly. "And this is supposed to heal him?"

Theba looked shocked. "That's not for us to say, Jackie. It's the will of the Lord."

Theba led Jack to the area across from the hospital room and he looked inside. It wasn't a doorway in the true sense. The hallway walls were made of glass. From the nurses' station around the corner, you could actually see into the room. The privacy curtain was not in use and was neatly tucked out of the way. Still, Jack couldn't see his grandfather. His line of sight was blocked by a man in a cheap suit who'd scooted a chair up to the bedside and was kneeling on the seat with his hands outstretched. He was muttering in a singsong fashion. Jack couldn't make out much of it except for an occasional "almighty God!"

It bothered Jack to think of the old man lying there, helpless to control what was going on. Jack had put off thinking about his grandfather for almost six hundred miles of travel. Now he was here just a few feet away with Theba's husband muttering some kind of incantations to fill up all the space around the him. It was smothering.

"Theba, if you could get 'the preacher' out of there, I'd like to see Bud."

"Oh, go on in," she answered. "It won't make no difference to the preacher. When he gets on a roll like this, he hardly knows anybody else is even around."

Jack didn't attempt to explain any further to Theba. There was not a timid bone in Jack's body. He knew that if he wanted something done, he had to simply insist upon it. He walked past Theba and through the door. He went to the old man's bedside, without even glancing in his direction. He was focused on what he was going to do.

He grabbed the preacher by his hand, and the man opened his eyes.

"Glory hallelujah!" the man shouted.

"I beg your pardon," Jack said with deliberate quietness. "My grandfather is sleeping."

"Oh, you're young Jack," the preacher said, suddenly pumping his hand with enthusiasm. "For a minute there, I thought I was seeing Uncle Bud come to stand beside me in an incorruptible body of resurrection."

The suggestion was so strange, Jack didn't know how to comment on it. He just stared at the man. Conrad McKiever was a small man, significantly smaller than Theba. His sparse hair on the top of his head was gathered into one steel-gray curl that hung down on his forehead. His eyes were unattractively spaced close together, but his smile was huge, displaying a bright gold tooth in lieu of a left incisor.

"Your granddad was as dear to me as any in my own family," the preacher continued. "And I've been praying here for the Lord not to take him until the two of you have made your peace."

Jack's annoyance at the man slipped into full-blown dislike.

"There is no 'peace' that needs to be made between my grandfather and myself," he said. "Our relationship was completely friendly."

"Well praise the Lord for that!" the preacher responded and slapped Jack on the back companionably. "I was thinking that because you never come around or nothing that there was bad blood between you, or harsh words spoken or some such."

"No," Jack said simply.

This guy might be married to a second cousin, but he was not privy to Jack's life. And even if he were a clergy-man, he had no business speculating about other people's family relationships.

"I'd like to be alone with my grandfather," he told the preacher very firmly. "My wife and I have come a long way to be here and we'd appreciate some privacy."

"Oh, sure, son," Conrad said, apparently oblivious to the coldness that Jack was sending in his direction. "Theba and I just stayed up here cause we didn't want him to be alone."

"Thank you," Claire said. Jack hadn't realized that she'd followed him inside the room. "We really do appreciate having you here with him," she said. "But you both must be exhausted. Can you keep each other awake well enough to drive home safe?"

Both Theba and the preacher were smiling broadly at Claire as if she were a dear, lifelong friend. They'd just met her two minutes ago! His wife's ability to walk into any situation and make total strangers friendly and comfortable was one of the things that had attracted Jack to her when they'd met. And typically it was one of the things about her that now drove him crazy. She was so kind and so conciliatory as she unhesitatingly urged Theba and Conrad to the door. They left smiling and pleased, instead of angry and insulted. Which, strangely enough, was what Jack wanted them to feel. He knew it was crazy. He was mad and Theba and Conrad were just an easy target. Knowing that didn't make him feel any less annoyed.

As they left, his attention was finally captured by the occupant of the room. At first glance it might as easily have been a stranger as Jack's own flesh and blood. The old man's body was covered to the armpits with a sheet. His arms were a tangle of tubes and wires, needles in his hands and neck were connected to bags of medicine hanging above him. His face was distorted by an apparatus that filled his mouth, connecting him to a flexible blue hose of a breathing machine.

Jack looked for something familiar. The tall proud senior of his memory was difficult to recognize in the silent, pale invalid in the hospital bed. He stood by the bed, uncomfortable, waiting.

Jack had plenty of experience with hospitals. His stepfather had taken him on Saturday rounds when he was a kid. It was supposed to be a treat, a reward usually for good behavior. His stepbrothers always loved it. Jack had never been able to appreciate it that way.

At least the majority of Ernst's patients would be conscious, even chatty. They always made a fuss over Jack, which helped to tamp down the squeamishness he felt around sick people.

Occasionally, Jack had seen some that were as seriously silent as this, but not often. And the thing about rounds was that his stepdad had always had things to do. He didn't come and sit and bide his time. He was in and out. When he was in a room he was busy. When he was no longer busy, he left.

Tonight, Jack couldn't do that. He folded his arms. Then unfolded them. He stood on one foot, then the other. Balancing equally on both, he swayed for a few minutes, hands at his side. Finally, he began to pace.

Claire returned from escorting out the unwelcome family members. To Jack's surprise, she walked straight to the bed and took the old man's hand in her own.

"Bud," she said, not loudly but conversationally, "it's me, Claire. Jack and I are here with you."

"Do you think he can hear you?" Jack asked her.

Claire shrugged. "I don't know. Does it matter?"

"You don't care whether you're just talking to yourself?"

She shook her head. "I don't care," she answered. "Even if he can't here me, I can hear myself and what I say to him is probably more important to me than it is to him."

Jack snorted and shook his head.

"What?" Claire asked him.

Jack didn't answer that question. He didn't want to fight anymore. He was tired, uncertain and out of his element. Claire, on the other hand, seemed so sure of herself. It was as if she knew exactly what to do in a room with a dying old man. She had no more experience with this than he did, but nothing in her actions suggested that. Jack found it annoying. And found himself annoyed with Claire. The argument from the trip still lingered in him just below the surface. He didn't want to stoke those flames. Instead, he resumed his pacing.

Claire pulled up a chair beside the bed and continued to talk to Bud and stroke his arm. She wasn't saying anything important. It seemed to Jack that if you were talking to someone who was dying, you would only have important things to say. There was nothing of significance in his wife's words. Yet they hardly could be described as useless chatter. She talked about the children and the weather. Surprisingly, she talked about Jack's business and his new project. When he'd told her about it, he'd thought she was hardly paying any attention. But she spoke about it to Bud with great thoroughness and there was pride in her voice.

Jack couldn't listen anymore. He needed action. He needed to be doing something.

He pulled his cell phone out of his pocket thinking he'd call Dana and check in with the office, find out what was going on. When he realized what he was doing he shook his head at his own idiocy. It was nearly one o'clock in the morning. If Dana were awake, she surely wouldn't be in any frame of mind to discuss business. Besides, he'd come all the way to Oklahoma to take care of his grandfather. That's what he needed to be doing.

He walked out of the room and around the corner to the nurses' station. The woman, Lucy, was talking on the phone. Jack waited, not very patiently, until she finished.

"What can you tell me about my grand-father?" he asked the minute she hung up. He knew his voice was harsher, more confrontational than it needed to be. Somehow he couldn't stop himself.

The nurse's back stiffened. She was a hardworking professional and longtime veteran of the night shift. She could do the niceties of interacting with patient families, but she was not about to be roughshod by anyone.

"Mr. Crabtree has had a stroke and a head injury. Beyond the fact that he's stable right now, I can't really tell you much of anything," the nurse answered. "You'll need to speak to his doctor."

"Where is his doctor?"

Lucy's expression was incredulous, but she did manage to keep most of the sarcasm out of her voice. "At this time of night, I'd think that he'd be home in bed."

"So there's nobody that I can talk to?"

She shrugged. "I could wake up the resident, but I doubt he'll be able to tell you more than I can."

Jack felt helpless, which made him angry. Deliberately he said nothing to keep from saying something he'd regret.

"Look, you and your wife should get some rest," the nurse told him. "His doctor makes rounds between eight-thirty and ten in the morning. You can ask all the questions you want then."

Jack shook his head — he didn't even give consideration to the suggestion.

"No, I need to stay here." He was emphatic.

The nurse nodded. "Okay," she said. "Why don't you go get some coffee for you and your wife. You'll need it if you're staying up all night."

Jack listened as she gave directions to the vending area around the corner, then headed purposefully along that route. It all felt so much easier when he had something to do.

With an instant flash of insight he realized that was why Claire was in that hospital room talking to Bud. That made him feel better.

The huff of the breathing machine and its continuous groan muffled all other sound in the room, engulfing Claire in a cocoon of white noise that was somehow safe and intimate. She was alone with Bud, and although she kept her voice light and chatty, he gave no appearance of consciousness. He was so helpless, so vulnerable. She felt a swelling of tenderness for the old man. She wasn't sure if that was a universal response or something she'd gotten from her own parents, the potent outpouring of compassion for the weak. And Jack's grandfather seemed very weak indeed. His skin color was grayish, looking almost blue around his fingernails. Unlike Jack's, Claire's busy, globetrotting childhood had exposed her to some of the starker realities of human existence. She didn't need a consultation with Bud's doctor to realize the seriousness of his condition.

She felt sad about that. Not so much for Bud. He'd lived a really good life. The last of it undoubtedly very hard. And he missed Geri, Claire was sure about that. He still had a lot to offer to the world and Claire sent up her own silent vow. *If he gets well, we'll come and see him more often.* She wished now that he knew the kids and that they knew him. But she'd failed to make that happen and it might well be too late.

It was Jack's fault. She would never say that aloud to him, but she knew it was true and she could hardly blame herself. Jack simply had never seemed to have a lot of interest in his grandparents, and as the years passed, he had less and less.

Claire had always liked Bud and Geri. She'd connected with Jack's grandparents in a way she had never been able to with Toni and Ernst. Jack's parents were nice, but she just wasn't close to them. As she stroked Bud's hand, she wondered if the physical resemblance had anything to do with it. The long tapered fingers of the hand she stroked were an older, more weathered version of the ones hers had trembled within when she spoke her marriage vows.

They had stood facing each other in the courthouse chambers. The ceremony may have been the most serious thing either of them had ever attempted, but they were both so nervous they couldn't stop giggling.

The solemn tones of the judge along with the bored expressions of his clerical staff drafted as witnesses only made it worse. Promising unity until death while laughing so hard she was afraid she might pee was not part of Claire's childhood wedding fantasy.

But they were sober enough the next morning. After a romantic twenty-four hours wandering the Riverwalk, dinner by candlelight and one long-stemmed red rose on the bed of their little honeymoon heaven at the Fairmont Hotel, the clear light of day meant owning up and confessing all.

Claire remembered so distinctly how Jack had wrapped his arms around her. She felt so safe.

"It doesn't matter what anyone says today," he told her. "Your parents, my parents, they are all going to be mad. They're going to say we made a mistake and that we don't know what we're doing. But we do know what we're doing. We're going after what we really want, and that's being together."

Claire realized she'd quit talking when Jack stepped back in the room. He was carrying two white disposable cups, both steaming with hot liquid. He handed one to her.

"They didn't have the yellow stuff, only

the blue," he said, referring to her preferred sweetener.

"It's fine," she told him as she took the coffee. It was slightly bitter and not that hot, but she appreciated the gesture.

Jack took a seat across the room from her on the windowsill. Behind him she could see downtown Tulsa and the lights of the Williams Center building in the distance, a tall lonely sentinel among the squatty unimpressive office buildings and upwardly striving church steeples. More attractive was the early twentieth-century Mid-Continent Tower with its terra-cotta facade and dark green metal roof sparkling like an emerald against the night sky.

"Did you run out of things to talk about?" he asked her.

Claire nodded. "I guess I did. Hard to believe, huh? Truth is, when I get beyond you and the kids, I don't really have that much to say anymore."

Jack nodded. "I know what you mean," he said. "I only talk about my job."

"Yes, we used to be able to talk to each other about it," Claire said. "But these days I don't even know what's going on."

"I thought you explained it pretty thoroughly to Bud," he said.

She shrugged. "I am paying attention,"

she assured him. "I know that your work is important to you. It's important to all of us."

He didn't comment, but Claire detected a raise of his eyebrows indicating skepticism. Claire knew he was trying to avoid another fight. He was tired. She was tired. And they'd already said everything that could be said about that stupid house at least twice already. And the house was tied to his job, to his work with Dana, to his relationship to his parents, to his own vision of himself. From Jack's perspective the house was more than a house. And rejecting it was rejecting him.

Claire was beginning to worry that he was completely right about that. And yet giving in felt too much like giving up. None of the dreams that had brought them together could be nurtured in that house.

She changed the subject.

"I was just noticing how much Bud's hand looks like yours," she said.

Jack was surprised.

"Really? Mom always said that I looked like the Crabtrees. I suppose it's true. I got my looks from my father and everything else from her."

Claire stroked the aged, lined hand she held in her own. "I think Bud must have looked a lot like you when he was young."

Jack shrugged. "I remember him from when I was small," he said. "You know I stayed with them for a while. Probably a summer, I guess, when I was very little."

"Oh, yeah?"

He nodded. "I don't remember much, mostly I remember being outside with him. But my memory of when Mom showed up is very clear. It's as vivid to me as things that happened yesterday. It was the first time I'd seen Ernst. The two of them came to Bud and Geri's little house to get me. Mom looked so beautiful and Ernst was so tall and had a shiny blue Caddy." Jack was smiling as he recalled it.

"It must have been a happy time," Claire said.

Jack nodded, then shrugged. "You know, I always think of it that way," he said. "But I also remember that Geri was crying. And that when I hugged Bud goodbye, he held me too long, like he didn't want to let me go."

Claire was thoughtful as she stroked Bud's hand. "Maybe he felt like he was losing his last contact with his son."

"Yeah, that makes sense," Jack said.

Claire agreed. "That must be the worst thing that can ever happen to you," she said.

"Losing a child, even a grown one, must be the very worst."

"I can't even imagine it," Jack said.

"How much do you know about what happened?"

"Practically nothing," he admitted. "My dad was killed in Vietnam before I was born. I guess he was just some grunt with a gun."

"What did Toni say about him?"

"Nothing much," he admitted. "I don't think she really even knew him very well. They met when he was stationed in San Antonio and got married just before he shipped out." Jack's brow furrowed. "I don't remember there ever even being a photo of him in our house."

Claire considered that and chose to give her mother-in-law the benefit of the doubt. "Maybe she was trying to move on with her life and reminders of your father made her sad."

Jack nodded in agreement.

Claire gestured toward the old man in the hospital bed. "Did Bud and Geri ever talk about him?"

He shook his head. "No, I don't think they really ever did. And I never asked."

"Why not?"

"I knew they missed him," Jack said. "I remember when I was ten or twelve and I was there for a weekend and totally bored. I went into Bud's shop to find something to build a skateboard ramp. There was this pile of boards on one of the shelves in there. They'd been planed and mitered, but they were just piled up weathering. So I borrowed them."

His expression bore the guiltiness that Claire had seen on her own children's faces more than once.

"Anyway, I set it up on the blacktop road in front of the house. I propped the boards against the edge of a cinder block and it worked perfectly. I'd only launched off a few times when Bud showed up, looking horrified. He grabbed the boards off my ramp. I thought he was mad at me for skateboarding, or afraid I'd get hurt or something. I told him I was really good at it. At first he wouldn't look at me. And he wasn't talking. But I followed him into the workshop and saw that he was all teary-eyed. I demanded to know what I'd done wrong, and he said that the boards were for a treasure box that my father had been working on for Grandma Geri."

"Oh, gosh," Claire said.

Jack nodded in agreement. "I felt terrible, but there was nothing I could do."

"You were just a kid," Claire said.

"Even kids feel guilty when they inadvertently step on somebody's feelings."

"How about your own feelings?" she asked him.

Jack's brow furrowed and he glanced at her with incredulity that bordered on amusement.

"Personally, I have no feelings about my father," he said. "I mean, how can you miss someone who died before you were even born?"

Suddenly on one of the monitors above the bed a red light came on. A loud, intolerable buzzing commenced.

Claire started and Jack jumped down from his perch.

"What's happening?" they asked each other. "What's happening?"

# BUD

The water was cold. It was so cold. I couldn't feel my legs anymore. My legs were gone. No, the fact that I couldn't feel them meant that they were there. I'd seen guys with legs ripped off. The missing legs hurt like hell. The legs were still there because I felt nothing of them at all. I had to keep swimming. I had to keep moving. My shoulders were screaming with pain, but I had to keep moving. I had to keep moving, I had to find somebody if I wanted to live.

The *if* hung there in my consciousness. Did I want to live?

Survival is a part of a man that doesn't reason well. It was all good and well to believe that you have nothing to live for. It's an entirely different thing to allow yourself to die. Even when you crave death, when you fear living, even then something binds you to the earth and it's hard to shake it.

I was willing to die. Somehow if I'd had a

loaded gun I'd have willingly put it to the side of my head. That was an action, and action indicated power. But killing myself by inaction, that was unacceptable. I redoubled my efforts to cross the water. When I realized I couldn't move my arms or legs, I got scared. Deliberately, I tried to control my breathing. If I could control my breathing, I could keep panic at bay.

Breathing was surprisingly rhythmic. I didn't need to make effort at all. I was in the hospital. The reality of that settled around me like a warm blanket. I was dry and safe and warm. I could smell the antiseptic and hear the annoying scream of the machines, but that was okay. Being in the hospital was much better than being in the water.

I felt myself relax. I wasn't alone. There was a flurry of activity around me. It was like the men on the boat that day. I was aware of everything, but I wasn't a part of it. I'd become an observer of my life, not a participant in it.

"I guess you just know when to do and when to let others do for you," Geri had told me laughing, when I'd relayed the story to her.

It was one of the things that I loved about Geri. I knew that what I'd said had scared her. But even when that girl was facing the most terrifying thing in the world, she wouldn't cower. She'd stick that little chin of hers in the air. And if she couldn't laugh about it, she'd likely come to blows.

Of course, I didn't always understand that about her. I didn't understand it in 1941 when the war started. Back then, there was so much that I didn't understand. That year, my senior year of high school, was busy, eventful and challenging. At least I suppose that it was, what with a Halloween party and basketball games and Les and I working together on his car. But in truth, when I think back on it, the whole time seemed to boil down to that first Sunday in December in a place I'd never heard of, half a globe away from where I lived. That day the world changed. And my life changed with it.

Roosevelt's declaration of war affected Catawah like an electric shock. We'd been going along, scraping by, introspective, pleasantly ordinary when suddenly the outside world existed for us as it never had before.

Several guys from my class had joined the reserves. It seemed like a good deal — five dollars a month just for what seemed little different from Boy Scouts. The only reason I hadn't signed up was that the meetings occasionally conflicted with basketball games.

Those boys were gone almost immediately. The McKiever brothers among them. They were sent to boot camps in Washington and Louisiana. We'd heard reports from all sorts of places I'd never been. And they were headed for places I'd hardly heard about and some I didn't even know existed.

I was jealous and I was angry.

As that cold winter warmed into spring, the war was all anybody talked about. Several guys I'd played basketball with were already in uniform. Stub and Hackshaw had begged recruiters to let them sign up, but had been rejected. Apparently the army didn't need guys with one arm or bowlegs. Orb quit school and enlisted, but he hadn't been able to pass the physical. Frank Trotter had gotten arrested for whiskey-running, and the judge had agreed to let him go into service as soon as he finished ninety days in jail.

But not everybody was so keen on serving the country. Piggy Masterson used his uncle's farm in Pott County as a convenient way out. He claimed he had a farm exemption, but when our draft board got close to him, he'd move down to the farm. And when it looked like he might be called up down there, he moved back to Catawah.

Les and I had no immediate plans to join up, but for very different reasons.

The problem with Les was that he was in love. He and Berthrene Melrose had become officially engaged. She was all blushes and I'd see her staring across the room at him as if he'd hung the moon. Les was equally google-eyed. And he didn't even rise to the bait when I teased him about becoming an old married man before ever bothering to be a bachelor.

I allowed my own feelings for Berthrene to die a natural death. Les was my best friend, so that was that. I deliberately put her out of my mind. I went out of my way to avoid her when she was by herself. When she was with Les, I was always friendly, but I tried not to look her in the eyes. I was afraid she might see something of my heart.

Truth to tell, it wasn't all that hard. With all the excitement of the war — and excitement was what I felt most about it — I gave very little thought to girls at all. What I prayed for, hoped for and dreamed about was being called up. Mama would never allow me to volunteer, but if I was called, well, I'd have to go. I began to look at the draft board as my savior. All my ambitions centered on the hope of being a Selective

Service Inductee.

In May, graduation seemed almost an aside. I marched into the high school auditorium in my long black robe and mortarboard and sat on the bleachers set up on the stage against a backdrop of burgundy curtains. I don't recall a word of the speeches that were made that day. What stands out in my memory is the color of olive drab all through the audience.

Mama had stirred herself to watch me cross the stage and receive my diploma. But by the end of the program, she was exhausted. I took her home and put her to bed. She was shaky and weak, but she was surprisingly happy, babbling like a child about all she'd seen and who she'd talked to.

She uncoiled the bun at the nape of her neck and began unloosening the braid. It was no longer the same dark brown as my own, but now had strands of silver that shimmered in the lamplight. I handed her the hairbrush, but instead of taking it she lay her palms on either side of my cheeks and urged me toward her as if trying to see me more clearly.

"I'm truly proud of you, son," she told me.

"Thanks, Mama."

"You've always done right by me. No mother could ask for better."

"Thanks."

She smiled up at me. "Now, you run along to your graduation party," she said.

I shrugged. "I'm not all that interested."

Mama raised an eyebrow at that. "It's high time that you should be," she said. "That Sapphira Stark seems like a sweet little thing."

"Saffy?" I was stunned at the suggestion. The grocer's daughter, and class valedictorian, had scarcely spoken a dozen words to me ever. I shook my head. "Oh, no, Mama."

She tutted. "Now I noticed that she's not all that pretty," Mama said, "but pretty doesn't count for much in the long run and marriages are for a lifetime."

"I'm not ready to get married."

"Well, maybe you're not ready to tie the knot, but you should be thinking about it."

At that moment I felt compelled to say something, to at least provide an inkling of what I hoped my future would hold.

"Mama, there's a war on," I told her.

For an instant she looked puzzled, then she actually laughed. "Oh, that's way off somewhere," she answered. "It has nothing to do with us."

"Didn't you see all the men in uniform

122

tonight?" I asked her. "Fellows are being called up all over town. I could be called up, too."

She shook her head. "You're my only son, Buddy. No one would take you from me. I have no worry on that score. Now go on to your party. Have a nice time, flirt with some girls. But no drinking," she insisted. "Not one drop."

I nodded.

I'd gone up to the gym where a very lackluster graduation dance was taking place. There were more chaperones than seniors. A few couples danced on the hardwood floor. A herd of unattached females stood self-consciously on the sidelines. I knew immediately that the reason I was greeted at the door so warmly was more for the desperate need of guys going stag.

I smiled at everyone. I drank two glasses of fruit punch. And just so I could report it to my mother, I danced one dance with Saffy Stark. She was all dressed up in something frothy and pink. But her depth perception seemed to be bad without her glasses. She stepped on my foot about three times.

When the music ended, I escorted her back to her place in the line of wallflowers and thanked her politely. Then, pretending to head for the punch bowl once more, I ducked out the side entrance.

Beyond the lights of the doorway, the town was dark and ordinary. The sliver of moon overhead was the only illumination until I got up to the highway. There I turned south and headed for the edge of town. This main artery in and out of Catawah was two narrow lanes of pavement with deep drainage gulleys on either side. A pedestrian had to either walk in the road or on the steep edge of the ditch. I chose the former, preferring to risk my life rather than my good shoes.

I didn't have to walk far. Les drove by me and then made a U-turn in the street to come back my way. His 1934, five window coupe was a little scarred and faded, but it was still a luscious car, and between the two of us, we kept it running like a sewing machine.

"Hey, Bud," he called out as he pulled up alongside me. "You headed home or to the Jitterbug?"

I raised my hands and shrugged. "I haven't decided. I've had all the punch and cookies I can stomach. What's a guy supposed to do on his graduation night?"

Les smiled broadly. It was the kind of grin that came so easy to him and was so appealing to all of us. It was more than just straight white teeth and a handsome face that the girls so admired. It was the energy in his expression that made me believe that life might be bigger and more exciting than I thought. Like me he was still dressed in his graduation suit, but he'd discarded his coat somewhere.

"Well, we've got some plans," he said.

Beside him, Berthrene gave Les a small ineffectual punch in the shoulder. "Remember, it's a secret," she admonished him.

Les's grin didn't falter, but he did roll his eyes. "It's only a secret for tonight. By tomorrow everybody in town will know. We're running off to Fort Smith tonight to get married."

I stood there, mouth hanging open, stunned into silence. Berthrene filled in the gap.

"But you can't tell anybody!" she said, shaking a finger at me.

"I won't say a word," I assured her.

An old truck turned down the highway behind Les. He glanced up into the rear-view mirror.

"Hop on," he said to me. "And I'll drop you off at the Jitterbug."

I stepped up onto the running board and threaded my arm through the window for a handhold. Les cruised down the highway with me on the side. The wind blew through my hair and the speed was surprisingly exhilarating, like a carnival ride. I let out a holler of enthusiasm. In the distance I spotted the multicolored lights strung along the roofline of the Jitterbug Lounge. The front door of the place was propped open with a wedge of wood and the music spilled out into the dusty parking lot.

Les eased off the side of the road and came to a stop.

"Thanks for the lift," I told him, jumping off.

He pulled on the brake and shut down the engine.

"I'll be right back," Berthrene told him as she hurried out of the car and headed for the door of the Jitterbug.

Les stepped out of the car and we walked around to the back of it. He leaned back against the wheel well and pulled out a pack of Lucky Strike cigarettes.

"When did you take up smoking?" I asked him.

Les shrugged. "This is my first pack," he admitted. "All the guys in service smoke 'em, so I thought I'd get the jump on it." He held out the pack to me. "You want one?"

"Nah, I tried it once when I was a kid," I told him. "Dad-blamed tobacco made me sick as a dog."

Les grinned. "That's something I admire about you, Bud," he said. "You never feel like you've got to prove anything to anybody."

I propped a foot on the bumper and crossed my elbows on my knee. "I don't have to prove nothing to the knot-heads in this town. I was born smarter than most of them will ever become."

Les chuckled. "And you're such a modest guy, as well."

I laughed with him.

Turning to glance toward the music coming from the honky-tonk, Les's mood turned more somber. In that gap I poured in the words that I'd been too stunned to speak at the side of the road.

"Congratulations," I said. "Getting married, that's . . . that's really something."

Les nodded. "Truth is, I know she wants a church wedding and all the trimmings. But we both feel like our time is so short. I don't know when I'll be called up, but I think it's soon. Dr. Phillips said that the draft board was scraping the bottom of the barrel April and May to get their quota. They've been licking their lips to see us all graduate from high school."

I nodded.

"Berthrene and I just want to be together every minute that we have the chance," he said. "I was thinking that it was nobler to not marry her until I come back, but we both know I might not come back. And I want to be with her now."

"Sure," I agreed. "That makes sense. You two are really lucky to have each other."

"Yeah, I know," Les said. "I want you to be my best man."

"Me?" I shouldn't have been surprised, but I was.

"Berthrene's in there getting herself a bridesmaid. She seems to think that just about anyone would do. For me, it just wouldn't feel right if I had anyone stand up with me but you."

"I'd be honored," I told him.

We stood across from each other but I felt as if we were on a precipice. The future spread out before us was a stark and dangerous place. But the waiting was harder than the falling — we were both filled with an eagerness to jump.

"We're ready!"

I turned to see Berthrene hurrying out of the club. Inexplicably, her companion was Geri Shertz. If she was surprised to see me,

128

she didn't show it.

"I'm so excited for you two," she said to Les. "When I heard there was going to be a wedding, I just couldn't miss it."

"Geri was the only girl in the place who felt like she could just not show up at home tonight and nobody would worry," Berthrene explained.

Geri didn't show so much as a smidgeon of embarrassment by that explanation of selection as bridesmaid. Instead she held up a brown paper bag.

"And I brought the hooch," she said. "You can't have a wedding without a toast of celebration."

"All right!" Les agreed.

We didn't ask how a sophomore, no more than a kid really, could come up with liquor. It was a poorly kept, small-town secret that Geri was an underage hostess at the Jitterbug. She had access to anything that was available.

Les took the bottle from Geri, reached inside the paper to unscrew the cap. He offered a drink to his bride-to-be. Berthrene took a dainty sip, immediately complaining that it burnt her throat. Les chuckled and then tested it himself. He made a face.

"This is really cheap stuff," he told Geri.

She agreed. "But the cheap stuff will get

you just as drunk as the stuff that costs more money," she said.

Les raised an eyebrow at that and handed the bottle to me. I tasted the whiskey. It had to be 150-proof bathtub Scotch. It nearly choked me to death before I tried to hand it back to Les.

"Keep it," he told me. "You're going to need it, bouncing a hundred miles in the rumble seat."

He opened the driver's side door and Berthrene scooted in.

Geri looked at me and smiled, a little hesitantly.

With a sigh of resignation, I handed her the whiskey bottle, stepped on the running board and opened up the small pop-up seat on the back of the car. Once I got in, I turned to her. I took the bottle and then offered a hand in. She scrambled up beside me, showing a goodly amount of shapely leg that I tried not to notice. We scooched together too cosily for my comfort in the tiny seat. I'd ridden back there before, but never with a girl I was avoiding or with a bottle of rotgut.

"You all okay?" Les asked.

I nodded and knocked on the window affirmatively. We took off down the highway.

Beside me Geri said something.

"What?" I asked her.

She tried again.

"I can't hear you."

"I said, I knew it was you out here," she said. "I wouldn't have come if I didn't know it was you."

I nodded. It was true, and there was really nothing to say about it. I unscrewed the cap on the liquor bottle and took another swig. Les hit a pothole in the road, and I got a little more than I wanted, splashing down my shirt as well as my throat.

Beside me, Geri was grinning.

"You're a crazy girl, do you know that?"

She agreed.

I offered her a drink and she took one. Unlike Berthrene, she had no trouble with the burn of cheap booze. The night was dark and black and clear. There was a good-size moon on the horizon. Not a full one, but better than half. It could barely penetrate the trees as we twisted through the farms and woods along old Highway 64. It was too noisy to talk, and we had nothing much to say to each other. We drank our way to Fort Smith. As the night got later and we both got drunker, she snuggled up against me. I should have resisted it. But she was small and sweet and soft. It's hard for a man to turn up his nose at that, even when he knows that's what he ought to do.

To avoid the thoughts that plague a young man of eighteen, I began instead to concentrate on what Les had said to me and to think about the future. I really hoped that he was right. That we would get called up in the next few months. Unlike him, I was looking forward to it with such eager anticipation. I might go to Europe or North Africa, China or the South Pacific. It didn't matter to me if I only got so far as California or Norfolk. I wanted to get out of Catawah. I wanted to go so much. And I knew that sometimes when you wanted something so much, fate was fickle enough to ensure that you never got it. Like Berthrene. I had loved her from afar for so long. And I would have fought any fellow for her heart. Except of course, Les. Les was my best friend. Because she loved Les, I would bow out. And that was that.

I couldn't help but be concerned that my escape through military service might prove to be just as elusive. As I sat, snuggled up with Geri in the rumble seat, the wind blowing in my face, I worried about Doc Phillips, heading up the draft board. He made a house call to see Mama every other week. He knew her condition, her dependency. And he knew I was taking care of her. Was

132

it possible that he'd use that knowledge to make his decision? Suddenly the fear that I might get passed over went through me and I shuddered with it like cold. The bottle of whiskey I held was a handy remedy.

By the time we reached the home of the justice of the peace in Fort Smith, I was very unsteady on my feet, but feeling no pain at all. Les got annoyed with me. He was trying to rouse the guy by politely knocking on the door. I decided it would be quicker just hollering and raising a ruckus on the man's front lawn. Les, Berthrene, even Geri tried to hush me, but it was my rowdiness that finally got the man to the door.

Angry and in his bathrobe, the bald, fat man with a muttonchops moustache allowed himself to be placated by Berthrene's tender pleadings. Within minutes we were ushered into the family's parlor.

It was a well-appointed old home with high ceilings and a massive brick fireplace. The lady of the house came down to join us. She seemed totally unperturbed at having her sleep interrupted by a drunken lout and his friends desperate to be married. She was a tall, lanky kind of woman with a horsey face and a long gray-streaked braid hanging down her back. There was a naturalness about her. She had that kind of confidence that kept her as sure of herself in house-dress and slippers as she would have been in an elegant gown and tasteful jewels.

"I can see you young gentlemen are in need of some coffee," she said as cheerfully as if we were honored guests. "I'll brew a quick pot. Why don't you make yourselves comfortable. Augustus will fill out your paperwork."

Neither Les nor Berthrene could take a seat. He paced the rug. She managed to stand in one place, but she continued to pick nervously at her fingernails. I glanced over at Geri on the sofa beside me. She looked pale and scared, as well.

I wasn't jittery at all. Somehow, in the back of that rumble seat I had come to a momentous decision that I was certain would put my life on the track I longed for. The relief I felt about it had me almost giddy. In fact, I couldn't recall when I'd felt better. I was so relaxed and the sofa was so soft. I could have easily stretched out and enjoyed a nap.

"Are you boys joining up?" the judge asked.

"We're waiting to be called," Les said. "But we expect it soon."

The judge nodded.

"Our son, Cedric, is in Britain," the judge said.

His wife walked in carrying a silver tray filled with coffee paraphernalia. "And our youngest is in Corregidor," she added.

"Vivian!" the old man scolded her. She blushed.

"I'm sorry," she said. "I'm not supposed to speak about it. Loose lips sink ships, I know. But he's my baby and I worry about him."

Berthrene and Geri nodded sympathetically.

The judge sighed. "Women!" he complained under his breath.

"So," he said, more authoritatively. "We're here to marry Lester Andeel and Bertha Irene Melrose."

"Us, too," I piped up. "Jack Crabtree and Geraldine Shertz."

Three sets of eyes turned on me in shock. Berthrene issued a little gasp. Geri was silent. Les was not.

"Are you drunk or crazy?" he asked.

"Neither," I answered, lying.

"You can't marry her, she's just a kid."

"Oh my!" the judge's wife tutted. "How old are you, dear?" she asked.

When Geri didn't answer, I spoke up for

her. "She's seventeen," I said. "That's plenty old enough to know her own mind."

The judge's wife looked concerned, but her husband apparently wasn't. "That's legal age here in Arkansas," he said. "Do you want to marry this young man?"

Geri glanced over at me and then raised her chin in typical defiance. "I don't believe I've been asked," she pointed out.

I couldn't stop myself from grinning at her. "I thought you were the one who asked me," I said and then added, "Crazy Girl, what do you think about us hitching up?"

She didn't hesitate an instant.

"All right," she said with a definitive nod.

Around us, suddenly everyone was talking, questioning and arguing. But suddenly, unexpectedly, their words were drowned out by the overwhelming rhythms of "Beat Me Daddy, Eight to the Bar."

I could still see them all talking but the music was too loud for me to hear what they were saying. Was the radio on? I tried glancing around the room and realized that I couldn't move at all within what was a dream. The music was not there, it was not in the past — it was here in the present, in the hospital room where I lay strapped down and paralyzed. The beeps of monitors and the whizzing hiss of the machine that

covered my face was here and now, but so
was the big band. Was this hospital upstairs
from a juke joint? It seemed impossible, but
hearing was believing.

# FRIDAY, JUNE 10, 6:17 A.M.

The sun rose over Tulsa, illuminating the east sides of the downtown buildings. In the hospital room, Jack was far enough away to view the beauty of it. But far too tired to care. He'd caught a few minutes of catnap through the night, but he'd been more or less awake for twenty-four hours.

He glanced over at Claire. She had twisted herself into a fetal position in the chair by the bed, but he knew that she was only sleeping in little fits and starts. They had discovered through the night that Bud's thrashing and gagging was cyclical. Just when they thought he was finally resting comfortably, it would begin again.

Claire would hold his hand, whisper to him, try to soothe him. Jack figured that was some kind of mothering thing, a propensity for nurturing. Claire hardly knew the old man, but she knew how to care about him. Jack had known him all his life, but didn't really feel comfortable with him. He didn't know what to say to him. Or even why to say anything at all.

The old man was quiet now. Everything was quiet. Jack could almost let his mind wander back to San Antonio and his life there. He thought about Butterman and pictured the lay of the land in the man's backyard, mentally conjuring up his ideas for the pool. It was going to be great. Jack fumbled in his pocket for writing materials. He could always think better with a pencil and paper in his hand. He'd spend this slack time getting a few drawings done. He hunched over his paper, using the window-sill as a desk. It wasn't ideal but, despite the discomfort, he was grateful for the distraction. Rebar and concrete, gravel and pipe, these were the materials he worked with. The calculable gradient or the instability of the bedrock were things that could be understood. Maybe they couldn't be controlled, but he could build in flexibility that could make them manageable. When it came to human relationships, flexibility was still something he struggled with. He believed he was giving it his best. But somehow his best just wasn't good enough.

A stirring buzz of activity outside Bud's room caught his attention. It wasn't sound so much as an alertness. The languid we-are-the-only-ones-awake feeling disappeared like a vapor, and it was a get-up-and-get-moving morning as clearly as if an alarm had gone off.

Jack speculated that it must be the change of shift, but discarded the notion a minute later when a thirtysomething man pushed into the room without so much as a hesitation. He jerked back the curtain, causing Claire to startle awake abruptly. Behind him the Nurse Lucy followed rolling the computer chart.

The man glared at Claire and then at Jack. He was clearly all business and didn't offer so much as a greeting. As he washed his hands in the sink he surveyed the blinking, beeping equipment. Nurse Lucy did the same. Drying his hands, he approached the bed.

Claire slipped out of her chair and made her way to Jack's side. Her steps almost tiptoes, as if trying not to call attention to herself.

The man didn't give her a glance.

He tossed his paper towel into the bedside trash and began moving the myriad lines and hoses out of his way as he examined Bud's face. He pried open the old man's eyes and shined a light into each for a couple of seconds. He clicked off his tiny light and slipped it back into his pocket. Then he tossed the sheet back, surveying the thin body covered in a cotton hospital gown. From around his neck he retrieved the stethoscope and set the phones in his ears. He listened to Bud's chest for several minutes, moving the sensor to several sights, including turning him slightly in the bed to place the shiny metal circle on his back. When he'd carefully laid Bud back down in the bed and covered him with the blanket, he placed the stethoscope back around his neck. Then he asked Nurse Lucy for scissors and pulled on a pair of latex gloves. He cut the bandage from the side of Bud's forehead and examined the wound. It was angry, swollen, black and blue, made more unattractive by the raised line of stitches across the middle of it.

Jack felt the familiar queasiness that plagued him around blood and scars and wounded body parts.

"At least that looks good," the doctor said. It was the first words he'd spoken.

He turned to Lucy. "Get him rebandaged," he said. "And get me an update eval on his lungs."

She nodded.

He walked over to the nearby sink and

began washing his hands again.

"I suppose you people are more of the family," he said without turning to look at Jack or Claire. "I'm Dr. Marchette, the neurologist."

"I'm Jack Crabtree and this is my wife, Claire. This is my grandfather."

The doctor made a noncommittal *hmm* sound.

"We got in from San Antonio late last night and came straight to the hospital," Claire explained. "We know it's not visiting hours, but we wanted to stay until we were able to talk to somebody about his condition."

She was so apologetic, so conciliatory, Jack resisted the temptation to hush her up. Claire was always this way with strangers, meek and empathetic. Jack supposed that it worked for her in the way that sexiness worked for Dana. It was just a ploy to grease wheels in her direction.

Jack had his own way of handling people. He was not about to allow this doctor, a fellow not much older than Jack himself, to pull any superiority crap on him.

"We have been and continue to be concerned about his care," Jack told the man. "My stepfather is on the board of the Methodist Healthcare System in San Antonio. When Grandfather is stable enough, we may need to move him to a more highly rated facility down there. This place is basically the county gunshot and stabbing hospital, isn't it?"

He then had the immediate attention of both Dr. Marchette and Nurse Lucy.

The doctor, his face red and his cheeks bulging, answered quickly and sharply. "We do have an urban trauma center in this hospital," he said, "as well as our share of indigent services. But I can assure you, Mr. Crabtree, that all our expertise and equipment is thoroughly up-to-date and our patient care is top-notch."

Jack repressed a grin. He'd managed to get on a new footing with the doctor, even if he had to use his stepfather's connections to do it.

"That's very reassuring to hear," he said, less belligerently.

Dr. Marchette relaxed a little and then added. "And I don't think it will be feasible to move your grandfather at the present time."

Jack nodded. He, of course, had no intention of transferring the old man, but he wanted to give the impression of having options.

"Because of his condition?"

"Yes," the doctor answered. "At this point, I think the less jostling around the better." He turned toward Lucy and held out his arms. She handed the computer chart to him. "We've been relying rather heavily on EEG readings rather than transport him for regular MRI scans. I'm trying to give him as much time as possible."

"Time to wake up?" Jack clarified.

"Coma is not a complete lack of consciousness per se," Dr. Marchette answered. "We associate it with unresponsiveness to stimuli and limited brain activity. Although we have not been able to interact or communicate with Mr. Crabtree, we believe your grandfather to be suffering from what we call locked-in syndrome. This differs significantly from what you've probably seen or heard about on TV, and it's very difficult to definitively diagnose, but we believe the evidence indicates that your grandfather has significant brain function — periods of sleep and wakefulness and knowledge of his surroundings. But all the conduits to his ability to interact with us have been shut down. He doesn't have control of his muscles, and therefore he can't speak or squeeze our hands or blink an eye."

Jack nodded. "And this is part of the stroke."

"Yes and no. Unfortunately, the stroke symptoms are being masked by significant internal bleeding in his brain."

Jack nodded slowly.

"My wife was talking to him as if he could hear her," he said. "Do you think that's possible?"

"I think it's very possible."

"What's going to happen to him?" Claire asked. "Is he going to get better?"

The doctor shook his head, uncertain. "I can't really tell you that at this time. He's in good general health, but he is elderly and it's a significant injury. We're trying to get the bleeding stopped. As it goes on, the pressure builds up and that may rupture more blood vessels. It's a bit like repairing the foundation of a building with cotton candy. It may work, but it is hardly ideal. His body needs to be immobile to make the repairs in his brain. But the rest of his organs deteriorate with inactivity. His lungs, his heart, his kidneys, all of them are at risk."

Jack glanced at Claire. She was eyeing the old man in the bed sympathetically.

"Last night he had that episode where he was thrashing around," Jack said. "If he's paralyzed how can he do that?"

"He's not physically paralyzed," the doctor answer. "His thinking brain can't initiate movement. The thrashing occurs during his periods of sleeping. There's apparently still some function in that state and that's a very promising sign."

"So he can make himself move when he's asleep, but not when he's awake."

"Yes. We don't want to overmedicate him for that, but we do need to keep him as still as we can. So I've authorized the very prudent use of restraints."

"You're going to tie him down?"

"Only when his movement endangers him," the doctor assured Jack.

"Why is he fighting so hard?" Claire asked. "Is he afraid or in pain?"

"No, I don't think so," the doctor answered.

"Then why would he struggle like that?"

"He's having nightmares," Dr. Marchette answered. "We believe that what we're seeing is a typical effect from his PTSD sleep disorder."

"His what?"

The doctor looked momentarily surprised.

"Mr. Crabtree has a PTSD sleep dysfunction," he said. "Posttraumatic stress disorder."

Jack was incredulous. "How would you know that?"

"It's in his medical history," Dr. Marchette answered. He pulled the stylus out of the side of the chart and tapped a few places on the screen. "He was diagnosed in 1986. PTSD associated with being shot down over the Pacific in 1943."

Jack frowned.

Claire spoke up. "He was shot down in World War II? I didn't know that."

She looked at Jack questioningly. He hadn't known it, either, but he refused to give any indication of his ignorance.

"It happened in 1943, but it was thirty-three years before he was diagnosed. Did he suffer all that time?"

Doctor Marchette shrugged. "Probably," he answered. "It's, unfortunately, not all that unusual for the old soldiers. Back in those days they told men to just buck up. The symptoms grow more manageable over time and most just lived their lives, secret intact. But a relapse can be triggered that sends people into treatment. That may have been what happened."

He looked over at Jack for confirmation. Jack kept his expression blank. He knew nothing about posttraumatic stress or old soldiers. He only had a vague idea that his grandfather had even been in WWII.

The doctor was looking at the chart again. "It says he suffered insomnia and intermittent night terrors. Pretty typical." He looked up from where he was reading and glanced over at Bud again. "So that's what we think the thrashing is about. He's just reliving his usual nightmares."

"Oh, that's horrible!" Claire's voice was distraught. "That's actually worse than if he was in pain."

Jack's cell phone vibrated on the bedside table. Claire heard it for about the twentieth time. Beside her, Jack was deeply asleep. He had that ability. He had slept through half her labor when she had given birth to the twins, innumerable childhood illness that had kept her busy all night, and every alarm clock he'd ever bought. And he slept through the annoying buzzing of his stupid phone.

Claire reached over and picked it up, squinting at the caller ID. It was Dana's number at Swim Infinity. Now she was not only awake, she was annoyed.

The back bedroom of Bud and Geri's little Catawah bungalow had two big windows on the west side. The late afternoon sun was shining through brightly, making the room uncomfortably warm. Claire was only covered with a thin cotton sheet, but she threw it off and rolled to a sitting position on the bed.

Her feet didn't touch the floor. Why anyone would have a bed so high off the ground, she didn't know. But there were a lot of things that she didn't know and she managed to get through the world just fine without them.

She scooted off the bed and ran a weary hand through her hair. She needed a cut and a style, but she hadn't had time in ages. She'd grown accustomed to just pulling it back into a ponytail and calling it done. Her mismatched T-shirt and pajama bottoms had seen better days. The logo for the Red Fireball Stars, Zaidi's soccer team, had been washed almost completely into oblivion. But that was the thing about cotton, the more you washed it, the better it felt. Claire was all about comfort these days.

She padded through the tiny house and into the little kitchen. She got a glass out of the cabinet and filled it at the sink.

In the dish drainer a coffee cup, saucer and cereal bowl sat clean and dry. Bud must have washed up after his breakfast, she thought to herself. It was a sad thought.

She glanced up at the clock above the refrigerator. It was shaped like a loaf of bread with several slices ready for buttering. Both hands pointed directly at one of the furthermost slices. Twenty after four. They'd gotten here from the hospital about eleven-thirty in the morning, and it had taken them maybe a half hour to get to bed. That meant almost four and a half hours of sleep. It wasn't enough, but Claire supposed it would have to do.

She needed to call the hospital to see how Bud was doing. She needed to call her mother-in-law and talk to the kids. She needed to take a shower, get dressed and try to find something to eat. Instead she wandered out into the utility room, or as Grandma Geri had called it, the wash porch. The washing machine was still in its place, but nothing much else was recognizable. The room was piled high with old newspapers, magazines, dozen of plastic jugs and stacks of glass jars of every size and description. Claire was genuinely startled. The house was as neat as a pin, but this one room was a disaster. There were bins full of cans and boxes full of junk mail. Coils of wire hung on nails high up on the wall. A gigantic basket was piled high with threadbare rags. It was a huge truckload of trash.

Maybe, she thought, poor old Bud couldn't get his stuff to the curb anymore. While they were here, she'd have to clean the place out and make arrangements to get it hauled off.

Claire opened the back door to air out the room. She stepped onto the back steps and stood there for several moments admiring the flower garden. It had been Geri's.

"When you grow flowers around your house," she'd told Claire years ago, "it's a commitment. It means more than just your intention to stay. It says that you're making the best of what you have. Maybe your ground is rocky or your soil is alkaline. You figure out what you can make grow and find contentment with that."

Even back then, as young and silly as she had been, she knew that Jack's grandmother had been talking about more than a few pretty blossoms. Claire was reminded about her own garden back home. Not just the hibiscus and petunias, but Zaidi and the twins, as well.

She made her way back into the house and into the small intimate living room. The twelve by twelve square was tiny by modern housing standards. Half of one wall was overwhelmed by a huge fireplace, but the four oversized windows let in a lot of light. Bud's grandfather had built the house in 1904 when it was in the middle of a cotton field. Bud and his father and Jack's father had all grown up there. This was a room where a lot of living had been done. Lots of happy birthdays and sad funerals. It had been touched by all the people who had lived in it. To Claire's way of thinking, that was what a home was supposed to be.

She sat down in the aging recliner that was closest to the telephone. She dialed her mother-in-law.

Toni answered on the second ring.

"I just called to find out if my children are driving you crazy yet," Claire told her.

Toni laughed. "From time to time," she answered. "Seriously, they are doing great. They have their moments, but you know kids are always better behaved with other people than with their parents."

"I'm counting on that being the truth," Claire said.

"Right now, everybody is at the hospital."

"Ernst took all of them?"

"No," Toni answered. "Even *he* wouldn't take on a job like that. Keeping Peyton at his side will be tough enough. But we do have the advantage of having three doctors in the family. Zaidi went with Ben and Presley went with Nick."

"Oh that's great," Claire said. "Anytime my kids can get some one-on-one attention, they always behave better."

As she listened to her children's grandmother lovingly and enthusiastically report on their antics, their bravery, their intelligence, Claire smiled and luxuriated in the moment. It was so rare to get any feedback about her kids. As a parent she made a thousand judgment calls a day, trying, hoping, praying that she was doing right. But she was never sure if her kids were doing okay because of her efforts, or in spite of them.

As she sat there in Bud's chair, her eye was drawn to the lamp table beside her. On it was a neatly folded, two-day-old newspaper, a metal lid with a handful of screws inside and a family photo. Claire had seen the picture many times. It was vintage 1960s. Bud, looking grim and uncomfortable in gray suit and narrow tie. Geri, with a teased-up hairdo so high it looked like a giant balloon around her head. And J.D., Jack's dad, just a boy with a mischievous grin and teeth too big for his face.

Claire had not realized until that moment how much that grin was like the twins'. She always thought they looked like her family, but looking at young J.D., she was not so sure.

"Claire? Claire are you still there?"

"Yes, sorry."

"I thought I'd lost you for a minute there."

"No, I guess my mind wandered," she said by way of apology. "I haven't had a lot of sleep."

"I suspect not. How is it going up there?" Toni asked. "How's Bud?"

"He's still hanging in there," Claire answered. "We talked to the doctor this morning. He didn't promise us anything, but he wasn't as pessimistic as Bernard."

"Well, that's good," she said. "Or at least I think it is. Sometimes drawing these things out can be very hard. But it's important that Jack be up there. And I'm glad you're with him."

"Yeah," Claire agreed, hoping she sounded more sure than she felt.

"Bud just lays there breathing for hours and then he has these . . . these . . . attacks. He starts struggling and gasping and fighting the covers."

"Oh, honey, I'm sorry."

"Yeah, me, too. I thought he must be in pain. But the doctor thinks he's having nightmares."

"Nightmares?"

"Yeah. Did you know that Bud had a history of posttraumatic stress disorder?"

"Really?" Toni sounded surprised. "No, I didn't know that. J.D. never said anything."

"I think J.D. had already passed away before he got diagnosed."

"I knew Bud was in WWII," Toni said. "He was a big hero of some kind. That was probably the most important reason that J.D. joined up with the air force. He got a high number in the draft lottery, so he probably wouldn't have been called. J.D. was very proud of his father's service. I remember him talking about a little box of medals that was stored under his bed. J.D. wanted to be just like his father. And he wanted Bud to be proud of him."

"I'm sure he was."

"Have you seen any of the family?" Toni asked.

"Theba and her husband were at the hospital when we got there," Claire answered. "And Bernard came by this morning and gave us the key to the house. We had every intention of staying in a motel in Tulsa, but he was nearly horrified at the idea."

Toni chuckled. "Yes, the Crabtrees are firm in their belief that commercial lodging is for people who have no family."

"Apparently so," Claire agreed. "Now we're forced to commute from this small unfamiliar house in Catawah to the hospital in Tulsa, forty miles each way. It doesn't seem like the best plan, but I didn't want to cross any of the family and Jack was too tired to argue."

"Well, make the best of it," Toni said. "I'm sure Bud has probably left the place to Jack, so it's probably good for him to familiarize himself with it again."

"It doesn't seem like he was ever familiar with it at all," Claire said.

There was a long pause on the line as Toni hesitated before her response.

"Actually, Jack spent a lot of time there," she said. "I lived there with Bud and Geri when J.D. was overseas. I was alone and pregnant and they just took me in."

"Really?"

"Yes, they were good people," Toni said. "I don't think I would have made it through those first few months without them."

"And they were grieving, too."

"Yes, yes, they were."

Toni paused. Claire wasn't sure if she was examining a memory or conjuring up something to say. When she spoke, it turned out to be both.

"I decided to leave Jack with them when I came back to San Antonio," she said.

"I wasn't aware of that."

"I told them that I wanted to go home and they helped me. They were great to me," Toni said. "And to Jack. I went back to my old life, attended college, dated and managed to get remarried while they raised my son."

"Wow, I can't believe I've never heard that before."

"Well, it's not something I'm really proud of," Toni said. "I mean, it really sounds even worse than it was. I dumped my son on his grandparents and went on my way. I thought it was the right thing to do at the time. And I think they did, too. But we paid a high price. I missed so much with Jack, his first tooth, his first step, his first word."

Claire could hear the anguish in her mother-in-law's voice and she felt it herself. As a mother, it was hard for her to even imagine not being there with her baby.

"I did grow up a lot," Toni said. "And then, when it was convenient, I just drove up there with Ernst and picked Jack up. I had no idea what I'd missed until I had Ben and Nick."

"Jack has never said a word."

"He never says anything to me about it, either," Toni said. "And I'm so grateful. I feel terribly guilty about it. I never bonded with him like I did with the other boys."

"Oh, don't be silly, of course you did," Claire assured her. "He's just different from his brothers, that's all."

"And different can be good," Toni stated. "I've always believed that. Unfortunately, I'm not sure that Jack does."

# BUD

I awoke to a hissing sound, a terrible, terrifying hissing sound. It was the sound of air escaping from my raft. The rafts weren't much to speak of. And like the escape chute, a G.I. never knew if the damn thing was going to work until it was too late to do much about it. Mine had worked perfectly. Maybe because I was the newest man with the newest equipment on the crew. Or maybe just because I was lucky.

But with that hissing sound, I didn't feel lucky. If the raft failed, I'd be in the water. The water meant almost certain death. The Solomon Sea was full of predators. I'd already seen what they could do. I'd seen Lt. Randel. The memory nauseated me. Deliberately, I forced my mind away from it. I couldn't think about Lt. Randel or Sterno or Mugs or any of them. I had to think about myself. If I was going to live, I was going to have to think about myself.

And I was going to have to stop the air from escaping from my raft.

I followed my ears as I moved my hands over the rubber and found the tiny hole. It couldn't have been in a worse place. It was on the near underside, just above the water line. I could hold it secure with just one finger. Relief washed over me, quickly followed by despair. I had to hang one arm over the side of the raft in an uncomfortable position and keep a finger atop the hole. How long would I be able to do that? Six . . . eight hours? A day?

No one was coming for me. That truth skimmed across the pervading terror in my head. Nobody knew I was here. Nobody would come looking. It had taken them three weeks to find Eddie Rickenbacker — and they were looking for him. He was an important man. A hero. Bud Crabtree was a nobody. A lowly private from a town nobody had ever heard of. With nobody to mourn him. Almost nobody. The blow would probably kill Mama. And then there was Geri. My wife, Geri. Or not exactly my wife.

The night in Fort Smith, after we'd married, I walked my bride out into the fresh air of the night and then vomited in the rosebushes. Berthrene made no attempt to hide her disgust. Even Les was visibly annoyed with me. But Geri wiped my face with a damp handkerchief and soon we were back in the rumble seat and on our way. The motion made me feel worse. I laid my head in her lap and she stroked my forehead, the way my mama had done when I was a baby. It was comforting.

Les stopped at a circle of Traveler's Cabins just outside of town. He rented one for himself and Berthrene.

"Have you got any money, Bud?" he asked me.

"Eighty-three cents," I managed to croak out as an answer.

"It's okay," Geri said. "You all go on. We'll be fine sleeping out here in the car."

Les and Berthrene moved a little away from the car and seemed to be in deep discussion for several minutes about something. Then Les came back.

"You can share the room with us," he said. "You girls can have the bed and Bud and I will take the floor."

It sounded like a good idea to me. I sat up, a little too abruptly and the world spun.

"Don't be silly," Geri said. "This is your wedding night. Bud and I will be just fine out here in the car. It's a pretty night and there is nothing like camping under the stars."

The newlywed couple didn't take that much convincing. And in the end they brought us blankets from their room. Geri and I snuggled up together in the front seat.

By morning I was cold sober, my pounding head seemed swollen to three times its original size. My mouth tasted like some mangy mountain critter had crawled inside it and died. I was stiff and sore and grouchy as a bear. I was also married, though I had not availed myself of the privileges of a husband. My seventeen-year-old bride was still a virgin, not from any great sense of chivalry on my part, but because I'd been too drunk to function. Well, perhaps not that drunk. I made a groping attempt, but was basically pretty naive about the mechanics. After a couple of unpleasant gasps of pain from Geri, I just decided it wasn't worth it and went to sleep.

In the clear light of day, I was grateful. Geri and I could swear Les and Berthrene to secrecy. We could quietly get the dang thing annulled and nobody would be the wiser. I wondered if the judge could do that this morning.

"What time is it?" My first question of the morning to Geri.

"It's after ten o'clock," she answered. "If

you're worrying about your mother, there's no need. I called Stark's Grocery and asked to have Skeeter stop by your house and mine when he went out on morning deliveries."

"What reason did you give?"

Geri looked momentarily puzzled at my question.

"I didn't need a reason, I just told the truth," she said. "We got married in Fort Smith last night, and we didn't want our folks to worry about us not coming home."

"You told Mr. Stark that!"

"Well, yeah."

"Then everybody in Catawah knows by now!"

"So what? Everybody in Catawah was going to find out anyhow." Her eyes suddenly narrow. "Oh wait, you were hoping they wouldn't find out. You were thinking it could be some kind of secret marriage. You're ashamed to be wed to one of the trashy daughters of Dirty Shirts."

"No, no, nothing like that," I insisted with all the shocked self-righteousness of a liar. "I just wanted to tell Mama myself. I don't know how she'll take it."

Geri nodded. "I may not be exactly who she was wanting for you," she admitted. "But I'll make her like me, Bud. I'll be so good to her, she won't want to live without me."

I nodded grimly at that.

We didn't discuss it again until mid-afternoon riding once more in the rumble seat headed in the direction from which we'd come.

"This is what I'm thinking about this marriage thing," I yelled at Geri over the noise and wind. "We can both get what we want here."

She looked at me expectantly, her chin raised slightly almost expecting a fight.

"I want to go into service as quick as I can," I told her. "With you, as my wife, taking care of Mama, I could do that."

"Okay," she said.

"I'll probably be killed," I said with all the bravado of youth and inexperience. "If I am, you'll get my military insurance and you'll always have a home with Mama, if that's what you want."

She hesitated for a long moment.

"And what if you do come back?" she asked.

The answer that hung in my mind was *I'm never coming back.* Even if I lived, I wasn't going to live in Catawah. I was going to start off anew somewhere else. Somewhere exciting and adventurous. Someplace where living wasn't just day-to-day drudgery. I was going to leave Mama in Geri's care and never look back.

I was smart enough and deceitful enough not to share any of these thoughts with her.

Instead, I grinned broadly and winked. "If the Krauts or the Japs don't get me, Geri, then I'm all yours."

She smiled back at me. It was the first genuine smile I'd seen on her face all day. To the surprise of both of us, I leaned forward and kissed her.

Geri moved into the house that evening. Old Dirty Shirts brought her and her meager bag of personal things over to the house. He stood awkward and uncomfortable in the front room.

"That Geri, she's stubborn near to the point of stupid and goes after what she wants," he told my mother. "She had her eye on your boy for years now. I figured it wouldn't come to nothing, but here it is come to wedding."

Geri blushed, her defiance disappearing completely in her embarrassment.

To her credit, my mother made her weary way to the front room to greet the man. She treated him with politeness and respect, as she did Geri. What she actually must have thought, I'll never know.

But the wedding was done and everybody knew and wished us well and no one asked questions about why a couple that had never dated should suddenly up and marry. It was a time of surprise weddings.

Not being any more of a cad than I could bear to be, I decided that I would not have intercourse with Geri. Rationally, that seemed to me the most correct way to handle things. It would be wrong to leave her with Mama *and* a baby.

Of course, the right thing, the intelligent thing is sometimes the toughest thing to do. Especially when it involved lying as chaste as a monk alongside a soft, healthy, sweet-smelling young woman. After about forty-five minutes on the very first night, I moved to the living room. But even my nights on the couch were sexual torture.

It was that temptation that spurred me more quickly into my military service. After little more than a week of married life, I got up before dawn and drove into Muskogee to enlist.

Mama couldn't believe I was leaving. She insisted that she would write a letter to President Roosevelt and that he'd understand that I was needed at home. Geri told me not to worry.

"I'll take care of your mama. She'll be

fine," she said. "You just take care of your-self. I'm counting on you coming back to me."

"I'll do my best," I promised, though I still had no intention of returning to her.

The most difficult part of taking my leave was that I felt obligated to be serious, duti-ful and stoic, when what I wanted to do was celebrate. I was appropriately subdued, but the minute I boarded that bus for camp, there was a smile on my face.

I got to see some places I'd probably never have seen, like Ft. Sill, Oklahoma and Alexandria, Louisiana and Wendover, Utah. I met some people who were so different from me, it was like we were from different planets. And I learned some things about myself. Some of which I felt good about and others that I wasn't so proud of. I got two good stretches of leave that year. I didn't head for home on either one of them. I spent one of them learning how to ski. The other I traveled up to Massachusetts to at-tend a bunkmate's wedding. It was the only Polish wedding I'd ever been to in my life and it was memorable for the strangeness and exuberance. I think he was hoping to fix me up with his sister. But, of course, that couldn't happen. I hadn't mentioned to anyone that I was married, which would have made going out with local girls a bit dicey. I didn't feel married, so I just conveniently pretended that I was not.

If I tell the truth, I didn't immediately discover a love of military life. I learned from the jump go that there was a right way, a wrong way and an army way. I'd been my own man almost my whole life and suddenly there were NCOs and officers who didn't seem to have one jot more sense than I did, and they were busy every moment of their lives telling me how to do everything from wiping my ass to firing a rifle.

Some of the fellows thrived with the discipline, regimentation, the routine. And others, like me, chafed at it.

I'd never ridden in a plane and the only thing I knew about radios was turning the dial to hear Charlie McCarthy. The army shifted me into the air corps and taught me to be a radio operator. I figured out pretty quickly that since there are two ends to a communication and one of them is going to be stuck at base, I applied for and was accepted into gunnery school.

That was better. I was eighteen years old, not the age to be interested in talking my way through a world war. I wanted to shoot at something, even if it was only a target with a Hitler moustache.

I guess I was too good, or not good enough. While most of my classmates went on further training on newer planes, by June 1943, with less than a year in service, I found myself shipped to the South Pacific as a replacement.

The crew didn't exactly welcome me as a long-lost brother. The first time I saluted my pilot, he looked at me as if I was an idiot.

"Could they have sent us anybody greener?" he asked rhetorically.

There were grunts of agreements all around. Then Mugs, a wry-spoken sergeant who was the flight engineer and waist gunner spoke up.

"We don't have green in this man's army, Lieutenant," he said. "We call it olive drab."

That comment provoked hoots of laughter and was the source of my nickname. The fellows began calling me Olive, which quickly and fortunately was shortened to Ollie.

I remember my first mission in the Martin Upper, the Plexiglas cupola of the plane. I was as excited as I'd ever been.

"Just do your job, Ollie, and try not to get us killed," Mugs told me. "Up in the turret you've got better than 180 degrees of slight-line, the best view on the plane. We've been keeping *Libby* out of trouble since Guadalcanal. You're going to have to be alert to do the same."

I assured him that I would, with all the bravado expected of a ignorant kid.

Our plane, *Lusty Libby,* was a C-class B-24 Liberator. It had four Pratt & Whitney Twin Wasp engines, eight guns, a bomb bay with a maximum load for 8,000 pounds and a seven-man crew. Libby had seen significant action in the Thirteenth Air Force, the Jungle Air Force they called it. And I was anxious to see some action myself.

For takeoff I crouched down in the fuse-lage, but I climbed up into my position as quickly as I could. The clear Plexiglas bubble sat atop the plane and could be rotated in any direction. I sat on what could only be described as a bicycle seat and spun around, taking in the sight. It was beautiful, it was incredible. It was more fascinating and exhilarating and totally thrilling than anything I'd ever done in my life. I'd been in plenty of planes in training, but I'd never actually trained in the Martin. And I'd never been over the water before, the sea and the sky both brilliantly blue. I thought it was wonderful . . . for about five minutes, until I realized how dad-gummed cramped and miserable it was. The sun came directly through the Plexiglas cooking me, but the air blowing up from below was freezing.

Down below I could hear Mugs and Jed-lowski laughing at me.

"Now you know why you get the upper."

"Yeah, newest guy, lousiest position."

That's how they felt, but not me. I had the best view in the whole war. When we were strafing for landing assists, I saw the guys running up on the beaches with nothing but a gun and guts. I was very happy to be above the fray. I sat in the Martin Upper basically for the duration. And when you're fighting, you're not hot or cold. You're just acting on training and instinct and you keep at it.

In the next six months, I got good at my job. We saw lots of action. We were the heavy bomber in the area, flying in support at six thousand feet. Bombing is a strange business. Flying in tight formation, all the way to the target, you know you're just an explosion waiting to happen. Any fighter with a half-good shot can blow you all the way to kingdom come. And you're likely to take the next plane with you when you go. There's a heaviness. You can feel it in your chest, you can hear it in the voices of the crew on the radio. And when the pilot gives over control to the bombardier, you hold your breath. Then it's bombs away. And strangely your fear goes with them. The lightened plane lifts and your spirit does, too. Of course, the danger is not over, but somehow, because you've completed your mission, you have confidence that you can withstand anything that happens. And things do happen.

In the Pacific we also did a lot of near-ground-level strafing, just above the small arms fire, but too low for ack-ack, the anti-aircraft guns. I liked that. I hated the ack-ack. I'd much rather be shot outright by another fighter. But the worst for me was flak, the impact-bursting shells shot into the air just hung there, suspended, waiting for a plane to fly in to explode. Just seeing the stuff made my skin crawl. Sometimes the whole sky seemed filled with the small black clouds. If we were alone we could pull up or down, but if we were in formation, we just had to hold position and fly right into it.

Up on the top, I could always see it coming. For me, the helplessness of that was worse than a squad of zeros homing in. But then, fighting the fighters was my job. On short runs we'd have escorts, fighter planes whose mission was to keep the enemy away from us. But in the Pacific, distances were great and the flying range of those tough fighter planes was not. Once we got too far, we were out on our own.

My position was the watch on top, making sure no fighters slipped in over us to get a bead. I had two .50-caliber guns that could shoot five hundred rounds per minute. Of course, you couldn't do that for long or they'd get hot enough to burn through your gloves. Short bursts were best. Short bursts, on target. After a time or two I didn't even have to remind myself. It became as natural as breathing.

As time went on and missions were completed, I came to truly like my perch in the Martin. And I had ample opportunity to give it over to someone else. We got two new crew members in that time. Dupre came down with malaria and was sent to the field hospital in Espiritu Santo.

"See," Mugs told me. "You don't need a war to die in this place. You can go from natural causes."

Dupre didn't die, he got better, but they sent him home.

Hawkins, our bombardier, was taken out by a zero over Bougainville. The Jap plane was coming straight at us. He had a thick trail running behind him, so he probably knew he was gone. I didn't really notice when Hawkins bought it, but I just looked that pilot in the face and kept firing. I must have hit something, because his plane blew up and we flew straight through the pieces of it. Something hit my turret and nearly knocked me out of place. But I was fine, the Plexiglas was only scratched and we got the kill. I didn't know until we were nearly back to Henderson that Hawkins was dead. Mugs and I cleaned his brains and blood out of the greenhouse nose. Even without that, the trail of bullet holes in the plastic told the story.

He wasn't the first guy I knew who died. It was a war and guys were dying every day. You expected it, you got used to it. But a crew is like a family when you're fighting. It was like a death in the family.

I found myself thinking a lot about family. Guys talked about that the most, their homes, their wives, their girlfriends. Surprisingly, in that beautiful place, among interesting people and more excitement than you could ever really enjoy, the thing that meant the most to me and that I appreciated most were Geri's letters from home.

She wrote me every day, but they'd arrive in a great big bundle. I would pounce on them like a starving man and then linger over every word as if it were an endless banquet.

"Crazy Girl," I often muttered under my breath.

I loved hearing from her. I thought it was just the lure of the familiar. Hearing about places and people that I'd known all my life. And the news was always good. She'd bought some brooder chickens, and they were big and fat and in high demand. The spring rains had been just about right and she'd canned string beans and crookneck squash till she thought her arms would fall off. She put by sixteen quarts of peaches from the tree in the backyard and two dozen pints of pickled beets, half sweet, half sour. Sitting on a tropical beach with all the coconut and breadfruit a man could eat in a lifetime, my mouth watered for those pickled beets back home. She'd been able to share her meat rations with her sisters. She'd gotten Mama to get outside and help with the victory garden. And Berthrene was in the family way.

I read each letter with a smile on my face. They were all signed the same way, "Your wife who's waiting for you at home, Geraldine."

If she meant to fill me with guilt, the line worked very well.

From a distance I heard music playing. I looked up and down the beach line and out

175

into the sea. It seemed to be coming from that direction, but there was nothing out there but some PTs and an L-10. No horns or clarinets, but the sound of Benny Goodman playing a sad and sentimental "Hour of Parting" floated clear and crisp on the morning air.

Then the unbearable beauty of the South Pacific faded back into the memory that it was, and I knew I was in the hospital once more. That strange dark hospital where the big band music played in the hallways.

# FRIDAY, JUNE 10, 5:30 P.M.

Jack had slept through the buzzing of the cell phone, the padding of his wife around the house, the smell of coffee brewing, but when he heard the footsteps of an unknown person sneaking around the house as quietly as possible, all his senses came on alert. He opened his eyes and was on his feet in one motion. But he was saved from some ancient midbrain fight-or-flight response by the sound of his wife opening the wash porch door for the supposed intruder.

"Hi there," Claire said. "Can I help you with that?"

"I was just leaving this on the step for you," the stranger answered. "Everybody thought you'd still be asleep and we didn't want you to wake up hungry."

Jack sighed with relief and flopped face-first down on the bed once more. He was exhausted, physically and emotionally. His muscles ached from the long night in the hospital's chairs. He stretched that ache across the bed as far as he could. What he really wanted was a nice long swim.

He relaxed into the memory of it. He didn't actually recall his first venture into the water. He did remember lessons at the club. And he'd liked it immediately. The splashing around, jumping off the diving board or going down the slide. It was all fun. But ultimately it was the silence that lured him in. When the laughing kids and scolding mothers and competing radios got to be too much, he'd slip into that cocoon of silence under the water. The rest of the world didn't disappear. But it would be muffled, distant and of no concern. That's what he wanted this morning, the sanctuary of the swim.

It had been surprising to him how accepted his interest in swimming turned out to be. His mother and Ernst were most often disparaging of things that appealed to him. The two were either completely befuddled or openly critical. They always made great efforts to steer him in some more acceptable direction. To their way of thinking, why would he want to disassemble the lawn mower when he could play chess instead?

With swimming, however, they seemed

very pleased. They immediately got him a private trainer, which took some of the fun out of it, but nothing could obliterate the temporary escape the water provided.

By high school he was making an impressive showing at almost every meet. He was fast off the blocks and could rack up decent times on any of the strokes. But it was the distances that he loved, distance where he really shined. He was at his best in the fifteen hundred meters. It was a length that coaches often meted out as punishment, but for Jack it was pure pleasure.

Swimming had another benefit back then: it gave Jack an identity. Everybody had to be in some group. By virtue of the swim team, Jack was a jock. With that designation came its own expectations. Fortunately, those were expectations Jack could live with. Jocks didn't worry too much about grades. Jocks didn't need other activities or organizations. Jocks got girls just on the strength of being jocks.

So Jack allowed himself to be absorbed into the whole persona of being a swimming jock. And part of that meant narrowing his world to pools. In sophomore year, when Ernst and his mother discussed with him the possibility of volunteering at the hospital in the summer, Jack quickly acquired his lifeguard certification and lined up a full-time job from June to August. By senior year he was part-timing for the City Parks Department pools year-round. So it really wasn't that miraculous that he was given the assistant manager job of Dellview Pool that first summer he was home from college. He opened and closed the facility, ran the receipts for both the gate and the snack shack and supervised all the personnel, including the lifeguards.

That was how he had gotten to know Claire. He had noticed her the minute she'd walked onto the deck. It was not just that she was female or had a nice figure. Almost half the staff were girls and all of them looked good. There was some indefinable difference that had caught his attention. Maybe it was the modest one-piece swimsuit. Or it was the quality of her speech, slightly more precise than the rest of girls'. As one of the crew had put it, "She has no twang in her Texas."

Or perhaps it was some vague exotic quality that Jack liked. She was not like the other girls. And Jack was very sensitive to being an outsider.

At first he was only trying to make her welcome, to ensure that she felt included. Within only a few days it had become something more. He really liked talking to her. She was so smart and interesting and upbeat. People immediately loved her. He found that he did, too.

"Do you have brothers and sisters?" she asked him.

"Two brothers."

"Are they like you?"

Jack shook his head. "Not at all," he answered. "They're both geeky science guys. Middle school scholars, pasty white and addicted to Dungeons & Dragons."

She laughed, open and throaty. It was a clean sound and at the same time very sexy.

"Still," she told him, "it must be nice to have siblings."

He shrugged an agreement. "You're an only child?"

"More than just *only*," she answered. "I'm an only child sent to boarding school. Therefore, I refer to myself by the technical name *alonely* child."

Jack chuckled. "Sounds pitiful enough," he said.

Claire nodded feigning seriousness. "Yes, indeed, all the downside of being an orphan without the glimmer of hope that someday a loving adoptive family will come and take you home."

"Hey, being raised in the bosom of the

181

nuclear family isn't all that it's cracked up to be, either," he declared. "Especially when you really don't fit in all that well."

"You don't fit in with your family?"

"You've heard the story of the swan raised by ducks, right? I'm the duck raised among a family of swans," he said. "I just go quacking along being myself and my parents give each other these horrified looks of 'Where did we go wrong?'!"

Jack smiled as he remembered that first fun summer they shared together. He hadn't meant to fall so hard for Claire, but he'd found her admiration for him, her belief in him, very hard to resist.

"Hey, sleepyhead," she called from the back bedroom door. "I thought I heard you stirring around in there."

Jack propped himself up on his elbows. "I woke thinking the barbarians were storming the castle and I needed to rescue my damsel in distress. But then I heard you taking care of it. How are the barbarians, by the way?"

"They brought home-cooked food," Claire answered. "It was very nice of them."

Jack sighed. "They probably feel about restaurants the same way they feel about motels," he said.

"Oh, come on," she chided him. "Staying here in Bud and Geri's house is very homey.

And I much prefer eating home-cooking in my pajamas over having to go out and find a restaurant."

Jack could hardly argue that, so he didn't.

"Are you hungry?" he asked instead.

"Starving."

"Well, let's see what they brought us."

Jack rolled out of bed and slipped into his signature khaki shorts and padded barefoot into the kitchen.

Claire was unpacking a brown cardboard box and inspecting the contents of all of the containers. Jack immediately pitched in to help her.

Some things went into the cabinet, some into the refrigerator and some things straight onto the table. Claire rounded up a couple of plates, and Jack attempted to relearn the technology of ice-cube trays, as they put together a meal.

He couldn't remember the last time they had worked together on such a mundane task. When they were newlyweds, every breakfast was a team effort, every supper was a collaboration. When had they stopped doing that, and why?

She filled him in on her call to his mother. He wasn't surprised that the kids were doing fine. Though he had mixed feelings about the news that they were doing rounds with his father and brothers. Jack had never really liked the hospital that much, though he had craved the attention he had received at the side of his stepfather. Everyone from the custodian to the hospital administrator knew Ernst's name and treated him with respect. Jack had basked in the glow of that.

"Who is this little fellow?" a pretty blond nurse had asked once.

"I'm his son!" Jack piped in the answer in a youthful soprano.

The nurse seemed momentarily surprised.

"Stepson," Ernst corrected.

"Oh." The nurse laughed as if that explained everything. "I was wondering about all that gorgeous dark hair."

She ran her fingers through it and smiled at him. Jack remembered that, but the feeling of the moment stood out stronger than the features of her face. His stepfather had not claimed him. Ernst was not his dad and even strangers had a right to that information.

"Why can't he just be my father, too?" Jack had asked his mother so many times.

"Because you already have a father," she answered.

But Jack didn't want his father, the dead father. He wanted Ernst, the cool father, to be his father.

He only hoped that his own children wouldn't end up feeling the same. "I could take the kids to work with *me* sometime," he said to Claire.

Claire, who was pouring ice water in glasses, raised her head to look at him curiously. It was as if his suggestion had come out of nowhere.

"You tried that, remember," she answered. "You took Zaidi for me when the twins were down with the flu. You said she was in the way all day."

He had taken her, he recalled it now. And she had been in the way.

"Maybe I'll try again," he said.

"That would be great," Claire told him. "I'm sure the kids would love being with you. No matter how many hours you spend at home, there never seems to be enough 'dad-time' to go around."

Her words didn't seem like a criticism, so Jack didn't take them as such. Claire knew how hard he worked and why. He could never do the work that he wanted, build the business and support them in the lifestyle that he wanted, without putting in long, long hours. Claire never heaped parental guilt on top of that. Jack was grateful and he told her so.

She shrugged. "The kids love you and

know that you love them," she said. "You don't have to be a scout leader or coach soccer to qualify as a great dad."

"Thanks," he answered, and then added, "If I haven't said it lately, I appreciate how you always pull up the slack with the kids. Whether it's T-ball or a piano recital I know you'll be there even when I'm not."

"And I know you'll be there when you can," she said.

Jack realized that hers was a perfect opening for a new battle over the house. This was one of her arguments, that if they stayed in their old house he could cut back on work hours and have more time for the kids. Mentally he braced himself for the first volley. Surprisingly it didn't come. Instead they sat down to eat their makeshift meal in peace and congeniality. It was very welcome, very pleasant. It made the food taste even better than it was. Jack wondered why they didn't have meals together this way more often.

Claire came up with the answer without Jack's even voicing the question.

"Your phone's been vibrating away all afternoon," she said.

"Oh my God!" Jack was stunned, both by guilt and disbelief. He hadn't talked to the office since late the previous day. It wasn't as if he were some cog in a big machine. His was a very hands-on business and his hands were on every part of it. Every design, every decision, every account was personally managed by him. He pictured all his employees standing around the office, uncertain what to do, and Laura, the receptionist, buried in those little pink *WHILE YOU WERE OUT* notes. Wordlessly, he left his plate on the table and hurried to his cell phone on the bedside table in the bedroom. He clicked it open it to see nine missed calls.

He immediately dialed the office.

It rang several times with no answer.

He glanced at the time. Of course there was no answer. Everybody had gone home for the day. He was just about to disconnect when somebody picked up.

"Swim Infinity."

"Oh . . . ah, hi," Jack said, momentarily taken aback by the voice on the other end. "Dana? Are you still at the office?"

"Hi, Jack," she answered. "We've been calling all day. No, I had Laura forward the switchboard to my cell. That's what you do, right?"

"Yeah . . . yeah. We wouldn't want to miss any calls."

"And we won't," she assured. "Stupid son

of a bitch! Get your lazypoke ass outta my way!"

Her screech momentarily caught Jack off guard.

"Oh, you're driving," he said.

"Yeah, Stone Oak Parkway," she answered. "Every stupid, lousy, thousand-year-old driver in America must be out here testing the road. Take a bus, grandma!"

Jack pulled the phone away from his ear and shook his head.

"So do you want to call me back or can you talk?" he asked her.

"I can talk," she said. "I do some of my best thinking behind the wheel."

Another curse sprang from her lips, saving Jack from any comment.

"I talked to Big Bob today," she volunteered.

"What did he want?"

"I called him," Dana said. "You know, just to touch base, have him keep us in mind and let him know that you are hard at work on the design."

Jack frowned. "I don't know if that's necessary, Dana," he said. "Butterman's a busy man. We don't want to become a nuisance."

She laughed. It was a throaty sound.

"*You* might become a nuisance," she said.

"But a gorgeous woman on the phone is always welcome. I got right through to his direct line."

Dana was obviously delighted with herself.

Jack was not as pleased, but he figured Dana's little personal girl-games were harmless. And Big Bob probably was flattered to get a call from her.

"Is that what you called me about?"

"No," she answered. "I think Laura was doing most of the calling. I told her not to bother you. I can handle things while you're there among your hillbilly kinfolk."

Jack ignored the jab.

"One good thing about that old man passing on, you'll be able to deep-six the phone numbers of those cousins and completely forget that you ever knew those poor relations."

Jack was momentarily struck by the harsh suggestion. She hadn't even politely inquired about his grandfather's condition. It seemed so unkind, so heartless. Then he reminded himself that Dana's opinion of his family had come directly from him. He was the one who had groaned aloud when he got a call from Catawah. He was the one who could never see clear to take his family to Oklahoma for a visit.

Not wanting to dwell on that thought, he

changed the subject.

"Did Crenshaw get his crew back out to the site today?"

"I suppose so," she answered. "I didn't see them sitting around here, anyway. I had lunch with Matt Carmelo from the bank. He wanted to know if you're going to take a construction loan for Big Bob's start-up or get more up-front money for the design."

"I haven't decided."

"Well, I think we could get a really good rate with Matt."

Dana continued to talk and Jack tried to stay in the conversation. Surprisingly, he found it difficult to get wrapped up in the mundane details that normally filled his day. He felt removed from it as if the distance between San Antonio and Catawah was more than physical.

Jack interrupted her. "Well, it sounds like you've got everything under control," he said. "I'll keep my phone with me. And if you need something, don't hesitate to call."

If his ending of the conversation was a bit abrupt, he didn't really care. He stuck the phone in his pocket and returned to the kitchen. Claire was no longer there.

He sat down at the small kitchen table to finish his meal, but eating alone, the food somehow didn't taste as good. He resisted the temptation just to wolf it down. Eating seemed to take an inordinately long time. It wasn't as if he never ate alone. He frequently ate alone at his desk. And two or three nights a week he arrived home late and ate dinner after the rest of his family had gone to bed. Of course, he was usually on the phone or listening to the TV or checking e-mail. Here, he was forced to simply take bites and chew them. With nothing to take his attention from what he was doing except the neat little yellow kitchen, with the drop-leaf table and the ancient white fixtures. It was a small room. About the size of the his-and-hers closets in the master bedroom of the house he was building.

The kitchen in that house was expansive, with restaurant-grade appliances and casual seating for twelve. It had a walk-in pantry large enough to park a car and forty thousand dollars worth of custom cabinetry. And the hundred square feet of countertops were still waiting for Claire to choose the granite. She hadn't picked out any flooring, either. Personally, Jack was hoping for travertine.

He glanced down at the faded linoleum of his grandparents' kitchen. Inexplicably, he smiled. There was some memory, just beyond his grasp that was triggered by that floor. Connecting squares of mismatched size in red and black. He'd driven tiny metal trucks and cars along that roadway. He was sure of that now and he tried hard to recall exactly the time, the moment, the people nearby. He couldn't quite retrieve this tiny glimpse of the past, but he could smell biscuits baking in the oven and hear laughter all around. It made him feel warm and safe and loved.

Jack knew he shouldn't just continue to sit in the kitchen. He needed to get moving. He needed to clear the table and put dishes in the sink. To get showered and shaved and dressed. He needed to get over to the hospital to see about the old man. Yet he lingered in the kitchen, staring at the faded floor as if it were a window into his own soul.

Night was already upon them and visiting hours nearly done before Jack and Claire arrived back at the hospital. But they needn't have worried about Bud being alone. They could hear the clatter of the family as soon as they got off the elevator. The Crabtree-Shertz clan was having an impromptu family reunion in the corridor of the neurology/neurosurgery wing. There must have been fifteen people milling about in the small waiting area and hovering around the doorway. In the center of the commotion sat three matriarchs, two in wheelchairs and the third had her walker parked against a chair nearby.

"Lord a-mercy, it's our boy Jackie. Come give your Aunt Jesse a big wet sugar!"

The words of the woman in the wheelchair were accompanied by outstretched arms. And Claire watched as her husband stiffly but dutifully succumbed to a hug from her, the other older women and basically anyone who could get within grabbing distance.

Claire also found herself being swept up into familial affection as nearby cousins simultaneously introduced themselves and embraced her as if they were long-lost friends.

"I'm Patsy, Aunt Viv's daughter by her first husband," a heavyset woman in thick glasses told her.

"I'm Wilford, Aunt Sissy's boy," a thin man leaning unsteadily on a cane said.

She noticed that, like the older women, he pronounced the word *aunt* more like *ain't.*

A handsome, distinguished man in his late sixties with a straight-shouldered military bearing spoke to her in a deep and rich baritone. "I'm Aunt Cleata's oldest, Julius Shertz, or Julie for short."

Claire was not aware of any Aunt Cleata,

but she was distracted from any question on that point by the thought that *Julie* might be the worst nickname possible for a man. A few minutes later she was dissuaded from that.

"Nice to meet you, Cousin Claire. I'm Leo, but everyone calls me Poot. I'm Theba's son. I think you met Mama yesterday."

"Yes . . . yes, I did."

"But you didn't meet me," interrupted a woman who looked very much like Poot except for an abundance of bleached hair and heavy makeup. "I'm Reba, Theba's twin. She's the one married to a preacher. My husband is more like a pagan, but he's a lot better-looking than her man."

The names began swimming in her head. Claire would never be able to keep the identities of all these people sorted out. And apparently that was what was expected.

"Patience Carlene, I'm Aunt Sissy's great-niece and Rudy's baby's mama. He's Bernard's youngest. Try not to mix me up with Kindness Sharlene — she's my sister and Aunt Jess's grandson's wife."

The hubbub of introductions finally quieted as Jack asked for an update on Bud's condition. Viv was the spokesperson. Using medical terminology gleaned from her personal experience with doctors, she both stated the facts and interjected her own opinion.

"Basically it comes down to this," she said. "When it comes to the brain, they don't know come here from sic 'em, but nothing looks good. It might be two months, it might be two days."

Claire watched Jack nod with appropriate gravity. It was a little bit wooden. Even knowing her husband as well as she did, Claire couldn't tell if that was a reaction of grief or simply Jack going through the motions of an expected response.

"If I was a betting woman," Aunt Viv began and then hesitated glancing around the crowd until she spotted the face she was looking for. "And for the record Preacher McKiever, I am not prone to gambling of any sort. I'd say poor old Bud's going to meet his maker sooner rather than later."

This was not really news. Bernard had said as much with his first telephone call. But there was great poignancy in hearing it from the aunts, who had known Bud longer than any person living on earth.

While the socializing continued, family members took turns sitting in the room by the hospital bed. Claire was hurried into a turn after only a few minutes in the crowd.

Bud looked much as he had the night

before. The muted light over the bed left the face in shadow. As she seated herself beside him she noticed one difference that clutched at her heart. Padded tethers now braceleted his wrists and were attached to the bed rails. She had seen him agitated, the bad dreams made him struggle and fight. And she knew that with the bleeding in his head, the doctors were trying to keep him as still as possible, but it hurt to see the wonderful old man tied down.

Claire stroked his hand and began to talk to him.

"How you doing, Bud?" she asked. Without waiting for an answer she continued. "It's Claire. You sure have a lot of friends and family outside who've come to see you. And even people who aren't here, they're thinking about you." She hesitated only a moment. "I talked to Toni today. You're in her thoughts and prayers. She talked about all that you did for her. Taking her in after her husband was killed and taking care of Jack while she went back to school. That was a very good thing that you and Geri did. I can't even imagine how hard that must have been. After just losing your own son, taking on a baby to raise. I can't even imagine it."

For several moments she just sat there

thinking about Bud and Geri and what little she actually knew about their lives, feeling regret that she didn't know more. That she and Jack hadn't made them a priority. That her children would never know them at all.

Deliberately she stopped the direction of her thoughts. Regret was a cheap and frivolous emotion, especially when time was growing short. Immediately she began to speak again.

"The children went on rounds today with their step-grandpa and uncles," she said with a light laugh. "Wouldn't we have loved to have been a fly on the wall to see how the crazy Crabtree kids did among the stoic and stalwart doctors Van Brugge."

Claire hoped that somehow, on some level, Bud could hear her. She wanted him to know Zaidi and the twins, to know them as she knew them. And for him to have no regrets.

The time next to the hospital bed did not pass quickly, as it never did, but when Jack touched her shoulder she smiled up a him. There was a sad frown creased in his brow, but his words sounded light, almost teasing.

"Do you think he hears you today?"

She shrugged. "Maybe."

He raised an eyebrow. "Then he'll be sorry to have me cutting in. I'm not much of a talker at the best of times. With him lying there like that, I can't think of anything to say."

"It doesn't matter what you say," she told him. "Just chat about anything."

His brow was still lined, but his mouth widened into a grin. "Guys don't chat, Claire," he pointed out. "They argue or complain or explain, but they never chat."

She laughed lightly and nodded agreement.

"Why don't you try thinking aloud," she suggested. "I think the sound of a human voice is as important as anything. Tell him about the Butterman project. I know you're already designing it in your head."

"Bud was never interested in my swimming pools," Jack reminded her.

Claire shrugged. "So now he'll have to listen to you whether he wants to or not. I guess the unconscious are the ultimate in a captive audience."

Jack helped her to her feet and then, to her surprise, he kissed her on the top of the head. It was a sweet gesture that at one time had been very ordinary between them. She couldn't remember the last time he'd done that. And she wondered when and why it had stopped.

Back in the hallway the crowd had thinned

significantly. She wondered if her husband had simply told his family to go home. She wouldn't have put it past him. He was not particularly sensitive to these people, this family that he didn't try to know.

Claire seated herself among the three aunts who eagerly demanded her attention.

"Plant yourself right here next to me," Jesse said. "Viv, get that horse of yours out of the way, so the little gal can sit here next to my chariot."

Claire smiled at the old woman's nicknames for the conveniences mentioned. Viv's, in fact, was a walker with yellow tennis balls on its feet. Sissy sat in a regular wheelchair, and Jesse rode in a bright pink self-propelled scooter.

Viv was a tough-looking woman, slim and lanky with a lived-in face. Her steel-gray hair was clipped very short and she was wearing men's blue overalls. In contrast, her sister, Sissy, was heavy, big-busted and feminine, dressed in a yellow-flowered muumuu that had seen better days. Her voice was high-pitched and hesitant.

"We sent the children down to get some dinner," she said. "We thought it might give us a chance to talk to you two."

"That's right," Viv piped in. "Sisters and me are hungrier for you two kids than all the overcooked chicken and limp green beans in the county."

The old woman giggled delightedly at her own little joke, her eyes disappearing in the laugh lines of her face.

"That Vivy, she's a card," Jesse explained. "But we do love seeing you. And you're looking so good!" She pinched Claire's thigh like it was a baby's cheek. "I worried when Jackie brought you home and you were such a stick of a girl and all, but you're finally getting your womanly curves."

Claire could have dissected that compliment and found multiple slights, but instead she took it in the open welcoming way that she was sure it was intended.

"Thanks," she replied. "Having three kids does tend to pack the pounds on me."

"Don't pay any attention to Jess," Viv told her, waving away her sister's comment. "She talks so fast she doesn't mean half of what she says. You are now, and always have been, a beautiful young thing. And everyone, Bud and Geri included, were pleased as punch when Jackie brought you home."

The use of the word *home* to describe this strange, unfamiliar place that she and her husband visited so irregularly was not lost on her, but she didn't comment on it.

"You and Jackie are the cutest couple,"

Aunt Sissy said.

"Absolutely the cutest couple since Bud and Geri themselves," Viv agreed.

"Of course, you're not a thing like Geri," Aunt Sissy said.

"Well, not in the way you look," Jess agreed. "You're a tall, stately gladiola and she was a peppy little pansy, but you're both beautiful and hardy flowers. The beauty is a nice thing, but you'll need that hardiness being married to that man of yours."

The last statement caught Claire by surprise. Her reaction was apparently evident in her face.

Viv shushed her sister. "Jess doesn't mean anything by that," she said quickly. "It's just those Crabtree men are thoughtful and too sensitive by half. Why, I've been widowed three times and if you added up the musing of a lifetime for all three of them, it wouldn't make half a typical day for a Crabtree."

"Well, I don't know if that's true," Sissy said. "I thought your Winslow was a very thoughtful fellow."

Viv shrugged. "Maybe so. He thought about sex a lot. He couldn't do anything, but he did think about it."

The three old ladies cackled. Sissy shyly covered her face as if she didn't want to be caught giggling about something so risqué.

Claire was smiling, too.

"Seriously," Viv said. "We're not criticizing no one, no how. The Crabtrees are peculiar men, but in a very good way. We love Jackie and Bud and we dearly loved J.D., God rest his precious soul."

All three were now nodding solemnly.

Jesse spoke. "I sure to the world could never understand why, if the Good Lord had to take one of our boys, he didn't take Julie instead."

"Sister!"

Aunt Jesse was undeterred by the other women's scolding. "I'm just speaking aloud what we've all wondered in our hearts." She made eye contact with Claire and spoke more quietly. "Julie is our sister Cleata's boy," she said. "Cleata was violated as a young girl and Julie was the rendering of that. Our sister kept him and did right by him as best she could, but she was never close to him like her other children."

Sissy piped in. "Julie run off to the army at seventeen with just the purpose to get himself shot, we were thinking. He did a full tour of that Vietnam and didn't get so much as a scratch. So he came home and became one of those hippies. Lord, that was a sight. And for all his good looks he could never keep a woman for more than a week at a time. Never had a child."

"And there's J.D., who everybody loves," Aunt Jesse said. "The light in his parents' eyes. He had a new wife and a baby on the way. And he's just lost to us. It's beyond all understanding."

"Not that we're not glad to have Julie back," Viv interjected. "He's a fine man, honest and upright and good to his mama till the day she died, no matter who his father might be. But sometimes a person just wonders what in the world God must be thinking as he's picking and choosing."

"Well, I just wish He'd quit picking this family altogether," Jesse said. "Opal's first husband, Melville, is buried in the Hurtgen Forest. We just got Bud back from the Pacific by the skin of his teeth. J.D. came home in pieces. And now our little freckled-faced Corbin is over in that Middle East desert somewhere. I'm about ready to beat my sword into a plowshare, if you want to know the truth."

Viv was shaking her head. "But you can't stop men from going," she said. "No matter how hard you try. Bud and Geri would have done anything, said anything, to keep J.D. from risking his life."

Claire frowned. "But didn't J.D. go into the service because he wanted to be just like Bud?"

Each woman nodded and sighed. "More's the pity," Aunt Jesse said. "J.D. was always more of a Shertz than he was a Crabtree."

"What do you mean?" Claire asked.

Viv gave her sister a look as if to suggest that she'd spoken unwisely. But before she had a chance to change the subject, Aunt Sissy piped in.

"I guess it's part of growing up as a big family crowded together," she said. "We Shertzes don't get a thought passing through our brains that we don't share with anybody who will listen. The Crabtrees are secretive."

"Secretive?" Claire was surprised at the word.

"No, not secretive," Viv corrected. "*Discreet* is a better word for it. The Crabtrees keep to themselves. Oh, they talk and are sociable and all, but that's all for show. Their real feelings they keep locked up inside. You can never be sure what's really going on with them."

"J.D. hadn't figured that out yet," Jesse said. "The poor boy died without understanding a blessed thing about his father."

# BUD

I awakened cold, my body was cold, my face was burning up. The sky above me was bright blue. It wasn't the blue of the sky above Catawah. It was South Pacific blue, a beauty so brilliant it was almost unbearable. I lazed in it, smiling. And it was quiet, so quiet, except for the persistent little hissing sound. Water sloshed around my waist.

"Oh, sweet Jesus!" I screamed aloud.

Wrestling with what was left of the raft, I managed to find the leak again and put my finger over it. Cupping the other hand I began bailing furiously. If I lost the raft, I was doomed. If I lost the raft, I was dead. I didn't want to die. I wanted to go home to Geri, to go home to J.D., my baby boy.

That thought caught me up short. In the raft, I hadn't thought a thing about Geri, and my baby boy wasn't even born. I had survived. I had come home.

It was just my dreams again. More of my

bad dreams. Wide-awake a man could go on, he could live his life. But in dreams the water was never far away.

I'd survived the water and gone back to the war. I'd been a country boy in a gun turret before I was shot down. Afterward, I was a warrior in flight. I didn't want to be anywhere but in back of my guns. They sent me to New Zealand for an R & R, but I was miserable. I wanted to be in the air. By the time I mustered out, I had a sleeve full of hash marks and a chest full of medals. I wasn't some kind of hero. But I was comfortable in my turret and confident about my job. I would have been willing to continue doing it forever.

When the Japanese surrendered, we all celebrated. But I was in no hurry to leave. I had nowhere I wanted to go. After the war ended, we ferried POWs back to the States. It wasn't fighting, but I felt good about it. In late 1945 they disbanded our unit. I volunteered to stay in the Pacific. With communists coming out from behind every bush and trouble brewing in Korea and China, it seemed sure that things would heat up again. So I asked to stay. I'd found my place in the world and I wanted to hold on to it. I maneuvered. I stalled. I transferred. I pleaded with the brass that the air force was my home. But they relieved me of duty.

It was the dreams that did that, too.

All the missions I'd flown, all the kills I'd made, they didn't mean much after the war. Everybody'd flown, everybody'd killed. But *I* was the one who woke up in the middle of the night screaming.

"Shell shock, combat fatigue, whatever you call it, it's incurable," the flight surgeon told me. "Go home and learn to live with it."

I'd gotten used to following orders, so I took a train to Tulsa. I walked from the station to the bus depot and then got on a Greyhound to Catawah. Though I had little reason to do so. I knew there was nothing left there for me.

In late '44, Mama had written to say that Mrs. Stark, the grocer's wife, had passed away and that she'd agreed to marry the grocer. I read her letter a half dozen times, finding it completely unbelievable.

Geri's letter arrived a few days later explaining my mother's whirlwind romance.

"Mother Crabtree has finally decided to get out of bed and get on with her life," Geri wrote. "But it took a world war to do it."

The next day I sent Mama and Stark a card expressing congratulations. And I wrote to Geri and told her I was getting an annulment.

I'd talked to the CO and he'd made me talk to the chaplain, but they both agreed that since I hadn't slept with her, I could be done with the marriage without much fuss. By the time I got back to base in the States, all the paperwork was in order. I was out of my marriage almost as quickly as I'd gotten into it.

"It's no big deal," the company clerk assured me. "Since V-J day, I'm requisitioning more divorce forms than toilet paper."

Geri never wrote me again. Somehow I expected to hear from her. I expected her to argue that I was reneging on our agreement. She'd kept her part of the bargain, I should, too. In my spare time I practiced my arguments for why she had to let me go. But I hadn't heard one word from her when I stepped off the bus in Catawah at three-twenty in the afternoon of Wednesday, October 10, 1946.

The afternoon was not a bit cold, but the smell of autumn was in the air. It was so familiar and yet so surprisingly unexpected. There had been no autumn in the South Pacific. Not even in San Diego, where I'd mustered out, had there been any sense of fall. But it was here in Catawah. The leaves on the birch trees that lined Main Street were bright yellow and the various oaks and ashes and maples in the city park were just as vividly colored.

I swallowed hard. There was a kind of catch in my heart that I hadn't expected. All the guys talked of home, but except for Geri's letters I thought it meant nothing to me. Now that I was in my hometown again, it did seem somehow to be my hometown.

The bus stop was in front of Lyler's Drug Store. I stood there for a moment taking it all in. Then a voice called out to me.

"Who ere ye, soldier?"

I glanced up to the sidewalk bench where a trio of decrepit old men watched passersby. They were all squinting, trying to make me out. I recognized all of them. I'd once stolen a huge orange pumpkin from Clevon Ramsey's patch. Ned Gunderson was Orb O'Neil's grandfather. And George Collier had been sitting on that bench spitting tobacco on the day I'd left town.

"Crabtree," I answered simply.

I'd begun to think of myself as a one-name guy. Bud was some young fellow that I'd been before I'd left here.

I turned to walk up the street.

"You're headed the wrong direction," Gunderson called out. "Your mama's at Stark's grocery."

I knew that, but I kept walking. I wasn't ready to talk to anyone. I was still trying to get a handle on how little things had changed. I felt like I'd been away a lifetime. But it was as if in Catawah no time had passed at all. I walked down Main Street to the highway and headed toward the house. The walk did not in any way dispel the sense that I'd just stepped back in time. The streets were the same. The houses were the same. I recognized the cars at the gas station. The path beneath my feet was so familiar I almost felt I should be dragging my duffel bag behind me on a little milk wagon rather than hoisting it on my shoulder. Even the stray dogs looked to be the same mutts that had been around before I left. I was totally different. Catawah was just the same.

Despite appearances, I knew that there were changes. For one thing, it occurred to me that our house might not be my home anymore. For all I knew Mama might have sold the place. Or Geri might still be living there.

As I made my way along the path at the side of the highway, I considered my options. Mama and Mr. Stark would probably offer me a place to stay for a night or two. If they didn't, I was not too proud to rent a room. But if I had no home in Catawah, I had the perfect excuse to go elsewhere.

Elsewhere had always loomed large in my aspirations. But now elsewhere was a specific place with a familiarity that both drew and repulsed me. Elsewhere was the Pacific. If I couldn't live there, then I must live here. Otherwise, I felt I would just simply be lost.

I was not doomed to be lost, however. Not long after I turned off the highway on to Bee Street, I could see that the house seemed empty, perhaps even abandoned. As I drew closer, I realized it was the one place that seemed very different. When I'd left, it was a stark place, a bit shabby and badly in need of paint. Back then it looked, in fact, like what it was: a property kept up by a young boy, resentful of the work and ungrateful for the good fortune of a roof over his head. As I approached it now I saw that it had been well tended. The remains of summer flowers were evidenced in beds cut out of the sparse lawn. The rickety floorboards on the porch had been replaced and everything had a clean coat of whitewash. It looked like somebody's home. I couldn't remember the place looking so fine since before my father died.

I was stunned. I was puzzled. Then I reasoned that this must have been how

211

Stark courted my mother. He undoubtedly paid fellows to come down here and fixed up Mama's house. In gratitude she'd felt obliged to marry him. It was a very plausible explanation. I could hardly resent it, but somehow I did.

I stepped up to the front door to find it locked. Undeterred, I reached up and ran my hand along the top of the doorframe and sure enough, the key lay up there. I unlocked and walked in, dropping my duffel inside as a doorstop.

Immediately I had the answer to the question of someone's living there. The house had been closed up for some time. It was dark and dusty and so stuffy it was almost airless. I began pulling back the curtains and opening up the windows.

The sunlight revealed the aging furniture I remembered very well. The overstuffed horsehair sofa was still in its place, though the rip in the arm had been sewed up. The spindly rocker where, on her good days, Mama sat, was still next to the fire, though the cushions for the seat and the back were changed to a dark blue fabric. The blue caught the colors in the newly braided rag rug that now covered a broad circle of front-room floor.

I sat down on the arm of the sofa and just

stared at the room. It wasn't that I was lost in thought. I didn't have any thoughts at all. I'd made it home. It was something I'd never intended. Beyond that, I knew of nothing else to do. I don't know how long I sat there. I couldn't summon the will to make my next move.

Then I heard the creep of a car coming down the road. The pop of branches and rustle of trees let me know that it had pulled up into our driveway. Wearily I got to my feet.

I glanced out the front door, but didn't recognize the car. Still, I stepped out onto the porch, certain that whoever it was, they were here to see me. When the driver stepped out, I knew Mr. Stark immediately. He hurried to open the passenger door, but Mama didn't wait for him. She thrust it open with her own strength and came hurrying toward me arms outstretched.

"Buddy!"

She embraced me, burying her head against my chest as sobs escaped her throat.

"You're home," she declared. "You're home and safe."

She was shaking with emotion. That was when I first realized how numb I had become. I could hardly summon a response.

"Don't cry, Mama," I told her. "It's all

over. It's all over."

She would hardly release me long enough to catch her breath. Stark handed her a handkerchief and she wiped her eyes.

He offered me his hand and I shook it. "Welcome home," he said.

"Uh, thanks."

"Now, Dumplin'," the man said to Mama, "turn off your waterworks. Your boy is here and he's fine."

Mama nodded, but continued to cry, offering an explanation broken by sobs.

"When I didn't hear . . . and I didn't hear . . . I just didn't know what to think. Geri told me . . . she was sure you were back in the States . . . out of harm's way, but as time went on —"

My own callousness shamed me. Why hadn't I put a penny postcard in the mail? I could have even called Stark's grocery. I could have let her know where I was and what I was doing. I didn't even think about it. I'd thought, if I'd thought at all, that she was busy with her new life. It never even occurred to me that she might worry.

"You shouldn't have been scared," I told her. "You know the army would let you know if something happened."

"That's what I told her," Stark said.

She waved away their explanations. "I just

214

don't think I could go on if something happened to you, Buddy," she said.

I didn't doubt my mother's sincerity. And not being able to go on was a condition with which she was quite familiar. I'd just not expected her to feel that way about me.

"Let's go inside," I suggested.

Stark, who had brought some groceries, went out to the car to get them while I settled Mama into her rocking chair in the front room.

"I was afraid you might have sold this place," I admitted to her. "With the housing shortage and all, I figure you could get a pretty penny for it."

She looked surprised. "It's your house, Buddy. It's the only inheritance you'll ever get. I wouldn't sell it for anything."

I nodded, but the idea of it being mine didn't fit perfectly with my perspective on things. I'd convinced myself that there was nothing left in Catawah for me. And now I was confronted with the facts that I had a mother who loved me and missed me as well as a pretty good house on a nice piece of ground. More than a lot of G.I.s I knew could brag about.

"Well, the place looks really nice, Mama, the way you and Mr. Stark got it all fixed up."

Her brow furrowed, momentarily puzzled. When the truth dawned on her, she shook her head and laughed.

"Oh no, Bud, I didn't fix up this place," she said. "I've just got no knack for even seeing what should be done, let alone doing it. It was Geri that made the place so nice." Mama smiled. "I thought you were out of your mind hooking up with her, but she's got a good head on her shoulders and none of those Shertz girls are afraid of work, I'll sure give them that."

"Geri fixed up the place?" I was completely dumbfounded.

Mama was nodding. "She'd get that little government check and she'd stretch it out until she'd feed half the town with it. Then she'd barter with folks for whitewash or roofing or canna bulbs. I've never seen a person who could do so much with so little."

I looked around the room feeling distinctly uncomfortable.

"You know we've had our marriage annulled," I told her quietly.

"Oh Lord, yes," Mama answered. "Geri came down to the store and told me the day she got the papers. She wanted to make sure that I didn't give a moment's grief about it. She said she'd been wondering how the two of you were going to find a way out of your hasty mess without a bevy of harsh words and a big scandal."

When I heard this, I'm sure my mouth must have dropped open. Geri had been in love with me for nearly a decade. And she'd written me all those letters, every last one of them signed *Your wife who's waiting for you at home.* Somehow discovering that she might be as eager to dissolve our bonds as I was tilted my world even further.

Stark puttered around the kitchen brewing up coffee as Mama caught me up on the local news. Piggy Masterson had opened an automobile dealership in what had been Cut Melrose's bootlegging warehouse. The community was thrilled about the new use of the property. And Stub Williams, Piggy's friend forever, was now working with him to make a go of the place. The McKiever brothers had married sisters they'd met in Scotland. Tim had been killed in France, but Tom had brought both the sisters home with him. Nobody in town could understand a word they said, but they were pretty as peaches. Mr. Stark's daughter, Saffy, had finished college and was teaching at the grade school. Coach Burne claimed a good crop of youngsters this year, and speculation was that the basketball team might do really well.

I listened, nodding, feeling like a visitor, a casual observer in some foreign universe. But I tried for Mama's sake to show an interest.

"Is Les back? Geri wrote me that Berthrene had a boy."

Mama blanched, her eyes wide. Immediately she turned a pleading gaze to Stark.

The man looked me in the eye and didn't mince words. "She lost Les in March near the Rhine. I'm sorry to be the one to tell you. I know he was a good friend."

I don't believe the words truly surprised me. I was beyond being caught short by loss. I accepted it with the same stone-faced expression that had become my trademark, and I allowed myself only the briefest moment of dismay and grief.

Catawah without Les? I'd been wrong. Nothing about my hometown was the same and it never would be again.

I spent the next few days settling in. At least as much as a man could settle in when he didn't have a plan for the future or any idea of how to build a life for himself. I made a couple of trips downtown, but I really tried to avoid people. Not an easy thing to accomplish in a place where everybody has known you since childhood and feels as though they had a hand in your upbringing.

Mostly, of course, I was alone and I was grateful for that. I wandered through the house looking for nothing. Accomplishing nothing. The autumn chilled into winter, and the first dusting of clean white snow settled over Catawah. I spent hours at a time just sitting and shivering on the back step as I gazed at the remains of the summer garden. It was all frozen, just gray stalks standing withered and broken. The remnants of a half dozen rows of roasting ears. The tiny hills of turned earth that had been Irish potatoes and yams. The trellises lined up like planes in formation, the scraggly vines upon their wings had not so long ago been bright with red tomatoes. I liked the leftover garden. After a day or two I even dragged a chair out into the middle of it so I could be surrounded by it, maybe even be a part of it. I felt comfortable there. I could see what it had been. But I was completely satisfied with what it was now.

I was sitting out there on the day that Mr. Stark came to see me, without accompanying Mama. He walked around the house, calling my name. I pretended not to hear him and kept completely still, hoping he'd not see me and go on his way. But he spotted me and waved me over.

"What are you doing out there?" he asked.

I didn't answer, but reluctantly I rose to my feet and made my way toward him. Deliberately, I painted a smile on my face and held out a hand in greeting. I needed to be polite. He was Mama's husband. I didn't resent him or dislike him for that. I was grateful. I didn't want to be his friend or for him to be mine, but he seemed to be doing Mama a lot of good.

"I've been wanting to talk to you, Bud," he said without ceremony. "Can we go inside or would you rather sit out on the porch?"

I indicated the porch. I hadn't gotten around to sweeping out the inside of the house, or washing any dishes or my clothes. In fact, since I'd pretty much given up sleeping, I hadn't bothered to even put sheets on the bed.

I knew enough to keep these facts to myself.

We walked around to the porch. I sat down in the swing. Mr. Stark preferred to stand. He seemed determined to say something, but loathe to spit it out.

"I haven't wanted to intrude upon your homecoming," he began. "I'm sure you know that all of us, the entire community, we're grateful for your sacrifice, for putting yourself in harm's way for your country."

I didn't respond. There was no response to make.

"With your time overseas, it's understandable that you've earned a bit of time off. And I'm sure you have a nice little pot of money saved from your combat pay."

I emitted a sound that was vaguely positive.

"But I don't think that you realize," he continued, "how quickly the jobs are being snapped up by there turning soldiers. The refinery and the production work crews went begging for help just a year ago. Today they're turning away experienced men. Easily a quarter of jobs that called for strong backs when you graduated high school are now being done by machines. And for every machine out there, there's three guys vying for a chance at the controls. The war years have been solid for Main Street, but we're not so far removed from the breadlines that we don't remember what that's like. There's a job shortage in this country and you need to be aware of that."

"Thanks for letting me know."

My glibness didn't sit well with Stark. His brow furrowed and his mouth thinned into a line of disapproval. But he kept himself from stating what he must have thought.

"I'm here," he began again, more quietly, "to make you a very attractive offer." He began to pace back and forth in front of me, never looking me in the face. He might as well have been talking to himself. "Since your mother and I wed, you are now a part of my family. I believe strongly in family and in the inherent importance of family connections. Mrs. Stark and I are totally in agreement on that."

It took me a moment to recognize that when he said *Mrs. Stark* he meant Mama. And that what he really meant was that Mama had sent him down here to give me this lecture.

"My intent has always been to give my boy, Jonas, a partnership in the store when he graduates from high school next spring. I can't disappoint him on that. But we've been busier than usual the last few months, so I'm willing to offer you a job."

Stark stopped and turned to eye me as if assessing my potential.

"I'm not too much concerned about your lack of experience in the grocery business," he said. "I'm not unaware of your willingness to work. You did take care of your mother even back when you were just a boy. So I'm certain you have a natural inclination to better yourself. With a secure job and this old place, you'll definitely have a leg up in that direction."

He just stood there, looking at me expectantly. It was all I could do not to laugh in his face.

"I'm not interested in working for you," I told him finally.

I witnessed an instant of relief that swept across his face, followed almost immediately by indignation.

"This is quite a plum I'm offering you, Bud," he said. "I hope you realize that whilst you're so quick to turn it down."

"No doubt it's a good job," I assured him. "But I've got . . . I've got some other plans brewing that I'm not ready to talk about yet."

The lie so pleased the grocer that I almost wished I'd said so earlier. Fortunately, he didn't press me for details.

"Your mother will be delighted to hear that," he said. "She's been worried that you don't get out much — she never sees you chumming around with your old friends and you haven't been to church since you got back."

"You tell her not to worry," I said.

Stark nodded. "I'll do that," he said. "I'll surely do that. Now you stop by the house just anytime. I want you to know that you're always welcome. Dinner is on the table every day at six-thirty sharp and I'm sure you miss your mama's cooking."

I couldn't even remember my mother ever cooking. The idea that she might on a daily basis put a meal on the table was just more evidence that the world had shifted.

After Stark left, I went back to the chill of the garden and sat some more, huddled in my old cane seat chair. But I had a harder time staring into nothingness. The outside world was pushing in and I didn't know if I had the strength to push back.

It was all too true that I would have to find some kind of work. I'd been surprised when I'd gone downtown to cash my mustering-out money and discovered that I actually had a tidy little stash in the bank. Apparently Geri had set aside a good portion of my pay that the government had sent her. It would get me by for a while, but it wouldn't be enough to set me up for life. Like everybody else in the world, I'd be expected to make a living.

That wasn't going to be easy.

For a few self-indulgent moments I toyed with the idea of ceasing to live. Of course, I couldn't just shoot myself in the face — that would be too hard on Mama. I'd have to be killed in a way that would appear to be a tragic accident. I considered climbing the light pole and electrocuting myself. Or perhaps I could burn the house down with me inside.

I knew that I couldn't really do any of these things. For three years, I had been in the middle of a shooting war actively trying to get myself killed. If I hadn't been able to do it there, I sure wouldn't be able to do it here.

When the sun went down, the night got colder and I went inside. All I could find to eat in the kitchen was a hunk of cheese and a handful of crackers. I walked aimlessly through the house. I was so tired I could hardly keep my eyes open, but I did. I sat in Mama's rocker focusing on a piece of peeling plaster on the ceiling.

I felt myself starting to drift off and I startled myself awake.

I got up, found my jacket and stepped outside. The cold would keep me wide-awake and the garden was still there.

But it was different at night, darker. With only a sliver of moon to light it, the potato hills and remnants of rows looked like waves on the water. The night water was the worst, the very worst. Deliberately I turned and walked as fast as I could around the house and to the road. I would not run. I held myself in check. My heart was pounding and when I reached the road I began to walk up it toward the highway, purposely, as if I had someplace that I planned to go. One foot in front of the other, I just kept moving.

The dreams didn't occur so frequently during daylight. My sleep in the sunshine might be fitful, but the dreams didn't always come. At night they haunted me so badly I tried not to sleep. But if they began to haunt me while I was awake, how could I go on?

I don't know when I began to hear the music. It was on the edge of my consciousness for a minute, and then I realized I was listening to it. Up ahead I saw the multicolored lights of the Jitterbug Lounge. Slowly, it pulled me out of the dark shadow that followed me. I was not hurrying away anymore; I was heading in that direction, my step lighter and my thoughts, as well. The music had saved me once. Maybe it could again.

I recognized the song, it was one of my Glenn Miller favorites. It had been on the jukebox before I'd left for the war. And Tokyo Rose had played it on her broadcasts in the South Pacific. As the jiving tune came to its pause, I spoke the now infamous phone number aloud.

"Pennsylvania 6-5000!"

My own voice was loud in the darkness.

The joint was really rocking. The little vacant lot beside the building was jammed with cars, and more were parked all along the ditches of both Bee Street and the highway. As I made my way to the door, it looked to me not much changed from the way it had always been. I ignored the knots of people standing around outside. Some were too young to enter, others were socializing in the shadows with bottles of bootleg liquor. The repeal of prohibition had meant very little for Oklahoma. Watered-down beer was still the only legal alcohol in the state.

I wasn't interested in drinking, it was the music that drew me there. I kept my gaze straight ahead. I heard a vaguely familiar voice call my name but I kept walking.

Left over from its speakeasy days, the Jitterbug Lounge had both an outer and an inner doorway, with a tiny foyer in between. This night, both were propped open with wooden wedges allowing the light and sounds to spill out into the night.

The entryway was crowded. I had to squeeze by to get inside. The smell of cigarettes, stale beer and cheap perfume somehow mingled into a scent that was almost pleasant. The long mahogany bar along the north side of the building was crowded with customers. The group of musicians on the bandstand would never grace the stage at Macambo or the Blue Note, but they knew the songs and played them faithfully enough that everybody could dance.

And lots of people were dancing. I'd been in swing clubs from San Diego to Chicago, Manhattan to Manila and back again. Not a one of them had been any more crowded or loud or rowdy or giddy with desperation for a good time than this one here in this dinky, wide spot in the road.

This piece of strange truth made me smile. I'd become so unaccustomed to the expression that it felt unnatural to me and quickly disappeared. But I felt myself relaxing. The place was well-known to me and the music so familiar. I could almost put myself back into the boy that I had been. I could hear what he heard and see what he saw and feel how he felt. Almost.

I edged myself into a corner where I could view it all without really being a part of it. I let my attention wander from the musicians to the drinkers and finally to the dancers. The whole room was swinging and swaying and jiving it loose in every kind of way. I didn't notice the fellows, though I'm sure there were some who could really cut a rug. It was the girls whom I watched.

That was a natural. I might not be a normal guy, but I still had normal urges. And I was not a monk. I'd found out that a woman could offer some relief from the tension, some respite from the dark shadows.

That night I was only looking. I was not seeking any comfort in Catawah. The hometown offered no anonymity. And I didn't need any complications. But even a damaged man could hardly avert his gaze from a pretty girl. It wouldn't even be polite.

So I allowed myself the luxury of observing the chubby blonde and the long-legged redhead. I assessed the assets of the big-busted gal who was so drunk she was reeling on the dance floor.

A couple emerged from the center, rocking and reeling. They were good at it, I suppose. But what caught my eye was the girl. She had her back to me, but it wasn't her face that I was looking for. She was small, delicate, but her bottom was nicely rounded and looked especially fine in a red pencil skirt with only a tiny row of kick pleats near the hem. Her dark brown hair had been twisted and primped into a thousand loosened pin curls that bounced with every move she made. I was curious about the rest of her figure. And leaned slightly to one side to get a better view. From what I could tell, her breasts weren't all that big, certainly not as impressive as the blousy gal, but I thought she filled her little sweater very nicely. Her legs were not so long, but they were well-shaped and the calves tapered attractively to her ankles and the straps on her perilously high heels.

I was really enjoying watching her and was disappointed when the music ended. She applauded the band as her partner leaned over to steal a kiss. Easily she dodged him and I found myself chuckling in admiration.

It was then she turned in my direction. From across a distance of a half dozen yards our eyes met instantly, and I'm sure my jaw must have dropped open.

My rational mind made no decision to go to her, but my arms and legs acted upon instinct. A second later she leaped into my arms, and I was pressing my face in her soft, sweet smelling hair.

"Crazy Girl, my crazy girl!" I said over and over again.

"I'd forgotten how much it is that I love you," she whispered against my ear.

The musicians struck up another tune, the catchy "Is You Is or Is You Ain't My Baby?"

Then I caught sight of the bandstand and saw they were taking a break. The music was not there in my memory, it was here in my hospital. I lay still, strapped down to my bed as I listened to the song. My wife was gone. Everything from way back then was gone. But I held the memory of Geri in my arms and it felt good.

# Saturday, June 11, 2:12 P.M.

Jack Crabtree had time on his hands. That wasn't something that normally happened in his life, and he wasn't quite sure what to do about it. He wandered aimlessly and uncomfortably around his grandparents' house.

They'd gone early to the hospital, following Aunt Viv's instructions. Even in her state of decline, she behaved as the family matriarch, and everyone, including Jack, went along with that.

Her edicts included insisting that Bud never be left alone in the hospital.

"When your health is poor, being handed over to strangers can only make you feel worse."

The hospital shouldn't be overrun by relatives.

"We'll have shifts of pairs, so Bud's never left alone and nobody in the family is overwhelmed."

And that everybody must be involved.

"The only way young people learn how to take care of their family is by trusting them enough to let them do it."

For that reason, Viv wanted the nights and weekends to be left up to the twentysomething nieces, nephews and cousins who had less flexibility in their schedules of work, school and kids.

This was all very foreign to Jack. He was his grandfather's closest relative and could easily imagine himself not having come here. It was beyond understanding for him to think of being a twenty-one-year-old college kid sitting up all night with an ancient great-uncle. But the kids in the Shertz family seemed to accept it as the normal thing to do.

Jack wondered, not for the first time, how different he might have been if he'd grown up here among these people, as one of them. He had been much better off, he was certain, amid the intellect and affluence of the Van Brugge household.

Aunt Viv had drafted Jesse's granddaughter, Lisa Marie, who was apparently home bound with five children, to create a suitable schedule that would ensure that Bud was never alone, and that no one was overly burdened by his hospitalization.

Jack and Claire had been relegated to two hours that morning. And now, in mid-afternoon, they were back at the house in Catawah. Claire was making herself useful to Theba, who'd come over on some errand. Jack had no idea what they were up to, but he was determined to steer clear.

He stood uneasily on the front porch for a few minutes. He glanced at both the wicker chairs and the swing, but he was too antsy to sit. Instead he propped his foot on the bottom crosspiece of the railing and leaned forward, elbow on knee staring out into the open land across the street from the yard and thinking. One of the slats had broken loose from the railing. It momentarily captured his attention and Jack began to wiggle it with his foot.

He pulled the cell phone out of his pocket, flipped it open and then stared at the face of it for a moment. There wasn't anybody he really needed to talk to. He'd spent most of his two hours at Bud's bedside making business calls. He didn't feel like that was so bad. Claire wanted him to have conversations with Bud and that talking about anything was fine. Jack decided that he could extend that idea to speaking with other people and allowing Bud to just listen in.

He stuck the phone back in his pocket and wondered about the concept of free time. He never had any free time and always thought he wanted some. Now he wasn't so sure.

The problem, of course, he told himself, was that he was here in Catawah. If he'd been in San Antonio with several days off, there would have been plenty to do. Even on nights and weekends he spent endless hours on the job. And when he wasn't working, there was the new house. He couldn't just hand the contractor a check and expect the place to turn out to his liking. Every trim piece and electrical outlet had been his decision. Claire should have done more. But she wouldn't lift a finger to help him. He'd made every choice himself. Now all that was left was paint, tile and carpet. And it looked as if those decisions were going to fall to him, as well. He didn't really mind doing it, but it was the principle of it. It was *their* house. She should be involved in it. Claire was just too stubborn. Every wife in the world wanted a new house, a bigger house. But not his wife. No, she wanted to stay put in a starter home that was too small for their family and not lavish enough to entertain his clients.

As Jack felt his annoyance rising, he

deliberately pushed the problem to the back of his mind. It wasn't fixable. Claire was being unreasonable. There were no solutions to that except very bad ones. So he just wouldn't think about it at all.

But he had to think about something. With his foot he'd managed to significantly worsen the problem of the broken slat on the railing. He squatted down, assessing the situation. It wasn't critical, but Bud was certainly in no condition to repair it. Jack decided to make himself useful. This was something that he *could* fix. He headed around the side of the house, looking for tools.

The shed was padlocked. Jack assumed the key was one on the line of hooks hanging on the wall inside the screened back porch. He glanced over in that direction to see the door propped open and to hear the voices of his wife and his cousin Theba. He still wanted to avoid them. Immediately he looked at the hinges and frowned. He hoped his grandfather hadn't believed he was actually securing anything inside. Using a penny from his pocket as a screwdriver, he managed to free the hinges from the frame and folded open the still-locked door.

Inside it smelled like sawdust and linseed oil. Jack felt along the inside wall in the darkness for a light switch and finally noticed the long piece of string hanging down from the bulb. Electricity revealed a small, neat and well-organized workshop. His grandfather had been meticulous about the care of his tools. Bud's preference, it seemed, was for hand work. He had a couple of power saws and an electric drill, but the expensive nail gun on the shelf was still in its plastic packaging and sported a faded red-and-green bow, a ghost of a Christmas past.

Jack quickly found a small-size crowbar, a claw hammer and a mallet. He carried all three back to the front porch. Although he'd never done this particular job, he was confident. He'd been naturally gifted with his hands since boyhood. The way things were put together had always made sense to him. Without help, supervision or even permission, he'd built a treehouse in his backyard. His mother was so leery of it that she'd paid a retired building inspector to assure that it was safe. The guy had looked it over and given the thumbs-up.

"You'll always be able to find work in the building trades," he'd told Jack.

He'd been delighted by the praise.

His mother had put a damper on his pride later that day when he proudly relayed the story over dinner.

"Well, of course you could be in *the trades,*" she'd said, dismissively. "But you're bright and gifted enough to aim higher. What do you think, Ernst? Maybe architecture? Architecture is not so blue collar."

Jack squatted down to pop out the slat as he recalled the memory. He wondered, not for the first time, how his natural parents had ever gotten together. A regular G.I. grunt like J.D. Crabtree could never have met his mother's high standards.

He removed the rotten board from the railing and found two others that were almost as bad. He was just pulling out the third when he heard the crunch of footsteps on the driveway gravel. Glancing up he saw Preacher McKiever, Theba's husband, and he sighed aloud.

"Hullo!" the man called out to him. "Keeping yourself busy, I see."

The preacher didn't look much like a preacher this morning. He was an angular man, far too thin and with a face stretched so closely across the front of his skull that he looked ghostly even in the prime of health. He was dressed in faded overalls, T-shirt and a scruffy ball cap that advertised a septic-tank service.

Jack rose to his feet, acknowledging the

man with cold politeness. He didn't want to encourage this guy. It was bad enough that they were related by marriage, but he had no interest in forming any kind of social connection.

"I do what I can," Jack answered. "Theba's out in the back with Claire."

It was Jack's hope that the man was merely picking up his wife. Though the fact that it was she who brought the car and that the preacher had arrived on foot didn't give him much hope.

"I know," he answered. "I've been up at the church shoring up some plumbing problems." The last was spoken with a gesture explaining his attire.

"How's your granddad doing this morning?" he asked. "Theba and I aren't on the schedule at all this weekend."

"He's the same," Jack answered. "The doctor said that the swelling in his brain is going down, which actually makes the bleeding worse. The monitors indicate periods of consciousness, but nobody's actually been able to get a response from him."

McKiever nodded solemnly. "Well, I want you to know that he's on our prayer chain. And we've got some world-class prayers among our little congregation."

"Uh . . . thanks," Jack said.

"Actually, I came down here to make sure you got a personal invitation to come to service tomorrow," he said. "Being away from home and living in and abiding now in such a valley of uncertainty, you'll be requiring some sacred time with the Lord."

Jack raised a skeptical eyebrow, but didn't comment.

McKiever glanced at the wood in Jack's hand. "Are you going to try to reuse those slats or cut new ones?"

"I thought I'd cut new," he answered. "This one I might be able to plane down enough, but these other two are practically powder."

The preacher nodded. "Did you find everything in your granddad's shed?"

"I found the tools," Jack answered. "And there were a few old boards on the shelf that I might be able to use."

"If not, I know where he stores his wood-pile," McKiever said.

The two made their way back around the house.

The preacher noticed Jack's folded back door. "I think the key to this padlock is on the back porch," he said.

Jack nodded. "I figured as much, but I didn't want to interrupt the ladies."

McKiever laughed. "I doubt if you could interrupt," he said. "But you might very likely be drawn into whatever project the two of them have set their mind to."

Inside the shed, Jack walked over to the west wall and reached for a small pile of cut boards in the corner of the top shelf. He examined one of the boards closely.

"I was going to use this," he said. "It looks like it's been sitting there for quite a while, but this is better wood than you use on a porch rail."

He handed the piece to McKiever for verification.

"It looks like walnut," the preacher said. "That's high-dollar lumber nowadays. Is all that up there the same?"

"I think so." Jack brought all of the wood down and they laid it out on the worktable. There were nine pieces in all. Two had been carefully dovetailed. Jack slipped them together and the grain lined up perfectly.

"He must have been making a drawer to a cabinet or something," McKiever said.

Jack was quiet for a long moment. "I think I know what this is," he said.

"What?"

"I remember getting some boards out of here when I was a boy," he said. "Bud scolded me and said they were for a treasure box my father had been making."

McKiever gave a little gasp of surprise and surveyed the boards more carefully. "Do you know the story of Geri's treasure box?" he asked.

Jack should his head. "No, I haven't heard it."

The man remained hesitant. "I'm sure Theba could tell it better than me," he said. "Your grandma Geri always kept her special things, things that were dear to her under the bed in J.D.'s room. What I recollect hearing is that young J.D. was on leave from the service and got it in his head to make her a treasure box. He wanted to make it real pretty and he wanted to make it brand-new, cause everything that woman ever had was castoffs. It took him awhile to find just the right wood. He finally settled on some black walnut. And he worked on it for a few days before he went back to his base. He was going to finish it next time he came home."

Jack nodded thoughtfully, surveying the wood differently now.

"But then, when he got to San Antonio, the boy got busy. He fell in love and then got married. He did get back home for a few days before he headed overseas. But mostly I guess everyone understands why a fellow would rather spend his last days home with his new bride rather than his old parents." McKiever chuckled lightly and shook his head. "I think everybody just forgot all about the treasure box, figuring he'd finish it when he got back from Vietnam."

"But he didn't come back," Jack said.

"No, he didn't. Bud never spoke a word about it, but Geri told her sisters that he was just stuck. He couldn't bear to finish it, but he couldn't give the wood away. I suspect that this is that wood."

Jack nodded wordlessly. He pictured himself once more using this fine walnut for a skateboard ramp. It was amazing that his grandfather hadn't been more angry. Jack began gathering up the pieces and putting it back on the shelf it came from.

"So where's this woodpile?" he asked McKiever.

The preacher at least understood when a subject didn't require further discussion.

"There's a flap door underneath the back of the house — he keeps it on a palate down there."

Claire had awakened that morning when her husband had reached for her. The old cast-iron bed was bouncy and squeaky, but

243

there were no children who might wake up and no place she needed to be on time. She gave herself up to the pleasure of having intercourse with him. Even from their earliest days together, it had always been good. It was one of the few things between them that hadn't changed. And beyond the welcome physical release, there was the embrace, the affection, the kissing and cuddling that were actually more dear. Sex had its substitutes, but there was no alternative to the touch of another human being.

So their day had begun on a high note, but had become twangy later and she was convinced that Jack must be tone deaf.

At the hospital something had changed. Claire sensed it from the nurses. Nothing was said to that effect. The doctor said that there were no notable changes in his condition but from the moment she walked into the room, Claire sensed that something was not right. In the hallway she said as much to the nurse. The woman nodded.

"I had that feeling, too," she admitted. "But everything we look at —" She indicated the computer screen on the rolling unit she manned. "Everything seems very much like yesterday."

"But it's not," Claire stated flatly.

The nurse didn't attempt to dispute that.

"Everybody has good days and bad," she said. "It may not be an irreparable setback, just a temporary wavering on his road to recovery."

Claire tried to be mollified, to take on a more positive attitude, but back in the room her husband didn't make it easy.

Jack was using his time with Bud to phone his office. No one was supposed to be working on the weekend, but somehow Jack always managed to catch up with Dana.

Claire sat across the room from him as he talked to her. It didn't matter that the two discussed drainage and impervious cover restrictions; it was the way they talked to each other, the way his voice softened into a tone that was so familiar to Claire and, she had once thought, exclusive to her.

When he finally ended the call, Claire couldn't bite her tongue fast enough not to scold him about it.

"Couldn't that have waited?" she asked sharply.

Jack shook his head. "Dana has a meeting tonight with Butterman, I wanted to be sure that she was completely up to speed on the project."

"She has a meeting *tonight?*" Claire's voice was incredulous. "What kind of business meeting happens on Saturday night?"

"It's a last-minute thing. I'm not even sure what the man wants to know. But Butterman's a busy guy with a lot going on," Jack said. "I'm sure he has to fit building contractors in wherever he can."

"I'm sure he holds a spot open on Saturdays for those building contractors with really big boobs."

Jack sighed heavily and gave her a stern look. "This pointless cattiness doesn't look good on you, Claire."

To avoid any further discussion he began phoning once more and spent the rest of the hour touching base with current clients.

By the time their replacements showed up, two middle-aged cousins named Sherry and Bob Lee, Claire was past mad and into near despair. She didn't understand Jack anymore. They didn't value the same things. If she met him now, she would never have had any interest in him. Their marriage hardly stood a chance.

Driving back to Catawah with Jack only eighteen inches away from her, she effectively avoided him by calling the children. Standing in line to ride the roller coaster at Sea World, the kids were laughing and acting up so frantically, Claire could hardly get a word in. Finally she got Zaidi on the phone, but that wasn't a perfect conversation, either.

"Guess what, Mom?" she burst out, not allowing Claire to even hazard. "I got my ears pierced. Toni bought me some amethyst studs that I just love. I can't wear them until my holes heal, but they are completely yowling!"

"You got your ears pierced?"

"Toni said I could." Her tone was partly defiant, partly pleading and partly just passing the blame.

"Well, that's great," Claire responded forcing herself to sound happy about a circumstance that couldn't be changed. "And I'm sure the new earrings are perfect. Your grandmother has excellent taste."

Continued discussion yielded the fact that having purchased the jewelry for Zaidi, "in order to be fair" she bought a new and very expensive game system for the twins. Claire tried to be cheerful about that, too. But what she wanted was to be with her kids. To stop them from getting all starry-eyed about the things that Toni could buy for them. She believed that children needed limits. She even believed that adults needed them, as well.

When Presley asked to speak to Daddy, she handed Jack the phone. She listened to him talk to the kids. Or rather she listened to him listening to the kids. Laughing with them, enjoying their excitement. There was no deliberateness about his conversation, no concern about saying the right thing, encouraging in the right way, maintaining the balance between instilling values and fostering independence. He was just parenting from the hip. Jack was good at that. Claire was not.

When he finished the call, he glanced over in her direction, smiling. His expression changed immediately.

"What?" he asked.

"Nothing," she answered immediately. It would have been more truthful to have said *everything:* Dana, the house, the kids, his job, his attitude toward Bud. Or maybe *nothing* was the correct answer. Because *nothing* her husband did, thought or said seemed all right to her anymore.

Claire kept silent for the rest of the trip and got out of the car the minute they pulled into the driveway. She needed to put some distance between herself and her husband. Inside the house she slipped into what she now considered her work clothes. From a stack of vintage blue jeans she'd found in the back-room closet, she recovered a well-worn and faded pair that fitted comfortably. She'd matched that up with one of Bud's old shirts, tying the long length of it in a knot at her waist. And finished off the look, which might aptly be described as hausfrau hobo, by wearing Geri's green plastic gardening clogs she'd found still sitting where the old woman had left them by the back door. She pulled her hair into a ponytail and stepped outside.

The scent of flowers and the buzz of bees lured her out to the garden. She'd been weeding and watering for the last two days. It was not perfect, but it was very close. Only Geri herself could have made it look better. She was tempted to piddle with that perfection, but steeled herself to accomplish something more substantial. Claire turned around and marched back into the house.

The screened wash porch was full to bursting with piles of junk. Crates and boxes of jelly jars, rubber hoses, cardboard packaging and plastic bottles were stacked to the ceiling. The table and chairs that had once been the room's furniture were hidden among it. Claire didn't know where to start. Why had Bud kept all this trash? And what was Claire going to do with it? The answers to those questions unexpectedly came walking around the corner.

"Hello."

Claire glanced up to see Jack's cousin Theba.

"Oh hi," Claire responded.

"I was up at the church with the preacher and I thought I'd just stroll down here to see how you two are doing, find out if you need anything."

"No, I think we've got everything. The whole community has been so generous," she said. "If one more pie shows up here, my backside will never fit in the airplane seat, going home."

"Oh, don't be silly," Theba said. "A woman's suppose to have a womanly figure. Those models in the magazines, they're just clothes hangers."

Claire chuckled. "Well, there doesn't seem to be any danger of me turning into that."

"What are you doing?"

"I've decided that I have to do something about all this stuff," she said, indicating the wash porch.

"Mercy!" Theba exclaimed and then laughed. "I guess Bud's not been keeping up with the recycling since Geri died."

"Recycling." Claire shook her head at her own obtuseness. "Of course, it's the recycling. There was just so much, I couldn't imagine what it was for."

Theba nodded. "Geri was a big saver, all

the Shertz sisters are," she said. "You know they grew up in the junk business. People like them were the original recyclers."

"I don't guess I knew that," Claire admitted.

"Yeah, my old granddad made a living from other people's castoffs," Theba told her. "And I don't imagine that was easy during the Depression when nobody was casting off much of anything that had value."

"No, I guess not."

"My mama's just like that, too. Can't throw anything away, no matter what. When the old man died, the county was going to just bury his junkyard, make it a landfill. It was just one giant mountain of refuse. The sisters spent weeks up there picking it clean before they'd let it go."

"Wow."

"You can say that again," Theba agreed. "Geri knew where to recycle everything. It was really important to her. I suspect Bud wasn't able to keep up with it."

Claire nodded.

"Maybe if I get it sorted, I can figure out where to recycle it," she said.

"I'll help you," Theba said. "Between the two of us, it won't take that long."

They dug into the work, creating new piles on the back lawn — things that could go to the town's recycling center, household items for the Goodwill thrift shop, books for the library's annual sidewalk sale, metal parts and wires for the salvage company, electronics and car parts that would require special handling and disposal. If Theba thought that her mother's generation knew a lot about this process, Claire was very impressed about Theba's store of knowledge. They worked well together and they made lots of progress.

"I really appreciate your help," she told the older woman. "I'd never have been able to figure this out without you."

"Nonsense, you would have done fine," Theba said. "And I'd much rather be doing this than fetching tools for the preacher while he tries not to curse at the church's plumbing."

Claire laughed.

"Your husband's church is near here?"

"Yes, it's right up at the highway," she said. "You have to pass by it every day."

Claire remembered the long, odd-shaped building on the corner at the highway that had all the earmarks of an ancient honky-tonk. "I thought that's, like, a Mexican church," she said.

"Hispanic," Theba answered. *"Iglesia de Jesus."*

Claire managed not to smile at her pronunciation. It was probably only here that the son of God might be called *Hay-Zoos.*

"I didn't realize that you and the preacher spoke Spanish," she said.

"Oh Lord, I wish that we did," Theba said. "It would sure make things a lot easier. But I just know a few words and the preacher is even worse than me."

Claire was momentarily incredulous. "How did he get to be the pastor of a Hispanic church without speaking Spanish."

"Oh, he was called by God," Theba explained. "You ought to hear the story from him, 'cause he tells it much better than I do. But the gist is, God called him to preach, but he could never find a church to give him a chance. Then one morning about three years ago, he was sitting in the coffee shop and the place was full of Hispanic people. They were all yammering to each other in their language and the preacher was resenting it. He was wishing that they were gone and that the town would be back to the way that it used to be before they came. Back when everybody knew everybody else and everyone was the same."

Claire was a little surprised at this politically incorrect admission.

"So then right there in the coffee shop,"

Theba continued, "it was as if the Lord brought his finger down through the cloud and popped the preacher right on the breast bone. He told him, 'if you don't know these people, it's because you choose not to. Get to know these people because they need you and you need them.' "

Theba clasped her hands together, shook her head and glanced up toward heaven.

"It changed our life," she said. "The preacher began to talk to them. Most everybody speaks a little English, though, for some it's not much. And we had come to find out what these people needed was a church. They didn't feel welcome in any of the ones we have, they wanted one of their own. The preacher had just inherited the old Jitterbug Lounge up at the highway — it had been a nightclub and dance hall for years. The preacher wouldn't have nothing to do with that kind of business and didn't know what he was supposed to do with the building. Then he realized it could be a church for these people."

Claire tried to hide her surprise.

"Aren't most Hispanic people Catholic?"

Theba shrugged. "We don't let that bother us," she said. "We all worship the same God. Sure, it's different than they expected. But the nearest Catholic church is forty miles from here. They can always make that trip if they really have to. But mostly folks around here get by. They make do with what they have until they reach the place where they realize it's exactly what they want."

Claire gave her a little half smile, as much puzzled as amused.

"You should come tomorrow and meet our folks yourself," Theba said. "You can learn a lot by watching people putting square blocks in round holes."

Claire wasn't so sure.

# BUD

I was floating, floating down as if I had not a care in the world. My escape from the plane had been without injury. We'd been so flaked that one engine was knocked out and two were badly sputtering. When I saw the far right one burst into flames, I knew we were in trouble. The captain ordered us out of there and nobody hesitated. Mugs jumped just ahead of me. It was only after my chute opened that I realized that his hadn't. I watched him fall to his death as I floated on the breeze.

In the distance, the plane tipped its wings near perpendicular to the horizon and then slipped into the water as neatly as a diver eager for a summer swim.

A quietness settled over the moment. There was no sound on the breeze, no birds or bugs or engine noise. Even the sea made no noise if there was nothing for the waves to lap against. It was peace. I wanted just to close my eyes and enjoy it, because I knew the future would be uncertain.

Instead I forced myself to look for other chutes. I saw only three. Jedlowski had been dead in the plane and Mugs had bought it on the way down. In a ten-man crew that made four unaccounted. The B-24 was notoriously hard to get out of. The G.I.s in the European Theater had nicknamed it the flying coffin. But we'd dropped our bombs. That should have made the catwalk from the flight deck to the tail exit a lot easier.

I guessed it wasn't easy enough.

I drifted down so gently into the Solomon Sea. As soon as I hit the water, I detached myself from the chute and let it go. My life vest, a Mae West, inflated successfully. It was not sturdy enough to keep me upright for long. I had to tread water if I was going to stay alive.

My first priority was to rendezvous with my crewmates, but after hours of fruitless swimming, I was content to just drift, bobbing and treading water, waiting for rescue. The other planes in our squad must know we were out here. When they got back to the field, they'd send a boat to look for us. In the first hours I was certain of that. As the day got longer, my hope wavered. These waters were notoriously shark-infested. We'd flown over huge schools of the beasts many times and marveled at the numbers. Remembering that, I tried not to kick so noticeably and I was keenly on the lookout for the sight of fins.

Suddenly, I did spot something that was much more welcome. It was debris from the plane and it was floating. If it was floating, I could maybe get onto it. I swam as hard as I could in that direction.

As I got closer I recognized it as the plane's five-man survival raft. The raft, stored in the tail, was supposed to be released when the plane hit the water. I'm not sure when I realized that there was somebody clinging to the side of it. But I do remember my joy. I hadn't realized how alone I'd felt until I saw someone else.

"Hullo!" I called out, stopping to tread water and cup my hands as a megaphone before raising my arms in the air to get his attention. With more energy and eagerness I swam toward the raft, stopping to holler in that direction several times. His back was turned to me. He couldn't hear.

I felt so much better, I felt almost safe. It was a part of our evac plan to rendezvous in the water. But after hours of swimming in the direction I'd seen other parachutes, I'd given up. They'd seen me, too, and the current was in their favor, not mine. So I'd waited for somebody to find me. And now, somebody had.

"Hey! Over here. I'm here."

The person hanging on to the raft still didn't move. I swam harder to get to him. As I got close my stroke slowed. I knew before I reached him that the man was dead. I'd already seen a lot of death. Without thinking my body steeled itself for the horror. I'd seen worse, I reminded myself.

It was Lt. Randel. I identified him from his jacket, there was nothing else recognizable about him. It was hard to tell if he'd grasped the cords on the raft to save himself, or been trapped in them accidentally to fall to his death. I untangled him and let him go into the sea.

I took a deep breath and heaved myself up into the raft. It took two tries. My arms, the young muscular arms of a nineteen-year-old, had inexplicably turned to jelly. Finally, I got myself high enough to fall inside. The relief was so tangible that I actually laughed out loud. I was exhausted, but I was out of the water. It was only after that I noticed Lt. Randel still bobbing on the waves. I'd forgotten to take off his life vest.

Don't remember. Don't remember! *Don't remember!*

On the first night I'd fallen to sleep with Geri in my arms, I'd remembered.

For several weeks since that night at Jitterbug Lounge we'd been dating. If *dating* is what you call two people who had been chastely married for three years, now unmarried and spending every possible moment together having sex. We didn't talked about the past. We didn't talk about the future. Come to think of it, we didn't talk much at all. We let our young, eager, lusty bodies say everything that needed to be said between us.

In any other era in Catawah, we would have shocked the village. But after the war, there were a lot of couples just like us. Kids who'd married too fast, guys who'd seen too much, girls who were widows too young. It was a crazy time. And it was as if our elders, who had always maintained the highest of propriety for themselves and insisted on the same for their offspring, turned a blind eye to what was going on. It must have been like a gift to us, to our generation from their generation. They gave us some time and some latitude. From what I saw, and as for Geri and myself, we really needed it.

Sex together back then was wild and frantic. I couldn't get enough of her and she apparently felt just the same. The first time we barely managed to get inside the house. We did it on the living room rug that she'd so carefully braided and sewn.

"That was good. Oh my God, that was so good," I told her after.

"Me, too," she said snuggling up next to me and resting in the crook of my arm. "You're not disappointed are you?" she asked me after we'd had time to catch our breath.

"Disappointed?"

"That I'm not a virgin."

I hadn't noticed. But then I didn't know what to notice. The few women I'd been with had been, if not professionals, certainly very experienced.

"It doesn't matter," I said.

"It does to me," Geri said with a sigh. "I should have waited. I should have had faith that once you were back home you would love me."

I remembered my long-ago plan to just dump my mother on her and never come back.

I put my fingers atop her lips. "Sweetheart, lots of things happened in the war. Lots of things that just don't bear speaking about. Now we're never going to talk about this again."

That was my choice and hers, too. We

didn't talk about the war. We were both willing to put it all behind us.

But it wouldn't stay there.

I was still spending my days listlessly. At night we'd meet at the Jitterbug Lounge. We'd have a couple of beers and we'd dance and laugh and then we'd walk down to my house and we'd have sex. Our evenings frequently lasted until the middle of the night and then I'd walk her back to her old clunker Ford and she'd drive home. I'd walk home and begin my day. Which meant wandering the house until the sun was up and then sitting in the garden once it was.

Then one night came when we fell asleep. There was nothing different from other nights, except maybe the winter cold had passed and the spring was finally on us. The windows were open and the perfume of the honeysuckle on the trellis outside my window enveloped us.

"I love you," she whispered in the moment our passion was spent.

"Me, too," I'd answered and pulled her up against me, spooning our bodies so comfortably as I caught my breath. She was warm and smooth and I was so relaxed beside her. The softness of those brunette curls were a perfect pillow.

I drifted off. Off to that place I never

wanted to visit, but couldn't stay away from. I was back in the water. I don't recall which of the dreams it was. Lt. Randel or the leaky raft or the worst, alone in the water. But I woke up screaming and flailing as I always did. It was just that this time I was not alone or among crewmates who'd seen as much as I had. I was in bed with a beautiful, gentle and caring woman who loved me.

When I realized where I was, she was cowering at the foot of the bed. The first rays of morning sun lit the room well enough that I could see her brown eyes wide with shock and fear.

I managed to get control of myself. Or at least as much control as I could take immediately. My hands would sometimes shake for a quarter of an hour. There was nothing I could do about that but clutch them together.

"I'm sorry," I said. "I'm . . . I'm just sorry."

I climbed out of bed desperate to get away. I grabbed my pants and pulled them on as I left the room. I had no shirt, no shoes, but I headed straight out the back door and walked up the rows to the middle of the garden where my ancient cane-bottom chair was waiting.

I'd been caught. My secret had been revealed. All was lost. I expected Geri to get herself dressed and out the front door as quickly as possible. I knew she'd never come back to the house with me again. And I'd be lucky if she didn't tell people why when they asked her what happened.

I really underestimated that woman.

The back-door screen slammed. I glanced up to see her standing on the step. She must have made the noise on purpose warning me that she was there.

I purposely looked away. I remembered the fear in her eyes and I couldn't bear to see it again.

She was walking toward me, I could see that in my peripheral vision, but I refused to turn my head to look at her. I still thought if I kept my distance, she would, too.

But she didn't.

"Here," she said. "You can't be sitting out in this cool morning breeze half-naked."

I glanced, then, at what she carried. My shirt and shoes. I took them from her and busied myself with buttons and socks and laces.

"Thank you," I said quietly. That was her cue to leave, but she didn't take it. After a moment I added. "I'm fine now."

Still she didn't go. Instead she squatted down in front of me and took my chin in her hand, forcing me to make eye contact.

"Is this what's going on with you?" she asked me.

My first impulse was to lie. Anybody can have a nightmare. It's no big deal. But that little heart-shaped face, those flashing, determined eyes, I couldn't belittle her by deceit.

"Some things happened to me out there," I answered.

Her brow furrowed with concern. "You had to kill people," she said. "That could give any man bad dreams."

I might have left it there, but I needed to tell it out loud and her trust, her love, gave me that courage.

"It wasn't the killing," I told her. "The killing was easy. It was the dying that was hard."

There was no change in her expression, not an iota of judgment, not the batting of an eye.

"The man you loved, Geri," I told her. "That man died out in the Solomon Sea in 1943. Everything that happened since then, all the kills I made, all the medals I won — those went to a dead man. That's how I did what I did. I had no fear of getting killed, 'cause I was already dead."

Geri continued to look at me. I tried to

look away, but she wouldn't let me.

"These last weeks I've not been making love with a dead man," she told me at last.

I didn't answer.

"You can't tell me that you don't feel alive when I touch you, Bud. This shadow may come back on you, but when you're in my arms you're alive."

I nodded. "Yes," I admitted. "For those few moments it's like the war never happened. You make me want to try to live."

Those words dangled in the air between us for long moments.

"Do you know how I got you to love me?" she asked finally.

I was surprised at the change of subject.

"Wearing that tight red pencil skirt?" I suggested.

She laughed and shook her head.

"That was just the last straw," she told me. "Every day of my life, every day since I was a kid, I pretended that you loved me. I walked like you loved me and I talked like you loved me. I even married you like you loved me. Each day it got easier and easier. And even when you said you didn't love me, I'd gotten so used to pretending that you did, that I didn't believe you."

She took my hand in her own and caressed it and kissed the knuckles.

"Then one day, you did love me," she said. "It was a miracle. But one I'd worked for, waited for, struggled for, for years. Sometimes miracles are like that. I wondered many times why it had to be so hard. Now I see exactly."

"Why?"

"Because it's going to take a miracle to bring you back to life," she said. "And I've already learned how to go about getting one."

I was skeptical.

"Trust me," she said. "I've already proved this works. Together we'll pretend that everything is fine. We'll pretend it every moment of every day. We'll pretend that the war never touched us and that our life is normal. We'll pretend we're a regular couple. Nothing out of the ordinary about us. We'll pretend it day after day and if we're lucky, someday we'll forget that we're pretending."

I wasn't sure her plan would work, but I cared enough about trying to make her happy that I had to try.

The first thing we did was get married again. We meant it to be just a small, private ceremony in the Pentecostal church. The Shertz family showed up, which filled half the church. Old Dirty Shirts was widowed

267

now and frail in both body and mind. His daughters and sons-in-law helped him to his pew, but he didn't seem much aware of his location.

"Daddy, this is Bud, you remember Bud don't you, Daddy?"

The old man looked up at me, his eyes rheumy.

"No milk today, boy. Go on now, no milk today."

"At least he knows who you are," Geri's sister Viv said. "Even if he don't know what decade he's in."

On my side of the aisle I expected only Mama and Mr. Stark. But surprisingly Saffy and Jonas showed up. They were, Mama pointed out, my stepbrother and stepsister. And Berthrene came, as well. I was shocked to see her. I'd taken great pains to avoid her since I'd come home. Like facing the night terrors, I approached her and thanked her for coming.

"I was there for the first wedding," she said, laughing. "I could hardly miss the re-run."

Our first wedding had also been hers and Les's. It couldn't have been easy remembering that. I said as much to her.

"The hurt of remembering those you've lost is not as painful as not remembering at all," she said.

She was undoubtedly right about that.

The kids we saw nightly at the Jitterbug Lounge showed up, as well, which filled up the groom's side of the aisle nicely. And all in all it seemed as nice and fancy and full of good will as any normal wedding for normal people. Geri and I pledged our vows of love, honor and fidelity once more. And this time I listened to her words and I meant my own.

She wore a blue dress and pinned her hair up with a funny sort of beaded cap on her head. She looked young and pretty and happy. I had on my high school graduation suit, which was two inches short in both the sleeves and the trouser hem, and hung on me like a sack. I hadn't realized I'd gotten so thin.

People threw rice and everyone went to Mr. Stark's house afterward. My mother had a fancy cake with a sweet candy wedding bell on top.

It was official once more. We were Mr. and Mrs. Crabtree. And this time I wanted everyone to notice.

Geri, always practical, always willing to make do with whatever she had, began our marriage not from the perspective of our problems, but rather from our opportunities.

"You need to get a night job," she told me.

"Huh?"

"If you can't sleep at night, then you need a reason to be awake. You go up to town and see who needs a watchman or a booze runner or whatever kind of jobs people do at night."

"A booze runner?"

"Well," Geri said, with great seriousness, "it would be better to do something legal. But at this point any job would be better than pacing inside these four walls all night."

Fortunately, I didn't have to pursue a vocation in crime. I began asking around. My willingness to work the night shift quickly became a positive. I got hired at the *Catawah Daily Citizen,* helping the typesetter and running the presses. Before the war there had always been a newspaper in town. And the bankers and merchants read it and the working men sometimes looked at the sports page. During the war, however, the news became something that everybody wanted to know, needed to know. Timbuktu wasn't just a place you couldn't pronounce, it was somewhere that someone you knew was hunkered down.

After the war, the reading habit lingered. The G.I.s who'd seen the world were still interested in it. And the folks from the home front who'd kept up with the world for years now just couldn't let it be. Circulation at the paper was up, which meant that advertising was up. And that meant the number of pages had to be increased, meaning more time and more hands running the presses at night.

I showed up at deadline, 10:00 p.m., and worked until the paper was on the street, usually four o'clock or four-thirty. Then I'd walk home, climb into bed with my warm and rested wife and we'd play love games until breakfast time. I found it to be a near-perfect situation.

Of course, nobody can stay awake night and day. Geri saw how comforted I was about being in the garden, so she got a cot and set it out under a tarp right in the middle of everything. I told her she was crazy, but the truth was, I could rest better out in the open like that, until the day got too hot.

"You need a fan to keep the heat off you," Geri said.

I laughed. "Why that'd be perfect, Geri. You just get one of those big palm fronds like the slaves of the pasha have in the movies and you can just fan me all day long."

She laughed. "What? Are you trying to

ruin my reputation as the meanest wife in town, making her poor husband work all night long."

Ultimately, I ran an electric line out to my tarp pole and pulled in a brand-new oscillating fan that kept me as cool as cucumber.

Geri teased me about that, too.

"I'm going have to plant pole beans real thick around your camp or the neighbors will start thinking you're living the life of Riley."

Her reference to the popular radio show gave me an idea. I dragged the radio out into the garden and plugged it in, as well. I played it all day long and it kept me from sleeping really deep. And without sleeping really deep, the dreams were less horrible and less frequent.

In the late afternoon and evenings I did my chores around the house, patching the roof or painting the walls. When the water and sewer mains got laid down Bee Street, I dug ditches for my own lateral pipes and stole the interior portions of both bedrooms to put in an indoor bathroom.

Mama was appalled. Although the Stark home already had indoor plumbing, Mama insisted that the room only be used for bathing.

"It's disgusting to use the pot in the same

building where you eat and sleep!"

Geri and I only snickered at her behind her back. We were young and progressive and the world was new. We were trying to be alive and that meant embracing change.

Once I'd constructed the new room, I realized how much work the house still needed and I began to try to make our home a nicer place. I was pulling in good money and Geri could make a nickel stretch nearly to Tulsa and back. Our life together was good. The dreams had not gone away, but I was learning to live with them. And Geri was, too.

Just before Christmas in 1949 we got some news that should have been expected. For a couple who went at it like rabbits, the news shouldn't have been much of a surprise. But I was completely caught off guard.

"Pregnant? Are you sure?"

Geri nodded excitedly. She was obviously delighted.

I felt as if somebody had punched me in the stomach.

"Dr. Mayes said that everything looks perfectly normal and I should deliver near the end of July."

She was smiling so brightly, looking at me so eagerly, I didn't have a clue as to what I should say.

"Well . . . Geri, that's . . . that will be real nice."

I excused myself and promptly headed for the garden.

Geri caught me before I made it past the kitchen.

"You're not happy about the baby?"

"Of course I am," I began, before surrendering to the relentless honesty that she expected from me. "I'm just worried that a baby will upset things. I'm doing better, but what if that stops. What if I get . . . what if I get in a bad way again. A child needs a responsible parent, not a . . . a damaged one."

"A child only needs people to love it," Geri answered. "We're not going to borrow trouble on this. We're going to take it one step at a time. You're going to be glad about this."

She was right. On June 30, 1950, Jack Dempsey Crabtree, Jr. was born at Prattville Memorial Hospital near Catawah. He had all the requisite arms and legs, ten fingers, ten toes.

"He's perfect," I told Geri.

"He's beautiful," she corrected me. "Just like his dad."

She was sitting up giving the baby her breast in the eight-bed maternity ward, our privacy provided only by a thin white sheet that encircled the bed.

I ran my finger along the chubby pink cheek that suckled so greedily at his mother.

"I don't want him to know about me," I whispered.

Geri looked up surprised.

"I want him to know everything about you," she said. "How you are kind and hardworking, how you took care of your mama through your whole childhood, risked your life for your country and chose to love me, even if I pushed you into it."

I chuckled lightly at her little joke, but leaned closer. "I mean about the other thing," I said softly. "I don't want him to ever know about that."

She gave me a smile of reassurance. "Your son will know everything about you that he needs to know. And nothing that you don't want him to know. I think that's fair."

"Can we keep it from him?" I asked. "What if he hears me . . . you know . . . having a dream?"

"Don't worry," she said. "We'll make sure Daddy always gets to sleep in private."

The music began playing. I was momentarily startled before recognizing the tinkling ivories of "Pompton Turnpike," my favorite Charlie Barnet tune.

But, of course, there had been no music in Prattville that long ago. The music was here now, in this hospital in Tulsa where I lay connected to these tubes and wires. Here the music played at odd times of the day and night. I was getting sicker, feeling weaker. Was I just treading water, waiting for the inevitable?

# Sunday, June 12, 5:00 A.M.

Jack awakened when the headlights of a car flashed through the bedroom window, followed by a thump on the front porch. He rolled over and wrapped his arms around his wife. She was warm and soft and sweet-smelling. She was also sound asleep. He feathered some kisses on her neck, hoping to wake her. They'd had sex the morning before. And since the birth of the twins, their frequency had really slacked off. But this was a vacation, sort of, he reasoned, and there was no reason why they shouldn't enjoy themselves.

No reason except that Claire wouldn't wake up. He stepped up from neck kisses to full body stroking and got little response beyond a whining groan of complaint.

"Sweetheart, sweetheart, are you awake?"

Clearly she was not. Finally, he was shaking her shoulder. "Hey, sweetheart, it's morning."

"Morning," she responded finally turning into his arms. Her voice was still gravelly with sleep. She rolled over into his waiting arms and promptly fell back into sleep.

Jack held her there, considering whether to continue trying to awaken her. In the darkness he could only see the contours of her face, but her breathing was so relaxed, so peaceful, he didn't have the heart to rouse her out of that.

He pressed a kiss on her forehead and disengaged himself from her arms as he slipped out of bed.

In the kitchen he measured coffee by spoonfuls into the filter basket and then filled the machine with water. He waited for a minute to make sure the rich morning brew was dripping into the pot, and then he went out to the front porch to get the newspaper.

The sun had yet to show itself over the eastern horizon, but the silver shimmer of predawn was illuminating the edges of the landscape. There were no sounds of traffic or neighbors, no leaf blowers or boom boxes. But he noticed that it was far from quiet. The sounds of birds in the trees was not hesitant little tweeting, but strong, insistent calls. He didn't remember noticing the sounds of birds before. He frowned slightly as he tried to imagine why not.

Water features.

He realized instantly that in most of the backyards he spent time in, all that he'd designed, he'd gone to excessive lengths to ensure the constant sound of water. Whether it was a waterfall of rocks, the circulation from smaller pools at different levels or just the drop-shelf return of the infinity design, he made certain that the sound of water was as prominent in his layouts as the sight of it. That's what pools were about. And it was important for the occupants of the house to be drawn to the pool. It was a part of the total sensory package. Swimming alone was not sufficient to give pools their allure. He'd always understood that it was much more complicated. To be successfully integrated into a house, the pool must be an asset to the theme of the decor as well as part spa, part Zen garden. It was not enough that the occupants of the house would want to show off a pool to their friends at parties, it also had to be as much about everyday relaxation and peace as it was exercise.

Those were all good things. Until this moment, Jack had never considered what those positive experiences might be masking. Uncensored nature also provided a welcome respite.

He went back into the house to get his coffee. He left the Sunday paper unopened on the kitchen table and instead returned to the front porch with his drawing pad under his arm.

He seated himself in the old wicker chair and propped his feet up on the railing that he'd repaired yesterday. It still needed painting, but it was now significantly more sturdy. In the low light, he could hardly make out what he was sketching, but somehow he didn't want to intrude on wakening the world around him. He began working.

Designing pools was an accidental vocation for Jack. After he and Claire had married, their disapproving parents had cut them loose.

"If you expect to make decisions on your own," Ernst had said, "then you'll need to support your wife yourself."

Jack hadn't offered even the slightest complaint. In truth, he'd been almost cavalier about it. Claire had a scholarship and he didn't care so much about college. He figured that he'd get a job and she could continue in school. He took a full-time spot on a construction crew. But it didn't take them long to figure out how expensive an education could be and how hard it was to stretch a workman's wages.

He began doing pool care on the side for extra cash. Cleaning and maintaining was low-paying, but Jack was working for himself. He could put in extra hours on nights and weekends. He taught Claire how to do it and they expanded the business further. It was a nice addition to his regular paycheck. He might have continued doing that, but one fateful Sunday one of his client's neighbors asked advice on building a pool. The man wanted something special and hadn't seen what he wanted in any of the stock structures from the local pool builders.

Almost without thinking, Jack had offered to design and build it. And once he'd done it, Jack never wanted to do anything else.

His pencil moved purposefully across the paper. As the morning light heightened he could see more easily, but the sounds retreated. The birds were still there, still whistling and singing among themselves, but they were joined now with the barking of dogs and the whirr of car engines up on the highway. Fortunately, the memory of the early hour lingered in his mind and translated itself onto his paper.

The sound of the screen door caught his attention.

"Morning," Claire said.

She was still dressed in her sleepwear, a pair of baggy pajama bottoms and a mismatched T-shirt. She hadn't brushed her hair yet, and it was tousled and a little wild, giving her a surprisingly youthful look.

"You're up," he said.

"I smelled the coffee," she answered, indicating the cup in her hand.

She sat down in the swing, drawing it forward slightly so that she, too, could rest her heels on the railing next to his.

Jack smiled at the comparison of the two pairs of peds. His feet were very long and narrow, with little tufts of dark hair on each of his toes. Hers were wide for a woman, but they had a high arch that kept them from looking blocky. Her toes were long and thin and her nails were painted with a bright pink shimmer.

"What are you doing?" she asked him.

He handed her the sketch pad.

"Oh wow," she said. "This is really different. Is this for Butterman?"

Jack shook his head. "Oh no, it's much too . . . discreet for that guy. It's just something I thought up this morning."

"I like it," Claire told him. "It's kind of hidden in the landscape."

Jack nodded. "That's what I was thinking," he said. "I was thinking of a quiet pool that doesn't draw attention to itself."

"Where is it?" she asked.

He shrugged. "No where, it's just something I dreamed up."

"Really? It looks kind of familiar, somehow. I thought it was maybe somebody's backyard, maybe one of your brothers or a friend or someone we know."

"Nope."

He took a sip of his coffee. He wanted to share the feeling of the morning with her, but he wasn't sure exactly how.

"It was the birds," he said.

She glanced at him with a skeptical frown. "Birds?"

"Yeah," he said. "I came out here to get the paper and the birds were singing like crazy. It was kind of nice. I realized that I never design anything with birds in mind, so I just came up with an idea for a grotto unobtrusive enough to hear the birds."

Claire glanced up into the trees around the yard and Jack followed her gaze. There were a lot to look at. Jack recognized the big-breasted robin, but most of the birds he didn't know. They were small and gray, sparrows or wrens. His one year of Cub Scouts didn't make him any expert.

"Oh look, a cardinal."

Jack followed the direction of her finger to

find the brilliantly bright red bird with its peaked feathered crown. He'd seen them before in pictures or in passing. But now he really looked at the bird.

"Do you see his mate?" Claire said. "On that limb just a little higher and on the right."

Jack didn't see the other bird at first, expecting it to be just as vividly colored. Instead it blended in with the color of the bark, and he'd looked past her a couple of times before the bird moved and he saw it.

"Oh, yeah," he said.

The bright red one then flew up to where the brown-colored one was. He had something in his mouth that he shared with her.

"She must be sitting on a nest," Claire said. "The male feeds her while she's doing that."

"That's a pretty good boyfriend, I guess," Jack said, joking.

"Husband," Claire responded. "Cardinals mate for life."

"Really? I didn't know there were animals that did that."

"A lot of creatures do," Claire said. "Monogamy is not so artificially imposed as many men like to pretend it is."

Jack raised an eyebrow, refusing to take the bait.

They watched the male cardinal fly away, perhaps to find another seed.

"Birds," Claire said thoughtfully and shook her head. "I can't remember the last time I thought about birds, let alone listened to them."

"Me neither," Jack said.

"The last time was probably when Zaidi was doing that school report on emus and we drove out to the wildlife ranch."

"Who could forgot that fiasco. The twins strapped in car seats, still managing to throw the emu feed at each other."

"The stuff was all over the car."

"And Zaidi complaining because it was *her* report and the backseat of the minivan has the worst view."

"I agreed to trade seats with her, but she was afraid for us to open the door, so both of us had to climb over the seats and crawl the entire length of the vehicle."

They laughed together.

"You should do that more often," Jack said.

"What?"

"Look happy."

Claire frowned uncomfortably. "I guess there's just not a lot of reasons to be happy these days."

She took a big sip of her coffee and immediately rose to her feet. "I told Theba that I'd come visit their church this morning. So I'm headed for the shower. You should call the hospital to check on Bud. We'll talk to the children in the afternoon."

Jack returned his gaze to the sketch pad before the screen door shut behind her. Then, thoughtfully, he gazed up at the redbirds once more.

Claire typically went to church on Sundays. That was as much for the children as for any great insight she received from the pulpit. Her venture on this particular Sunday stemmed from similar motives. Theba and McKiever had been very helpful to Bud and Geri. Though that was true of the whole family and no one seemed to take it as anything special, Claire wanted to be supportive of them. And if they had their whole church praying for Bud, she wanted to acknowledge that, as well. There was no clearer way to do that than by showing up for the morning service.

Claire understood her own motives, but she was completely clueless as to those of the man who walked beside her up Bee Street toward the highway.

Jack rarely attended church at home. He was either "working through the weekend"

286

or he was "taking a day off from everything." He always seemed somewhat cold and distant from his family in Catawah. And on this trip he'd seemed to take a particular dislike to the preacher.

Nevertheless, he'd donned his suit, combed his hair and tied his tie.

"Guess I'll go with you," he'd said. "There's nothing much to do around here."

In fact, she'd been surprised at all the things they'd found to do. Yesterday, while she'd spent her time sorting and hauling off the recycling. Jack had made some repairs to the front porch and had marked several other small repair projects that needed his help. This morning, however, they were taking time for spiritual reflection.

Claire didn't know what to expect of Theba and the preacher's church, but she'd grown up walking into situations that were not familiar. She could give her parents credit for that. They were brilliant, charming, insightful people. But dragging their daughter from New Guinea to Zambia and then Bulgaria and back was not Claire's ideal of child rearing. It did, however, make her comfortable in all types of situations and with strangers. In truth, she sometimes craved that adventure, of seeing the lives of other people so different from her own.

Perhaps that was why she was enjoying these days in Catawah. Yes, she admitted to herself, despite missing her children and the sad nature of the visit, Claire was feeling happier, more upbeat than she'd felt in a long time. Jack had said as much on the front porch that morning. She'd rewarded his insight by turning sullen and walking away.

*It's because Dana's not here with us,* she thought to herself spitefully. Of course, she knew that wasn't true at all. Dana was only a very frequent phone call away, just as if they were in their own home in San Antonio. Still, something was different. Maybe it was like Jack's design for the "quiet pool." Simply getting away from the normal routine inspired him to look and think differently about his designs.

Maybe this unfamiliarity could inspire Claire to think differently about her life, too.

The *Iglesia de Jesus* did not have that sweet, homey white frame and tall steeple look of a country church. It was long and narrow with a low-pitched roof and was devoid of ornamentation. It looked like the roadhouse that it had been for so long. And the exterior paint job didn't help. Perhaps they had chosen based on cost rather than aesthetics, but for whatever reason, the building was painted a dull, dusky pink with dark burgundy trim. Claire thought it might have been an attractive combination for a prom gown, but it was certainly not traditional for a place of worship.

The grassy patch on the east side of the building was already full of parked cars. There were more along the edges of Bee Street and a few parked off the shoulder of the highway. The vehicles were mostly older, more sedans and pickup trucks than SUVs.

The front door was open. A portly man in his early fifties stood there shaking hands and offering greetings.

"*Bienvenidos,*" he said to the couple who went in just ahead of them. As they stepped up, he offered Jack his hand. "Welcome to our church," he said in only slightly accented English. "I am Jorge Trevino. You must be the old uncle's grandson."

"Jack Crabtree," he answered. "This is my wife, Claire."

The man acknowledged her with a nod as he took her hand in his own.

"*Mucho gusto,*" Claire said to him.

The man's eyebrows shot up and his smile brightened.

"*Habla español?*" he asked.

"*Un poquito,*" she answered, modestly.

289

"My wife is fluent in four languages," Jack told him. "Unfortunately, I don't think Spanish happens to be one of them."

Claire nodded agreement. *"Hablo bastante para entender y nada más,"* she told him — *I speak only enough to get by.*

"I am the same with English," he replied, understating his ability.

He ushered them into the tiny vestibule, and with Jack's hand resting on the small of Claire's back, they made their way into the sanctuary. The place was obviously make-shift. There were no pews, just rows of folding metal chairs lining a center aisle. On the west side the long mahogany bar ran the length of the building. The far end held several long rows of small, lit candles. The shelves behind were used for books. At the end of the room was a raised stage with a plain wooden mourners' bench in front. Above it an equally simple podium served as the pulpit. The place was no awe-inspiring cathedral. Despite the gleaming floor and the fresh white paint on the walls, it looked rough and poor.

The people in the seats did not. The well-dressed men in conservative suits sat next to fashionable wives with neat and scrubbed children under the watchful eyes of their parents.

There was much potential for Claire and Jack to feel like interlopers. It seemed to be a close-knit group of no more than a hundred people, counting the children. The opportunity was ripe for fear and distrust of strangers. But Claire felt none of that sentiment buzzing around her.

They sat down about midway up the aisle next to a young women with a bright-eyed baby on her lap. Between her and her husband at the end of the row were three more kids — the oldest couldn't have been more than six or seven.

*"You have very handsome children,"* Claire told her in very rudimentary Spanish. Being fluent in French was a great help in understanding Spanish, and living in San Antonio she'd had some practice, but she was aware that she often sounded either childlike or foolish. That, Claire believed, was her secret to learning languages. You have to put your ego aside and be willing to sound like an idiot. Having done that a lot, she knew how difficult and lowering it could be. Which was why she admired other people's willingness to do the same.

"You kind," the woman said to her in English. "The children very noisy. I'm sorry. Here. Sometimes. Very noisy."

Claire smiled at her. "I have three myself,"

she said. "They can be very noisy in church, too."

"Three?" the woman asked, incredulously holding up her fingers. "You are young."

Claire accepted the compliment gratefully. She was fairly certain that this woman was her age or perhaps even a few years younger.

*"Mi niña tiene ocho años,"* Claire told her — *I have an eight-year-old girl.* "Y tengo dos la misma edad, niño y niña. Twins, *como se dice?"*

*"Mellizos,"* she answered. *"Que suerte!" You are so lucky,* the lady said.

The service began with a familiar hymn with unfamiliar lyrics. Claire took her cue from the preacher, who belted out the words in a croaky English baritone as his congregation sang them in Spanish.

Claire had had exposure to a number of different religious traditions and was inclusive enough to find spiritual renewal and common ground with many of them. At *Iglesia de Jesus* she found the quirky mix of Southern evangelical and Latin America to be surprisingly compelling. McKiever's preaching was very typical of what she'd heard from evangelical pulpits elsewhere. However, after each thought he uttered, the preacher paused to allow Jorge Trevino to repeat it for the congregation in Spanish. Claire noticed, after only a few passages, that Trevino was not doing a literal translation. Even with her limited understanding of the language, she could detect the much more lyrical and stylized presentation of the words in a tonality that was old church liturgical. Protestantism for Catholics, she thought to herself. All the guy needed was a thurible of burning incense to wave back and forth.

After the benediction the congregation filed out into the grassy area in front of the building. Claire and Jack were with them. Everyone seemed friendly, open and welcoming.

"We wanted to thank all of you for praying for my grandfather," Jack said to a middle-aged woman who was acting as spokesperson for the congregation.

"We think of Mr. Crabtree as one of us," she said. "He is not a member of the church, but since his wife died, he comes some Sundays just to sit with us."

"Really?"

Claire was surprised and from the look on Jack's face, she knew that he was, as well.

"Yes," she said. "He would come in some Sundays. He would sit in the back. I asked him once and he said he liked to be here to remember his wife. He said this was the place he felt most close to her."

"Did Geri go to church here?"

"No. I met her a few times," the woman said, "but she never came here. But I guess any house of the Lord is close to heaven, yes?"

# BUD

On the sea at night the predators come. Across the water tiny microscopic plants that live there have a phosphorous glow. Anything that disturbs the water shows in the dark depths like a beacon attracting those that feed. I sat in my tiny raft, less than a flyspeck on a giant ocean, wishing myself smaller. I knew what the monsters of the deep could do. I'd watched them eat Lt. Randel. He was dead already. He couldn't feel a thing. It was only the remains of his body bobbing on the surface. I was at quite a distance by then and what my eyes mostly viewed was a thrashing of water as they swarmed him. My imagination filled in the detail. And a bump underneath the raft sent me screaming, screaming, screaming.

I heard the other voice. I was not screaming alone. Was it Randel? No, no, of course it wasn't, I realized, as the sun streamed in upon the chenille bedspread that covered me. It was J.D.

Geri came rushing into the bedroom, the baby in her arms.

"I didn't mean to wake you," she said, her eyes wide. It was a fearful look. My dreams and my screams scared her. But she never ran from them, from me. She was still that defiant little waif with her upturned chin daring Piggy Masterson to try to get the best of her.

"I'm so sorry," she said. "I don't know what's wrong with him. He may be teething or coming down with a cold. I think he's too big for colic."

I threw back the covers. It was a chilly fall day, but the dreams had left me wringing wet with sweat. I climbed out of bed.

"You haven't slept long enough," Geri cautioned. "You need at least a couple more hours before you've rested enough to work. I don't want you getting a hand caught in those presses."

"I'll catch another nap later," I lied. Sleep was my biggest enemy. If I never had to close my eyes again, I could be happy with that. "Give the little guy to me. We'll walk the floor together."

Geri handed me the baby. The furious little fellow was reluctant to let go of his mama. He looked up at me with Geri's eyes and her determined chin. Then, as if he'd thrown a switch, thrust himself into my embrace and clung to me crying miserably.

"Oh yeah, poor little guy. Are you having a hard time, today? I know exactly how you feel."

I bounced him slightly in my arms as we walked.

"You go on and do what you have to do, Crazy Girl," I told her. "We men will take ourselves a short stroll through the garden."

She winked at me and stood on her tiptoes to give the baby a tiny kiss on the forehead.

It's strange when you realize later how one thing affects another thing, and that affects something else, until your whole life turns out to be different than you thought it might be.

Because the bad dreams affected my sleeping, I decided to take a night job. Being home during the day allowed me to be closer to my son than maybe a lot of fathers of my day could be. He was a strong, healthy baby. He had his mother's looks and, I thought, her temperament. He didn't give up easily on anything he might try. When he was ready to eat, he'd scream bloody murder until he made it to his mother's breast. But he was no crier. He was stoic through the requisite bumps and bruises of a little fellow still unsteady on his feet. And I knew I couldn't always be there to catch him when he fell. But I caught him when I could and trusted him to take it well when he landed on his own.

As the years passed Geri took care of more than just our house and our garden. She took on every good work in town and made sure all of her sisters' husbands had jobs and all of her nieces and nephews had shoes. I watched J.D. as he moved from crawling on all fours to running full tilt. I made him a stick horse with a strip of real leather for a bridle, we went fishing together at the river bluff and built a tree house among the branches of the catalpa tree.

When I slept Geri kept him at a distance. Her father, by then very ill, took up a lot of her time, and she had her sister schedule his care so that she and J.D. could be at his house during any of my possible dream time.

I walked him to school his first day of kindergarten, with great relief. He'd made it through childhood at home without ever knowing my nightmares, and now he would be safe at school when I was sleeping.

Awake, I was able to keep him close. We played all the sports. We passed the football in the fall. We shot free throws into a basket on the side of the shed in winter and used the garden for the foul line when we batted in summer. As he got older and had his friends from school, I spent more of my time as a coach than as a participant, but I enjoyed his childhood much more than I'd enjoyed my own.

I was philosophical when I watched them racing around carrying plastic guns and pretending to shoot each other with great enthusiasm. It was just a game, I assured myself. Girls play with dolls and boys play with guns. That's just the way it is growing up.

"Were you in the war, Daddy?" J.D. asked me one time over the supper table.

I was momentarily mute, so Geri filled in for me. "Of course Daddy was in the war," she said, laughing lightly. "Almost all the daddies were."

J.D. nodded solemnly. "Lester's father, his real father, was killed in the war."

"I know," I answered. "Lester's father was my best friend."

J.D.'s little eyebrows shot up in surprise. "Really and truly?"

I nodded.

"I'd make Lester my best friend," J.D. suggested, "but he's a lot older than me. I don't know if he'd want a younger kid for a best friend."

"I thought Kevin was your best friend."

"Well, yeah."

"You wouldn't want to give up Kev for a boy who's older and that you don't know so well."

"No, I guess not."

"A boy can have lots of friends," I assured him.

"What did you do?"

"Huh?"

"In the war, Daddy, what did you do?"

I tried to form appropriate words in my head.

"Phil's pop was a leatherneck and Kevin's dad was a swab jockey. What did you do?"

"I rode in a plane," I answered.

"An airplane!" J.D. exclaimed. "You rode in an airplane?"

"Yes."

"That's neat!" Across the table I exchanged a glance with Geri. J.D. seemed delighted with what he'd learned. I hoped then that I would never have to say more.

But that wasn't to be the end of it. I suppose it was their generation. Maybe it was the comic books or the movies or TV, but our youngsters seemed fascinated with the war of their fathers.

I remember lying on my garden cot and

listening to the boys playing in the yard. I was amazed that sites like Anzio and Omaha Beach cropped up in the game along with the persistent verbal "rat-ta-tat-tat" of their weapons. They were just children and their war was make-believe. I took comfort in that.

By age eight, J.D. and his buddies were all heavily involved in Boy Scouts. It was in my workshed that he earned his merit badges for woodworking, electricity and gardening. When the troop went for their overnight camping trip out to Sand Hills, I volunteered to chaperone. I figured I was perfect for the job, since I knew all the kids, I liked the outdoors and I would be awake all night long. Though there would be swimming, and I made it clear that I didn't swim and I wouldn't lifeguard. I didn't even want to be a spectator when the boys were in the water.

Frank Trotter had cleaned up his rough and rowdy ways and now served as the scout leader. He accepted my limitations and assigned me to stay at the camp. I had expected that and I was pleased.

What I hadn't expected was the talk around the campfire at night.

I thought there would be ghost stories and jokes, but Frank was more serious than that. He'd done time at a Japanese prisoner of war camp, and he apparently thought it was important to share some of that experience with the boys.

"The first day they brought me a bowl of rice," he said. "And I said to myself, 'I can't eat this, it's full of maggots!' " The boys universally made a sound of disgust. "About the third day, I was so hungry, I began picking the maggots out and eating it anyway." The boys expressions were grim. "By the end of the week, I was looking through that bowl, eagerly eating the maggots first. They were the best part — that's where all the protein was going to be."

Frank was a good storyteller and a likable guy. Just his good humor about survival was an important lesson. But I was totally taken aback that night when he turned his attention to me.

"You know," he said. "Mr. Crabtree is also a veteran. He was in a bomber wing that was responsible for protecting more than eight million miles of Pacific from the enemy. They fought from Guadalcanal to Tokyo."

"Were you a pilot?" one of the scouts asked.

"I was a gunner and backup radio operator on a B-24."

"That's safer than being in the infantry,"

Tommy Giest said. "My dad was in the infantry."

"The infantry is very close up," Frank told the boy. "And I'm sure your dad's record is impressive. But bombing is actually a very dangerous job. The air corps had a high casualty rate."

"Maybe because the enemy didn't have to shoot you right in the chest," Kevin O'Neil piped in. "If they just knocked a big old plane out of the sky that was enough. Yyyyyyyyyy-pow! You're dead."

"If you're a gunner, then you're knocking the Japs out of the sky, right?" Bucky Williams exclaimed. "How many did you kill?"

I was so taken aback that I didn't answer. I never talked about the war. Once I arrived in Catawah, I'd been determined to keep my "kills" all in the past. Frank misinterpreted my hesitance.

"Boys, you don't ask a soldier about killing," he said. "Soldiers keep count of missions flown, aircraft downed, positions overrun and targets neutralized. Killing is the unfortunate necessity of war, it's nothing a man takes a bow for."

All the eager scouts looked appropriately solemn by his words, except for Bucky who just seemed as much annoyed as sobered.

My eyes immediately went to J.D. He was

just a little boy. He didn't need to know anything about war and soldiers and killing. I wanted to protect him from this, to keep him from knowing anything at all about it. But his expression was one I hadn't expected. He was looking at me with undisguised awe.

"Did you win any medals?" he asked.

"Yes," I answered, hesitantly. "Like almost everybody who's been in combat, I have a few. I . . . I was awarded the Bronze Star in Okinawa."

"Wow!" the word was uttered in a chorus of awed respect.

"What did you get those others for?" Kevin asked.

"My unit," I began slowly, "bombed and strafed our way from the Solomons to the Philippines. I received one for an air strike against a place called Truk. Another for bombing oil refineries in Borneo."

I hadn't wanted to talk about the war. I never wanted to talk about the war. But now, looking at the admiration in my son's eyes, I fooled myself into believing that there was no danger in toying with those demons.

"Man, I'd really like to see those," Bucky said.

"Me, too," J.D. admitted.

That night, as all the boys slept in their pup tents, I tended the fire and arranged my thoughts. Why not show the medals, why not grasp the good in the memories that I was working so hard to be free from? Both the American Legion and the VFW had invited me to join. I'd avoided them both. I didn't want to wear a uniform cap and hang out with the fellows who could talk about the good ol' days in combat. Those who returned were divided into two groups. The ones who wanted always to remember and those who wanted nothing more than to forget.

I was staunchly among the latter, but now I was thinking that maybe I was wrong. Maybe it was good for our boys to admire us. To recognize our sacrifice. To remember friends like Les, who we lost. If I did that, then maybe it could all end up making sense. That somehow we could render down all the horror and have nothing left but honor.

I talked to Geri about it.

"Your dreams are less frequent now," she pointed out. "You seem much more rested, more healthy than before."

I nodded agreement. "I feel a lot better. I only have the nightmares maybe once, sometimes twice a week now."

"So I guess they might just get to fewer and fewer until they go away completely," she said.

That seemed like a reasonable assumption to me. Geri had made it happen. I felt that I was more alive than dead. And part of being alive was seeing the war the way that the people around me now saw it, a great and glorious victory for democracy, a noble triumph of good over evil. If the gory, gritty details of how that came about were lost to memory, then so much the better.

That next weekend I showed J.D. my service medals. I usually slept while Geri and J.D. went to church. But that day I didn't sleep. I got the shoe box out from under the bed and after Sunday dinner I spread the contents of it on the dining room table.

J.D.'s eyes were as big as saucers.

"You're a hero," he told me in an awed whisper.

"No," I assured him. "I just did my job."

I don't think he even heard me. His eyes were completely filled with shiny metal and bright strands of ribbon. We looked through all of it. The Air Medal with its bronze clusters, the Asiatic-Pacific Campaign Medal and the Victory Ribbon, the Good Conduct and Marksmanship medals and, of course, the Bronze Star.

That one attracted J.D. immediately, but because of his time in Boy Scouts, he knew that sometimes the ribbons meant as much as the flashier medals. He asked questions about everything. I answered factually, but not completely. I told him what it all was, but never revealed what it all meant. Or who I'd been back then. And I never mentioned anything about the water.

"What about the Bronze Star?" J.D. asked. "They only give that for something special."

I answered that easily. It had happened late in the war, and when I thought about it, I felt next to nothing.

"We'd completed our mission, dropped off our escort and we were headed back to base. Our plane was in the back of the formation. For some reason I looked over to my left and in the distance I saw a zero. He didn't seem interested in us, and I realized that he was too far from home to ever get back and that he was headed in the direction of the carriers supporting the landing. There was nobody in the sky but us. So we pulled out of formation and flew over and took him out before he could kamikaze himself into the carrier."

"Did you shoot him out of the sky yourself?"

I nodded. "Yes, I think so. But the whole crew got the kill."

The pride in the boy's eyes almost unmanned me. "He was a dead man already," I tried to explain. "He'd already made that decision. We just made sure that he went out alone, not taking a bunch of our guys with him."

J.D. nodded gravely.

"Why don't you ever talk about the war, Daddy?" he asked.

I shrugged. "I try not to live in the past. I want to spend my time thinking about you and your mama and what we do today."

He accepted my answer, but his brow was furrowed. I knew he really didn't understand.

"But when you've done something big like this," he said. "When you've been a hero, people ought to know that."

"I'm not a hero," I told him again.

"I guess what you mean is like what Mr. Trotter says sometimes. The real heroes didn't come back."

That wasn't truly what I meant, but I wasn't sure I understood myself. It wasn't going to be possible to explain it to my son. At least not then. When he's older, I promised myself. When he's older I'll try to tell him everything.

Until then, I tried to make him proud. I joined the American Legion, hung out with the aging G.I.s and did volunteer work for my community. I found it to be a significant strain, but I marched in parades and served as honor guard at funerals. Either of these duties during waking hours was likely to result in more water dreams in my sleep.

Things finally made a turn for the better in the early sixties. With the organization of our local civil defense, I found my niche. American Legion volunteers constructed the alarm tower at the highest point in town, just east of the cemetery. Though supposedly built to protect Catawah from a Soviet nuclear attack, CD mostly kept watch for spring weather and bad storms. By taking on civil defense as my civic duty, I was freed from sharing war stories with the guys. I was still a man my son could look up to, without having to look back on the past. Instead, I was high on the tower above it all, and I kept my eyes and my binoculars on the horizon, looking for danger.

But of course, I never saw it coming.

The music was playing again. I was in that dad-gummed hospital where the music played. And I knew all the words as I listened to the song "It's Easy To Remember and So Hard To Forget."

I could hear the hiss of the machine on my face and the consistent beeping of the monitors. There was someone in the room with me. It was a woman. I couldn't see her, of course, but I could smell a feminine perfume. Was it a nurse? No, there was nothing professional about this person. She was holding my hand and she was talking to me. I tried to focus on her. I really tried to hear what she was saying to me, but the music was too loud. It completely drowned out every word.

# Monday, June 13, 9:37 A.M.

Jack and Claire met up with the doctor just as he was leaving Bud's room. The man had his head down and might have walked right past if Jack hadn't stopped him.

"How is my grandfather?" he asked.

The doctor gave a shrug that was not at all reassuring. "He's about the same. He's not really improving, but he's still hanging in there."

He gave Jack a pat on the shoulder that felt more like condescension than compassion. Jack was grinding his teeth unpleasantly as he entered the room. Bud lay propped up on one side facing away from the door. The change in position gave the impression of movement, but Jack had already learned that his grandfather had to be turned regularly to prevent bedsores. The long blue hose down his throat had been replaced with a clear mask over his face. His wrists were still tied to the rail and a

311

brace on his head had been added to keep his thrashing to a minimum. It was a strange helplessness for a man who'd always been so active.

It made Jack sick to his stomach to see it, and his reaction to his feelings was to take a seat across the room and retrieve his cell phone from his pocket. He knew Claire was looking at him reprovingly, but he refused to meet her gaze. Instead he pressed the speed-dial code for his office.

Laura picked up. "Swim Infinity."

"Hi, it's me," Jack said, expecting correctly that she could always recognize the boss's voice. "Everything going along well there?"

"Yes, sir," she answered. Her tone was slightly off. "The crew is out at the Jacobsons'. They're filling the pool this morning and finishing up the landscape. Miguel was having some trouble with the client. She's complaining about the sago palms. She wants them planted closer together, but he says they have got to have room to grow."

"Miguel's right," Jack told her. "I'll call Mrs. Jacobson and convince her."

"Great. Josh and Crenshaw are at the Guillermos'. They were supposed to do the pour at seven-thirty this morning, but as of a half hour ago, the truck still hadn't shown up."

Jack focused on what Laura was saying, but his eyes watched Claire as she sat beside Bud's bed. Holding his hand and chatting with him like she always did.

"Have you followed up with the cement company?"

"I called when he called me," she answered.

"Well, keep calling. Call every fifteen minutes and remind them how many guys we have over there that are on the clock."

"Okay."

"Anything else?"

"Ah . . . no, not really."

She didn't sound that sure.

"Let me talk to Dana," Jack said.

It was almost imperceptible, but Jack could tell that Claire was listening as soon as she heard the name mentioned.

"Well . . . ah . . . she's not here."

"Oh. Where is she?"

"I . . . I really don't know."

"Did she just step out?"

"She . . . well . . . she never came in this morning."

That revelation momentarily left Jack speechless. After perhaps a ten-second pause he recovered. "Did she call in sick?"

"No, she didn't call in."

"Did you call her?"

"Yes, I did. But she didn't pick up."

"How many times have you tried?"

"I don't know," Laura said. "Maybe ten times. I've left her voice mails on both her home phone and her cell and sent a red-flagged e-mail to her BlackBerry."

"That's strange," Jack said. "Well, she must be really busy with something. I'm sure she'll call in when she gets the chance. And I'll try her myself later."

He hung up. Glancing up, he saw Claire watching him. Their eyes met and there was disapproval all over her face. She quickly looked back to Bud and began talking again.

Jack placed a metaphorical chip firmly on his shoulder. He was making a living. He was supporting his family. That was what a man was supposed to do. And the man's wife shouldn't be trying to guilt him about it.

He made his other calls, deliberately taking his time. He spent twice as much discussion on the sago palms as necessary, verified the arrival of the cement truck with Josh, and then, after unsuccessfully trying to contact Dana, finally slipped the telephone in his pocket.

Jack glared over at Claire defiantly. She looked just about ready for a fight. Unfortunately, or maybe fortunately, they both detected the telltale sound of a person scooting down the hallway.

"It's one of the aunts," Claire warned just before the door opened.

Jack found himself sitting up straighter as if he had been caught doing something he shouldn't.

Aunt Viv shuffled in on her walker with the yellow tennis balls; a big brown purse was hitched to the front like a saddlebag. The old lady was out of breath, but she smiled when she saw them.

"Oh good, I caught you two," she said. "These dad-gummed hospitals are as bad as airports on keeping one thing as far as possible from everything else. And this rattletrap of a metal horse of mine just has one speed."

Today, Aunt Viv had left the overalls at home, but the man's long-sleeved shirt and navy trousers she was wearing didn't do any better at fostering a more formal image.

Both Claire and Jack rose from their seats, but the old woman preferred the chair next to the bed.

"How's the dear old fellow today?" she asked Claire.

"I don't like his color much," she answered.

The two women gazed together for a moment into Bud's face. Jack raised a befuddled eyebrow. He hadn't noticed anything different about the guy. But then, he realized, he hadn't actually looked at his grandfather in the face since he'd walked in. That's what he was here for. Why hadn't he done it? He pushed the question away. He'd had phone calls to make.

The old woman continued to pat Bud's hand, but glanced up at the two of them.

"I came to see Bud, of course, but I wanted to have a minute or two to visit with you children," she said. "That's the best news about making up the schedule. I always know who I'm going to run into when I come up here."

"Well, we're glad you ran into us," Claire said.

"Here, take my seat," Jack said to his wife.

She waved him away. "No, I think I'll go get a cup of coffee," she said. "You stay here and talk with your aunt."

Her retreat left Jack alone with the spirited senior. Not something with which he was particularly comfortable. What did a guy say to a really old lady?

Jack smiled in a way that he hoped looked

pleasantly sincere.

"How are *you* feeling today, Aunt Viv?"

She laughed. "You know, Jackie, at my age I don't ask myself how I'm feeling anymore," she said. "If I wake up and I'm still breathing, I just figure that's good enough. Bud here is my example. When I keel over, I want to be up doing something that people will remember, not laying around on a couch or worse yet, sitting on the damned toilet. That's my worst fear — dying undignified, on the pot or some such. I'm more scared of that than of dying itself."

There was no response that Jack could make to that.

"What's that look?" Aunt Viv asked him.

"What look?"

"That look on your face," she said. "It's kind of like a cross between 'the fort is surrounded' and 'I ate something that's gone bad.' "

Jack felt himself blushing. "I . . . uh . . ."

She shook her head and held up a hand to forestall his explanations or apologies. "Don't mind anything I say, Jackie," his aunt told him. "Jesse is right about me — what comes into my head just goes out my mouth and I'm nearly helpless to stop it."

"That's a good quality," Jack assured her, not sure if he were lying or not.

"Yes, I think that it is," Viv agreed. "But there are a lot of people who don't find it all that appealing."

Jack smiled gingerly, trying to be noncommittal. Aunt Viv found that amusing enough to laugh aloud.

"So I hear you're doing some repairs around the old house," she said.

Jack shrugged. "I'm just keeping busy," he said. "If you'd schedule me to be here at the hospital more, I would be."

The old woman glanced down at the occupant of the hospital bed and patted his hand.

"You won't get too much in touch with Bud in this place," she said. "It's too late for that. You'd be closer to him at that house, among his things, his memories, than would ever be possible here."

"You don't think he's getting better?"

Viv raised an eyebrow at him and shook her head. "It was hard enough for him to scrabble up a reason to live before the stroke," she said. "Even with all our family around, he's been really lonely since Geri died."

The words somehow felt like a reproof. Jack was surprised at that. No one in the family had ever suggested that he should have visited more often. He had a busy life, three kids and a business to run. He couldn't have been running up here to Cat-awah to see the old man.

Even as the words ran through his head, he recognized them for what they were. A rationalization. He hadn't visited, he hadn't brought his children up here, because he hadn't wanted to. These people might be related to him by kinship, but the Van Brugges were his family. That thought didn't quite ring true, either. He was odd man out in that group, as well.

"I heard you went to Theba and the preacher's church yesterday," she said. "I bet that was an eye-opener."

"It was Claire's idea," he said. "But it wasn't so bad. Not that different from a lot of churches I've been in. I was surprised to find out that Bud attended."

Viv smiled. "Yessir, since Geri died, he made his way up there pretty regular. But I don't think it was for the preaching and singing."

"Oh?"

"He and Geri used to really cut the rug in that old dance hall when Bud got back from the war. I think he just goes back there to remember."

Jack smiled. "Is that when they were dat-ing, after the war?"

Viv raised an eyebrow. "I guess that you could call it dating," she said. "They'd been married before Bud went into service. But by the time he came home, they'd had it annulled."

"Annulled? Really?" Jack had never heard that.

Aunt Viv nodded. "I think he just married Geri to change her name and give her some protection."

"Protection? Protection from what?"

It was the old woman who then looked as if she had a bad taste in her mouth. "From the fine citizens of the community," she answered. "If you haven't figured it out yet, Jackie, it's one of the nasty realities of human nature that everybody wants to look down on somebody. And in our town, it was our family that got looked down upon. And once everybody's looking down on you, there are those who are just one opportunity away from doing you harm."

Viv was momentarily lost in memory, memory that didn't appear to be at all pleasant.

"The Shertz girls were in great need of protection and our mama and daddy, they were good people, but they were weak. They couldn't do nothing to help us. We had to take care of ourselves," she said. "Cleata left town. Opal married when she was just fifteen. I turned myself into a boy. Jesse was just too smart for them. And Sissy struggled to make herself invisible. Your grandma Geri loved Bud from the time she was a little girl. She always said that he'd saved her. But you know, I think when he came back from the war, it was her turn to do the same."

"After the war, she saved him?" Jack asked, confused.

Viv's brow wrinkled and she pursed her lips with self-disapproval. "I've said too much. My mouth just gets to going and I say things that maybe should never be said."

"Why shouldn't they be said?" Jack asked. "I'm family."

He was surprised at his own declaration.

"I know that you are," Aunt Viv said. "And I know that Bud and Geri just loved you to pieces. And maybe they wouldn't want you to know everything. Maybe that's why they never told you."

"Or maybe they never told me because they didn't have a chance," Jack said. "I haven't been up here a dozen times in the last thirty years."

Viv thought about that and slowly nodded.

"I don't know so much," she said. "But I do know that Bud was messed up after the war. He was strange. He wasn't wounded, but something terrible had happened to him out there in the Pacific. Something that preyed upon his mind."

Jack nodded.

"The doctor said that he'd suffered post-traumatic stress disorder," he told her. "I guess that sort of thing is pretty common in combat. And from what my mother has said, I understand that Bud was a big war hero."

"Gracious Lord!" Aunt Viv exclaimed and then in a whisper added, "Don't let Bud hear you say that, he'd have a fit."

The old man, breathing into the mask, said nothing.

Claire had been so grateful for Aunt Viv's arrival. The interruption had given her a chance to put some distance between herself and the man she wanted to choke, aka her husband. Why in the devil had Jack even come to the hospital if he was going to spend his time talking business and playing phone tag with Dana?

In the vending area she decided to forego the thick black coffee and went straight for sugary soda and a dollar-size chocolate bar.

She sat down on a long, uncomfortable couch. She called to check on the kids. They seemed to be having the time of their lives. At Toni's house, every day was a holiday. And every holiday meant presents.

Claire tried to be firm with her mother-in-law.

"It's not good for you to overwhelm them with *stuff*," she said.

Rather than being rebuffed, Toni laughed. "Oh, let me spoil them just a bit," she said. "They miss their parents and getting a few shiny new things can be a welcome distraction."

Though all three answered positively about what they were doing and how they were feeling, Toni was right about needing distractions. Peyton and Presley seemed especially keen on her coming home.

"What's the deal with that old man? He should just get better and go home," her son declared.

"He's trying, honey," Claire told him. "But sometimes it's not as easy as you think."

"Well, if Pops was taking care of that guy, he'd be well by now."

"Peyton, don't speak of Bud as 'that guy.' He's your dad's grandfather. He means as much to Daddy as Pops does to you."

The little boy only considered that for a minute.

"Naw, mom, I don't think so," he responded.

Claire didn't try to argue the point.

Once she got off the phone, she actually missed the kids more than before she'd called. As the thought passed through her mind it occurred to her that she should lock it down in her memory banks. So much of the time the idea of being away from the kids for a few days sounded like heaven on earth. The reality of it wasn't even close.

Claire tossed her candy wrapper in the trash and headed back down the hallway to Bud's room. Jack and Aunt Viv were sitting in the small corridor waiting room. As Claire approached he answered the question that she had yet to ask.

"The nurse's aide is washing Bud up. She said it would only be a couple of minutes."

Claire nodded and seated herself on the one remaining chair in the alcove.

"Would you like something to drink, Aunt Viv?" Claire asked. "There are vending machines just down the way. I can get you a soda or some candy."

She shook her head. "Oh no, sweet thing. I don't eat nothing anymore except peppermints and black coffee. That's been my way of life for years. My doctors say that's not nutrition and it's sure to kill me. I say,

324

it better hurry up or I'm going to die of old age first."

Viv chuckled, delighted at her own humor. Claire shot a glance at Jack. Neither of them knew whether to laugh or be appalled.

"So how are your little young'uns?" Viv asked. "I swear before I get to see them they'll be in college."

"Not quite yet," Claire assured her. She gave a quick, positive report on her offspring, including the current excesses of their grandmother.

Viv chuckled. "That's Toni, she's something else, no doubt about that. Jackie, when your daddy brought that gal home he could have knocked us all over with a feather. She was so fancy and sophisticated. She's like quality people and I swear I got tongue-tied every time I tried to talk to her."

Claire found it hard to believe that anyone could intimidate Aunt Viv to the point of muteness.

"I'm sure she was as nervous around you as you were around her," she said.

"Toni, nervous?" Aunt Viv laughed. "That gal has as much confidence as she had good looks. And who wouldn't, with J.D. all calf-eyed and totally smitten."

Claire smiled at the image and glanced at Jack. His expression was more serious.

"I don't think it was the romantic love match that you imagine," he said. "It was a quickie wedding. My parents hardly knew each other."

Aunt Viv seemed puzzled at that statement.

"Things did happen fast between those two," she said, "but it was no lighthearted fling with wedding bells. Those crazy kids were true hearts united. Soul mates they call it now."

Jack appeared incredulous. He looked as if he was ready to dispute his aunt, and Claire thought it might be better to smooth out any difference of opinion on the subject.

"They were just newlyweds when they were together," Claire pointed out. "And then Toni was a widow. The image you have of her is probably very different than the woman we know."

Aunt Viv nodded, for once more wise than talkative. "I'm sure you're right about that," she said.

The subject changed and a couple of minutes later they were back in Bud's room. He'd been turned onto his back again. He was freshly scrubbed and his hair parted neatly on one side and combed. To Claire he looked both very much like himself, yet completely different from the vibrant, active man she knew him to be.

As if she felt the same, Aunt Viv began telling stories. Not about the sadness in Bud's life or the obstacles that he and Geri had faced. She told funny stories. Like the Saturday night dance contest where Geri and Bud were one of the last three couples on the floor. After a very successful twirl, the hem on Geri's skirt got caught in Bud's belt buckle. For a frantic few seconds Bud tried to get it unhooked. When he couldn't he simply spooned her backside against him and danced her right out the front door.

She also related an incident when a local circus was camped in a field a half mile away. Geri looked out her window and saw an elephant in the flower bed. She grabbed her weapon of choice and ran out the back door to chase the creature away. Bud would say for years thereafter that she was the only person in the world willing to battle an elephant with a flyswatter.

Claire found herself laughing at story after story. April Fool's jokes they played on each other. Family foibles. J.D. dragging his potty chair to the dining table when the preacher was over for supper. Geri slipping on the ice in the driveway, sliding under the car, and Bud coming to her rescue and then asking her, tongue in cheek, if she could lube the chassis while she was down there.

The entertainment made the time go faster. And when the nurse came in to take Bud's vital signs and declared she thought he was looking better, Claire could hardly be surprised. Their own light spirits had somehow been conveyed to his own.

Driving back to Catawah, Jack commented on it.

"When Aunt Viv started telling those crazy stories," he said, "I thought it was a bit inappropriate, like Aunt Viv herself. But you know, I feel better and apparently Bud was better. It's amazing, really."

Claire agreed.

"And I think I learned more about Bud and Geri today, as a couple, than I had ever figured out by visiting them."

Jack nodded. "They seem a lot more likeable when you hear it from Viv's point of view."

"Likable?" Claire was surprised at his words. "You didn't think they were likable."

"That's not it exactly," he said. "I just didn't think they really liked me very much."

"Of course they liked you," Claire said. "They loved you. Why would you think otherwise?"

Jack hesitated as if he were getting his thoughts in order. When he spoke it was almost defensive. There was a hurt in his voice that told Claire he'd been hanging on to these words for a long time.

"Well, they never came to San Antonio to visit us when I was growing up," he began. "Every summer there was Little League, Scouts, summer camp. They never came to be a part of that. They never even saw me swim. I went to the state swim meet two years and my own grandparents never even watched me get wet. In that little house full of photo frames there are no pictures of me with my trophies. There's not even my high school graduation photo. They have more pictures of our kids, who they've never met, than they do of me."

Claire was surprised at Jack's admission.

"Because I sent them," she pointed out. "Photos don't just appear by magic. Toni had a lot of social obligations and two other boys to manage. Maybe she never got around to keeping her former in-laws in the loop. Did you ever mail them anything?"

Jack's brow wrinkled. "No. I guess I thought that was somebody else's responsibility."

Claire raised an eyebrow. "You would never assume something like that at the company. You might delegate, but you'd never fail to follow up. Family is not so different."

He shrugged. "But that doesn't explain their attitude toward me as an adult."

"What was wrong with their attitude?"

"I try to do something nice for them and they just throw it back in my face like it's worthless."

"What are you talking about?"

"Don't you remember when I offered to put a pool out in the back for them," he said. "It would have been a gorgeous locale and great exercise for them. And although cash was tight for us back then, I was willing to pay every penny of the expense myself."

"Of course I remember that," Claire said. "But Geri really did love her flower garden and she didn't want to give it up."

"That wasn't it," Jack said. "I watched Bud's eyes when he said all that about Geri and her flowers. He was lying. He didn't want my gift. He was disgusted by it and he threw it back in my face."

Claire found that revelation shocking.

"They didn't like me," Jack insisted. "I don't know if I reminded them of my father or if I wasn't enough like my father, but they didn't like me and didn't want anything to do with me."

"That's just not true," Claire said. "Toni told me that it nearly broke their hearts when she took you away from them."

Jack glanced over at her, his jaw hanging open. "Took me away from them? What are you talking about?"

Claire remembered clearly that Toni said Jack never talked about it. Claire realized that was because Jack apparently didn't know about it. She was hesitant to be the one to tell him. But it was too late to back away from it now.

"Toni told me that she left you with Bud and Geri when she moved back to San Antonio and went to college," Claire said. "You lived with them until after she'd married Ernst. So you must have been four, maybe five years old."

Jack just sat still, staring at the highway in front of him.

"Are you sure about this?" he asked finally. "Maybe you misunderstood my mother."

"No, we talked about it a couple of days ago."

He continued to drive in silence. Claire didn't want to say any more. She wondered if she should try to change the subject. But that seemed wrong. The facts had been ignored too long already.

Finally Jack spoke. "You know, I don't have any memory of life with my mom as a single parent," he said. "When I try to think back to preschool childhood, I can't come up with anything that doesn't include Ernst. I guess the reason that it always seemed as if my stepfather was there is because he always was."

"But you don't have any memories of being here, with Bud and Geri?"

"Yes, I have a few," he admitted. "Since we've been here, there've been some things that have seemed somehow special. And that memory I told you about, when Mom came to pick me up in Ernst's blue caddy. That must have been when I went back to stay with her."

He hesitated again.

"The things I recall, from way back, they're all loving, good things. So I must have liked being with them."

"So they had to love you," Claire stated.

He shrugged. "I guess so, back then. But something happened, somehow I didn't live up to things."

"Of course you have," she insisted. "They were always so proud of you."

He shook his head. "There's only one thing that I really feel confident about being able to do well, and that's building swimming pools. They wouldn't let me do that for them."

# BUD

The hissing sound awoke me with a start. The raft couldn't lose any more air. It'd already lost too much last night. If I wasn't vigilant, my safe haven would collapse beneath me. I'd be back in the water. I'd be back in the water, like Lt. Randel. I put my finger over the hole once more and screamed at the ache in my arm and my back. The position I had to maintain to keep my hand over the leak was excruciating. Exposure to the salt and the sun had made my skin raw. I felt as if I were covered in boils. I no longer could think about rational reasons to stay alive. I was surviving on instinct and even that will was beginning to fail me.

Would it really be worse back in the sea, treading water, than in the leaky raft, forced to maintain an immovable position?

*Randel,* the answer reverberated in my head. *Remember Randel.* It was my own fault. If I'd taken Randel's life vest, he would have drifted to the bottom of the sea. But I hadn't taken the vest. And Randel's body had bobbed and floated on the waves. Sometimes it was far. Then I would look up again and it would be close. I kept my eyes on it. Somehow I couldn't look away. So I was glad when the sun began to lower on the horizon. I would be in darkness, unable to see the remnants of a man floating nearby.

I hadn't counted on the glow in the water. I hadn't thought about the predators under the surface.

"No!" I screamed into the sunshine as the memory assaulted me. I didn't want to remember. I didn't want to see Lt. Randel. I began to cry again. I hadn't thought I had enough water left inside me to shed more tears. But I did.

Randel was already dead, I reminded myself. He was already dead and you can't hurt the dead. It's the only way to be truly safe, to be untouchable. I longed to be safely dead. I envied my crewmates. I was jealous of nameless marines I'd seen strewn across beaches. I even begrudged my own sweet Geri her final rest.

Wait, Geri was not dead. Yes, yes, she was. I realized I was not in that raft in the Pacific.

I was here in the hospital. The hospital with the music. And the stabbing muscle cramps I felt in my arms, back were in the here and now, not the long ago.

I'd made it back from that raft in the Solomon Sea. Back, more dead than alive. Truly more dead. I'd considered myself dead. And by being dead, I'd had no fear of dying. And with no fear of dying, heroism had come easy.

"Zero at seven o'clock," I hollered into the radio. "He's headed out to sea."

"Does he see us?" the copilot asked.

"He doesn't care about us," I answered, knowing it was true. "He's too far out to have fuel to go back. He's headed for the convoy. He's going to kamikaze himself."

"Damn," I heard someone say.

"Is there a way we can warn them?" someone else asked.

"Where are the fighters?"

"They're already circling the field."

"We're too slow to catch him," the copilot said.

Captain Price wasn't so pessimistic.

"If we angle that direction at about sixty degrees, we might be able to intercept. What do you think, McSween?"

"It'll be close, sir," he answered, after the slightest hesitation.

"Captain, I'll get him if you can get me close," I promised.

He banked the big bomber and we flew in low. Our top speed was three hundred miles per hour and the zero was pushing that or better. I could see him the entire way. He never saw me. He never once glanced to the left or to the right. He was a dead man. He'd already decided that. But he wanted to take some of our guys out with him. What he couldn't know was that I was a dead man, too. And I was taking as many with me as I could, as well.

He was a little faster than we thought. We were a little slower than we hoped. We came in well over a mile behind him.

From the greenhouse nose the bombardier cursed. "We missed him."

"I got him," I assured the captain.

"You'll never hit him at this distance," someone else said.

"We've come this far and I've got plenty of ammo," I replied.

"Knock him out of the sky," the captain ordered.

I did just that. I put so many holes in the tail and fuselage, it must have been like trying to fly a block of Swiss cheese. The bombardier was also shooting, and the zero burst into flames.

He went down into the water within sight of the ships.

Through the radio headphones I could hear the other guys cheering. I felt nothing. Dead men don't have feelings.

But it was hard to get that across to anyone. I wouldn't have even tried to explain it to J.D. And I didn't.

On gray, rainy days he would go get the shoe box from underneath the bed and he would lay the medals and ribbons and assorted paraphernalia on the table to examine it.

For the first few times he'd ask questions.

"Now what's this one?"

"That's the American Defense Ribbon."

"Oh yeah, right. American Defense Ribbon."

But quickly he knew them better than I did.

It was all harmless, I told myself. Little boys like to play soldier. And I made sure that it was never too much a game. I reminded him of all the men, like Les, who hadn't come back. And that instilled the proper reverence, but I still worried. Geri waved away my concerns.

"He's a child," she reminded me. "Children need to be proud of their parents."

I knew she spoke from her own heart. Her

father, who'd been the town joke for her entire lifetime, passed away that winter of 1959. His six daughters had been devastated. In the strange way that they always decided things, they refused to have Darby Shertz transported from the church in a hearse.

"Daddy always hated being shut up in cars," she explained to me.

Instead, the pallbearers had loaded his coffin onto the pushcart that he'd rolled a million miles through the dusty streets of Catawah for one last trip through town.

We walked behind it.

But in our little, small-minded town a funeral procession was not enough to restore a man's dignity. I could hear the young boys call out as we passed them on the street corners.

"Dirty Shirts!"

"Did you bury him in a dirty shirt?"

"He's finally off to that laundry in the sky."

They laughed at their own cruel jokes. I wanted to jump out of the procession and race over and break somebody's nose.

Instead, I took my cue from those women. With heads high and stance proud, they followed that coffin, deaf and blind to anything or anyone outside their circle of mourners. Even J.D., walking with his cousins, Julie and Leo and Bernard, gave no inkling of having heard the hecklers.

We were all deliberately dry-eyed as the old man's body was lowered to his final resting place. The Shertz daughters gave no outward clue to the grief that simmered below the surface.

That evening after visiting with family and eating a hasty dinner, J.D. announced that he was tired and going to sleep. It was more than two hours before his bedtime. And he rarely adhered to the requirement without complaint. Worried, I followed him into his room to tuck him in.

"You want me to read something?" I asked.

He was way too old for bedtime stories, but I felt I needed to distract him somehow.

I shouldn't have worried. Even with oversized front teeth and dressed in cowboy pajamas, J.D. was wise. He shook his head.

"I think Mama needs to cry about Grandpa," he told me. "She won't do it in front of me. It's important to be brave about family things, but I don't want her to have to be brave any longer."

His insight stunned me. That he looked so much like her, with his tousled brown hair and pointed chin, was an accident of his birth. That he understood his mother so well was a beautiful gift.

I kissed him on the forehead. "Goodnight, son."

He rolled over on his right side and I tucked the covers around his shoulders.

I found Geri cleaning up in the kitchen. I opened my arms and she slipped into them, allowing all her emotion to come pouring out. I don't think I had realized until then how good it felt to give comfort. In our marriage I was so often on the receiving end. But that night I held her as she sobbed and shook and relinquished all the grief and hurt and loss she felt. I knew that she'd long since forgiven her father for being the man that he was. That night I think she was finally able to forgive herself for being ashamed of him.

It was late at night when she finally fell into an exhausted sleep. I got up and walked to work. Up Bee Street toward town. It was a Friday night and the Jitterbug was busy. But the music had changed. There were no swing bands coming into town now. The place had become a honky-tonk. And all the songs were for crying into your beer.

I had no reason to cry. I wasn't dead anymore. I'd gotten a new life. A life I'd never expected and one I knew I didn't deserve. My dreams still haunted me from time to time. But they were just dreams now and I was no longer afraid of them.

In the weeks after the funeral, Geri and her sisters made an unexpected discovery. In the back of the kitchen pantry, behind the flour barrel and umpteen jars of home-made preserves, they found a half dozen one-pound coffee cans. Each one stuffed solid with paper money. And from the looks of it, much of it had been buried in those cans for years. The sisters were completely dumbfounded. Their father had lived the life of the poorest of paupers. For years they took turns paying his light bill. Every Easter they'd taken up a collection among them-selves to pay his taxes. The only clothes he owned were other people's castoffs. His pantry stayed full because of the generosity of his daughters and their husbands. And now, now that it was too late to ask any questions, they discovered that he had more money than any of them. Counted up, the cash in the cans amounted to more than $30,000, a fortune at that time.

Geri put her share in a savings account at the bank.

"That's going to be your college money," she told J.D. "No one's ever going to tell you that you can't afford to finish your education."

The little guy nodded, unconcerned about the future.

"So when you go to college you can study what you like," I tried explaining further. "You can be a doctor, a teacher, an engineer, whatever you want."

He smiled up at me.

"I just want to be like you, Daddy," he said.

My heart caught in my throat.

"I'll expect more from you than that," I said, trying to make a joke of his words. But I was serious.

"Well, it's way too soon for you to decide," Geri piped in. "And besides, I was hoping that you'd follow family footsteps into the trash business. Whether those are family footsteps or someone just tracking in, either way, you're a natural for it. Your room is always littered."

J.D. giggled along with his apology. "Sorry, Mom."

It was too early, I suppose, to think about his future. But the future has a way of rushing toward you when you least expect it.

In the fall of 1965 the newspaper went from a daily to a weekly and my job disappeared. I kicked around that winter, trying to find work I could do that had decent pay that allowed me to be on the night shift.

I finally got hired on to do sorting at the post office substation in Glenpool. There was a strange camaraderie at the place. Lots of aging G.I.s like me. No one ever spoke about it, but I felt strongly that I was not the only soul in the place who was still haunted by the past. Geri worried about me making the long drive every night and morning. And we talked about selling the house and moving closer. But home was home. And J.D. was growing up among his aunts and uncles and cousins. And we thought that was a good thing.

Too quickly his bicycle and beanie flip gave way to Beatles records and basketball. Before I had a time to even savor his childhood, he was a teenager. He grew to full height in this thirteenth year. He didn't have long, athletic lines. He retained the small, slight build of the Shertz family. But he never let that stop him. Only five foot nine on his tiptoes, he couldn't post up on the court, so he made his points scoring on jump shots and dribbling inside for layups.

Geri and I never missed a game, not even in the early years when he did most of his minutes on the bench. Tuesdays and Fridays from October to February, our calendar was filled.

"It's because you only have the one boy,"

Hackshaw Hurst told me. The father of four sons and two daughters, each of whom played sports, he was never expected to show up at any particular game. "When my kids see me, it's a big occasion and they're grateful. J.D. takes it for granted that you'll always be there."

I knew he was probably right, but I didn't care. I wanted to be there. I wanted to share every moment of his young life.

Of course, there were some moments when I wouldn't have been welcome. Geri and I were both caught a little off guard when he started dating. He'd never shown a lot of interest in girls. At first it seemed harmless enough. He went to a class party with the sister of one of his teammates. And then to the movies a few times with the Methodist preacher's daughter. But by junior year he seemed to be exclusively steady with Melinda Masterson.

Melinda was blond and peppy, with bright eyes and a great big smile. She was an average student and socially quite a bit more popular than J.D. She was a cheerleader and one of the runners-up for homecoming queen. She had a pale little voice, but could carry a tune and sang soprano in Sunday choir. We might have thought their pairing to be a perfectly nice one, but in a small town, you always know way too much about other people's lives.

Melinda's mother, Bertie McNeil, had been a local beauty who at the tender age of nineteen had gotten involved with Piggy Masterson. She got pregnant out of wedlock, which was not unheard of in any generation. However, instead of hastily making an honest woman of her, Piggy decided to wait until the baby was born and could be certified to be his. This action suggested that Bertie was not merely a girl in trouble, but also an immoral girl. Her family's humiliation was horrible. Bertie hid out at home until she'd had her baby, but that didn't help. Everybody knew and disapproval was unanimous.

After Melinda was born and a blood test revealed that Piggy was the likely father, a fact that Bertie had insisted was a certainty from the start, the two were married. But Bertie could never really forgive what he had done to her. And I doubt that Piggy tried very hard to make it up to her. They divorced a few years later.

By the time Melinda was in high school, Piggy was on his third wife and had two other children, both boys. He was very proud of his pretty daughter, but he didn't have much time. What he did have was money and he lavished it on her. He made sure she always had plenty of nice clothes and spending cash. And for her sixteenth birthday, he bought her a baby-blue Ford Mustang.

So throwing into this mix a healthy, active teenage boy, who we, his parents, feared might have a sex drive as strong as our own caused Geri and I a lot of worry.

"You have to talk to him," she insisted.

"He knows all about the birds and bees," I assured her.

"Yes, but does he know how determined a teenage girl can be when she puts her mind to getting her claws in a certain guy."

"I assume you're speaking from experience," I teased. "That didn't turn out so bad, did it."

Geri waved away my attempt at humor. "I just want to give him a chance to choose a girl himself, before this one does all the choosing for him. You two need a father-son talk."

So on a pretty autumn Saturday, I encouraged my son to help me wall in the wash porch to make another room. In truth, it was more me helping him. I was a competent carpenter, but J.D. had a knack for seeing how to put things together. I wouldn't have thought of making the wash porch into a room, but J.D. recognized the possibilities. And when he pointed them out, I felt almost stupid for not having seen something so obvious myself. We worked well together, understanding instinctively what we needed to do for each other. Few words were required. By midafternoon I hadn't quite managed to bring up the all-important subject.

I suggested we take a break. We sat down in the shade of the steps each with a glass of cool water.

"That Mclinda, she's a mighty pretty girl," I began.

He glanced up at me and raised an eyebrow, a grin on his face. "I noticed that," he said. "In fact, most of the guys in school have noticed that. But I guess I'm a bit surprised that you would notice."

"I may be old, but I'm not blind," I told him.

"Does Mom know that?"

I laughed "That woman knows more about me than I know myself." I hesitated for a moment and then decided that was exactly the right track to go down. "You know, your mother and I, we have such a good marriage. We're happy. And our life is full and fun. Some people would say we don't have much. There's not enough paint on the planet to cover up the flaws in this old house. We're never going to be rich or have a lot of nice things. But we have each other and we love each other."

J.D. nodded thoughtfully.

"When trouble comes," I told him. "And it does for everybody, money and property and what you've accumulated, that stuff doesn't mean much. But if you have the right person beside you, you can get through a lot."

"I believe that," he said. "I see how you and Mom are and that's what I want someday. Someday, not very soon, though."

I managed not to sigh aloud with relief. "If Melinda is the one," I said, "she'll wait for you."

His grin broadened and he chuckled aloud. "Melinda's not the one," he said. "Don't get me wrong. I like Melinda. She's got a cute face and nice figure and fabulous legs."

That was all true, but I was taken aback to have him inventory her assets aloud.

"You know what I like best about Melinda, Dad?"

I tried to think of what he might not have mentioned. "Her smile?"

His expression sobered into deliberate seriousness. "Her baby-blue Mustang," he answered.

We laughed, both of us. It was very funny, but I had to remember my place as father, so composed myself as quick as I could.

"Son, I don't want you to marry that girl, but I don't want you to break her heart, either."

"I won't," he insisted.

"Are you sure? Girls can be very fragile and tender-hearted."

J.D. shook his head. "She only goes out with me because her father dislikes me so."

"What? How could he not like you?"

"He can't stand me," J.D. said. "To Melinda's face he refers to me as Dirty Shirt-tails. He's scared to death that his precious daughter is going to tie herself to the trashy Shertz family. So she pretty much dates me to annoy Piggy."

"Oh my gosh!" I was shocked.

"Melinda and I are perfect together. She gets to needle her dad and I get to drive the Mustang. It's a match made in heaven."

J.D. laughed again.

I remember that face, that young, strong face with the wide grin. Of all the photographs we have, he never smiled like that in any of them, yet it's that smile I remember most.

It was so long ago. So very long ago. I had

failed my son. And now he was gone. Geri was gone, as well. I was all alone in the world, all alone and trapped in this bed in this hospital room. There was someone beside me. I tried to open my eyes to see, but my body would not obey my will. I was weak as a kitten, unable to so much as lift my hand.

The music in the hallway was playing again. As soon as I recognized the tune I wanted to laugh at how completely appropriate it was to hear "Papa's in Bed with His Britches On." The band could not be Dizzy Gillespie's, but they were almost as good. I relaxed into my pillow. Maybe all the music in this place wasn't so bad after all.

# Monday, June 13, 4:35 P.M.

Jack had been unable to get Dana on the phone all day. She didn't pick up anywhere and that was not like her. He'd begun to worry. And to make it worse, he'd called Swim Infinity a little before four and Laura had put him off with, "Let me call you right back." More than a half hour later, she still had not phoned. Mondays could be very busy, he reminded himself, and with Dana out, Laura would be fielding calls from both the work crews and the clients. But he didn't like it. He needed to be there. He needed to be working. The very last thing he wanted or needed was to have time on his hands to rethink his own past.

Women liked that kind of thing. Well, maybe not all women. He couldn't imagine Dana being keen on it. But Claire certainly was. It was as if she was determined to understand everybody's perspective, everyone's reason for actions taken. Even now she was sorting through the photos and mementos stored under Bud and Geri's bed. As if coming across some scrap of paper would explain everything.

This is what they were thinking when they took you in.

This is what they were thinking when they gave you back.

"It's very typical for children who were very young when they lost their parents to feel abandoned by them," she'd said to him. "Maybe your feelings about your grandparents are complicated by anger associated with your father's death."

Jack had rolled his eyes. "I think you've gone one *Oprah* show over the top on that one," he told her.

But he did wonder if all his impressions, his certainties, about his relationship with his father's family, might be flawed.

He had to find something to do.

He pulled his cell phone out of his pocket, making certain it was operational. It was, but he had no missed calls and no messages. He needed to be busy. He'd repaired about everything he could see that needed repairing. He'd even painted the railing on the front porch. Which, of course, made the whole house look as if it needed a fresh coat.

He'd changed the oil in both Geri's car

and Bud's truck. And he'd given them both a nice wash and wax.

He'd cleared the yard and mowed the grass. He was amazed that Bud still used his push mower. It worked fairly well, but Jack took great pride in sharpening the blades.

He'd looked over the garden, abundant with flowers. He could probably hook up an automatic watering system for it. But he'd have to pull out a lot of plants to do it. And even to his eyes, the garden looked as if it had been very well kept.

At a loss, Jack walked into the shaded work shed and looked around. The smell of axle grease, the dirt floor and the lingering scent of sawdust was an aromatic cocktail he found compelling and intoxicating. Surely, he thought to himself, there's something in this building that is just screaming to be done.

As soon as his eyes settled on the neat pile of cut boards on the top shelf, he knew what he needed to do. His father had wanted to make a box for Geri to keep her treasures in, but he hadn't had the time to finish it. And Bud hadn't had the heart. Jack figured he had both time and heart to do the job.

He pulled the wood down and spread it along the work-bench. The raw wood had aged considerably since it had been cut. The pieces on the top of the stack now showed a rich dark patina, as did all the edges and corners. He smoothed his palm across the grain of the wood and ran his fingers along the carefully detailed slots of the one completed dovetail corner. It was a strange feeling to know, without question, that his father's hands had done exactly the same. He'd made a through joint, the strongest of all dovetails and the easiest to work by hand. Jack fitted the two pieces together. It was a perfect fit.

He smiled. From his Cub Scout days, he'd always had a keen interest in building. And he just seemed to have a knack when it came to using tools. His talents had always been a mystery to his Van Brugge family. His brothers had fine motor skills that were better than Jack's own, but they never seemed to get the feel for wood, or to have the desire to create something from its raw materials. Their scientific curiosity had always been directed toward plants and animals, while Jack was more fascinated with the geometry of structure and function. It was just another working-class anomaly, something that made Jack different, something in which he'd been embarrassed to take any pride. But at this moment, and maybe for the first time in his life, Jack had an inkling about the source of his natural ability.

He took the pieces apart once more and looked around for paper and pencil. Without plans to work from or a picture of what the finished product was supposed to look like, he would have to imagine the intent his father had by looking at the evidence of what was already done. Not a foolproof method, but Jack took up the challenge. His woodworking skills were rusty, but he needed to do something. And this was, he realized, what he wanted to do.

He found paper and carefully traced the patterns of the cuts already made. He was somewhat surprised by the size of the box. It was supposedly for his grandmother's treasures, and from what Jack had seen Claire dragging out from under the bed, that would require a box of considerable size. What these boards represented was clearly something considerably smaller.

From around the room he gathered the tools he would need: an adjustable gauge, a square, a dovetail saw and a half-inch chisel. Not everything was as easy to find as he'd hoped, but he did find his grandfather's shop to be surprisingly intuitive. It took only a few moments before he was working.

From the traced patterns he marked the wood with a pencil. Then he clamped a board secure to the work-bench and began to saw with a special blade, narrow and designed for fine crosscuts. Still, it would only be close to the right dimensions. The wood required hand chiseling to achieve the perfect snug fit.

Keeping busy was a wonderful way to keep errant thoughts at bay, but today they followed him. And because they did, Jack forced himself to concentrate totally on the task at hand. He was accustomed to doing that. It was how he got by most of the time. The more vexing or complicated his life became, the more he would direct his focus to his work.

He paused in midmotion as that realization came to him.

When mankind was admonished "know thyself," it had never really been explained that the information was most often arrived at in dribs and drabs.

Reasonably, Jack began to consider the accusation that Claire so often made that he was hiding out with his work.

He might have pursued this direction of self-discovery further had his cell phone not gone off. He pulled it out of his pocket. It had been nearly an hour since Laura had said she'd call right back. Finally, she had. But the office should be closed by now and his receptionist should have been on her way home. He flipped open the phone.

"Yeah," he said by way of greeting.

There was a momentary silence on the other end.

"Hello, Laura?"

"Um, yes . . . Mr. Crabtree," she stumbled. "I meant to call you sooner, but . . . well, it's . . . well . . . ah, you know Mondays."

"What are you still doing at work?" he said. "It can't be that busy. Did you manage to get in touch with Dana?"

"Uh . . . well." The hesitation was beginning to annoy Jack.

"Laura, what the devil is going on?"

With a gush of anxiety and concern, the receptionist answered with a demand.

"Mr. Crabtree, you've got to come back here," she said. "I'm not completely sure what all is happening, but none of it seems to be good."

Jack couldn't even imagine what she might be talking about. "I've only been gone four days," he reminded her.

"A lot of things can change in that amount of time," she said.

"Like what?"

"Like . . . well, like Dana going out on her own."

"Out on her own?"

"She's starting her own business," Laura said.

Jack was genuinely surprised to say the least. He'd always figured that Dana would eventually go out on her own, but she hadn't yet acquired the knowledge or experience to compete with most of the guys in town. Most of her ability was in sales. She did have a good eye, but her understanding of construction was very limited.

Jack responded with generosity. "I wish her well, but surely she'll stay on at Swim Infinity for a while," he said. "It takes time to get a new business on its feet. She'll have to find a prime location, hire some good people, do some advertising and all of that takes money. She'll need a really top-notch business plan to go to the bank."

"She doesn't need to go to the bank," Laura said. "Mr. Butterman is paying. She's already setting up in one of the auxiliary shops next to his store near La Cantera. And she's offered jobs to most of the guys in your crew, with higher pay and Butterman's company benefits package. I think a lot of them are going to take her up on it. She doesn't want me. She said I'm not 'hot enough' for the front of her store."

The last was spoken with such heartbreak and disappointment, Jack thought the woman must be close to tears.

"So you've got to come back and do something," Laura said. "I need this job. I've got car payments every month!"

Jack had several monthly payments of his own. He wasn't worried, but he didn't like what he was hearing.

"I'll get a flight back as soon as I can," he told her.

The old iron bed in Bud and Geri's back bedroom was narrow and very high off the floor. Claire wasn't sure if this late nineteenth-century design was meant to keep vermin out of the mattress or to get the sleepers closer to the warmer air near the ceiling. Or if it was, just what it seemed, a practical arrangement that allowed for abundant under-the-bed storage. As soon as Claire got home from the hospital, she changed into her work clothes and got down on her knees on the little rag rug at the bedside and began dragging out the dusty boxes that were stored there.

She found old scrapbooks with orderly photographs held in place with black paper corners. In one picture there was a line of pretty young women standing in front of a brick building, the girl in the center in a graduate's cap and gown. Claire looked closely. It had to be one of the aunts, but she didn't know which one. She did recognize Geri, not because she looked like the woman Claire had known, but more because she reminded Claire of her twins.

There were newspaper articles cut out of the *Catawah Daily Citizen,* and later Claire noticed, from the *Catawah Weekly Citizen.* Many were obituaries of people Claire didn't know. There were also a lot of clips that featured a young J.D. either playing sports or getting some accolade:

### Crabtree Wins Leadership Award

Jack Dempsey Crabtree, Jr., known locally as J.D., received the Leader of Tomorrow Award from local American Legion Post 98. Crabtree, a senior at Catawah High, is an honor student, national merit scholar and three-year letterman in basketball and baseball. He was chosen for his schoolwork, his extracurricular activities and his service to his community.

In the last year he developed and initiated an antilittering program in conjunction with the Fellowship of Christian Athletes. The program, Catawah, Keep It Clean, was lauded earlier this year by Lieutenant Governor George Nigh as an example of local effectiveness in the state's new Beautify Oklahoma campaign.

When asked about his future plans, Crabtree announced that he has applied to the U.S. Air Force Academy. "If I don't get in," he said, "I'll join up."

Crabtree is the son of Mr. and Mrs. J.D. 'Bud' Crabtree, Sr.

Claire smiled and laid the yellowed piece of newsprint on the stack. She wondered if Jack had ever seen these. Even if he had, her children had not.

There were also articles about Bud and his volunteer work with civil defense, old "Ann Landers" columns on getting along with the neighbors and which direction to hang the toilet paper. Rather than wade through all of that, Claire moved on to other boxes.

Several contained old phonograph records, mainly from the big-band era. Lots of ancient and brittle seventy-eights by the orchestras of Tommy Dorsey or Artie Shaw, as well as later, minted LPs of greatest hits. She flipped through them with the thought-fulness and care that some might reserve for visiting a museum.

There was a lot of memorabilia of the Shertz family, including an old German-language Bible. Tucked inside was an aged and brown note in a poorly written hand: *Arrived* SS Hyde *June 16, 1854 Aldolphos Shertz 41 years, wife Willamina 34 years, sons Heinrich and Fredrich 11 years, daughter Ava dead at sea.* Claire placed the piece of family history aside, reverently thinking to herself, more twins, it clearly ran in the family.

One box contained only trophies and plaques, some for Bud but most for J.D. Jack's father played sports, made speeches and was good at history.

There was one box that was full of baby clothes. Claire couldn't help but sigh at the sight of them. There is just something about miniature sweaters and tiny stray mittens that touch a mother's heart. Her favorites were the lace-up leather shoes and a little pair of hand-sewn overalls. Most of the shirts and pants appeared not to be store brands but stitched up on somebody's sewing machine. All pieced together with love, Claire thought to herself. She happened on a round flattened beret of soft grayed wool with a note pinned to it. *Jackie's first cap, last piece knitted by Grandma Stark, 1972.*

Claire's jaw dropped in surprise. She'd assumed all these baby clothes belonged to J.D., but, of course, these could easily be those of her husband, as well.

The sound of someone knocking on the front door distracted her attention.

"Just a minute!" she called out as she extricated herself from the prison of boxes with which she'd surrounded herself. She made it to the front door to find a woman about her own age standing there. She was dressed in green crop pants, flip-flops and a T-shirt with flowerpots on the bosom.

"Claire? Hi!" the woman greeted, enthusiastically offering her hand. "I'm Mena Beverly. I'm sorry I didn't call. I left the house this morning with my phone on the charger and I haven't made it back home yet."

"I guess you're one of my husband's cousins," Claire said.

"Right, but isn't everybody?" She laughed. "Look, I hate to do this to you, but my grandmother made me bring her here. I've got a million things to do — would you mind letting her stay here on your porch. I swear I won't be more than a half hour. Promise. Absolutely."

"Uh . . . well sure," she answered, not having any idea what else she could say.

"Thursday's my day to get her out of the center and drive her around town, feed her family dinner and all that," Mena explained. "But my husband's doing roofing work out of town and my fifteen-year-old is arriving home from 4H State in —" the woman glanced down at her watch "— in about fifteen minutes."

"Oh."

"I'll just roll her right up here on the porch," Mena said. "She won't be any trouble and I'll be back in just a few minutes. Let me just get her out of the car."

"Sure, I'll help."

Claire had no idea which of the sisters might be in the car, but it didn't really matter. She was sure all these people had spent time taking care of Bud and Geri. It was a great opportunity for her to return the favor.

In the front seat of the minivan Aunt Sissy sat wearing a less faded version of the same muumuu she had on last time Claire had seen her. Her hair was freshly coiffed — probably from the local beauty shop.

Claire opened the door.

"Hi."

"Oh, I hope I'm not too much trouble," the old woman said in her tiny, childlike voice. "I just wanted to see you so much and Mena is so very busy."

"Please come sit on my porch," Claire said. "I was just getting ready to take a break."

Mena retrieved the wheelchair from the back of the van and opened it on the ground in front of the passenger door, locking it in place. With her granddaughter holding her around the waist, Aunt Sissy managed to lower herself from the car seat to a standing position. Once she got her hands on the arms of her chair, she easily seated herself. Mena lowered the footrests and placed her dainty size four-and-a-half shoes on them.

"There we go," Mena said.

The rough ground between the drive and the front porch was not easy on the wheels, but both women seemed accustomed to the terrain. Mena maneuvered the wheelchair backward up the one step to the porch and then moved a chair out of the way to put Sissy in a nicely shaded spot next to the swing.

"Thanks," Mena said to Claire and then added to Aunt Sissy in a higher voice, "I'm just going to run out to the school and I'll be back in fifteen minutes."

"Okay, honey," Aunt Sissy told her. "Don't worry about me. I'll be fine."

"Fifteen minutes," Mena repeated as she hurried to the car.

Claire seated herself on the porch swing and flashed Aunt Sissy a smile. She thought, not for the first time, that the name suited her. She appeared to be a tiny, vulnerable person with a natural expression that was forlorn.

Mena was backing out of the driveway almost as soon as she turned the ignition key. As she headed up the street, she waved.

Aunt Sissy returned the gesture, the small wrinkled and weathered hand seemed not quite big enough to support the plain gold band on her third finger. As the van disappeared up the street, she glanced over at Claire.

"Are you wearing a watch?" she asked.

Claire wasn't, but as Aunt Sissy continued, Claire realized the question was rhetorical.

"Take note of the time," the old woman said. "If that girl is back here in less than two hours, I'll give you one hundred dollars."

Claire's mouth dropped open, but she didn't know what to say.

"I don't take any offense of it," Aunt Sissy explained quickly. "The poor girl has her hands full. Working full-time with two teenagers in bloom. She and her husband are divorced."

"Oh, I'm sorry."

"Don't say I told you," Sissy suggested. "They don't think I know about it. They pretend that he's out of town working, but the fact is he moved to Tulsa last year. The kids are heartbroken about it. And you know they say two can live as cheaply as one. But when two who used to be one start living separately, that's something no family can really afford."

Claire nodded. "You're probably right," she said. "It's too bad, marriages don't last the way they used to."

Aunt Sissy laughed. "Oh, they never lasted the way they used to," she said. "Marriage has never been easy. Because neither husband nor wife is ever a saint. And if they were, well, that would just make it worse."

"But people stayed together back in your day."

She nodded. "Mostly, but not everybody," she said. "And even among those that did there were couples who hadn't given each other the time of day in twenty years. It's just back then they couldn't get a divorce. Too much shame."

Claire nodded as if she understood.

"I've got a friend at the center who's getting a divorce right now."

"Really? In the nursing home?" Claire was surprised.

"Yep," Aunt Sissy answered. "Her kids are fit to be tied about it. They say, Why do that when you're both living at different places and you'll probably never have to see him again?"

"That makes sense," Claire said.

"It does to the kids," Aunt Sissy answered. "But Belva, that's my friend, Belva says she couldn't bear to die with the whole world thinking she never had enough sense to leave that man."

"I suppose she has a point," Claire admitted.

"I told her that if she really wanted people to know how she feels, we should get ourselves a gun, go over to his nursing home and she should shoot his gonads off."

Claire's jaw dropped open and a shocked sound emerged from her throat.

"The old S.O.B. has got no use for them anyway," Aunt Sissy said. "The story would get splashed all over the six-o'clock news. And what are the police going to do to Belva? Once you're in a nursing home, you pretty much lose your fear of prison."

"Oh my gosh, what did Belva say?"

Aunt Sissy's face broke into a wide grin. "We had a great, good laugh just imagining it," she said.

She managed another one just by recalling the first. After a minute of enjoyment, her expression sobered.

"Seriously, I'm thinking that sometimes a couple just needs to break up," she said. "In marriage, where two souls are entwined, there can be things that can never be forgiven or forgotten. And that's just the truth. But most of the time it's just one disagreement that goes awry and two people who won't give in. They let it build and build on itself until they can't see any of the good they've got. And they let their anger destroy everything they ever made."

"Well, yes, I guess that's so," Claire admitted. "But sometimes people can just discover that they are at cross-purposes on what they want to achieve in life. They got married thinking they felt the same about things and then find out that the other person is not who they thought."

Aunt Sissy nodded sagely. "No husband ever turns out to be exactly what his bride thought," she said.

"Maybe not," Claire said. "But when your core values are not compatible, it would seem like you're doomed to divorce. So better sooner than later."

Aunt Sissy reached over and patted Claire on the hand. "Your mother is very far away these days, isn't she?"

The question momentarily caught Claire off guard. "Ah . . . well, they're posted in Moldova, but right now I think they're on vacation in the south of Spain."

Aunt Sissy clutched Claire's hand as if to imbue her with strength. "I don't think you and Jackie are doomed to divorce," she said.

Claire felt the blood drain from her face, just to come rushing back in an embarrassed blush.

"Oh, I wasn't talking about us," she insisted.

"Aren't you?" Sissy asked. "We couldn't help but notice that there's a distance between you two. And what was that boy thinking coming up here to Geri's funeral without you by his side."

"Well, there were the children. . . ."

"Who would have been perfectly welcome and made to feel at home with their cousins," she said. "Your husband needed you and you should have been here."

Claire felt as if she'd been slapped. "No, he said that he didn't need me. And he didn't want me to come. He didn't even want me to come this week."

Aunt Sissy shook her head. "Don't pay him any mind when he's like that. He doesn't know what he wants."

"Well, he knows he doesn't want me."

She hadn't meant the words exactly as they'd come out. She quickly tried to take them back, but Aunt Sissy would have none of it.

"Just spit it all out," she said. "Before it eats you up inside."

Claire hesitated, but found herself wanting to say it aloud.

"He's built a new house," she said.

"A new house? How nice."

"It's not nice," Claire said. "It's a huge palace of a place. It's showy and vulgar, designed just to impress. I swear the man would like nothing better than to paper the walls with hundred-dollar bills."

"A lot of women would love a nice, new house."

Claire nodded. "I'm sure they would, but I love the house that I have. It's not big or fancy, but it's ours. We bought it on a shoestring and I've painted and washed and waxed every surface in it. We brought our children home from the hospital to that place. And we've celebrated every birthday, every anniversary, every Christmas there. We know all the neighbors and it's in a great school system. We're close to everything. And the best part, we can afford it. We can afford it easily."

Aunt Sissy was listening intently.

371

"The new house is way out in a new area, surrounded by other giant Garage Mahals. The school district is only so-so and it's very overcrowded."

"Maybe you could send the children to private school," Aunt Sissy suggested.

"Jack says the same thing," Claire told her. "Just think how much that will cost. Jack works long hours now. So what happens when our mortgage triples and we start paying school tuition? The kids will never see him. I will never see him. I'll be living alone in a giant house that I don't want."

"Have you told him this?"

"We fight about it all the time," Claire said. "The thing is, it's more than just a house to him. It's like proof that he's a success. He wants everybody to see that he can make money. The people who love him don't care if he makes money."

Aunt Sissy chuckled. "I guess the people who love him aren't the ones he's worried about," she said. "He must have it in his head that some very important people don't love him."

That statement caught Claire up short. She gathered her thoughts for a moment before she spoke.

"It's really funny that you should say that," she told Aunt Sissy. "Because on the way home from the hospital today, Jack confessed to me that he didn't believe that Bud and Geri loved him."

"Why that's the silliest thing I've ever heard," the old woman said. "Why would Jackie think something like that?"

Claire shrugged. "Because they never came down to San Antonio to see him. And they wouldn't let him put in a pool for them?" Her answer was as much a question as a statement.

Sissy shook her head. "Bud and Geri never did any traveling. She always said that he liked to sleep in his own bed. And I don't think he cared much for the water, either," she said. "I don't think I've ever seen him go swimming."

"That Jack would even think that is just completely crazy," Claire said.

Aunt Sissy agreed. "It's sure crazy all right," she said. "About as crazy as thinking you don't share anything important with the man who's a loving father to your three children."

Claire had the good grace to blush.

"Pick your battles, girl," Aunt Sissy advised. "Where you are is not as important as who you're with."

Claire didn't openly agree with that, but she did consider that Aunt Sissy might know

373

what she was talking about.

She sure knew about Mena. After an hour and a half together on the porch, Claire asked her if she was hungry.

"It has been awhile since lunch," the old lady said. "And if you feed me, well that will be one less thing that Mena has to do."

Claire wheeled her inside the house back to the kitchen.

"You can have your pick of the leftovers," she told her. "The Shertz family has been sending over food like there's an army of eaters here. We've got ham and roast beef and even some very tasty tuna casserole."

Aunt Sissy glanced through the bedroom doorway and noted all the boxes scattered on the floor.

"Are you sorting things out in there?"

"Oh, I was looking at the pictures and reading through the old letters and mementos," Claire said. "That's all right, don't you think?"

"Absolutely," Aunt Sissy assured her. "I'm sure Geri saved all that for you and Jack and the children."

Claire nodded. "That's what I thought, too. I really hoped that I'd find Bud's war medals," she said. "Jack's never seen them, and Toni told me that they were very impressive."

The expression that came over Aunt Sissy's face was both shock and sadness.

"Oh, honey, you're not going to find them here," she said. "They were buried with J.D. I saw Bud put them in the coffin myself."

# Bud

Something bumped the raft and startled me awake. I hadn't really been asleep, but I'd been in that in-between place, that void of safety where neither the living hell nor the terror of dreams was in full control. I was still alive and I was trying to stay that way.

I'd managed to fix the hole in the raft, though I wasn't sure how well it would hold. Among the "provisions" stowed on the raft was a roll of adhesive tape. It was white and sticky and I think it was more for patching up flesh than rubber, but I got the leak stopped which freed me to move.

But I wasn't moving much. The sun was low, the oppressive heat was waning, but I was stiff and aching, sore and thirsty. There was no reason to lift my head up to gaze across the never-ending stretch of water on every side. I don't know what made me look up at that exact moment. Momentarily, I was startled by a man in the water. But it was only Randel. The body of Lt. Randel was still bobbing on the water. I should have taken off his vest.

He'd drifted away, but now he was drifting back. The day had not been a good one for him. The hot sun had done a lot of work. He was very much a dead man. Shrunken, sun-bleached, flesh missing. I might not have even recognized him as formerly human if I had not known he was there.

Maybe I'd have another chance of letting him go, I thought. It was what I should do. I didn't want to imagine his family, his wife, his mother thinking about him, praying for him and his body just stuck atop the water. It was like being trapped between heaven and hell. He deserved last rites. He deserved to have his body consigned to the deep. It was my duty to him as a fellow human being.

If I was going to do it, I couldn't wait. The sun was sinking and I'd lose sight of him. Paddling, I could get alongside in minutes. My decision was made, but my intention was never realized.

Everything happened so fast. At first I didn't realize what was going on. It was as if an errant wave rose up and swamped Randel. Then I realized the wave had teeth.

"Shark!" I screamed as the raft tottered

atop the violent movement in the water.

It rocked back and forth for an instant that seemed like an eternity. Then just as quickly the water stilled. It was as if an unholy quiet had settled upon the spot. I held my breath, waiting for the next horror. And I was not disappointed.

A minute after the eerie stillness settled in, Randel's vest popped to the surface. I gagged. Too frightened to lean my head over the side, I vomited all over myself.

No, I was trying to vomit, but there was something in my throat. I struggled to free myself from it, choking. Then I realized it was the breathing tube. I was in the hospital. I remembered now. But how real the raft had seemed! I wondered if that was what death was going to be for me. I'd believed that I had died out there in the water. Perhaps all these intervening years, the years with Geri, had been a gift and in the end I would find myself back there. Back in that most beautiful horizon of hell.

It was as good an explanation as any. Of course, death couldn't really be explained. You could see it, hear it, touch it, taste it and smell it. But humanly it somehow couldn't be understood, just endured.

Or maybe we can get a glimpse of comprehension by staring at its opposite: the spring that J.D. graduated high school.

My son became his own man that spring. He was strong and good-looking, funny and smart, hardworking and kind. He was captain of the basketball team and president of the senior class. Two girls took top spots in academics, but J.D. came in third with straight A's in all his classes.

He'd decided that he wanted to go to the Air Force Academy and he'd written a letter to Senator Mike Monroney asking for a recommendation. Military life would certainly not have been my first choice, even as an officer, but J.D. knew his own mind and what he wanted. He went after it.

He was working both early morning and after school at Stark's IGA. Old Man Stark had died and left the place to my stepbrother, Jonas. Mama retained enough influence to get her grandson a job.

J.D. was like his mother in the way that he scrimped and saved. You'd never catch him throwing away good money on beer or cigarettes or even flashy clothes. That spring he bought a brand-new Ford pickup. He paid cash for it and just drove it home. Geri and I were flabbergasted.

"It's not that I didn't want your opinion on this," he told me as he leaned over the big six-cylinder and listened to it purr. "I

379

just felt like it was something I needed to do on my own. Do you understand that?"

I smiled at him and wrapped an arm around his shoulder. "Sure I do," I told him. "When I was your age I got married without even giving your grandma a hint. It's your money, you worked hard for it and it's a fine vehicle."

"I thought I might start doing more grocery deliveries," he said. "I make as much in tips as I get in hourly wage. And then I'll have it to drive up to Colorado Springs in the fall."

But the fall was a long way off. There were so many busy days ahead. J.D. went to Boys State. He was a finalist for a public speaking award for Rural Electric Cooperatives and he and Melinda were definitely the cutest couple ever destined for a senior prom.

The rigidity of the new Baptist preacher, Brother Kelvan, kept the traditional dance out of the school gym that year. *He* didn't approve and so the rest of the community had to suffer. It made me mad. God and I weren't exactly on speaking terms, but I respected Him. What I didn't respect were those who could, with such self-righteous certainty, speak for Him. It didn't help my opinion that Kelvan put a big "My country right or wrong!" bumper sticker on his church bus. The man had spent the entire war on a base up in Minnesota. I suppose he was protecting us from the Canadians. He was one of the two biggest War Hawks in town. The other was Piggy Masterson, former draft dodger who now was with some carefully placed cash donations and draped in the American flag, a leader at Kelvan's church. More proof, if I needed it, that with money on the line, even people in small towns can have short memories.

I hadn't much cared for my senior prom. But nobody had said I couldn't have one. And my J.D. would never be a senior again, so a couple of days after the announcement, I went up to talk to Tom McKiever who was running the Jitterbug and we worked out a deal. He would close up the bar and he and his customers would steer clear. We, the parents, would rent the place, decorate it and serve nonalcoholic punch and cookies. We had no affiliation with the school whatsoever. We were a group of parents giving a private party and all the seniors and their dates were invited to attend.

Geri and her sisters did the decorating. They decided on a Dutch theme and the entire crew sat around our front porch every night for a week making tulips out of crepe paper. I got J.D. to help me put together a miniature windmill. We used an electric fan motor to turn the blades, though it took us a fair amount of engineering to get them to turn safely and slowly enough.

The night of the big dance, Geri and I put on our best clothes and went up to chaperone. Melinda was gorgeous in a bright pink gown, her hair piled high on her head in fat curls, like a stack of blond sausages. And J.D. looked perfect beside her in his white sport coat and pink carnation.

Geri and I watched from the wings as the kids danced the Jerk and the Watusi. When the band finally tried a slow number I took her in my arms and we danced as we had so very long ago on that very floor.

"You don't look grown up enough to have a son graduating from high school," I told her.

She raised her chin at me, feigning defiance. "I most certainly am," she insisted. "You've been the only fellow for me since I was five years old."

I leaned down and kissed her on the nose. She giggled.

"Hey, you two," J.D. said, easing his partner over in our direction. "No PDA on the dance floor."

PDA — public display of affection — was

one of the high school's most vigorously enforced prohibitions.

"It's all right, mister," I teased back. "She and I, we're married."

"Yeah, all you kids say that," he answered.

We had a great time at the dance. And we weren't the only ones. As the evening wore on, more and more of the couples were sneaking into the shadows for a moment of privacy, and who could blame them? They were young and full of life.

I even caught J.D. and Melinda when I went into the back room to fetch a canister of $CO_2$ for the soda fountain. My son was leaned up against a wall, and Melinda was plastered against him like a cheap summer suit.

"Don't mind me," I announced as I walked by them. And I got what I needed and made my way out of there without looking in their direction again.

I was happy for them. Happy for him. I trusted him to enjoy himself without getting into any trouble. Maybe it wasn't typical of what a father feels for a teenage son, but Crabtree boys grow up fast, I decided. My son was a man already and I was ready to accept him as that.

But the beauty of that spring faded too quickly. It was the last week of school, just a few days after the prom, with graduation coming up on the weekend, that I picked up the mail at the mailbox and saw the letter from the Academy.

I was excited and jumpy and hurried home to show it to Geri.

"We could call him at school," I suggested. "And he could come home and read it."

Geri shook her head. "No, he's got a calculus final this morning and European history in the afternoon. Just wait until he comes home for dinner."

So that evening after J.D. got off work, Geri sat the envelope on his plate while he washed up. He saw it as soon as he sat down and he glanced wide-eyed at us.

"When did this come?"

"This morning," I told him.

"Why didn't you call me at school? You know how anxious I've been to get this letter."

"Your mother thought you should take your final exams without this distraction."

"Mom," he said to her in a low-pitched tone that was heavy on long-suffering.

Geri laughed.

"You're here now," she said. "Go ahead and open it!"

He picked it up like he would tear into it, but she admonished him to pry it open gently at the corners.

"I guess she's putting this in among her treasures," he said to me.

I shrugged. "Once a junk collector's daughter, always a junk collector's daughter."

Geri slapped my arm playfully.

J.D. opened the envelope with a smile on his face. He read the words on the letter and then hesitated. As the moment lingered I glanced at Geri. The smile dropped from her face as quickly as from my own. Our son was a good student, a natural leader, he had excellent recommendations.

"I didn't get in," he announced.

"Why not?"

"What does it say?"

"It doesn't really say anything," J.D. answered. "They thanked me for applying and said that I'm allowed to reapply next year. That's pretty much it."

He laid the paper down on the table. I picked it up, but I was too agitated to read it. I handed it to Geri instead.

"It's a blow," I said.

J.D. nodded. "I should have been more realistic about my chances," he said. "Catawah is such a small school and the Academy is very competitive. I really shouldn't have gotten my hopes so high."

"It's good to have high hopes," his mother said.

I nodded. "We have to see this as an opportunity," I told him. "You're fortunate that this isn't your only chance for college. We've still got that money from Grandpa Shertz. You can go to Oklahoma State and take ROTC. It's the same four years and you'll come out with the exact same rank."

"I want to think about it," he said. "I just really need to think about what I need to do."

"And you don't have to decide right away," Geri assured him. "You certainly don't have to decide tonight. I've fixed your favorite meat loaf and mashed potatoes."

He pushed his chair back from the table. "Sorry, Mom, I'm not really hungry."

As soon as he walked out the front door, I was on my feet and I was cussing and headed to the phone.

"What are you doing?" Geri asked me.

"I'm calling those lousy S.O.B.s and giving them a piece of my mind!"

She decided to help me. Geri, who was normally too frugal to call her sister in Haskell because it was long distance, called Senator Monroney's office in Washington, D.C.

I was surprised to get a United States

senator on the phone, I was surprised to be screaming at him, but I was more surprised at the words that came out of my mouth.

"I served my country. I was a gunner on a B-24. I strafed as much ground, dropped as many bombs and killed as many Japanese as most men who went. I've got enough commendations and battle ribbons to choke a draft horse. Damn it! I was MIA alone on a raft for seven long days in the shark-infested Solomon Sea. I did this because my country asked me to. Now I'm asking something back!"

The big, important man never lost his temper. He took every angry phrase that I dished out and he promised he would do something. He was as good as his word.

The next morning, before J.D. left for school an Air Force recruiter from Tulsa showed up at our door. He was stiff and straight with more spit and polish than any of us guys had had in the Pacific. He had a few ribbons on his chest, but he couldn't hold a candle to the stack of pretty colors that I kept in an old shoe box.

"Senator Monroney's office called me," he said. "I'd like to talk to you, J.D. And, of course, your parents are welcome, too."

He sat down with the three of us in the front room.

"We want you in the Air Force," he told J.D. "We can see that you're smart, motivated and eager to serve. Are you familiar with the prep school?"

"Prep school?"

"As part of the Academy, the Air Force runs a prep school for young men who are good candidates for the Academy but need a little extra help to make the grade."

"I never heard of it," J.D. admitted.

"You're an athlete, I understand," the recruiter said.

"I play basketball and baseball," J.D. answered.

"Oh, that's great. The AF Prep Huskies have some great teams," he said. "You go a year there, play some ball, bone up on your studies, it will make you a lot more competitive for an appointment to the Academy."

"It sounds great," J.D. said.

He glanced at me for agreement. It did sound great. A little bit too great. My experience didn't include a lot of really great deals coming from the Air Force. Maybe things had changed.

"Okay," the recruiter said with a big smile. "Then let's get you started. We'll need to get you signed up for basic training and get you on the fast track. You sign up here for four years, but that's just a formality. Once you enter the Academy you make an eight-year commitment, I'm sure you know that."

J.D. nodded.

I guess with the sound of Air Force Academy still ringing in our ears, we didn't really hear everything that was said. But before J.D. finally trotted off to school, he'd enlisted in the Air Force.

We found out later, of course, that J.D. could have applied to the prep school without joining up. But we were assured that active duty would help him.

In July, instead of driving his car to Colorado Springs, he went south to San Antonio, Texas.

"I'll write you every week," his mother promised him.

J.D. chuckled. "And I'll phone in my replies," he answered.

We missed him when he was gone. But our life was full and busy. I was still working at the post office. Geri had hooked up with an odd assortment of people who were interested in resource conservation, which is apparently a fancy name for reusing junk. Using both her knowledge of the business and her contacts, she was very helpful to the group. Ultimately, she was named to the governing board of the Cannett County Friends of the Environment. I was proud of her, but she waved it off as though it were nothing.

It was late summer before we saw J.D. again. He looked like a different person. It was not just that his hair was missing and that he'd bulked up by thirty pounds, at least. He just seemed to be a grown-up, self-confident man. We loved having him home and hearing all of his stories. And there were a lot of them. He had a way of making the ordinary seem entertaining.

One night when he'd been home about a week he went in under the bed and brought out the shoe box with my war medals. He was looking through them inquisitively, as if he hadn't seen them all a hundred times and knew them better than referee signals.

"Do you know where I can get some nice wood?" he asked me.

"You planning a project?"

He gave a little smile. "I thought I'd make a box for Mama's treasures, something that doesn't look like it was dragged out of the garbage dump."

"Oh, your mother doesn't believe in garbage dumps," I said, with a teasing glance in Geri's direction. "These days we want everything to go into 'recycling.' "

She glanced up from the notes she was making on a pamphlet about composting.

"He's makes fun of me now," she said to J.D., feigning affront, "but he was pretty grateful when I rescued his worn-out soul from the trash heap of human existence."

I laughed. "And so, indeed, she did rescue me," I told J.D. "And we both have cause to be grateful. Me, 'cause I've had a great life and you, because Stub Williams would have probably been your father."

"Stub Williams? I would never have given that knothead the time of day."

J.D. chuckled. "Perhaps I wouldn't have been born at all. Thanks, Mom."

"I *am* the one you should thank," she said. "If I left it up to your father, I surely would have been an old maid."

"So to get back to the treasure box for the almost old maid. I think I know where I can get my hands on some gorgeous walnut."

The conversation proceeded and we eventually made it around to the future.

"Is it for sure that you'll be heading up to that prep school in the fall?" I asked him.

He gave a huff and shook his head. "No," he said. "The school year actually starts there in July, so I missed it, being in basic training. The Sarge tells me that I can apply next year."

"You must be disappointed." I said this, because it seemed natural that he would be, but he didn't look or sound disappointed at all.

"I'm rethinking all that," he said. "The Academy would be great, but Officer Candidate School works just as well. I'm just . . . I'm reconsidering my options."

"Okay," I agreed. "It's always good to consider all the options."

J.D. looked up at me and gave me a big grin that looked like his mama's. "Aren't you dying of curiosity to ask me why?"

I laughed. "Yes, but I guess you'll tell me if you wanted me to know."

"That's what I'll never understand about men," Geri piped in. "How they can beat around the bush and never ask the question. Why have you changed your mind? What's happened?"

"Those Shertz women — they've never had any patience and my crazy girl is the worst of them."

J.D. was still smiling a minute later when he answered her questions.

"I met someone," he said simply.

Geri's jaw fell open like a broken gate. I was equally confounded.

"Who? Where? When?" The questions continued.

I remember so distinctly the look on his face. There was a glow that came up from inside him as he talked about her. He didn't use gushy terms or fancy phrasing, but it was clear to me that my son was in love.

"Her name is Antoinette DeMoineaux, but everyone calls her Toni."

"What kind of name is that? French?"

"It is French, but she's not," he said. "Just an ordinary Texas girl. I ran into her, literally ran into her, coming out of Joske's Department Store. She had maybe ten bags of stuff she'd bought, and it was scattered all over the sidewalk, so I helped her pick it up and I carried it to her car and I asked her out to a movie."

"How could she resist you?" his mother asked.

J.D. chuckled. "Pretty easily, I imagine. San Antonio is full to bursting with fresh-faced flyboys like me, and my understanding is that we all look alike."

"Nonsense."

"Thanks, Mom," he said. "Anyway, I got my truck out of the garage and went to the address she gave me and it's like a palace. I'm thinking I can't date some girl who lives in a palace. But I guess she was watching out the window, 'cause before I had time to chicken out, she came trotting out to my truck and we were off."

"She didn't invite you in to meet her

parents?"

"No, in fact, I still haven't met them. They're a little stuffy, Toni says. I think they already had their eye on some guy they wanted her to marry."

"Marry?" I repeated the word, shocked. "You just met this girl, you're not talking about marriage, surely."

J.D. shrugged. "We're in love, Dad," he said. "Of course we're talking about getting married."

"There's no rush," I cautioned him.

He didn't seem to agree. "Sometimes the world moves fast," he told me.

J.D. was very right about that. In the hospital the band was playing again. It sounded loud enough to be right out in the hallway. And it was a Duke Ellington mimic who sounded just like the man singing "Taking the 'A' Train."

# Tuesday, June 14, 2:23 a.m.

The clang of the telephone awakened Jack with an unfamiliar jolt. He glanced accusingly at his cell on the bedside table, but when it rang again, he recognized it as the landline in the living room. Claire sat up and threw the covers off, but he hurried out of the bed.

"Let me get it," he told her.

Not bothering with light, he felt his way around the furniture and into the other room. He picked up on the third ring.

"Hello."

"Mr. Crabtree?"

"Yes."

"This is Lucy Fraiser. I'm your grandfather's nurse."

"Yes, is he all right?"

"He's not doing so well," she said. "He's taken a real turn for the worse tonight. He's not getting much renal output and his oxygenation has dropped quite a bit. I hate

395

to wake you, but I'd hate it more if he didn't make it through the night and I hadn't called."

"Right," Jack agreed. "Is somebody there? My aunts or my cousins?"

"Yes, there are a couple of young kids here," she said. "They've been playing cards in the room."

"Uh-huh," he answered. "Well, I'll be there as quickly as I can."

Jack hung up and turned to see Claire standing in a shaft of moonlight near the doorway.

"He's worse."

It was not so much a question as a statement. Jack nodded. He thought about telling Claire that she didn't have to go. That he could handle it on his own. But he found the idea very unappealing.

"Will you go with me?" he asked instead.

"I wouldn't let you go alone," she told him. Within ten minutes he was dressed and ready to head for the car. He could hear Claire in the bathroom brushing her teeth. He thought about the day ahead and the long hours they might get stuck at the hospital. He grabbed a tote bag from the kitchen and hurried out the back door to the work shed.

Inside he wrapped the cut dovetails in

newspaper and loaded them into the tote. He added a chisel and a couple of sheets of fine sandpaper. He carried it to the car. By the time he reached the driver's side door, he realized what a stupid idea it was, to try to do woodworking in the hospital next to a dying man's bedside. He turned to take it all back to the shed, but Claire was locking up the front door, so instead he just put the heavy tote into the backseat and took his place behind the wheel.

The night was clear and the highway was deserted, but Jack drove more cautiously than usual. On a lonely road like this a deer could easily dart out in front of a car. And it seemed lately that the unexpected was to be expected.

"Do you want me to call and cancel your flight?" Claire asked.

"Oh yeah, that would be great," Jack answered.

Claire dug the cell phone out of her purse and began dialing numbers and selecting menus to make the cancellation. Jack had gone to great lengths just a few hours before to get a seat on a flight back to San Antonio.

"I'll go back home, see if I can get things at the office stabilized and be back up here by the weekend."

She'd nodded agreement.

"I know you miss the kids," he'd said. "If you want to come with me, I'm sure the family can handle things here."

"No," she'd said. "Bud needs us. I wouldn't feel right about leaving him."

Jack had been stung by the criticism that was left unsaid. *He* was willing to leave his grandfather to others, but his wife was not. Now none of that mattered.

"I guess the business will just have to get along without me another day or two," he mused aloud.

"Everybody understands having a family crisis," Claire said.

Jack chuckled humorlessly. "You obviously haven't met our clients." He was joking, but it wasn't particularly funny.

"If our clients are so self-involved that they would think their swimming pool is more critical than your grandfather, then who needs them as clients."

"Our business is very competitive," Jack told her. "We can't pick and choose who we want to deal with. And we can't afford to disappoint anyone."

"You used to say that personal relationships were the most important part of the business," Claire reminded him.

"It still is," he admitted. "But you're thinking about the old days when our clients were Joe and Jane Sixpack wanting a place for their kids to swim in the backyard. These days our target clients are the most affluent pool owners in the community. They want something that presents the best features of their property. It's not so much about family as it is about business and social position."

"So? They still have families, they still understand emergencies."

"But you can't have that same kind of relationship with them," he said.

"No, *you* can't have that same kind of relationship with them," Claire said. "*You* can't do it because somewhere, somehow you got the idea in your head that you just don't fit into their world."

Jack blanched. "Don't be ridiculous."

"I'm not," she answered. "I'm just telling you what it looks like to me. It looks like you think they're better than you. That you're inferior."

"I'm not inferior to anyone," Jack insisted angrily.

"That's right," she said. "You're not."

Her agreement took all the wind out of his sails. Why were they fighting? They weren't. They were on the same side.

"I'm sure that everything at home will be fine," Claire said quietly. "And if it's not, then you'll do your best to set things right when you can."

"Yeah, I guess so," Jack said. "I'm still kind of stunned at Dana."

"Well, I'm not," Claire said.

"You never liked her," Jack pointed out.

"No, I didn't. But more than that, I never trusted her. And I didn't think that you should have, either."

"She's good at her job."

Claire didn't argue, but she restated her position. "She's good at doing whatever it takes to get ahead."

Jack shrugged. "That's what people do in business, Claire. It's a world where you live and die by the bottom line."

"I guess I never thought money was our bottom line."

Jack knew then that they were just one unconsidered comment away from another fight about the house. He didn't want to fight about the house. He knew all the arguments about the house. And it was hard to refute them. If they got rid of the new house, he wouldn't be under such pressure at work. They could easily afford the mortgage they already had. Their current house was in very good shape and in a neighborhood with good schools and lots of friends. They could continue to live there modestly.

Jack would have more time to spend with the family and they could still save for college and retirement. Jack knew all this and he knew it was all true. But something compelled him to ignore that judgment.

"Did you get the seat canceled?" he asked, already knowing the answer but choosing to change the subject.

She gave him all the details as they drove on through the darkness.

At the hospital, they found a couple of Shertz family teenagers in the hallway, looking bleary-eyed and out of their depth. The girl was a slightly pudgy brunette who identified herself as Michelle's daughter. Her cousin and card companion was a skinny, gangly guy over six feet tall who introduced himself as Darby Givens.

"They asked us to wait out here," the girl told Claire. "I thought about calling my mom, but the nurse said that she'd already called you."

Jack watched as Claire put a comforting arm around the girl. "You did exactly the right thing," she assured her. "We were on our way and there was no reason to wake your mother."

"He was just laying there like he always is," the boy explained. "And then when we looked up, he was different somehow and he was shaking."

"We are so grateful that you were there," Claire told him.

Jack had not given one thought to these kids, and they were little more than kids. He'd seen their faces, just as she had, but he hadn't wondered what they'd been thinking or feeling. Claire somehow knew that they were scared and guilty and worried that somehow this bad turn of events was all their fault. Her natural empathy was always a surprise to him. It wasn't the kind of talent that could be quantified or a skill that would show up on a résumé. It did have a very obvious value. The mood in the hallway lightened considerably.

"So who is who in there?" Jack asked, indicating the cluster of people visible through the glass doorway to Bud's room. "I only recognize Lucy, the nurse."

The boy answered. "The Asian woman is the resident," he said. "The man in the lab coat is from Respiratory Therapy. I don't know who anybody else is. They haven't really told us anything."

"Do you want to head on home now?" Jack asked them.

The girl glanced over at Darby questioningly. "My mom wouldn't want me out driving before it gets light," he said.

"That's good thinking," Claire told him. "Why don't you go down to the snack bar and get something." She turned to Jack. "Have you got any cash?"

"Oh, sure," Jack said, quickly pulling a couple of tens out of his wallet. It fit into the family's seemingly unwritten rule that the children, no matter who their actual parents were, belonged to everybody and that all were responsible for them. In turn, the kids seemed to treat all their elders with equal deference.

Both made a polite, if slightly embarrassed acceptance, and wandered off down the hall.

Jack and Claire continued to stand for a minute at the door. Lucy spotted them and came outside. She didn't bother with greetings, but went straight to the fact.

"Mr. Crabtree has spiked a temp," she said, using hospital lingo to describe an abrupt increase in body temperature. "The doctor will be out in a few minutes to talk to you. She's young, but she's really smart."

The nurse indicated that they should sit, so they did. For Jack, however, it was far from comfortable. He had jitters in his legs. He needed to be up and doing something. But there was nothing to do. Nothing but waiting.

"Do you want a cup of coffee?" he asked

Claire. "I could get you a cup of coffee."

The kids had asked the same question only five minutes before.

Claire shook her head. "I'm fine," she said.

Jack nervously took out his cell and then shoved it back in his pocket.

Finally, the room began to empty. The doctor came out with Lucy who spoke to her for a moment. She glanced at Jack and Claire, nodding and then turned to walk in their direction, hand outstretched.

"Hello, I'm Dr. Seng," she said. "I'm the resident on duty and I've been examining Mr. Crabtree."

They had been warned about her being young, but Jack found her age comforting. She was undoubtedly just out of school and she'd be quick thinking and up on all the new technology.

He introduced himself and his wife.

"Your grandfather's condition has deteriorated significantly in the last few hours," she said. "The respirator is doing more and more of the work to keep him oxygenated. And his kidneys are only barely functioning. He's getting a lot of fluid buildup in his chest, which is stressing his heart. Now he's developed a significant fever." She hesitated and took a deep breath. "Usually a fever means infection and we're treating him as if that's what's happening, although his white cell count doesn't back that up. Sometimes in a head injury it can be just a malfunctioning in that area of the brain that regulates heat. We're using antibiotics just to be safe."

"Okay," Jack said. He glanced over at Claire. She was biting her lower lip.

"As for the initial injury," Dr. Seng continued, "the internal bleeding has resumed. It's really more of a seeping than bleeding, but it's still not good."

"So he's not getting any better," Jack said.

The resident seemed uneasy with making such a declaration. "I think the next few hours are critical. Sometimes things can turn around."

Her voice trailed off putting pessimism into her hopeful words.

Jack nodded gravely.

"Is there any good news right now?" Claire said.

"We're confident that he's still in that locked-in state. He hasn't lapsed further," she said. "We aren't hopeful that he'll actually break through to communicate, but we are detecting frontal-lobe activity."

"So he might know that we're here," Jack said.

The doctor shrugged. "I can't tell you that," she said. "But sometimes I think when close family members are nearby, patients do fight harder. I'll be downstairs, two minutes away if I'm needed."

Left on their own, Jack and Claire entered Bud's room to find the situation changed. The old man's tangle of wires had increased. It didn't seem possible that there could be more blinking lights and beeping sounds, but there were. Bud lay on the bed, covered by a thin white sheet. He was shaking.

"Can you get him a blanket?" Claire asked the nurse's aide. "He's very cold."

"Not yet," she answered. "We need to bring the fever down a little bit and blankets don't do that. If we can get him down to maybe 100, 101, then I'll try to make him a little more comfortable."

Claire sat down beside the bed and began talking quietly to him.

Jack sat.

And then he stood.

And then he paced.

And then he sat again.

And then he stood.

The minutes passed by in agonizing slow motion. Even the quiet timbre of Claire's voice gave him no comfort. Bud's shaking, his obvious discomfort were more than Jack could bear.

"I'm getting something out of the car," he

announced at the exact moment the thought came to him.

His words, a little too loud, momentarily startled Claire out of her monotone.

"Oh, okay, sure," she said.

He was out the door before any explanation could be requested.

What Claire might have thought when he returned a few moments later with the tote bag of cut lumber, she didn't say. What she did say was that she needed to go to the restroom.

"I didn't want to leave him alone even for a minute," she said. "Not like this."

Jack nodded. "I'm here," he said.

She went out the door and Jack lingered by the chair next to the window. He always sat there, but the chair at the bedside looked very empty. He'd said he would stay with Bud, so he wouldn't be alone. With no one near, the old man might feel alone even with Jack across the room.

With a deep breath and deliberate decisiveness, Jack crossed the room and sat beside his grandfather. He looked at Bud, his trembling nearly hidden by the tubes and mask that kept him alive. His gaze dropped to the hand that was secured to the bed rail. It looked exceptionally large next to the aging emaciated body. The long, thick fingers were very similar to Jack's own, but the skin atop them was thin and weathered, with dark spots and lines and creases that evidenced eighty-four years.

From the tote bag Jack drew out two pieces of the cut lumber. He tried to interlock the two as a corner, but as expected it was not a close enough fit. He took out a newspaper and spread it on the floor around him. And then with the chisel began carefully winnowing the dovetails. The handwork required a bit of skill and because Jack was so rusty, he had to take it very slowly, carefully removing the excess wood a millimeter at a time, stopping to gauge his progress after each cut.

"I wish you could help me with this," he said aloud.

The sound of his own voice caught him off guard. He glanced up quickly to see if anyone had heard. He was alone in the room. His gaze went back to Bud. Maybe it was his imagination, but the shaking seemed to have lessened.

Jack didn't give himself the opportunity to try to think rationally or discount his own perception. Maybe his voice did comfort Bud, and on the chance that it did, it was a small thing. Jack didn't have it in his heart to withhold it.

"Claire had to step outside for a minute," he said, deliberately pushing himself to make conversation. "I'm sitting here with newspapers all around me doing handwork on dovetails. Anybody who walked in here would think I've lost my mind."

He gave a little humorless chuckle and observed his grandfather closely once more. It did seem as if his words helped, so he kept them coming.

"I'm working on this treasure box that my father was putting together for Grandma Geri," he said. "But I have to tell you honestly that I don't think this is it. She has enough treasures under that bed to fill a steamer trunk. This is just a little box. Bigger than a standard jewelry box, though. I think he must have had something specific in mind. Wish we could talk about it. Maybe we'd figure it out."

Claire made a detour after the restroom to check on the Shertz teenagers. She found them in the snack bar area. She couldn't tell if they were awake or asleep. Both were sprawled over chairs with eyes closed and their respective headphones plugged into their ears. On the chance that perhaps it was the latter, she tiptoed past them and got coffee for herself and Jack.

She was so glad that he was still here with her. And her gratitude made her a little guilty. If Bud had made his turn for the worse just a few hours later, Jack would have been back in San Antonio, dealing with work and Dana and all the day-to-day crises that gave him such a rush. How could a mere wife compete with that?

As she approached the room, she was surprised to hear Jack's voice. She assumed he must be talking to one of the nurses. She went inside to discover something entirely different. Jack was sitting in the chair next to the bed, doing some kind of carving on the wood that he'd brought and finally taking her advice. He was talking to his grand-dad.

He glanced up as she walked in. He looked a bit embarrassed.

Claire gave him a reassuring smile. She carried the coffee across the room and set his cup on the bedside table within easy reach.

"He isn't shaking so much," she said.

Jack nodded. "His temperature must be coming down," he said. "I thought that talking to him might help. If nothing else, it's a friendly noise in the room."

Claire resisted the temptation to say, I told you so.

She sat down with her own coffee in the seat near the window. She quickly realized in the ensuing silence that her presence was inhibiting her husband.

The moment lingered with the beep on the monitors and the *whoosh-klaa-whoosh* of the oxygen and the soft scraping of wood.

The nurse's aide returned to check on her patient, insisting that Claire and Jack keep their seats.

"He seems to be shaking less," Claire told her.

"Let's see if you're right," the woman said as she stuck a thermometer in the nook of Bud's ear. She waited a half minute until the devise signaled. "One-oh-one point four," she said finally. "Much better. I'll be back in a bit and I'll give him a cool-down rub. That should help, as well."

Jack nodded and the woman left the room. Claire picked up her coffee and followed her as if she had some reason to do so. The nurse's aide moved on down the hallway. Claire did not. Outside the room, away from the view from the glass door, she waited for a couple of moments until she heard what she was waiting for. Jack resumed his conversation with Bud.

Claire made her way over to the seating area. It was funny how she'd just been thinking how much she needed Jack to be here for her. When he really needed to be here for Bud and for himself.

She sat alone long enough to get very bored. The nurse and the nurse's aide made frequent checks inside Bud's room. Claire walked up to the doorway a couple of times to peek inside. Jack was still conversing with the old man as he worked on his pieces of wood. She wished she'd thought ahead and brought something to do with her hands. As soon as the gift shop opened downstairs, she would buy a magazine to read. She glanced at her watch to see that it was just a quarter after five.

The floor was so quiet that around the corner she could hear the elevator open. Then a whirring sound of electrically powered wheels commenced that she assumed was the movement of some big piece of hospital equipment.

She was wrong.

Turning down the hallway was Aunt Jesse in her bright pink wheelchair scooter. She caught sight of Claire and waved. She came to a stop in front of the glass door to Bud's room, watched for a moment and then moved on toward Claire.

Aunt Jesse was dressed in a knit pantsuit that still looked good on her, though it was about two decades out of style. The vivid purple color seemed coordinated with the pink scooter as if the latter were just another fashion accessory.

Rising to her feet, Claire greeted the older woman with a congenial hug and a look of surprise.

"What are you doing here so early?" she asked.

Jesse shrugged. "I don't sleep much anymore," she said. "So I called Darby to find out how Bud was doing. He told me that he and Missy were in the break room because the doctor had called you and Jackie in. So I just got in my car and came on down to find out what was going on."

Claire gave her a quick rundown of what seemed to be going on and what the doctor had told them.

The old woman shook her head. "Dying can be a hard job," she said.

"He may get better," Claire assured her quickly. "They say the next few hours are critical."

Aunt Jesse nodded. "Oh, I'm sure they are. But we're all old, sweetie," she said. "We may get through this year, but then there's the next. Not a lot of chances to get out of this world alive."

Behind her thick bifocals, Claire could see

the woman's eyes twinkling with humor. "Bud's had a good life," she explained. "He had Geri for most of that and J.D. for a lot of years. And you and your children have been a comfort to him, even so far away. I'm sure his regrets are few."

"I hope so," Claire said. "He's a good guy. He was always very nice to me. I have a few regrets, though. I wish we'd been here more. And I wish that he and Jack had been closer."

Jesse nodded. "Yes, that could have been a good thing," she said. "I suspect you're faulting Jackie for that, but it's hard to know, really. Both of them are so alike. I think that blame has to be shared."

"Jack thinks that his grandfather kind of rejected him," Claire said.

"I suppose in a way, he did," Jesse agreed.

The old woman sighed heavily and retrieved a handful of knitting from her bag. It was a large cable pattern in a garish teal color. She held it in her hands at an uncomfortable angle as she peered through the bottom of her glasses. Her hands easily picked up the movements as Jesse, still carefully watching her yarn, picked up the thread of the conversation.

"In the months and years after he lost J.D., Bud was hurting so badly," she said. "I

414

don't think there ever was a father and son more at peace with each other than those two."

"It must have been horrible," Claire said.

"Yes, I think so. But then, in the darkest of times a precious little light came into the world. Once Jackie was born Bud just cast aside all the bitterness and anger and guilt he must have felt and poured all his love into the baby."

The clicking sounds of Aunt Jesse's knitting needles was the only sound as the woman paused, choosing her words.

"A child belongs with his mother and none of us would ever say one word to contradict that, but when Jackie went back to live with Toni, it was devastating for poor Bud. It was as if he'd lost J.D. all over again."

Jesse shook her head sadly and continued to knit. "I suspect that he deliberately held himself back some after that. There's only so much heartbreak a man can volunteer for."

Claire sighed. "From the time I met him their relationship was so complicated. I'm just hoping that before Bud goes, it can all get simplified. That's why I've left Jack alone with him in the hospital room. It's the only way Jack seems comfortable enough to talk to Bud. I'm hoping that just by talking to him, Jack will manage to resolve some of the feelings he has."

"That's a good idea," Aunt Jesse said. "One thing I've noticed about men is they just don't talk enough. Maybe it takes having one of them in a coma to carry on a decent conversation."

Claire smiled at the woman's little joke.

"And your explanation eases my mind, as well," Jesse said.

"How so?"

Jack's aunt abruptly ceased her knitting to turn and look Claire straight in the eyes.

"I saw him in there and you sitting out here, and I was thinking that you and Jack couldn't bear to be in the same room together."

Claire was shocked.

"Good grief! Why would you jump to a conclusion like that?"

Aunt Jesse shrugged. "Sweetie, it doesn't take a mind reader to see that you two are going through a rough patch these days."

Too surprised to deny it, Claire questioned how anyone could.

"Jack and I never argue in front of anybody, not even the children."

"That's good," Aunt Jesse said. "It's terrible for the little ones. They can't understand how a marriage can ebb and flow. Sometimes you'll feel so close that even your breathing is synchronized. And sometimes it's like two strangers living in the same house."

"Well, we're not strangers," Claire said. "But there are times when I can't believe he's the same guy I married."

"You were very young when you fell in love," Aunt Jesse said. "You've both had some growing up to do."

Claire nodded but didn't reply.

Aunt Jesse took up her knitting once more. After a few stitches she spoke once more. "You're worried that it's less about growing up than it is about growing apart."

She shrugged. "It's so strange," she told Jesse. "I thought we wanted the same things, but more and more it seems like we're working toward living in two different worlds."

"What's your world like?"

"Mine?" Claire hardly gave herself a moment to ponder the question. "It's all about the kids. Our family being together. That's what's important to me."

"What's important to Jack?"

"His job," she answered. "He wants to be successful and make a lot of money and live in a big fancy house so that everyone will know he's successful and makes lots of money."

"Well, he has created his own business," Jesse told her. "I think that's something he should feel proud about. I'd bet he thinks all that money he makes has something to do with providing for the children."

"*We* created that business," Claire said. "I worked as hard at it as he did."

Aunt Jesse raised an eyebrow. "I suspect a lot of people have forgotten that," she said. "You miss not being a part of it."

"No, of course not," she answered quickly and then added, "Well, sometimes maybe a little. I was glad to give it up. I love staying home with my little ones. I want to be there with them. I want to see every moment of their childhood. But I wanted to share it with Jack, too."

"So," Jesse asked carefully as if sorting through some difficult formula, "you're doing what you want. And Jack's doing what he wants. But you're frustrated with Jack because he doesn't want what you want. And he's frustrated with you because you don't want what he wants. Does that about cover it? It's all a bit confusing."

Claire chuckled self-consciously. "When you put it like that, it sounds so petty," she said.

Aunt Jesse nodded. "It sounds petty

because it is," she said. "Most of the trouble between men and women falls into that petty category. If there is anything that ought to be clear to you sitting outside this hospital room it's that life is too short for this nonsense. Dig down deep inside yourself and find a way to be happy. Your husband isn't perfect. He's got the requisite number of flaws and blind spots. But if you don't let yourself get past him not being what you'd hoped, you'll never get to know him as he is. And that would be the real loss."

# BUD

The heat was unbelievable. I was not going to drown after all; I was to be cooked alive. What a great joke. To be stranded at sea, water in every direction and to die shriveled and dry. I reached for the metal can that held the raft's water ration. I screamed out in pain as my muscles complained about the movement. The water was disappearing by the hour. I was limiting myself to near dehydration, but it was evaporating faster than I was drinking it.

I wet my parched lips trying to remember how grateful I was for it and preparing myself for when it would not be there. I lay back down, closing my eyes, but the sun shone through the lids, I couldn't block it out anymore. I couldn't retreat into darkness.

"Go away!" I screamed at the hated hot orb.

The sun wasn't answering yet. But I

expected to have him talking to me very soon.

I longed to be back in the sea. At least there, death was cool. If the sharks came to get me surely it would be quick. If I thought about it rationally, it was the easier way to go. But I couldn't think about it rationally. I had become terrified of the thought of drowning. Terrified of the monsters that lurked under the surface.

"God give me strength to kill myself," I murmured to myself.

It was then that I heard it. At first I didn't think it was real or maybe at last it was God answering. The sound was not unfamiliar to me. I knew it from dozens of early mornings on various island bases. It was a plane overhead. And even without locating it with my eyes, I knew what kind of plane it was. The *whim-whim* sound was distinctive, a result of not synchronizing the propellers. There was a Japanese zero in the sky above me.

I should play dead. I should play dead. I knew my duty. I knew what I should do. I should give him no reason to waste a bullet. I surely must look dead. I almost felt dead. I merely had to do nothing and he would believe I was dead. He would fly on and I would continue to lie in the raft until

421

I was dead.

There are times when right and duty are at cross-purposes. I was supposed to stay alive, to suffer to the last. But I didn't want to suffer, I'd suffered enough. And my only other choice was to face the sea once more.

That thought, that fear, filled me with strength that I'd not felt in days. I opened my eyes and pulled myself into a sitting position. I saw him then. The little plane was flying low, it's one bright red dot on the fuselage easily familiar. As he curved around me, I shook my fist at him.

"Shoot me!" I demanded. "Shoot me!"

The croak of my voice was lost over the engine noise.

What if he didn't shoot me? He had no reason to. I was his enemy, but I was no threat to him. I had to make him shoot. I had to force him to kill me. I had no weapon. Only the water can. I grabbed it up and held it to my chest as if it were some strangely shaped tommy-gun. I made a shooting stance, forcing him to guess if the gun were real and raising the stakes if he were wrong.

Immediately he turned and headed for me. The sound of the engine grew louder as he accelerated. He began firing his guns.

And on the surface of the water pairs of fountains rose up out of the sea and came nearer and nearer. The whoosh of escaping air as a dozen bullets pierced the raft, the ping of metal, the splash of water, these were to be the last sounds that I heard. I was knocked backward to the floor of the raft, the sea was pouring in and over me. The saltwater didn't ease my pain, it stung and burned me. I gasped as my head cleared. I realized I wasn't hit. I was in the water and I wasn't hit.

I tried to scream. I tried to curse God. I could do neither. Beside me I heard J.D.

I turned my head expecting to see him in the water. But he was not there. I was not there. I was in a hospital bed far away from the sharks and the zeros. And J.D. was sitting beside me. He was talking calmly and quietly. He was doing something, working on something and talking to me as he did so. I couldn't quite see him but I knew he was there. That made me feel a lot better. He was so young and so full of life.

Like the day he brought his new bride to meet us.

They'd called us a couple of hours after they'd taken their vows.

"We didn't want a bunch of hoopla, so we wed at the courthouse," J.D. had said. "In the judge's chambers with his bailiff as our witness. No muss, no fuss, legally married."

Geri and I were both listening holding the receiver between us. She began to snivel a little bit.

"Mom? You're not crying, are you? Aw, please, Mom, don't cry," he said.

"I'm just happy," she assured him. "I'm just so happy. And the mother of the groom has a right to cry at her son's wedding."

"Well, you've got every reason to be happy," he told us. "Toni is the best girl I could ever even imagine. You are going to just love her."

"If you love her, J.D.," I told him, "then we love her already."

For his sake, we loved her from that very minute. Though it was more than a month before he got around to bringing her home to meet us. I have to admit that she was not at all what we had expected. It wasn't that she was fancy or looked down her nose at us. Toni was never like that. But she had grown up in a different world. She was, in her way, unflappable. Perfectly groomed and unfailingly polite, but her amiability seemed more studied than sincere. Not at all like Geri who gushed love from every pore of her being. J.D.'s choice was reserved and dignified.

What she thought of us, I can't even imagine. She never indicated, by even a look, that she was shocked by our plainness. But it was impossible for her to hide her unfamiliarity with the kind of life we led. As her story came out in dribs and drabs, I think we were able to appreciate how hard she was trying.

Her mother, a frail young woman, had died of asthma when Toni was just a baby. Her father brought her to San Antonio and left her to be raised by his aging parents. Rather than staying with them, her father moved out to California where he remarried and started a new family. They only rarely visited. Her childhood had been one of pampered princess, the darling of her grandparents' heart, much beloved. Then the old couple passed away within months of each other the summer she turned fourteen, and her father returned to San Antonio with his new wife. They took over the household and controlled the purse strings. The family had always been wealthy and prominent and her father and stepmother gladly stepped into those positions. With three growing children of their own, her new parents had little time or inclination to deal with a confused and grieving teenage Toni, whom they saw as spoiled, headstrong and rebellious.

It was undoubtedly this behavior that caused their reaction to her hasty, courthouse marriage.

"They hated me on sight," J.D. explained. "They told her to break it off with me or she would not be welcome in their house. We love each other, so we decided to get married instead. That really miffed them. Now they won't even talk to her on the phone."

The two laughed and joked about it as if family disapproval was a small thing. Geri and I shared a quick, worried glance with each other. But we only spoke about it in private.

"As hard as marriage is," she said, "starting out with your family against you is really getting off on the wrong foot."

I agreed with her. "I guess we'll just have to be doubly in favor of them to try to make up for her folks."

That seemed like a good plan, but it hit a snag in the middle of the Sunday dinner table. The day was very warm for May and by any stretch of reasoning, we should have been eating out on the cool, screened wash porch. But Geri, undoubtedly for Toni's sake, had opened up the drop-leaf dining table and had fancied up the meal as if it were Christmas.

"So will you be going up to Colorado Springs with J.D. come July?" Geri asked casually. "I hear it's a lovely town."

Toni glanced at J.D. He deliberately finished chewing his food and swallowed before he answered.

"I won't be going to Colorado," he told her. "The prep school doesn't accept married men. Besides the Air Force has other plans for me this summer."

"What plans are those?"

"It looks like I'll be heading off to Vietnam," he said.

"Vietnam?" Geri sounded shocked. "There's a war going on over there."

"It's not a war, Mom. It's a police action," he answered.

"Boys are being hurt and killed," she said. "I've seen it on the news."

"That's mostly army and marines," he assured her. "I'm in the Air Force, remember. I'll be up above it all. Best view of the war, right, Dad?"

I think I managed a smile. I tried for one anyway. But my stomach was rolling so sickeningly I thought I might vomit. I set my fork on my plate. The meal continued for nearly a half hour, but I wasn't able to force down one more bite. And I saw that

Geri wasn't eating, either.

I walked the garden most of that night, worrying and wondering and finally deciding that I had to talk to J.D. I had to make him understand. I wasn't sure that I understood it all myself, but I had to tell him more than I had so far.

Getting a moment alone with J.D. was not easy. Toni never seemed to be far from his side. And that suited him perfectly. He could hardly take his eyes off her and he hung on every word from her lips. That was to be expected, I suppose, from a couple of newlyweds. But as each hour passed, what I wanted to tell to him got more complicated and my thoughts on how to explain my experience became more tangled.

Finally, on his last morning at home, I got him to go out to the wood shop with me, under the guise of doing something about his treasure box project.

"Just leave it on one of the shelves out of the way," he told me almost as soon as we stepped through the door. "I'll finish it up next time I'm home. There's something I need to ask you about."

I sighed with relief. "I've been wanting to talk to you, too."

"First question," J.D. began before I could even form my own words in my head. "Why didn't you and Mom have any other children?"

"Huh?" I couldn't have been any less prepared for that inquiry. "I . . . ah, well, I don't know. We just didn't," I managed to get out. "We thought we might get you a brother or sister once, but your mother miscarried after just a few weeks. She had some kind of women's problem. The doctors said she probably wouldn't be able to have more children. And she didn't. We were sad, but we felt so lucky to have you."

J.D. nodded with understanding and then smiled at me. "When I was a kid I told myself it was because you could never love anybody as much as you love me."

I chuckled. "Well, there is that, too," I said and then added, "We couldn't love anybody *more* than we love you."

"Thanks, Dad," he said. "I want you to know how much I appreciate all you and Mom have done for me. I am very grateful. But I have to ask you a favor."

"Anything," I assured him.

"I need you to watch out for Toni while I'm gone," he said. "Oh, she's got her plans. We have our little apartment near the base and she's going to try to get a job in a dress shop, but I'm worried about her. This thing with her parents really took me by surprise.

I mean, I knew they didn't want any part of me. But I just didn't expect them to turn on her. I didn't think parents could be like that. Even if I went to prison, I know that you and Mom would show up on visiting day and Mom would probably bake me a cake with a file in it."

"She probably would."

"I just want you to keep an ear out in case she needs help," he said. "Now that she's my wife, that makes her your daughter and I want you to think of her like that, protect her like that."

It was hard to imagine that Geri and I could have any daughter as cool and reserved as Toni, but I didn't say that to J.D.

"Of course," I told him. "You don't have to worry about anything on that account."

"Good," J.D. said. " 'Cause I feel kind of guilty about leaving her. I mean, she's given up her family just to be with me. So what do I do? I set her up in a twelve-by-twelve efficiency and go off halfway around the world for a year."

"I'm sure she understands that you have to do your duty," I said.

"She does," he said. "And that makes me feel even worse. Now that I know I'm going, I'm really getting excited about it. I'm sure you remember, Dad, when the action's going on, you just hate not being a part of it."

I did remember.

And I didn't tell him any of the things I should have. I didn't want to dampen his enthusiasm. I didn't want to throw sorrow and grief and anger and fear all over his joy. I told myself that it would be all right. That this war wasn't like mine and his experience wouldn't be, either. That's what I promised myself. And that's what I can't forgive.

For the next four months Geri and I watched the evening news sick to our stomachs with fear. He was supposed to come back to see us again before he left, but he got busy.

"I'll see you when I get back," he promised.

And then he was there, like one of those boys in the news, the ones we saw lying on stretchers or wearing bandages on their heads.

He wrote us once a week. Little blue letters that arrived with an APO as a return address. He sounded happy, upbeat. He told funny stories about the people he met and the guys in his unit. He thanked Geri for all the mail. She wrote him, as she had me, with all the news of Catawah and our garden and the facts and foibles of his aunts and uncles and cousins.

In October we got surprising news.

*Toni is expecting,* he wrote. *She was on the pill, so we weren't thinking that this would happen. But for sure, we're both delighted. She says she's been sick most mornings, but that the doctor says she's healthy and should deliver in March.*

"We need to go get that girl and bring her here," Geri said immediately.

"What?" I couldn't even imagine it. "She'd never come here."

"That poor girl is alone down there in San Antonio, pregnant and with her husband in harm's way," Geri said. "She needs someone to take care of her, to care about her. And we're going to be the ones to do it."

I didn't argue. I made a point not to argue with Geri. Especially because she's usually right.

Within a week Toni had packed up their meager amount of possessions in J.D.'s truck and made the long drive up to be with us.

We settled her into J.D.'s room. Geri waited on her hand and foot and fed her until the girl pleaded for mercy. She wasn't the most approachable person I'd ever met, but I grew to like her. She and J.D. wrote to each other every day, and she found something to share in every letter she received.

Geri's sisters were not as welcoming as they could have been. They didn't like Toni from the jump go and found fault with most everything she said and did. They would get together and find reason to take Geri aside and make snide comments. For a while, she just let it go. Then finally she got her back up and told them so.

"This is my daughter-in-law," she said. "And it would be my place to defend her if she were the whore of Babylon. But she's not that. She's a lovely girl who is young and pregnant with her husband very far from home. Now you're my sisters and always will be. You can think what you want and are free to choose how you behave. You can treat Toni with the respect she deserves as a member of our family, or you can stay away from my front door from now on."

Her hard line shocked them into better behavior. They probably still picked the poor girl to death behind her back, but no one ever made a snide comment to her or in front of us again.

As the birth of the baby approached, we were all excited. Toni thought it to be bad luck to buy baby things before the baby arrived. Geri was certain that only meant the actual purchase of new items, something that she rarely did anyway. She got J.D.'s crib back from whatever family member had it last. I sanded it down a bit and restained the wood until it looked like new. She gathered up dozens of tiny T-shirts and sweaters and caps. And we rearranged Toni's room to accommodate both her and the expected new one. Geri's sewing machine hummed day and night as she stitched up baby bed linens and receiving blankets and plain cotton diapers.

J.D. passed the halfway mark on his tour and our spirits were beginning to lighten. We put up our Christmas tree in the front room with all the flashing colored lights and Santa and snowman bulbs. There were presents for all of us, including Baby. Toni helped Geri bake six-dozen peanut-butter cookies, J.D.'s favorite, which they shipped to him with some Christmas candy and new socks, the only gift he claimed to need.

I picked up a package from him at the post office and we could hardly wait until the big day to open it. For Toni he'd sent a cobalt box with a tiny jeweled frog inside. Geri got a large bowl made of tightly woven bamboo. I opened my small paper-wrapped present to find a miniature painting on a round piece of wood. The paint was applied water-thin, and the grain of the wood appeared as shadow on the tiny fishing village reminiscent of many I had seen in that part of the world.

In a funny way it reminded me of something he might have made in Boy Scouts. It was done by a much more talented artist than any of the kids in the Catawah scouts, but there was a simpleness about it, a beauty in the ordinary that appealed to me. I assumed that it had touched J.D. in the same way. I put it atop the bureau where I could see it every day.

We missed J.D., but it was as though he were always with us. We knew he'd be home before the baby was born, so we watched Toni's progress with even greater expectation.

On a cold February morning with the hint of snow in the air, I left work at the post office and slowly drove toward Catawah, careful of ice on the road. I'd finished up on time, but with the condition of the pavement, I suspected I wouldn't get to the house until eight-thirty or later. There were a few cars on the highway, but traffic was never a problem in our neck of the woods. I was in J.D.'s pickup. I had taken to driving it to keep the battery charged up and because it was a very sturdy, dependable winter vehicle. At some point along the trip

I noticed that the sedan I was following had a U.S. government license plate. That was not so exceptional — there were official cars in and out of the post office with the same type of tag. But later I noticed that the two occupants in the car were in uniform, and I wondered casually to myself what two G.I.'s were doing out on the road on this cold morning.

I'm not sure when my curiosity turned to anxiety. Maybe it was when we passed road after road and they never turned off. Or maybe it was slowing down on the highway through Catawah as if they were reading the street signs. When they came to a stop at the corner near the Jitterbug Lounge my heart was in my throat. When they turned east on Bee Street a wave of nausea clawed at me. I knew where they were going and I knew it wasn't good news.

In my imagination I saw J.D. bobbing alone and afraid in an empty ocean. It was my nightmare, but now I begged for it.

"Let him be missing," I prayed aloud.

As the official car pulled to a stop in front of my house I gunned it into the driveway and abruptly shut off the engine. I had to get to them before they spoke to Geri, to Toni. I had to keep the bad news from my door. I had to shelter the women under my protection.

I wasn't aware of everything that was going on. It was as if I were acting on impulse instead of thought. And from the reaction of the two airmen, I must have seemed aggressive. Both raised their hands, either to ward off an attack or to show they weren't holding weapons.

"My son," I managed to get out.

The man nearest me lowered his hands. He was so young. No older than my own J.D., surely they would not send such young men.

"Mr. Crabtree?"

"Yes."

The front door of the house burst open. Both Geri and Toni stood on the porch. I can never recall what words were spoken. I'm sure that something standard was said, that there were official condolences. I have no actual memory of that. But I will never forget the look on the faces of those women.

The next few hours, few days, blended into one long struggle with disbelief. I'm not sure how soon it was that I realized I was pretending. I was behaving how I thought a father would behave. I was stoic and soft-spoken with a display of strength. It was a sham. My actions were completely disconnected from what I was feeling. What

I was feeling was simply numb. I needed to be alone. I needed to sort it all out in my head. But that was impossible. The Shertz family has no appreciation of solitude. They believe strength is in numbers. Every family member showed up at the house, including Cleata and her son, Julie, who never came to Catawah for any reason. They were all there and I couldn't get away. I couldn't think.

I didn't realize what a blessing that was, until I was alone and I did think. That's when the guilt began pouring in. In my mind, image after image came of the face that I loved and it was always looking up at me with awe and admiration.

"I want to be like you, Dad," he always said.

And I had known what he meant. He didn't want to be a night-shift sorter at the post office or a woodworking piddler or even the guy who blew the warning siren when a tornado was spotted from the civil defense tower. He'd wanted to be an Air Force gunner flying high above the casualties in a cause that was right and good.

I saw him reverently sorting through that box of medals and ribbons, being able to name the what and the where for each.

Why hadn't I stopped him? Or told him

the truth? I wanted to scream at the heavens. But once again, God was not to blame. The guilt was mine. I was not some brave hero who risked my life for the good of my country. I was, at first, just a young, scared kid just doing what I was told. And then I was a dead man, risking nothing.

Why hadn't I tried to explain to him? I had told myself that maybe he didn't need to know. Maybe I could spare him the truth. But that was not how it had been. I had been unwilling to look small in his eyes. My pride had killed him.

I sat for long hours in the frozen chill of the garden at night. I could barely tell waking from sleeping. It was all about terror in the waves and emptiness of dying alone. I wanted to cry out to my son, to beg his forgiveness.

Then Geri was there beside me.

"Come into the house," she said.

"No, I can't. I want to be out here."

"Then I'll sit out here with you."

"No, you can't. It's too cold!"

"Yes, it is," Geri agreed. "But if you're here, I'm here."

So we ended up sitting in the kitchen all night.

"Stop blaming yourself," she told me.

"I should have stopped him from going,"

I told her. "It's my fault he's dead."

"And would it have been my fault if back in '43 you'd have truly died out there in that empty ocean?" she asked. "I made it possible for you to do what you wanted to do. Would it have been my fault?"

"No, of course not."

"Then J.D.'s death is not on your account, either," she said.

Her reasoning may have been compelling, but my guilt was stronger. It continued to be the vision in my eyes, the smell in my nostrils the taste on my tongue all through the next days of mourning.

When his body returned to Catawah, we were called to the funeral home to see him. I felt numb as I walked into the building. Geri was leaning heavily on me. Toni walked ahead of us, head high, without even a hesitance to her step.

It smelled like flowers, too many flowers, the scent nearly choked me. We were directed to the front viewing room. The door was open, but my eyes were drawn to the handwritten nameplate fitted into the plastic slot. *Airman First Class Jack Dempsey Crabtree, Jr., USAF.* The sight caught me up short. I was the dead one. It was supposed to have been my name. If I hadn't continued on after I was already dead, J.D. would

440

never have suffered this.

The fact that J.D. would never have existed and the world would have been a much sadder place was also there, but I couldn't grab on to it. My own remorse was too powerful.

The room where they laid him was too dark for the Fourth of July atmosphere inside. There were flags and bunting everywhere as if the florists had no other colors than red, white and blue. The only thing missing was a watermelon laid out on a picnic table. Against one wall the flag-draped coffin was nearly hidden among the sprays of flowers.

Harvey Crocker, the funeral director, seemed a bit too personally pleased by the display.

"We've gotten flowers from all over the state," he said. "The write-up in the paper helped a lot. And KTUL called me. They may come to the graveside to shoot some footage for the evening news."

Toni had walked forward and put her gloved hand atop the casket. Harvey quickly trailed after her.

"You didn't say if this was open or closed viewing," he explained quickly. "So I left it closed until I talked to you."

"May I see him," she said, so quietly I could barely hear.

"Yes, yes, of course."

Harvey scooted the flag down until nearly a yard of red and white stripes draped the end. Geri and I moved forward until we were right behind Toni. He opened the box at the center hinge.

Beside me Geri gasped and Toni momentarily stumbled.

I stared at my son in disbelief. What was so shocking was that he looked exactly as I remembered. I had seen plenty of dead men, corpses on the beach, bloated in the water, burnt beyond recognition as human. My son had been killed in a fierce gun battle with Viet Cong guerillas, and he lay there, spiffed up in his dress blues, looking only as if he were sleeping, so relaxed, so peaceful.

The unreality of it welled up in me with familiar anger and despair.

Back home that evening I rummaged underneath the bed in the back room until I found the shoe box that had so captured my child's imagination. The carton was so aged and oft-handled that the sides were coming loose. I took it into the kitchen and taped it completely all around. Then, as an afterthought, I taped the top closed, too. I didn't even look in it, I knew what was inside. It meant nothing to me. But every faded ribbon and shiny award was dear to

J.D. and they had taken his life. I didn't ever want to see any of it again.

The next morning as we left for the funeral, I carried the box in the crook of my arm.

"What's that?" Geri asked me.

"It's my war junk," I told her. "I'm burying it with J.D."

Her brow furrowed and I knew she was going to argue with me. I didn't let her.

"This box killed my son as much as any bullet from an enemy gun."

She never said another thing.

The funeral was gigantic. The entire town of Catawah showed up. The family alone filled up the right side of the Pentecostal church. I remember very little of what was said or done during the service. My eyes and my heart were focused on the flag-covered casket at the front of the church.

One of the airmen in attendance read a letter from J.D.'s commanding officer. The helicopter gunship had come under fire and J.D. defended the guys in his crew and the ones they were transporting as long as he could. The phrases were serious and solemn and heavily measured with words like duty, bravery and honor.

A half dozen Shertz cousins, with Cleata's boy, Julie, playing the guitar, sang "Where

Have All the Flowers Gone?" Some like Julie and Leo still had the clean-cut military look about them. Others had long hair and clothing decorated with peace symbols. They were our kids as much as J.D. had been. And if any one of them had been in the coffin instead, I knew J.D. would have wanted to sing, as well.

But mostly my focus was on the small shoe box beside me on the pew.

The crowd filed out and it was just the family, though that group was certainly numerous enough. They opened the casket one last time and back to front, everyone in the room filed past. Finally it was our turn. Toni was dry-eyed and completely composed. She bent forward and kissed J.D. on the lips. The whisper she spoke to him didn't carry as far as my ears. Geri openly wept. And even after she'd said her own goodbye she lingered as I stepped forward. I tucked the box into the near side of his chest. Then I looked at him. I didn't have a word to say. The dead can't hear your words of regret, and a million pleas for forgiveness would not give him back one minute of his young life. I stepped away and nodded to the funeral director to close the casket.

"Go help Toni," Geri said to me immediately. "She needs someone to lean on."

I did what I was told. Toni seemed the picture of control, but I needed to do my duty to my son's wife.

We made it out the front door of the church and down the steps to the sidewalk by the limousine. I was surprised to find that Geri was not right behind me. She seemed to have stayed in the church. I assumed it was something about flowers or consulting with the pastor. She emerged just before the pallbearers. And by the time they had carried J.D.'s body to the hearse, she was beside me once more. I needed her beside me. I remembered coming home from the war, thinking myself a dead man. How I wished I had been! How I wished I could have spared her, spared us, this pain.

We were all silent on the ride up to the cemetery. After the guns had fired, the flag folded and the coffin lowered into the earth, I walked zombielike toward the edge of the cemetery, trailing after the rest of the family. Inside the big black limo I looked up at the women in my life.

Geri looked as confused and hurt and, strangely, as guilty as I felt.

Toni was pale and looked so small.

"Are you all right?" I asked the girl.

She nodded. Then Geri reached over and patted her on the knee.

"You're doing so well," she told Toni. "J.D. would be so proud of you."

Toni gave her a brave little smile. "I can't lose control of myself and risk hurting the baby," she said. "I have to stay calm and not go into labor. That's what J.D. would want me to do. It's all of him that I have left. And he'd want me to put the baby ahead of my own feelings, even ahead of my feelings for him."

"That's what we'll all do," Geri said. She glanced over at me for support. "We'll save our grief for a more convenient time and put the baby first."

And that's what we did.

As I lay there in the hospital I was remembering and grieving. What better time for that than now?

I realized that it couldn't be J.D. sitting there in the chair beside me. We'd laid J.D. into a cold dark hole on the top of the hill a long, long time ago. It must be our little Jackie. Little Jackie no longer, of course. He was Jack, a grown-up man, married and with a family of his own.

Yes, it was Jack sitting beside me. He was doing something with his hands, but I didn't know what. And he was talking. He was talking and I was listening. I strained and concentrated, but I couldn't make heads nor tails out of the conversation. I could hear him fine, but somewhere in my head the understanding mechanism just wasn't in gear. I was sure it was important and I wanted to hear what he was saying, but it just didn't work.

Of course, that wasn't the case with that big band music. There was obviously some kind of concert going on out in the hallway and I could hear every note perfectly. And the sweet voices of the Andrews Sisters were as young today as they were the first time I'd heard them sing "Straighten Up and Fly Right."

By midafternoon Bud's condition was no better. The attending physician had been very blunt about his chances.

"I can't tell you that he'll make it through the next hour or the next three days," he said. "I'm honestly surprised the old gentleman has held on as long as he has. But I don't see anything good happening from here on out."

"What about the tears?" Jack asked. "When I was sitting with him last night, I swear there were tears coming out of his eyes."

The doctor waved off his concern. "That's pretty common in stroke victims," he assured him. "It doesn't mean anything."

Jack accepted the man's opinion, but he didn't quite believe it. His grandfather had been communicating with him with the one thing he had left, his emotion.

With the worst seemingly imminent, Aunt

Viv's visitation schedule went completely out the window. The Shertz family was once more present en masse, crammed into the little hallway waiting room like a tin of sardines.

Jack escaped the floor completely, finding a little coffee and snack shop on the first floor with thirty-foot glass views of the adjoining courtyard. He took the opportunity to try to figure out what was going on at Swim Infinity. None of the news was good.

Dana was still not taking his calls. Even at the new business number that Laura had come up with. She was apparently screening everything. Laura had started screening, as well.

"Between the customers asking where the crews are and the crew guys calling up to say they're leaving to work with Dana, it just doesn't seem worth answering the phone."

"Just keep answering," Jack said. "Apologize to the customers and tell the guys that they can't quit until they talk to me."

"Can I quit?" she whined.

"Oh, Laura, you don't want to quit," Jack assured her. "You want to give it all you can these next few days and when I get home, I'm giving you a nice raise. Okay?"

"Okay," she answered, still sounding forlorn. "The other line is ringing."

"Chin up," Jack encouraged.

He got off the phone and let out a big sigh. He'd had to offer the crew chief a bigger salary, as well. Jack didn't mind paying for quality workers and artisans, but he couldn't afford to get into a bidding war with Big Bob. Dana would certainly be able to pick off some of his best employees, but he hoped that camaraderie and company loyalty might hold some.

"Found you."

Jack glanced up to see Claire, gourmet coffee and chocolate chip cookie in hand, smiling down at him. He quickly made room for her at his tiny table.

"How's it going upstairs?" he asked.

She shrugged. "I really haven't had a chance to get back in there," she told him. "Aunt Viv's got everyone doing fifteen-minute visits, making Bud's hospital room busier than a bus stop. I'm glad we came last night and got to spend some quiet time with him."

Jack nodded. "Me, too."

"Though it's funny how we stayed awake all night and still look like we slept in our clothes," she pointed out, grinning.

Jack chuckled at the truth of that statement. They'd thrown their clothes on and hit the road. In the clear light of day, they both looked as if they'd dressed in the time it took them, except he was also sprinkled here and there with wood shavings.

"It's good to hear you laugh," Claire said.

Jack shook his head. "With all that's going on, I really shouldn't be. Poor old Bud just looks terrible. And things are really going south at the office. Laura was counting on me to come rescue her."

"What's happening?"

"Well, apparently Dana's new business is the real deal," he said. "She's undercut me with all the jobs that were upcoming but hadn't broken ground and she apparently has no qualms about stealing my design plans for those projects."

"Oh, my God, that's terrible," Claire said, though she didn't sound as if she were too concerned about it.

"It's the nightmare of the small businessman," Jack said. "You always worry that if you're not there to be on top of things every minute, it will all come tumbling down like a house of cards."

"Swim Infinity is not a house of cards," Claire assured him. "It's a strong, well-run business with a great reputation. It can't be wiped off the map so easily."

"No, but it can sure take some body blows."

"What can you do?" she asked.

"Well, I can't go after my clients. That's very bad for business. Besides, they're innocent. All they know is that the name of the business changed and that the price went down. I could sue Dana if I'm willing to take the time and money to do that," Jack said. "I guess it will be convenient since I'll already be in court."

"In court?"

"News flash: Mrs. Butterman is now threatening to sue us to get out of the contract her husband signed."

"*Mrs. Butterman* is suing?"

"Yeah, well, she's probably got a package deal going. The word is she's decided to divorce Big Bob. Something about him flying to Costa Rica for the weekend with Dana. It doesn't look good."

"How can all this happen in just a few short days?"

Jack shrugged. "You know Dana. When she decides she wants something, she really knows how to go and get it."

"You said those were good qualities," Claire reminded him.

Jack nodded. "And you said that I should be careful," he replied. "So I guess you win."

"Somehow it doesn't feel as good as I thought it would," she told him.

She reached over and took his hand in her own. Without thinking, Jack brought it to his lips.

"It's funny how being here, with Bud teetering on the edge can put a lot of things in perspective," Jack said.

Claire nodded.

"I even miss the kids," he said.

"Me, too," she admitted. "I wish Peyton and Presley were here right now arguing about inanities and trying to wipe snot on each other."

They laughed and groaned simultaneously.

"Why don't we take our coffee out in the courtyard," Jack said. "We can sit in the shade and give them a call."

Maybe it was just sheer exhaustion, but as the hours dragged on, afternoon into evening, Claire found herself more and more an observer of what was happening more than a participant in it.

She was hoping that the crowd of family members would dwindle as the day went on, but instead it seemed to get worse as no one left, and younger and more distant relatives continued to arrive.

The nursing staff finally had to put their collective foot down, and Aunt Viv's Center for Strategic Operations was moved to a larger waiting room downstairs.

Claire and Jack, declared to be the most important, were set up as permanent occupants of two of the hallway waiting-area chairs. The other seat was used as a sort of batter's circle where the next person to go into the room would wait their turn.

This had the unintended consequence of Jack and Claire being obliged to make conversation with every person in the family. Considering Jack's usual attitude toward his family, Claire fully expected that the bulk of this well-intentioned chitchat would fall upon her. Normally this wasn't much of a challenge, but after an interrupted night of sleep and fourteen stressful hours sitting in uncomfortable chairs, Claire wasn't sure how many simple pleasantries that she'd be able to offer. She didn't anticipate Jack making much effort to be conversational. But she was wrong.

Jack pulled the pieces of the treasure box out of his tote bag and showed them to every occupant of the chair. Ostensibly he was asking them to admire his handiwork, but more than that he was giving them an opening for a discussion of mutual interests.

All of the men in the family had at least a passing knowledge of woodworking, some of the women, as well. And those who had never darkened the door of a wood shop could still admire the beginnings of a fine box. Over and over, Jack showed it to them, told what he knew of the story, fitted the dovetails together for inspection and listened intently to their memories of the box and their advice on his project.

"This is a near perfect fit," Cousin Julie said as he joined the corners together. "Your grandpa would be really proud to see how well you've done. Did he teach you how to do this?"

Jack waved off the compliment. "I wish he had," Jack answered. "I'm self-taught. My stepfather didn't do any kind of manual labor. He didn't have any idea how to even get started. I was always good at it myself. So I guess it must be my genetics."

Bernard agreed when it was his turn to critique Jack's work. "This has got to be the Crabtree line," he said. "The Shertz family, we can make something out of nothing, but Bud and J.D. they could take something good and make it into something special."

When Poot showed up he had three different grades of sandpaper. "Everybody's talking about you being stuck up here while you're trying to finish up Geri's treasure box," he said. "I figured that at least you could get some sanding done."

Claire found herself observing her husband as she listened. This was the Jack she'd fallen in love with, she realized. He was relaxed, friendly, open, interested. So much of the time in the last few years, he would have been unable just to sit here. He would have to be up and moving, talking on the phone or text messaging. And it was now that she would have forgiven him for it. It was now, with things in such as uproar in the business, that she would have cut him some slack. But he seemed completely willing to sit here near his grandfather's door and pass the time.

When the preacher, Con McKiever, took the extra seat, he dutifully admired Jack's handiwork like everyone else. He looked strangely unclergylike in a T-shirt and gray cargo pants with brightly colored suspenders. But he was here on a mission and unwilling to be distracted by idle conversation. He clasped the hands of both Jack and Claire.

"Let us call upon the Lord," he said.

Claire bowed her head reverently and listened to his prayer to heaven that, in her thinking, was way over the top. The preacher called on the auspices of all the saints in heaven, angels both on earth and in sky, and the power that controls both the tides and the baby's cry to watch at Bud's bedside. "Almighty God, father of all things and ruler of the universe, we cry out for Your healing hand-ah!" he said loudly and quickly. "Knowing that in all things Your time is per-fec-tion and Your wisdom flawless, we bow to Your judgment in this and in all-ah. Blessed Savior-ah and Good Shepherd-ah, we beseech You in all things-ah that . . ."

Claire's mind wandered. It wandered away from the words in the waiting room to the dear old man lying alone in the hospital bed. She remembered his smile, so like Jack's and the dark eyes that sparkled like Zaidi's. He'd buried his only son, lost the woman he loved all his life and was practically estranged from his grandson.

*Please, no more suffering for Bud,* Claire pleaded silently.

McKiever's prayer went on interminably, voicing every biblical truth from the Garden of Eden to the Rapture, mentioning every prophet, poet and apostle and leaving no worshipful cliché unuttered. When he finally pronounced the amen, the preacher sighed as if a great weight had been lifted from his shoulders. He looked as if he felt much better.

Claire couldn't say the same for herself as she forced a smile to her lips while surreptitiously wiping her sweaty palms on her slacks. Jack stretched out his legs as if he'd been cramped in one position too long.

"I want you to know that our prayer chain is still secure and circling Bud and you two in a holy admonition."

"Thank you," Jack said politely.

A momentary silence ensued, but Claire had the distinct feeling that the preacher was just warming up for his next sermonette. Jack forestalled him. "You know, Con, there's been something I've wanted to ask you about your church."

"What's that?"

"How do you know if you're succeeding?" he asked.

"I don't catch your meaning," the preacher responded.

"What I'm curious about is what exactly you're trying to accomplish. Most of your parishioners are Catholic. So are you trying to convert them to Evangelicalism? I'd think that would be your goal, but after visiting your church it seems more like a way to continue with the faith that they already have until their own church shows up to minister to them? If that happens, won't it put you out of business?"

The preacher smiled and shrugged. "I can't know the answer to that one, son," he said. "Folks talk about the hereafter and how we can't know for sure what heaven will be like. That's so true. And for me, the here and now is the same. Things we don't expect have a way of happening. And the Good Lord continues to work in mysterious ways." He hesitated thoughtfully. "God gives me my job to do and I do it," he continued. "It's one foot in front of another, I keep walking the path. I try not to waste a minute gazing off in the future or imagining where I'm headed. Truth is, I just don't know. But God does. So I just have to trust him to get me there."

Jack nodded. "I guess I can see that," he said. "But shouldn't you have a goal? Doesn't every worthwhile endeavor require that?"

"My goal is to change the world," Mc-Kiever answered quickly and then laughed aloud with the humility of self-derision. "Of course, I don't actually get to change it myself. And I'm not even wise enough to say how it should be changed. But it's my job to make the opportunity for change within reach."

Claire liked his outlook. "That's kind of what we do raising children," she told him. "We can't make them become kind, hardworking and motivated adults. But what we can do is give them a chance to fulfill the potential that's already within them."

She glanced at Jack. He was smiling. "And for our kids, so stuffed with potential, giving them that chance is no job for the lazy or squeamish."

Claire laughed. "Hey, maybe if I'd finished college, I'd be qualified to manage a hedge fund," she joked.

"What you do is a lot more important than that," Jack said. "It's more important than being a heart surgeon. It is, for sure, more important than building swimming pools."

"Building swimming pools is what keeps our children fed and clothed and housed," Claire replied to Jack. "I don't want anyone bad-mouthing what my husband does."

Jack acknowledged her appreciation with a nod. But it was McKiever who spoke.

"The bible says that God 'established the work of our hands,' " he said. "I've always taken that to mean that whatever we're given to do, whether it's curing cancer or sweeping up French fries, it's equally important in God's plan."

460

Jack raised an eyebrow. "Now that's an interesting idea," he said to the preacher.

Claire continued to listen as the discussion so casually took on the broad scope of philosophy, theology and small-town horse sense.

Her thoughts drifted to San Antonio and the business and all the chaos that was now going on there. She found it remarkable that Jack, usually so focused on what was happening there, could seem so relaxed and thoughtful as he sat here.

She'd accused him of not having his priorities right. But clearly he did know the value of family, and he was willing to let everything else go on hold for someone who really mattered. She realized that she'd misjudged him. All the while thinking that he'd been judging her. She had been the one to insist on being a stay-at-home mom. It had been her choice, and yet, she resented watching him go off every day. He thought she'd been jealous of Dana. Maybe she'd thought the same, but in fact it wasn't another woman that she envied — Claire was jealous of Jack's work.

That thought caught her up short and she pondered it in disbelief. It was so obvious, it was difficult to imagine that she hadn't realized it before.

461

*So now that I know about it, what should I do?* she wondered.

The answer was easy. She could stop being dissatisfied and start helping her husband. She thought about the problems at the office. Jack was going to be short on help and she already knew so much about the business. Naturally, she was furious at Dana about stealing the clients, but this catastrophe could be turned into an opportunity. She and Jack just needed to talk it out. The two of them, together, had overcome so much. They could do that again.

And despite all the uncertainty ahead, Claire couldn't help but feel grateful, as if she'd dodged a bullet. If Jack had been more wealthy, Dana might have decided to simply steal him. And not many days ago, Claire had thought her husband would have fallen in easily with her plans. Looking at him now, Claire was not so sure. But Dana would have been relentless.

*Poor Mrs. Butterman,* she thought to herself. Of course, the woman was mad enough to sue them. She was probably mad enough to breathe fire. It was just too bad that she didn't know she was aiming in the wrong direction. But then, how could she know?

The answer came to her in a flash of

insight. Claire rose to her feet.

"Excuse me for a minute," she told Jack and McKiever and headed down the hallway. She took the elevator to the second-floor bridge, avoiding the rest of the family. She stopped at a shaded bench and pulled her phone out of her purse.

Toni answered on the first ring.

"Is it Bud?" she asked immediately.

"No, no," Claire answered and quickly gave the current update. "He's still the same. It's something else I wanted to ask you about."

"Oh good," Toni said. "What can I do for you?"

"Well, how about more of what you're doing now," Claire answered.

"I don't know what you mean?"

"Dana has quit the business," Claire said. "So by the time we get back to town, Jack's really going to be loaded down. I was thinking that when the kids start school in the fall, I would go back to work for him part-time. If you could help us get through this summer . . . I'm not asking for regular hours or big allotments of time, but if I could count on you for some backup, I could work from home."

"I can do better than that," Toni said. "Eloise's daughter is home from college.

She's an early childhood education major. She doesn't have a summer job yet and I've had her here helping out. She's great with the kids and they're crazy about her. Why don't I snap her up for the summer?"

"Oh, that would be great, Toni," Claire said.

"Good. What else can I do?" her mother-in-law asked.

Claire didn't even hesitate. "Do you know Big Bob Butterman's wife?"

"Natalie?" Toni responded. "Well, we're not close friends. We're both in Assistance League and have worked on a couple of committees together. Why?"

Claire smiled. "Would you like to do a nice favor for your son?"

# BUD

I was floating, bobbing on the water, in and out of consciousness. Time had ceased to exist for me. That's the good thing about death. There is no beginning or middle or end. Death had stopped looking like an enemy and looked now like a best friend. Maybe it was the saltwater. Drinking saltwater can make your brain go crazy. Awake I had enough sense to keep it out of my mouth. But when I'd startle from my bouts of stupor, my throat would be raw and my belly ached.

The zero had blown my little raft to bits, but had left me without a scratch. That was unlikely, I decided. It was very unlikely. With all the bullets that had rained into the water, I must have been shot. Not feeling pain undoubtedly meant that instead of getting off scot-free, I was dead in the water.

And the truth was, I wasn't that sorry. I'd seen lots of dead men since coming to the

South Pacific. I watched whole shiploads of dead men being ferried up to beaches by landing craft. They'd run forward, dodging, firing, not aware that they were dead already. With all of them dying, why should I be special so high above them? Did I think I was an angel or something that I could just watch them from the sky? No, I was no angel. Just another dead man, never to make it home.

I saw the sun just up from the horizon. This would be my last sunset and I wanted to watch. When that big orb disappeared below the water, the sharks would come. I'd already seen enough fins out here to know my fate. It just wasn't yet suppertime for sharks.

Is there a brave way to die? Or a good way to die? There's only dying and for me there was no cause to rail against it. Some lives are long and uneventful. Some lives are short and full of importance. My life was going to be mercifully short and pretty much meaningless. It was my fate and I couldn't resent it. Better men than me had already gone that way.

With my strength failing, I decided to take off my life vest and slip below the water. The sharks would still get me, but at least I wouldn't have to see them coming. I would free myself, watch the last sunset and go straight to hell. It was waiting for me just beneath the surface.

I began pulling at the straps on the vest. Wet and salty, they were rusted closed and I no longer had my knife to pry them open. My fingers were clumsy and swelled, what was left of my fingernails were as flexible as rubber. I tried to cuss, but my throat was too raw to speak. I thought maybe I could just pull it off over my head, but I didn't have the strength. The vest was stuck to me like a body part and like poor Lt. Randel, I'd just have to accept it as my shroud.

But I didn't want to miss my sunset. I turned my gaze in that direction and found more frustration. A great big fish had come up out of the water and was blocking my line of sight.

I waited impatiently. Whales only stay on the surface for half a minute, but this one lingered. It was huge and it lingered. And the most annoying thing about it was the music playing. That really made me angry. There was no music out on the ocean. It didn't make sense. I was tired of a world that didn't make sense. I was dead. I was a dead man in the water. But who could embrace death to the beat of "Little Brown Jug"?

It was irreverent. It was undignified. It made me suddenly furious. I was to be denied the final view of my last sunset as well as an appropriate funeral dirge. So be it! My throat was too raw to curse. I raised my arm out of the water and shot the giant fish an obscene gesture.

Then I lay back as far as I could and turned my eyes toward the dimming sky. I wouldn't shut my eyes. I was already dead and the dead have nothing to fear.

Surprisingly I found death to be easier than living. It was free from the confinement of the body and the pain of human frailty. I felt grateful for death. It was such a gift. Without it, living would just go on and on forever like an endless choppy sea. Only by being finite did life have any meaning at all. Like the sunset at the end of the day, it was what defined the day itself.

With a sigh of relief, I gave into it, ready for transformation.

"Hey! Hey, buddy!

I heard the voices. I assumed it was the other guys, the other G.I.s, the ones gone on before me welcoming me home.

Something splashed in the water next to me. I looked over at it puzzled. It was a life preserver. Where on earth had that come from?

"Hey, buddy!" I heard again and this time looked in that direction. The giant fish was still on the surface, bigger and closer than ever and there was a crowd of men standing on its back. The music that had traveled across the water to me was there with them.

One man dove into the water and began to swim toward me. I simply watched him as he closed the gap.

"Grab the float and we'll pull you in," he said.

I ignored the suggestion. How could he expect a dead man to grab anything?

"Come on, bud, there are sharks out here," he said.

When I didn't respond, couldn't respond, he began swimming closer. And then there he was right in front of me. I was stunned to see him. More stunned to find that I could speak.

"J.D., what are you doing out here?" I asked him.

But, of course, he wasn't J.D. J.D. wasn't even born yet.

I remember when J.D. was born. I relaxed into the memory of standing in the nursery, dressed in blue scrubs looking down at him with Geri at my side.

No, this wasn't J.D. I was getting confused. When J.D. was born I'd been relegated to the waiting room. That baby was Jack. Our little Jack, the child who healed the wounds of my heart.

Jack. I tried to speak the word.

"He's perfect," Geri said. "Big and healthy and perfect. He looks like you, I think."

"He's a baby — they all look alike," I told her. "How is Toni?"

"Exhausted," Geri answered. "But she did just fine."

Of course, she wasn't "just fine." Two days after the baby was born, we all went home together. Physically she was perfectly healthy, but it was clear that emotionally Toni was not doing so well. We'd all agreed that holding in her grief for the sake of the baby was a good thing. But now the grief was pouring out of her. She cried a lot. But worse than the crying was the silence. She just stared, listless, out the window, deaf to all around her.

Geri and I were still fragile as glass, but the baby gave us hope. He gave us a reason to keep getting up every day and every night. Geri, of course, in the days and me in the nights.

Toni obviously loved the baby and always kissed him and caressed him tenderly. But she did seem distant and we worried.

"What could anyone expect," our ancient

old Dr. Mayes said. "When you combine widowhood and baby blues, you're going to get some sad wistfulness."

But as the days turned into weeks and then into months, and Toni continued to stare out the window, showing less and less interest in Jackie, we worried.

Geri thought fresh air and exercise would help, so they took long walks together in the morning.

The weather was fair enough for me to be back at my sleeping camp in the middle of the garden, but I dolled up the place as nice as I could and offered it to her.

"Sometimes you'll just need to get away from us," I told her. "You can always come here. I find this garden very safe and comforting."

She thanked me and she did sit out there from time to time. I don't know if she found any serenity there, but hopefully a few moments of peace.

Geri's sister Opal came up with the best answer. "Call the medical people down at the Air Force. They're going to know more about this. They probably see it all the time."

So we called the Air Force and within a week all three of us, and the baby in his little car seat, drove down to Oklahoma City for a consultation.

Toni and Geri went upstairs and I was left in the waiting room with Jackie who slept peacefully in his little plastic carrier.

I was never one to sit idle. I glanced through the magazines, most were about fashion or had recipes, nothing much of interest to me. I did look at the one on golf, but having never played the game, I got through it rather quickly.

Across the room was a wall of brochures; I walked over there and looked through the titles. There were a couple on infant care that I pulled out. Most were about diseases I never heard of: *Coping with Schizophrenia* or problems I didn't have: *Overcoming Addiction.* But then I saw one that caught me up short: *The Facts about Combat Fatigue.*

Immediately I stepped back and retreated to my chair, glancing around, afraid that someone might have seen me with the pamphlet. There was, of course, nobody else in the room but Jackie and he was still sleeping. Sleeping like a baby. I could no longer remember when I had lain as peacefully as my grandson. It had gotten tolerable over the years. I didn't require as much sleep as other men, I'd decided, and a couple of naps during the daylight was plenty of rest. But when J.D. announced he was headed for Vietnam, the frequency of the dreams had gotten worse. At least now that the baby was here, I had a reason to walk the floors on the nights I was home.

I wasn't unfamiliar with the term combat fatigue. You couldn't be in the service long without seeing a share of it. Fellows with the shakes or guys who cried were the most difficult to watch. But the ones with the thousand-mile-long stare were everywhere. And we'd all heard about Patton over in Italy. How he'd slapped the guys in the hospital and called them cowards. I knew I was no coward. As long as we were fit to fly, I kept flying. And my restless nights might have kept my bunkmates awake, but they knew I wouldn't get them killed.

Ultimately, my bad dreams had drummed me out of the service. They'd kept my whole life off-kilter.

I'd managed to hide them from J.D. It was the secret I never shared. But as I looked down in that precious baby's face, the last remnant of my boy, I was wondering if I'd only succeeded in keeping the truth secret from myself.

I got up and walked over to the brochures once more. I took the combat fatigue one out of its place, and then I grabbed one on the problems with the aging prostate and put that on top. If someone caught me reading, I'd rather they assumed I was impotent or incontinent.

I carefully opened up the pamphlet. Under the heading *What is combat fatigue?* was written, *"Exposure to wartime trauma can sometimes produce lingering effects that follow a veteran back home."*

Well, that was certainly true of me. I continued to read the page, making mental check marks to myself. Anxiety — check. Lack of concentration — check. Emotionally disconnected — check. Nightmares — check. Fortunately, there were some things that I was grateful not to recognize. Violent outbursts, estrangement from friends and family, and abuse of drugs or alcohol were not on my list and I was very glad of that. I continued to read, nodding to myself in agreement until I got to the statement *"Symptoms may persist for days or weeks, most often spontaneously disappearing within six months."*

"Six months!" I repeated aloud.

I glanced down at little Jackie who was now wide-awake and staring up at me with those big dark eyes, so much like my own.

"Six months, my ass," I told him.

He was startled by my tone and his face screwed up as if he were going to cry.

"It's okay, Jackie," I cooed to him, more

softly as I detached him from his carrier and took him into my arms. "Grandpa's just an old, crusty, bad-talking man, but he's not mad at you, he's never mad at you. You are the little light of my life."

I held him close to my chest and bounced him a bit as I walked the floor. He decided not to cry after all.

A few minutes later, Jackie's mom and grandma returned for us. Immediately, I could see things were better. Toni looked more like herself than she had since the baby was born.

"It's just such a relief to get to talk about it," she admitted on the way home.

"But you know you can always talk to us," Geri told her.

"Yes, but you're sad, too," she said. "I don't want to make it harder for you. It's good to talk about it with someone who can't be hurt by anything I say."

Toni was put in contact with a group of women who met regularly in Broken Arrow, and she and Geri began attending the group nearly every week. They both seemed to get a lot out of it. And I was glad they did, but I stayed home with Jackie.

As the summer turned to fall and Jackie went from lying, to rolling and then crawling, I was happy and contented. Sure, sometimes I let myself imagine that he was J.D. and even when he clearly was himself and not his father, I pretended J.D. was just off somewhere and that he'd be home soon.

I wasn't out of my mind. I knew the truth, I knew J.D. was gone forever, but the quiet lie got me through one day after the next as our Jackie sat up and smiled and was happy and content with nothing more than a bottle of warm milk and some mashed-up sweet potato.

He was up on his feet by the winter. Holding on to the furniture and easing himself around to anywhere he wanted to go. And while I took pleasure in his new-found independence, I'd begun to worry that he might leave us.

Toni had continued to improve physically and spiritually. And she'd also reconnected with her family in San Antonio. With J.D. dead, her father had forgiven her and wished to let bygones be bygones. He was very anxious to see her again and to make the acquaintance of his grandson.

Therefore, it didn't come as a total surprise when Toni told us she was going "home" for Christmas. There was nothing we could do but wish her well. We took her to the airport. The place was all festive with lights and trees, and Jackie clapped his hands delighted with everything. I carried him on my shoulders down to the gate and we waited with her. He teetered around unsteady on his feet and then would drop into a crawl and take off like a shot in one direction or another. It was all I could do to keep up with him.

When it came time to board the plane, he unexpectedly clouded up. It was as if he knew how much we didn't want him to go. As she disappeared down the ramp, he was looking back at me and held one arm out as if to plead for rescue.

"See you next week, Jackie. We love you."

Our first Christmas without J.D. was quiet and lonely. But I think we must have wanted it that way. Geri had a half dozen invitations from sisters who would have welcomed us to join them for the holiday. But we wanted to stay at home. We wanted to eat a simple pot roast and pretend it was just another winter day.

Geri and I conversed over the meal but never much above a whisper. It was almost as if we were afraid to draw attention to ourselves. A stray word might catch God's ear. We both recognized what was coming and there was nothing we could do to keep it at bay.

"A young woman, any young woman, is

sure to get on with her life," I told Geri. "And there is nothing we can or should do to stop that."

"You're absolutely right," Geri agreed. "She's young enough to wed again and that's what J.D. would want for her. He'd want her to be as happy with someone else as they were together."

"And Jackie is her son. Of course she'll take him with her when she goes," I pointed out.

"Naturally," Geri agreed. "It couldn't be any other way."

So we deliberately made the decision not to get too attached to Jackie. He was *her* son. We'd had *our* son and he was gone forever.

It seemed like a perfectly reasonable, prudent and thoughtful strategy. We would always love Jackie, but we'd not make him the center of our lives.

Geri and I both agreed that was best.

And our good intentions lasted almost long enough to get the sleepy child from the arrival gate to the car at the airport parking lot. His smiles brightened everything. And when his tummy hurt or he was cutting teeth, all we could think about was his pain. He wasn't the center of our world, he'd become our universe and we couldn't resist him.

It seemed as if the motivation to keep him at arm's length might not be necessary. During our first meal with them back home, she gave us the news. We were sitting around the kitchen table. Jackie was in his high chair using his scant few teeth on a cooked carrot.

"My father thinks I should go back to college," Toni said. "Being a single mother is a big responsibility, and I owe it to Jackie to be as prepared as I can to provide for him."

My heart fell at her words, but I nodded with sincerity.

"That seems like a good idea, what do you think?"

She bit her lip nervously before she replied. "I want to do it," she said. "I always hoped I'd get a chance to finish school. And the only way I could really afford it is to move back in with my parents. I can do that . . . but I don't want Jackie being raised in their house."

Geri's brow furrowed and she glanced at me. "What do you mean, sweetie?" she asked. "Is something bad happening in that house?"

Toni shook her head. "No, nothing like that, nothing *bad*. It's just that my father and stepmother are so focused on money and social position. That was their whole objection to J.D., marrying him couldn't elevate my status. My half sisters are growing up to be little spoiled snobs. I don't want that for Jackie. I want him to feel loved and cared for the way I was loved by my grandparents and the way J.D. was loved by you."

"As his mother you'll be setting the mark on how he'll behave," Geri assured her. "And nothing will ever stop us from loving this child."

"I know," Toni said. "But it will all be tougher from the inside of my father's house." She hesitated. "There is something I want to ask you, but I don't want to pressure you or force anything on you. I would like to go back to San Antonio and go to college. But I would like to leave Jackie here with you two."

To say that Geri and I were delighted is to make the moment too small. It was as if a giant weight had been cast off my shoulders. I could have floated to the ceiling.

I'm sure it was difficult for Toni to leave the boy behind, but she was also excited and eager about getting back to her friends and the life at school. No one could fault a young woman on that, especially one who'd so recently had her heart broken to bits.

But we had one last good surprise. Geri and I discussed it long and thoroughly and were in total agreement. The day before she was to fly out, I went down to the bank and had our special savings account put into a cashier's check. We presented it to her after Jackie had gone to bed.

"This was J.D.'s college money," Geri said. "It's mostly proceeds from my father's business, and Bud and I put in more of our own when we had it. We want you to take it."

"Oh, no," Toni responded immediately. "I can't take your money."

"It was meant for J.D., so it should have been yours anyway," I told her.

"But you're going to have the expense of having Jackie here," she said. "And my father says that he'll pay for everything."

"We can easily keep Jackie in shoes and pull toys," I said. "With this money you could pay most of your own way. I'm sure your father's offer to foot the bill for everything is completely genuine. But sometimes it's better within a family for nobody to really have the upper hand."

So she returned to her family and a new life. And Geri and I were left in Catawah with the most fascinating child in the entire world to entertain us. All of our well-considered plans to keep a safe emotional distance and to prepare ourselves for his eventual return to his mother just disappeared in to thin air. He was ours. And the thrill of that swept through me like youth.

I heard the groan of an old man. I realized it was me.

I was far removed from my home and Geri. I was in the hospital. The hospital with the music. And the band that had been playing downstairs for the last few days had moved into the hallway right outside my door. They could really play, but their take on "Lover Come Back to Me" had a melancholy trumpet that made the heart ache. That was what had made me groan. My body seemed beyond hurt, only my memory could cause me pain.

# TUESDAY, JUNE 14, 7:12 P.M.

After fifteen hours at the hospital, it was unanimously agreed that Jack and Claire had to go back to the house to get some rest. Jack volunteered to drive so Claire could sleep.

"No," she told him. "Why don't I drive and you can talk to me and keep us awake."

Jack agreed and put his tote bag with the treasure box pieces in the back before taking the passenger seat.

It was not a difficult trip, there was still plenty of sun left and the rush-hour traffic had completely cleared out.

"Why don't you call Toni and give them an update," Claire suggested.

Jack pulled his phone out of his pants pocket and selected the number. Ernst answered. Jack quickly gave him the details of the bottom line — things were not looking very promising, but Bud was still alive.

"I'm sure that he's not in a lot of pain,"

his stepfather told him. "At this stage the groans he makes can be a good sign. Being able to verbalize at this point is an indicator of continued brain function. He's not that far away from consciousness."

"Thanks," Jack said. It wasn't hope, but it was reassurance.

"Toni and the kids are cleaning up the kitchen," Ernst said. "I'm sure everybody wants to talk to you."

Jack spoke with the children first. Zaidi sounded so grown-up.

"How is your grandfather, Daddy?" she asked. And when he answered, she responded with all the right conciliatory phrases.

"Don't worry about us," she told him. "We're great here with Toni and Pops. They're really keeping control of the twins. Toni makes them take naps in separate rooms. Mom could never get them to do that!"

If Peyton and Presley were truly under the thumb of their grandparents, they had apparently not yet noticed it. Both seemed happy and enthusiastic. Though Presley did have her one somewhat sad moment.

"We miss you, Daddy," she said. "When are you ever coming home?"

"As soon as I can," he promised. "As soon

as I can."

A minute later Jack's mother was on the phone and he gave her the same, if less clinical, version of the update he'd relayed to Ernst.

"Oh, honey, I'm so, so sorry," she said.

"I appreciate that, Mom," Jack answered. Then he almost changed the subject, to ask how the kids were getting along. But he'd already heard the answer for himself, and there was something else that was more pressing on his mind. "Claire told me that I lived with Bud and Geri when I was a baby," he said. "I guess I didn't know that."

There was a hesitation on the other end of the line.

"Yes, you stayed with them until you were almost five," she answered. "I phoned every Sunday and I flew up there about once a month to see you. I suppose I was hoping you didn't remember all that. It was the right thing to do at the time, I think. But I still feel guilty about it. Our children are children for such a short time. In hindsight it just feels very wrong to have spent so much of it away from you."

Jack was surprised at that admission. His mother always seemed so in control of her world. Somehow, hearing her admit to imperfection in parenting made him want to defend her.

"From my standpoint, you don't have anything to feel guilty about," Jack told her. "I had a great childhood. And my screwups, like not finishing college and marrying too young, those weren't your fault, they were mine."

"I don't consider those screwups," Toni said. "Not everybody has to go to college. And you were never the kind of fool to risk letting someone as right for you as Claire get away."

Jack glanced over at his wife behind the steering wheel.

"Thanks, Mom," he said.

"And I'm so glad she's decided to come help you in the business," Toni continued. "She's very clever and she keeps you focused on the things you really want to do."

Jack chuckled lightly, but his mind was still mulling her first statement.

"And tell her that I've spoken with Emily, Eloise's daughter. She's thrilled to work part-time with the kids."

"Uh . . . okay, I'll tell her."

They said their goodbyes and Jack snapped the phone shut and slipped it into his shirt pocket.

"Everybody's okay," he told Claire. "The kids miss us and Zaidi has matured so much she sounds about ten years older."

His wife smiled. "I hope that's just temporary," she said. "With Presley being so rough and tumble, Zaidi seems like the only little girl I've got."

Jack laughed. "Think of all the money we'll save not having to buy another round of those pink-and-purple princess outfits."

"True," Claire agreed.

"Mom said to tell you that Eloise's daughter has taken the job," he said. "And she said that she's glad you're back working with me."

Claire made a face. "Whoops," she said. "I guess I should have mentioned it to the boss before I rehired myself for the job."

"They say the husband is always the last to know," he replied. "It will be a big help," he continued. "I can't even imagine what kind of mess we're going to go back to. It will be wonderful to have someone I can trust to help me clean it up. Thank you for doing this."

"Don't thank me," Claire answered. "The truth is, I've really sort of wanted to come back to work. I'm really torn. I love being home with the kids and I think it's the most important job I can do. But I miss the action and I miss . . . I miss being in it with you."

Jack nodded thoughtfully.

"I'm sure there's a way you can still be part of the business and also do a lot of the parent things that you really want to do. There's no rule that says you can't work out of the house. And with phones and e-mail we can juggle a lot of things at the same time."

"That's what I'm hoping," she said. "I want us to set up an office at the house. Not just a corner of the dining room, but an area where I can get some real work done."

"Okay," he said. "We can do that."

"I was thinking of that room off the left of the foyer. I know it's supposed to be a little formal sitting room, but I think it's got lots of good light and with some shelving, it would be good to go."

Jack just stared at her at first not comprehending. Foyer? Formal sitting room? It was at least a half minute before recognition dawned.

"You mean in the new house?"

"Yes," Claire said. "It's so much closer to the office and there is a lot more room there."

"What about the school and the neighbors?"

She shrugged. "Anywhere you live you'll

have neighbors and whether they're good or bad depends a lot on you. And the school, well, of course the school is great and Zaidi will miss it. The twins have barely started, they won't know the difference."

"The new school is not nearly as highly rated," Jack pointed out. "And it has a genuine problem with overcrowding."

"Kids still manage to learn there," Claire said. "And our children are very bright."

"And bright kids deserve an excellent school."

"*All* kids deserve an excellent school," Claire said. "And some neighborhood schools are going to be better than others, but bright motivated educated kids come out of every school. And parents sometimes have other factors to consider."

Jack held up his hands. "Wait a minute, I'm getting confused," he said. "You're giving my arguments and I'm giving yours. Have we switched sides? Is that also something you forgot to tell me?"

She sighed slightly and then laughed. "I guess so," she said. "I just . . . I don't know . . . the situation has changed and . . . you know, Aunt Viv said something about picking my battles and Aunt Sissy suggested I wasn't looking at what's really important. And then I was thinking about Mrs. Butterman and how she's lashing out at our business when she's angry at Dana, not realizing she's aiming in the wrong direction. And it just made me think that I was looking at our . . . our problems just one way. So I gave myself the opportunity to consider your side of things and it seems like you make a lot of good points."

"Thanks," Jack said. "You don't know how long I've waited for you to say that. But you know what the bad news is? I've been thinking about this myself."

He settled down more comfortably in the seat as he gathered his thoughts.

"Being here in Catawah, being in Bud and Geri's little house, it's been kind of nice," he said. "It's not big or fancy in any way, but you have a sense that the place is home and that a lot of love has been lived through there."

Claire nodded. "That's right. It's almost as if the warmth of it oozes right out of the walls."

"I've been doing a few small repairs and fix-ups," Jack continued. "And I've remembered that I like that kind of thing. I actually find it kind of relaxing, maybe even purposeful. So I don't mind having an old house that needs a bit of attention."

"Yeah, I remember when we first moved

in our old place," she said. "Every weekend you were up before breakfast working on some project."

Jack agreed, then offered a heavy sigh. "With what's going at work, I don't even know how bad it's going to be yet. It may be just a few rough weeks trying to re-sell our old jobs and come up with some new ones. Or it may be a real problem. I feel like I don't even know Dana. I'm no longer sure that she wouldn't deliberately sabotage us."

"Surely she won't," Claire said. "It wouldn't even be in her best interests."

"Well," Jack said. "Whatever happens, happens. But I think I could be a lot less pumped up about it if I didn't have that huge extra mortgage hanging over our heads. I was thinking that I'd like to put the new house up for sale. The new owners could finally pick the tile and the colors."

By the time they'd arrived at the house at the end of Bee Street in Catawah, Claire was happy, smiling.

"I just feel so relieved," she told Jack.

"Relieved? Hey, you won, the least you ought to feel is jubilant," he teased.

"I'm too tired for jubilant," she answered. "Just let me get a few hours rest and something to eat and I promise I'll be dancing all over the place."

"Just so you don't forget to say nanny-nanny poo-poo, I beat you."

"I can't really use that," she told him, feigning seriousness. "You changed sides, so that makes you the winner and poor me, I'll probably never get a giant stucco mansion in the middle of a sterile subdivision."

They laughed together. It sounded very good to her.

"I'm going to take a shower, I'm all grimy," she told him.

"Okay, I'm going to see if I can glue these pieces together and get the clamps on them tonight."

He headed to the wood shop and she headed to the shower.

It felt so good to get the smell of the hospital washed from her skin, and the stream of hot water revived her. She found herself singing. It was not one of the songs of her teen years, or one she sang to the kids. It must have been from one of the old phonograph records under the bed. She la-la-la-ed in places where she didn't know the words to "Everybody Loves My Baby, but My Baby Don't Love Nobody but Me."

She was still humming after she shut the water off and dried herself with a towel. She'd meant to fix Jack and herself a sandwich. And she wanted to call the hospital for an update. But when she caught sight of the bed, she couldn't resist it and she just crawled right in. It felt so good to lie down.

Jack came into the room.

"You want something to eat," she asked him.

"No," he answered. "Too tired to chew. You?"

Claire's negative reply was partially muffled by the pillow.

A few moments later, she could hear him in the shower, and she realized he was singing. She smiled as she drifted off to sleep but roused a few minutes later when he got in bed beside her and pulled her into his arms. He held her close against him and rubbed her back. She hadn't realized how much it ached until it began to feel better. He ran his hands down the long length of her. Then he kissed her, softly and sweetly, allowing his lips to linger and then to trace the distance between her mouth and her neck. He buried his face against her throat and his sigh was a warm caress against her skin. She could happily lie there forever, but with a peck on his check she pulled away.

"I'll be back," she whispered.

He relinquished her unwillingly. "Where

are you going?" he asked.

"I need to put in my diaphragm," she said.

He didn't release her, but it was a moment before he spoke. And when he did, it was with laughter.

"You give me way too much credit," he said. "I'm so exhausted, I was barely able to brush my teeth. I know I can't make love. I just wanted to hold you. Is that okay? Can I just hold you?"

Claire snuggled back into his arms. "I'd love that," she told him.

Jack sighed.

"Are you worried about Bud?" she asked him.

"No, I just called up there. No news really, but he's still hanging in."

"Good."

"I was thinking about what it must have been like for them," Jack said. "You know, to lose your only child."

"Oh, God, it must have been horrible," Claire agreed.

"I can't even imagine it. When I think about Zaidi and Peyton and Presley, it just makes my heart pound. If anything happened to them, I just don't know how I bear it."

"I'm glad they had you," Claire said.

Jack raised up on one elbow to look at her.

"What do you mean?"

"I'm glad he had you here with them, to help them get through it," she said. "You know sometimes when we lose people we love, it becomes all about regrets. 'I should have done this or I should have said that.' "

"I should have visited them more," Jack said. "I should have brought the kids here so they'd know them."

"Yeah, that kind of thing," Claire said. "It's pretty typical for us to think like that. It's good that you can know that when it really mattered, when they were living the worst time of their life, you were here. And you made that time better for them."

"I can't take any credit for that," Jack said. "I don't even remember it and it was my mom's doing, not mine."

Claire ran her hand lovingly down the side of his face. "No, no credit," she agreed. "But also no regret."

# BUD

Dead in the water. The sun was setting and I was dead in the water. I was glad. Strange, the truth of that. I was glad. No one deserved to survive. I certainly didn't deserve it. And I wouldn't. If I could just get the buckle undone on my life vest, I could go down easy. But I didn't have the strength to pull on it. Dead men can't move their arms. Dead men just bob on top of the water until the predators come.

"Grab the float and we'll pull you in."

A man moved into the line of my vision. He was one of the men who'd been standing on the fish, the fish playing the music.

"Come on, bud, there's sharks out here," he said.

I wanted to ask him how he knew my name, but the saltwater had raked my throat raw — there was no way I could speak.

He swam all the way to me. Grabbed the lifesaver himself and then he grabbed me, shoving his arm down the front of my vest and then crooking his elbow as if he were hoisting a sack of fish.

"Pull us in," he hollered.

We began moving in the water, closer and closer to the music. I paid no attention to it. I was focusing on the sun on the edge of the horizon. It was my last sunset and I didn't want to miss it. In just minutes the sharks would come. I was glad I was dead and wouldn't be able to feel a thing.

Suddenly I was being dragged out of the water. Dozens of hands reached for me. I felt the coolness of the night, followed by the burn of a fire.

"Damn, how long has he been in the water? The flesh peels right off of him."

"Hold him by the vest until we get him belowdecks."

"Did you see all those fins in the water? The guy was five minutes away from being somebody's dinner."

"I just thought it was a pile of debris on the water," another said. "If he hadn't signaled me, I wouldn't have sent up the alarm."

A face appeared right above me. "Hey, flyboy? Can you see me? Can you hear me?"

I could see him. I could hear him. But I couldn't speak. I couldn't squeeze his hand or make any gesture. Finally I blinked. I blinked and I blinked.

"Okay," he said. "Okay, okay. Don't try to talk."

A medic examined me and someone dribbled some cool water down my throat.

"We're probably going to have to hurt you to get you to sick bay," the medic told me. "But that's just because you're sunburnt and your skin is so soft from the water. You're going to be okay."

"Yeah, you've just been rescued by the U.S. Navy," someone else called out.

It was unreasonable. Improbable. Unbelievable.

I never believed it.

I had been plucked out of the water and sent to rest in a clean, dry sick bay. No, that was beyond possibility, but here I lay.

But this wasn't sick bay and I hadn't just been plucked out of the ocean. It was just another dream. One of the dreams that weren't dreams. I finally talked about it, maybe understood, after Jackie left.

They say that in raising children the days are long but the time is short. That was only too true in the years after Toni had left for school. Geri and I were no longer kids, and at the end of the day we were always tired, but somehow the energy we needed to keep up with Jackie was always there when we needed it.

Jackie's first word was *Bud.*

He was sitting in his high chair, tired of being there and not at all interested in the bits of squash Geri was feeding him, even when she mixed them up in his favorite sweet potato. He wanted to be rescued and held up his arms to me.

"Bud!" he said.

Geri laughed. "That's Grandpa," she corrected him. "Say Grandpa."

"He can call me Bud," I assured her as I unhooked him from the seat and pulled him up. "We're pals."

"Let me get his bib off and clean his hands," she said, reaching for a napkin. "He's going to get his dinner all over you."

"What's a few vegetables between friends," I answered.

I don't think I can ever get over J.D.'s death. But having Jackie in our lives kept us moving forward in a time when we might have given up.

I continued to work nights as a postal sorter, though I could see retirement as the light at the end of the tunnel. The process was more and more mechanized every day. Being able to tinker with machines became as much of an asset as knowing nearly every zip code in the state.

Geri still did a lot of sewing, but a new interest now claimed her weekends. She'd discovered garage sales. It was as if it were her personal duty every Saturday morning to visit every front yard and driveway with a sign in front of it. She'd pour through every castoff in every box, and she'd come home with a car full of clothes and toys. And she refused to carry more than twenty dollars in her purse.

Jackie and I would pass this time walking up to Main Street, looking in the store windows and talking to the old timers. Everyone commented on how quickly he grew and how much he favored me in looks.

"That boy's going to be even taller than you, Bud," I was told. "For sure he's going to play Cedar's basketball."

I laughed off comments like that, knowing in my mind that Jackie would be long gone from Catawah by high school. I knew it was true. But I still lived my life as if he'd be with us forever.

Toni called long-distance every Sunday night. Sometimes Jackie would talk to her and sometimes he couldn't be bothered. She visited as her schedule permitted. We were always glad to see her, and happy that she and Jackie could be together. But we also cringed each time, fearing that she would say she just couldn't go home without him. Every time that didn't happen, it gave us a false sense of hope that we never spoke of aloud.

By the time he was three, he spoke of his mother as if she were some princess in a fairy tale. Geri or I would tuck him into bed and he'd demand a story. But he didn't want pirates or dragons or flying saucers.

"Tell me a story about my mommy," he would say.

We didn't know all that many stories, but we'd tell what we knew and make up the rest. The fact that he never asked about his daddy was curious, I thought at the time. I only realized later that, in our grief, Geri and I went through our days without ever speaking his name aloud.

About that time there was a small stir among the citizens of Catawah. A group of young people purchased the old Mehan farm south of town. Piggy Masterson insisted the long-haired freaks ought to be run out of the country. And every preacher in town was concerned that "Free love" was being practiced "in our very midst." As if that were something entirely new.

Maybe it was a shared interest in recycling. Or maybe it was because she knew exactly what it felt like to be an outcast in her hometown, Geri got to know those strange people and decided she wanted to be friends.

"Raising children has changed since we were parents," she insisted. "You and I are too old-fashioned and what Jackie needs is to be around boys and girls his age."

"He's always around other kids," I pointed out. "Your family is in and out of our house so much, I ought to install a revolving door."

"Family is nice, of course," she said, "but we don't want Jackie growing up thinking he's a second cousin to every person he ever knew."

So one sunlit Sunday when Jackie was a busy, curious two-year-old, we were invited out to the commune for an afternoon picnic.

The farm took up almost an eighth of a section, just shy of eighty acres. There were a half dozen young families all trying to live off that plot of land. I can't testify one way or the other about free love, but there were lots of kids and plenty of room to run, and Jackie, in his sneakers, did his best to keep up with them.

It was a bit tougher for me to fit in. I was nearly thirty years older than the men of the group. I was clean shaven and my hair, almost completely gray, I kept trimmed neatly above my collar. Many of these fellows had wild moustaches and beards and they all wore their hair long. Some of them just let it hang down to the waist, others had braids or pony-tails. I admit to being taken aback by this. But that didn't last too long. Maybe it was meeting so many different kinds of people during the war, but I found myself more curious than repulsed. And, of course, if they were Geri's friends, they must be all right. She was always able to see through to the heart of people.

They showed me around the place. They had huge expanses of vegetable gardens, the cleanest chicken coops I'd ever seen and they'd just gotten started keeping honeybees. They were heavily into recycling and composting, which I'm sure won over Geri's heart.

"We're hoping next year to get a cow," Brad, a very tall skinny blond fellow, told me. "It would just be so cool to make our own butter and cheese."

The other guys agreed.

"We had a cow during the Depression," I told them. "It kept us in milk and butter and earned us what little cash money we had. But I can't honestly say I was sorry to see old Becca go. I feel like I spent half my childhood snuggled up against her with my hand on her teats."

They laughed.

"I guess you kept her in a barn," another boy named Tom said.

"At night," I answered. "In the day I could open range her. That's getting harder and harder to do these days. I don't suspect your neighbors would appreciate it so much."

They all laughed again.

We compared knowledge on alfalfa and Bermuda grass. I suggested that they consider black-eyed peas, tasty to both man and beast. By dinnertime, we were companionable enough. The meal was set out on long tables in the shade. It reminded me of the old-time country feeds I attended when I was a boy. Although the food was not as I'd remembered. None of those light-as-air biscuits and everything seasoned with pork fat. At their table everything was nearly half raw and the bread was so grainy it sat on my stomach like a brick. But there was lots of conversation at the table and plenty of smiles. There was no children's table, nor a high chair to be seen. All the little ones were interspersed among us. Those less able to get along found themselves between two parents. Jackie sat between two girls about eight or nine, both with long, tidy braids. He seemed delighted by the attention.

"So the kid is your grandson," Brad said. "How'd you and Geri end up with him?"

"His mother is in San Antonio finishing college," I answered. "She thought he'd be better off here with us."

Brad nodded.

"Where's his father?" someone asked.

From all the way at the other end of the table, I could feel Geri stiffen. We were still not comfortable saying it aloud, but I managed.

"Our son was killed in Vietnam," I said.

There was a gasp from someone and a moment of complete silence at the table. Then across from me Brad spoke for all of them.

"Bummer, man," he said.

"Yes," I agreed.

The world continued to spin and I tried to keep moving. One crisp fall morning in the wood shop I put Jackie to work on a length of wood with six bolts to be tightened. It would keep him occupied and the pint-sized wrench wasn't all that dangerous. Geri's birthday was coming up and I had no idea what to get her. That morning, I got down the remnants of the treasure box J.D. had been building for her. It was a good idea, I thought, to finally get her a place to store stuff other than under the bed. But when I saw the pieces that J.D. had cut, my brow furrowed. It wouldn't make a big enough box for anything. I thought he'd meant to make something for her scrapbooks and photos, but this box was just slightly bigger than one you might put together for jewelry. Which, I suppose would have been fine, if Geri had been a woman who had jewelry or wore jewelry. She was a woman who neither owned nor was interested in the stuff. Anything she came across, she always gave to her sisters. And even her own wedding band was, more often than not, sitting on the windowsill above the kitchen sink.

What in the world had J.D. been thinking? I wondered to myself. He surely knew his mother better than that. I put the wood back on the top shelf.

"Maybe someday you can make a jewelry box for your mama," I told Jackie.

"Will it have bolts?"

"It will if you want it to," I told him.

Toni graduated with a bachelor's degree in sociology. She was pretty low-key about it.

"To do anything that intrigues me in my field, I need a master's degree," she told us.

A master's degree sounded fine to me. She could go to school forever as far as I was concerned. Jackie was settled in with us so well, a few more years wouldn't be a problem.

I'm not sure when I first heard the name of Dr. Van Brugge. Toni told us when she started dating again. She told us how strange it felt and joked about how the men at school all seemed like boys. The first thing I remember about the doctor happened after she'd been dating him for several months. She'd come for a weekend visit and we were sitting around a warm fire in the living room. Jackie was already in bed. I was shelling pecans as the women talked.

"Everybody respects him," she told Geri. "He is a very smart man with a kind heart and a wonderful future. A woman would be a fool not to fall in love with him."

Geri nodded sagely. "But you haven't been able to," she stated.

Toni shook her head. "He's not J.D.," she said. "I like him. I respect him. But I just . . . I don't know. J.D. was my soul mate. I don't know if a woman ever gets that again. Maybe a good provider who loves and cares about me is enough?"

I don't remember what Geri answered, but I gave the man no chance at all.

Less than a month later, Toni called us to

say that they were engaged.

I was flabbergasted. Totally caught off guard.

"You knew it was going to happen sometime," Geri pointed out.

"Yes, but not now, not him."

"It's not your choice."

Her parents wanted her to have the huge, society wedding they had been unwilling to give her when she'd married J.D. The thing was eight months in the planning alone. We were invited, but Jackie was not.

"My stepmother just thinks he'll be a disruption and will cause people to talk," Toni explained. "Ernst's mother doesn't like the idea, either. They'd both like to pretend I was never married before. But I've refused to wear white. All I can do to honor J.D.'s memory is to wear his favorite color."

She urged us to leave Jackie with one of the aunts, but we decided not to go. If Jackie wasn't going to be welcome, we didn't want to attend, either.

It's strange to admit it, but we weren't really so offended. We felt bad for Jackie, but for ourselves we were secretly hopeful. Maybe Jackie's presence could continue to be an inconvenience to Toni and an embarrassment to her new husband. If that happened, then Jackie stayed with us.

They went to Europe for three weeks on their honeymoon. With that and the busy schedule before the wedding, Toni had not been to see Jackie in almost three months. That's a very long time in the life of a five-year-old. Though she'd continued to call when she could, Toni had missed Jackie's birthday and he hadn't even noticed.

But just two weeks after they settled back into their life in San Antonio, Toni called to say they were coming up for the weekend. We told Jackie and he was more excited than if a circus had come to town.

"How many more sleeps before my mommy's coming?" he asked at least a hundred times in the three days that he waited for her.

And when Dr. Van Brugge's car pulled into our driveway, his dark eyes were as big as saucers.

I wanted to cry just remembering it. Or maybe it was the music. The orchestra at the end of the hall was playing the sad, melancholy melody of "I Don't Want To Walk Without You." And the notes were filled with such emotion that I could actually feel the music in my chest.

# WEDNESDAY,
## JUNE 15, 10:02 A.M.

Jack and Claire were seated in Bud's hospital room. They'd been there for three and a half hours already. Wilford had called them just after 5 a.m. to let them know that the night resident had said she thought Bud's death was imminent. They'd rushed back to the hospital as if their presence could really make a difference between life and death. He didn't look so much different than before. The grayish cast to his skin seemed more yellow now and the whoosh of oxygen into his lungs created some kind of rhythmic bass tone rattle in his throat. They sat listening. Waiting.

Jack didn't have any feeling of isolation or of being alone. He was grateful to have Claire beside him. He could have gotten through it without her, but he was finally able to acknowledge that it would have been so much more difficult.

But even the two of them weren't on their

own. In the three chairs out in the hallway family members waited with them. And in the lobby downstairs were a couple dozen more. They were there for Bud, of course. They loved and respected the old man. He was one of the few patriarchs left in their strange tribe.

Jack also understood that they were there for him. Not that he had done anything to deserve that. It had nothing to do with how successful he might or might not be. It wasn't anything he had earned by what he may or may not have done. They were there for him because he was family. And in this strange world where his father had come from, where his roots still lay, family was reason enough.

Jack shook his head thoughtfully as he realized that his life so far had been like one of those optical puzzles. Someone shows you a picture and at first glance you see it's a fish. You continue to believe it's just a fish until someone else looks at it and says, "Oh, it's a landscape" and suddenly you see it in a completely different way.

His whole life he had tried so hard to fit into the Van Brugge family. His stepfather and stepbrothers loved him and cared for him. His mother adored him, but somehow he'd always been odd man out. He felt different. He was just not like them.

His father's family were virtual strangers. He didn't know or understand them. Their curiously knit kinship and their apparent desire to live out of each other's pockets was as foreign to him as some of the strange tribes Claire had encountered in Africa. Jack didn't fit in here, either.

But now, today, with Claire at his side, he'd glimpsed the picture differently. He was not the inevitable outsider of two different family circles. He was the connection that held a long-frayed bond together. He, Jack Dempsey Crabtree III, was the living evidence that his father had existed and that he and Toni had once been in love.

Jack's own children would never know Bud and Geri, and he regretted that. And he'd never known his father, yet he now realized how much J.D. continued to be a part of his own life.

The door opened and Dr. Marchette and the R.N. on duty walked in.

Jack stood and accepted the man's handshake.

"How's it going?" the doctor asked.

Jack shrugged. "Maybe you'd better tell me."

Dr. Marchette nodded and patted him on the back. "I'd like to examine him, if you

512

and your wife could step outside for a minute . . ."

Jack offered his hand to Claire and was pleased when she clutched it tightly in her own. Once outside the door, she turned to him.

"You okay?" she asked.

"Yeah," he said. "I'm glad you're here with me, Claire."

"Me, too." She glanced down at the sketchbook in his hand. "You're working on the Quiet Pool?"

Jack nodded. "I figured out why the setting looked so familiar."

He held it up so she could look at it more closely. She studied it for only a minute.

"It's our backyard."

"Yeah, I think it is," he said.

He slipped his arm around her waist, hugging her close for a moment before they turned to the sitting area at the end of the hall. The three old aunts awaited them there, each with her own unique mobility accouterment. Aunt Sissy was wearing a bright purple muumuu. Jesse's pantsuit was a designer item from two decades previous. And Viv wore navy trousers with a blue-striped short-sleeve men's shirt.

"Is he still with us?" Sissy asked.

"Yes," Jack answered. "He's got a real bad

sound in his breathing, but he *is* still breathing."

" 'Course with that noisy equipment in there, I don't suspect you can tell how much is him and how much is the machinery," Aunt Jesse said.

Jack nodded.

"I really want to thank you for coming out here every day," he told the three. "I know that you want to be here, but I also know how difficult it is for you."

"You've come all the way from San Antonio to be here," Viv said. "It's not so much of a struggle to drive a few miles."

"Viv says that 'cause she wants to brag how she can still drive," Aunt Sissy claimed. "I have to be carted everywhere like a sad sack of feed. But I do think my kids feel fine about bringing me here. They think they can drop me off and if something happens, well, I'm already at the hospital."

"Just so they don't start feeling that way about the cemetery," Aunt Jesse joked.

The three women giggled together like girls.

Jesse reached up and took Jack's hand. "When you get our age," she said, "death doesn't have to be so dad-gummed solemn." Her words coaxed Jack into a small smile.

"When we were kids," she continued,

"Daddy stored a lot of his stuff in a place we called Coyote Canyon. It was a good-size dump and sometimes he navigated it by ropes. He'd string two ropes across, about four feet apart. He'd walk on the bottom rope and use the top one to hold on. Do you remember that?" The question was directed to her sisters.

"Lord, yes," Viv answered. "He could access the whole canyon that way. I've walked those ropes a mile or two myself."

"I know you did," Jesse answered. She turned again to Jack. "Viv was always tough and game for anything. But I was much more cautious and afraid of heights to boot. Those ropes scared me something fierce. I told Daddy I would never go across on them. And he was such a good man and so crazy about us girls, he'd never *make* us do anything. Which is why Sissy missed out on school almost completely."

"I never liked being shut into that place," she defended. "And I learned enough to get by."

"But you know, I watched Daddy and Viv and Opal and Geri and Cleata all crossing on those ropes a million times. Just like walking down the street. They did it and didn't think a thing of it. And one day, I needed to get a fender for an old Model T and I knew there was one on the south side of the canyon. It would have taken me nearly an hour to walk around and I just had more guts than I had time. I'd seen so many people I loved walk across on those ropes, so I just stepped up and made it across. It was a lot easier than I thought it would be and I never even bothered to look down."

The old woman smiled, remembering and then she gave Jack's hand a squeeze.

"That's what I think death is like," she said. "It seems like a very scary path. But once you've watched enough people go across, your turn seems less and less frightening."

All three women nodded.

"Poor old Bud has missed Geri so much," Sissy said. "It may be time to let him go."

Jack nodded. "I guess it is," he said. "Of course, it's not up to me."

"Oh, I think it probably is," Aunt Viv said.

Jesse shushed her sister and then apologized. "I told you how she is," Jesse said. "She says what she's thinking when she needs to keep her mouth shut."

Jack was confused.

"What are you thinking?" he asked Aunt Viv. "It's not a question of pulling a plug on the old man. He's not on life support."

Viv shook her head. "That's not my meaning at all," she said. "I just think . . ." She glanced over at her sisters and then looked once again at Jack. "I just think that you should kiss him goodbye and tell him that you're going to be all right and it's okay to go."

Dr. Marchette led the nurse out of Bud's room and said only a couple of words to her before coming directly to the family huddle at the end of the hallway. He didn't say anything that could be considered news. And he seemed almost apologetic about how long Bud had lingered.

"The day he arrived, I honestly didn't expect him to last the night," the doctor said. "And every morning I see him on rounds, I think it will be the last. It has to be nothing less than the will to survive that keeps him in there day after day."

Claire noted to herself that he had not talked so pessimistically at the time. She didn't know if that was revisionist history or sugarcoating for the family. But she was more inclined to go along with Aunt Viv. Bud continued to live because he still thought he had a reason to. And it very well might have something to do with Jack.

Aunt Viv was at Jack's side as he went in

517

to sit with Bud. Claire sat down with Jesse and Sissy.

"I'm so sorry Viv spoke out of turn," Jesse said. "But I agree with Viv and I sometimes think with those Crabtree men you've got to really make an effort to get them to see the obvious."

"That's for sure what Geri had to do," Sissy piped in. "She was perfect for Bud and she practically had to hit him on the head with a baseball bat to get the man's attention!"

Claire smiled.

"The thing about that," Aunt Jesse said, "is that once you've got their attention, you've got it. They're not the kind of men who are likely to stray, not Bud, not J.D., not Jack."

"And that's good," Claire said. "That's very good."

"How are you coming with the sorting of Geri's treasures?" Aunt Sissy asked. "Our whole family are a mess of pack rats, but at least Geri was good at recognizing the gold among the sawdust."

"Oh, I've found some great things," Claire told them. "I love all the old scrapbooks and photos. And the newspaper clippings tell us more about Jack's father than we ever knew."

"That's important to show to your young ones," Jesse said. "The first real sense of history a person can have is the history of their family."

Claire nodded. "And I looked through all their old record albums," she said. "I caught myself singing some old song in the shower last night."

"Geri and Bud were swell dancers," Sissy said.

Aunt Jesse agreed. "From the time he got home from the war until J.D. was born, they'd be up at the Jitterbug Lounge every weekend. They loved to dance. And they were good at it. They moved in perfect synch and were completely sure about each other. Lots of married couples would trade partners, but those two only wanted to move on the floor together."

"I think they missed it," Aunt Sissy said. "After they had J.D. and spent their weekends at home, Bud bought that record player. Those old tunes would be spinning against the needle all evening long."

"Those were good times," Aunt Jesse said. "They had a fine life. It wasn't easy and it wasn't free of troubles or heartache, but no life is. That's the secret, you know, to recognize the best times when you're living them and to have confidence that the worst times will disappear just as quickly."

"I guess Jack and I are just learning that," Claire said.

Aunt Sissy patted her on the hand. "You two are going to be just fine," she predicted. "For some couples, when trouble comes, it pulls them apart. But for others, like you and Jack, it can make you pull together."

"Thanks," Claire told her.

"But it's too bad about the medals," Sissy said. "Poor Bud was near prostrate with grief when J.D. died and angry and guilty to boot. I don't think he would have gotten rid of those military things of his if he'd been in his right mind. If he'd been thinking about Jack and Jack's children, he'd never have buried all that."

"Are you talking about that box of ribbons and such that Bud brought home from the service?" Jesse asked.

"Yes," Sissy answered. "Claire was looking for it, but I told her that Bud put it in the coffin with poor J.D. I remember that moment right now just as clear as any I've lived in my life. When Bud set that shoe box in the casket, it was as if he was sending his own heart, his very own life, to the grave with his son."

Claire considered that sadly and a brief moment of silence fell among the women.

"I have that box," Aunt Jesse said.

"What?"

Both women turned to look at her questioningly.

"I have the box," she repeated. "The one with Bud's medals."

"I saw him put it in the coffin."

Jesse nodded. "And when he'd left the church, Geri stayed behind. She had them reopen the casket and she got it out," Aunt Jesse said. "She came outside and handed it to me. She told me to take it home and not to let Bud see that I had it."

"Omigosh!" Sissy said. "You've had it all this time?"

"I took it home and put it in the top of my closet," Jesse said. "Geri never asked for it back and it's been there ever since. When she died, well, I didn't know if she'd ever told Bud, so I didn't say anything, either."

"So you don't think he knows?" Claire said.

Jesse shook her head. "I always felt very cross-purposed about the whole situation," she said. "These were Bud's things. If he wanted to bury them with his son, then he ought to be able to do that. I just felt like Geri knew that someday he'd want Jackie to have them."

"And I guess now he will," Aunt Sissy
pointed out.

# BUD

I had to keep swimming or I would drown. I had to keep swimming. I had to keep swimming. The water was dark. The water was full of sharks. I had to keep swimming.

"Flyboy! Flyboy! Wake up, you're having another dream."

For an instant I didn't know where I was. I thought I was still out in the Solomon Sea. But I was in sick bay. I was picked up by the S-class submarine *U.S.S. Perfidia* one week and three hours after *Lusty Libby* went down.

It was a miracle. I was a "goddamn miracle" the squadron commander said about it later.

The guys on the sub had seen the zero taking target practice at something and they'd cruised over to see what it was. One lone crewman bobbing on the water was not what they'd expected.

I guess that's true of life in general. It's

never what we expect. I had always known that Jackie would go home to live with his mother. Even when I secretly hoped it might not happen, I still knew it would. But when it did, it was not at all what I'd expected.

I thought I'd be sad, lonely. I thought I'd miss him. I had no idea I would go into a tailspin. I'd expected that Toni's husband would be a fairly decent fellow and would treat Jackie appropriately. The doctor, it turned out was a tremendously fine guy. He was great with Jackie from the moment they met.

"I want to be a father to him," he told me. "I want him to feel that he is my own son."

I would have thought that would make me happy. But it didn't. It made me sad. It was just what I wanted for Jackie. And none of what I wanted for myself. If Van Brugge was going to be his father, then what about J.D.? What about me? I managed not to voice my own selfishness about it, but it was a burden to me.

At first Toni called us every few weeks. We'd talk to Jackie on the phone and listened to all that was going on in his life. It all sounded good. He loved his new home, he'd started kindergarten. He was happy. He was settling in. It was exactly what we wanted. And yet, I just felt sick about it. Though, that wasn't so rare — I felt sick most of the time.

The dreams, the water dreams, had never really gone away, and after Jackie left, they returned with a vengeance. I suffered a lot with them when J.D. went overseas and after he died. But they had eased up a good bit. Once a month I'd wake up screaming. A guy could live with that. Especially if he slept only during the day and he had a wife who was understanding. But after Jackie left, it was every day. Every time I fell asleep. Every minute I closed my eyes. I couldn't stand it and I began to try just staying awake. I would stay awake for days on end and then collapse into near unconsciousness, the kind of sleep a guy could hardly wake from. Still the dreams would come.

My body was too old to put that kind of pressure on it. I started catching every germ that neared my neighborhood. I got every cold, every flu, one winter I got strep throat twice. Then there were the eye infections, the unexplained fevers, kidney pains and heart palpitations. On the job I spent more time on sick leave than I did showing up.

"Maybe it's time for you to think about retiring?" my boss suggested. "You've got enough time to do that, don't you?"

So I retired and then I had nothing. No job, no son, no grandson, no life.

"You can't just lay around here and watch TV all day, all night," Geri complained. "If you keep this up you'll be dead in five years."

"I've been dead since 1943," I told her. "Just leave me alone."

Geri being Geri could never do that. She pushed and prodded and nagged. She expanded the flower garden and painted the house and reorganized the kitchen. And naturally, she expected me to do most of the heavy work. She dragged me out to the hippie commune, having told them that I'd help them change over from a septic tank to a lagoon system sewer. And she volunteered me to help turn the old Ford dealership building into a senior citizens center.

Geri made sure I kept busy. And being busy helps pass the time, makes the years go by. But it doesn't make you feel better and it didn't help me sleep.

"Bud, you've got to snap out of this," Geri pleaded with me. "You got to try to get on with your life."

"Why should I?" I asked her.

"Because it was part of our bargain," she answered. "All those years ago. I kept care of your mother so you could go see the world. I did that, Bud. I did it because I wanted to have a life with you. You're the only man I've ever cared about. And when you don't care about yourself, it's the same as not caring about me."

The new senior's center held a Valentine's dance on a Tuesday night at the Jitterbug Lounge. Of course, it wasn't the Jitterbug Lounge anymore, now they called it Boot Scooters Dance Hall, but it was the same old place it had always been. Geri insisted that we go. I groused about it all afternoon and then all the way there. I refused to wear a suit and insisted I looked good enough for Catawah in a white shirt and suspenders. We went inside and the place reminded me of a prom. The ladies had decorated it in cardboard hearts and crepe paper streamers. Up in the bandstand the musicians in their white sport coats were as old as we were. They knew all of our songs and played "Stardust" and "I'll Be Seeing You" and "Stormy Weather."

From the moment we walked through the door, Geri wanted to dance. She didn't ask me directly. She was tapping her foot and swaying to the music. I left her alone and stood over by the bar just to be contrary. The ladies had laid out a variety of cookies and such on the bar. And the only drinks being served were soft drinks and lemonade. I found an empty bar stool and seated myself for the duration. I was tired. I was cranky. I was determined to be a stick in the mud.

Geri should have danced with someone else. Several guys came up and asked her. I watched her smile and thank them and shake her head. I knew my Geri. If she wasn't dancing with me, she wasn't dancing at all.

"Hey, Bud, how you doing these days?"

I turned to see Piggy Masterson. He looked just like he always did. Except of course that his hair now only grew around the rim of the back of his head. And his nose had somehow taken on unreasonably sized dimensions. Piggy took the stool next to me. He had a paper plate loaded up with chips and cookies and chunks of cheese. He had a coffee mug that he set on the bar. Even from a distance of four feet away, I knew he was drinking bourbon.

"I'm doing fine," I answered, not willing to claim the truth. "I'm retired now, just living the life of Riley."

Piggy sighed and shook his head. "I wish I could retire," he said. "What in the devil do I make money for if I don't get a stinking chance to go off and spend a dime of it."

"I thought your son-in-law was running the business now," I said.

"That numb-nut pinhead? I wouldn't trust him to clean my toilet, let alone run my dealership. I just let him work there to try to keep Melinda on my good side."

I didn't comment on that, but inside my mind I was remembering when J.D. said that Piggy didn't think he was good enough for his daughter. Piggy got just exactly what he deserved to my way of thinking, and I couldn't help but feel a tiny bit smug about it.

Myra Tobin walked up to us. I was surprised to see her. Her dress was too short and too tight and she was too young to even be at this function.

"Pig," she said, "if you're not dancing with me, I'm finding another partner."

"Go ahead, honey, have fun," he answered, as if giving her permission.

She walked away in a bit of a huff.

"What's that about?" I asked him.

He shrugged. "The gal is angling to be my fourth wife," he said. "I'm mostly resisting when I think about it."

I gave that a small chuckle.

"Your Geri sure looks pretty tonight," he said.

I followed the direction of his gaze. Geri

did look good. She'd never been a true beauty, but she was always attractive with that slim figure and the defiant chin. She was a woman who went out in the world and got what she wanted. It was hard not to admire that about her.

"You know," Piggy said, wrapping his arm around my shoulders. "I envy you. You found a woman who loves you. Not when you buy her things or take her places or do what she wants. She loves you all the time. Do you know how rare that is?"

The man was practically up in my face by then and the booze was strong enough to nearly knock me over.

"What in hell did you ever do to deserve that?" Piggy asked me.

I didn't have an answer. But I did think about it and a few minutes later after Piggy was gone and I was there all alone, I got up from the bar stool and walked across the room.

"Hey, Crazy Girl, you want to dance?"

As always with my wife, there were no recriminations, no tit for tat. She always found a way to forgive me, even when I couldn't manage to say "I'm sorry." Apologies weren't necessary, but I made one anyway. Not for leaving her a wallflower, but for everything else.

"I spend too much time thinking about all I've lost," I admitted. "And not nearly enough time on all that I still have."

She smiled up at me. "Well, at least you finally noticed," she teased.

"I would never have made it this far without you, Geri," I told her.

"You and I will just go on together," she said. "We still have each other and that's a lot, you know."

"Yes, I know."

"Bud, the only thing that I've ever really wanted was a happy life with you," she said. "I miss my son. I miss my grandson. I hate what that awful war did to you. But I can't let those things cheat me out of everything that I have. I've decided that I'm going to be happy, and like it or not, you're stuck with me, so you're just going to have to be happy, too."

I laughed at her joke, but I knew that she was also speaking truth.

"I haven't been able to give you much, Geri," I told her. "But I'll try my dangest to give you this."

I pulled her tightly into my arms.

"Bud, you're holding me too close," she whispered.

"Are you afraid the old ladies will gossip?" I asked.

She laughed. "More likely they'll all turn green with envy."

In the months that followed, I really did try harder to be happy. With the arrival of spring, I moved my sleeping camp back out to the garden and got by better that way.

During the summer, Jackie came up for the weekend with his family. Toni was expecting a new baby and Dr. Van Brugge was obviously delighted. But it was clear that he cared about Jackie and included him in everything.

"I don't want Jack to ever feel like he's not a part of our family," Toni told me. "Every boy needs a father and I'd like for Jack to think of Ernst as his."

That seemed like a reasonable consideration. J.D. would have wanted what was best for Jackie. He would not have allowed selfishness to stand in the way of that. Geri and I talked it over and decided that we would support her decision. We made a determined effort not to even speak J.D.'s name. Of course, having to guard our words around the boy created a strange wall between us. Geri and I could both see it, we both wanted to overcome it, but somehow we were never able to breach it.

In the fall a new doctor arrived in Catawah. Geri liked the young man, Dr. Williams, and trusted him. I was still struggling with my health so she insisted I go see him.

He looked me over head to toe, had enough blood drawn out of me to please a vampire and inquired in detail about my eating and drinking habits. I answered as best I could. Then out of the blue it seemed, he asked the question that nobody ever asked.

"How are you sleeping?"

I hesitated long enough that the man raised his eyes up from the paper he was writing on to look at me.

I was tempted to lie. If I just said, "Fine," that would be the end of it. I wouldn't even have to lie, I could say, "Same as always." Which would be the truth and have the same result as a lie. But I didn't do either of those things.

"I don't sleep unless I just have to," I admitted. "And then I don't sleep well."

He raised an eyebrow and set his clipboard on his lap and waited for me to explain myself.

"I'm troubled by dreams," I said. "I have been ever since the war."

"How often do you have these dreams?"

"Pretty often."

"Have you ever talked to anyone about them?"

I shrugged. "I talked with the flight sur-geon when I was still in the service."

"And what did he say?"

"Learn to live with it," I answered.

"Have you?"

"Well, I haven't committed hara-kiri, so I'd call that some level of success." I chuck-led at my own joke.

He nodded, but he wasn't smiling. "I'd like to refer you to somebody," he said.

"I'm not big on headshrinkers," I told him.

"They've learned a lot about this in the last few years," he told me. "I think he might be able to help you. At the very least, he can tell you more about what you're liv-ing with."

I wasn't too keen on the idea, but I was curious so I agreed. The fellow he sent me to was in Oklahoma City, which was a heck of a long drive to just sit and talk for an hour. I had my doubts about doing it. But after the first couple of visits, I found myself looking forward to it. It was such a relief to be able to say things that were in my head.

"The weirdest thing is that it's always about the water," I told the man. "I see it all exactly as it was and it's always the water."

The psychiatrist nodded without com-ment.

"Now that time in the water, that was bad," I admitted. "It was bad and scary and I gave up hope of living. But it wasn't the worst thing that happened during the war. I saw so many worse things. The years after that when we were taking those islands, my God, it was a damned slaughter day in, day out. I saw things that no human ought to ever put his eyes on. I never dream about any of that. It's always the water."

"What do you think was the difference in you, before the water and after?"

I hesitated.

"I don't know if I can explain this where it makes any sense to anyone else," I said.

"Just say it how you feel it and we'll try to sort it out," he said.

"It was like I died out in the water," I told him. "I gave up hope of being saved. I no longer cared about living. I decided to go ahead and die. If I'd been able to get that rusty latch undone on my life vest, I'd be bones scattered on the bottom of the ocean right now."

"But you're not," he said. "You're here."

I shrugged. "They pulled me out, but I'd already made my peace with death. Living had lost its value to me. When I got back to my squad, I realized what a great fighter that made me. It was like being a kamikaze

535

day after day after day. If you're already dead, then you can't be killed and those who can't be killed never hesitate."

"So you took your living nightmare and adapted it into a positive force — that's laudable self-preservation."

"Yes," I said. "I guess you could say it saved me. But it killed my son."

The doctor didn't say anything, he just waited in silence for me to say it myself.

"J.D. thought I was a hero. He thought I'd done all the things I'd done because I was brave and noble, and that I was willing to sacrifice myself for freedom and country. I let him believe that of me. He admired me and wanted to be like me. That got him killed."

The two of us sat for a few minutes letting the feel of those words soak in. Finally the doctor spoke.

"Let's say a man is walking by a house and hears a child screaming and looks up to see smoke billowing out of the window. He doesn't stop to think about what might be happening in the house, whether the fire has reached the roof or how dangerous the smoke might be. He rushes into the house to save the crying child."

"That man's a hero," I said.

"Are you sure?" the psychiatrist asked.

"What if that man was just coming from his doctor and had been told he had an inoperable brain tumor and that he only had six weeks to live? Would that make his action any different?"

I shrugged. "It might have made it easier to go into the house," I said.

"But it was the same act, the same heroic act," the shrink said. "And the child was saved, the man's motive or his future or lack of it meant nothing to that child, only the man's actions."

"Yeah, I guess so."

"Heroes are defined by heroic acts, not by the emotional baggage behind those acts," he said. "You are a genuine hero. There is nothing you can do to change that."

"But what about my son?" I asked.

"I am so sorry about your son," he said. "I can see why he wanted to be like you. And from what you've told me about the fire fight he died in, he managed to do that. Do you think that after seven months in Vietnam he hadn't learned as much about war as you knew? Give him some credit. He did what he did for the same kind of reason that propelled you forward. He made peace with death, too. He just didn't get a second chance to act upon it."

I continued to see the psychiatrist for the

better part of a year. I'm not saying the man cured me. He had me do relaxation techniques that helped me sleep better. The dreams still came, but I learned that they weren't really dreams, they were just stark memories. Knowing that's what they were and that they were in the past, helped somehow.

Geri and I continued to be happy on a day-by-day basis. Our ties with Jack got fewer and fewer. When he brought his new wife to meet us we were delighted. She seemed like she would be good for him. And we had hope that now he was grown, we could be closer. It didn't really work out that way, but we were happy for him. We bragged about him to friends and family and anyone who would listen.

"Our grandson, Jack, has a lovely wife."

"Our grandson, Jack, has a very successful business."

"Our grandson, Jack, has a beautiful, healthy daughter."

"Our grandson, Jack, is now the father of twins!"

Of course, we wished they lived closer and we could be more involved in their lives, but we weren't alone in that. A lot of our friends were in the same boat. That we lived long enough to *know* our grandchildren was probably gift enough.

When Geri died, Jack came home to stand beside me at the funeral. I was so empty, so at a loss, I couldn't even think of a word to say to him. Geri had always kept our conversation going. Without her, I found myself speechless, even among the people I loved.

And now I was here in the hospital myself. This crazy hospital with all the loud dance music. It seemed especially loud today. Then strangely, I felt a warm hand clasp mine.

"Grandpa Bud? Grandpa Bud, it's me, Jack."

It felt so good to hear his voice, his very human voice and the one most dear to me on earth.

"I just want you to know that I love you," he said to me. "I love you and I appreciate all the time that we had together. I wish we had more time, but I know you miss Grandma Geri. If you want to go to her, I understand. I just wanted to say goodbye."

*Goodbye,* I tried to say, but my lips and tongue and the breath in my lungs would not cooperate. *Goodbye, Jack, I'll miss you.*

# Saturday, June 18, 3:30 P.M.

Bud's funeral was held in McKiever's *Iglesia de Jesus*. The family section of the church was full to bursting with every Shertz relative in attendance. Jack was glad to have his own family, as well. Claire was at his side, and Toni and Ernst had driven up bringing the children with them. None of the kids had ever been to a funeral before, but they all behaved well through the songs and the eulogies, and at the ceremony at the cemetery where the American Legion did honors and folded the flag, which they handed to Jack.

Afterward the twins went racing off with their cousins, but Jack got the chance to show Zaidi his father's headstone.

"So you didn't know him at all," Zaidi said.

Jack shook his head. "No, I didn't get a chance," he answered. "Just like you didn't get a chance to know Grandpa Bud. But sometimes, even when you never get to know people, you can still know them through the people that they loved. So I know my father through the love that my mother and my grandparents had for him. And you can know my grandparents through the love I have for them."

Zaidi thought about that for a moment and then nodded.

"Cool," she said.

The community did a huge outdoor dinner at the house. It was ostensibly for the family, but in Catawah, a lot of people were part of the family, or were married to people in the family, or felt as close as family. A huge crowd showed up. Car after car parked up and down the street and every visitor brought a pie or a salad or a bean casserole.

Nearly all of these people had a story they wanted to tell about Bud. And Jack found himself learning more about the old man in death than he'd ever known in life.

Jack and Claire were the center of attention among the crowds of friends and relatives. They spent most of the afternoon shaking hands, meeting people and thanking everyone. There were the townspeople who'd been friends of the Crabtrees all their lives. There were professional people in the recycling industry who had known Bud and

Geri through their volunteer work. And the guys in the veterans organizations, who knew Bud from his war record. There were even members of the Stark family who claimed to be relatives. Though Cousin Reba made a point of telling him that the Shertz family didn't claim any kinship to them and warned Jack to keep his distance. Jack shook hands with a tall, robust man of about sixty. "I'm Lester Andeel," he said. "Bud and my dad were best friends in high school. My parents and Bud and Geri had a double wedding. That was the first time they got married."

Jack laughed. "You know I didn't even hear the two weddings story until a couple of days ago," he said.

"Yes, the four of them ran off to Arkansas on graduation night," Lester said. "My father was killed in WWII, but my mother stayed a friend to Geri and Bud all her life. She always bragged that she was the only person in Catawah who had been at both their weddings."

"There's so many things about my grandparents that I'm just finding out about," Jack admitted.

But he also learned some things about his father, as well. A very lovely older woman tugged on his sleeve.

"You're Jack, right?"

"Yes, ma'am," he answered.

"Oh, don't call me ma'am, it makes me sound like I'm a thousand years old. I'm Melinda," she said. "Melinda Carson, I used to be Melinda Masterson."

"It's nice to meet you, Melinda," Jack said. "Thank you for coming."

"I was your father's steady girlfriend in high school," she announced.

"Really?"

She nodded. "He was such a good guy," she said. "He looked a lot like Geri, but he was kind and decent and honorable, just like Bud. I miss them both."

"Thank you."

A few moments later Jack felt Claire come up next to him and he slid his arm around her waist. He felt stronger with her at his side.

The aunts were all there, sitting in the shade, talking, joking reminiscing. They waved the couple over. Jack and Claire worked their way in that direction. As always the three were unique. Jesse was wearing a classic business suit. Aunt Sissy's dress was blousy and unfitted. And Aunt Viv had on a three-piece man's suit with an actual watch fob hanging out of the vest.

Aunt Jesse handed Jack a worn and faded

pale green shoe box.

"I decided I'd better bring these to you today, in case I'm the one in the casket at the next one of these shindigs."

Her tone was light, but the whole day had been that way. Jack could not imagine a more upbeat funeral than the one they'd shared. It was all about the celebration of life and almost nothing about the sadness of loss.

"Is this the military stuff?" he asked. He would have peeked inside, but he saw that it was taped up.

Aunt Jesse nodded. "Geri had me save that for you," she said. "So now you'll need to save it for your children."

"We'll do that," Jack said. "I promise."

After a few more moments of conversation, other people came over and Jack and Claire moved away. They were walking toward the house when Jack suddenly stopped in his tracks.

"What?" Claire asked him.

"Come with me," he said.

He made their way across the yard as quickly as they could without being rude to any of the people who greeted them. Once inside the wood shop, Jack closed the door, ensuring their privacy.

On the table was the treasure box. It was

near completion, both the bottom section and the top had been completed and the locations for the lid hinges had been drilled. Jack had put the first coat of oil on the wood, but it would need several more after it dried.

He tested it for tackiness and was satisfied that it wasn't sticky.

"I think I figured it out," he told her.

Jack took the shoe box that Jesse had given him and slipped it inside the treasure box. It was an exact fit.

"Oh, wow," Claire said. "Your dad wasn't building anything for the treasures under the bed — he was making this specifically for the medals."

Jack nodded. "That must have been why Bud never finished it," he said. "He must have realized what it was for when he looked at the boards. Since he didn't have the stuff anymore, he didn't see any reason to finish the box. But he couldn't make it into anything else, either."

"This is where they belonged all the time," Claire said.

Jack nodded.

# BUD

It was the music that awakened me. If anything, it seemed even louder than it had been before. It was a couple of minutes before I realized it was because that breathing machine was not whistling anymore. I tried to see why and to my surprise my eyes opened right up. I had been too exhausted to even lift the lids for days. Now I could see the room with perfect clarity. Small, beige and maroon with two chairs, one by the bed and one by the window.

I could see myself, as well. All the wires and leads, all the needles and tubes and those terrible restraints that had kept me fastened to the bed, all of that was gone.

I sat up in bed. I felt fine. I didn't even feel light-headed.

Where was everybody? For almost the whole time I'd been here, I'd always had the sense that there was somebody with me in the room. But there was nobody here now. I sat there for a few minutes, listening to the music and waiting for somebody to come in so that I could tell them I was awake.

When nobody came, I decided to get up. I gingerly put my feet on the floor, but found there was no weakness in them. I didn't have my stick to lean on, but found that after a couple of steps, I didn't even need it.

At the doorway, I looked out.

"Hey, is anybody there?" I called out.

I didn't see a soul. And I doubted that anyone could hear me over the band that sounded a lot like Sammy Kaye doing a rousing rendition of "Daddy Swing and Sway." I glanced to the left toward the end of the hallway and there was a door. It looked vaguely familiar, but what captured my attention was the colored lights that gleamed in that direction. That's where the music was coming from. I shook my head with disbelief. Good grief, why would they have a nightclub in a hospital. It was the craziest thing I'd ever heard of in my life.

I headed down that way. I could hear laughter inside, so at least there would be someone to tell me where the nurses might be.

As soon as I stepped past the door into the anteroom, I recognized the place. It was the Jitterbug Lounge. I'd been in this place five hundred times and it was as familiar to me as my own name. But how could it be here? I didn't try to answer the question. I just walked inside.

I stood for a moment, watching the dancers, listening to the band. It was so familiar and yet there was a luster to it, a warmth and a thrill that I had never quite experienced. I felt young and strong again, young and strong and eager to dance.

"Dad!"

I heard the voice and turned toward it.

"Dad, you made it," he said.

I couldn't believe my eyes but there he was standing right in front of me, looking young and strong and exactly as I remembered him.

"J.D.?"

"Yeah, it's me," he said. "It's really me."

He wrapped his arms around me in a bear hug and the feel of it was like a flood of molten joy that poured all inside me and burnt away every whit of sadness and anger and disappointment I'd carried in me.

"Oh, J.D., oh, J.D., I've missed you," I said. "I've missed you."

"We're together now," he said.

Deliberately I pulled away from him. "J.D., there are things that I've wanted to say," I began. "I have such regrets. There are things that I should have told you and I never did."

"Dad, it's okay," he assured me. "It's okay. I know. I know everything."

"You know everything?"

He nodded.

"Do you forgive me?"

"There is nothing to forgive," he said. "But there is plenty to talk about. And now there's no reason why we can't talk about all of it."

"No, no, I guess there's not."

"But later," he said. "Right now, I'm going to duck out of this place. All this old fogey music, it's not really my scene."

He laughed and I found myself laughing with him.

"Besides," he said, "there's somebody waiting out there for you."

I glanced toward the dance floor. It was a mix of couples, lots of G.I.s in uniform and girls with bouncy hair and seams in their stockings. I didn't see anyone I really recognized. Then a girl caught my eye. She had her back to me. She wasn't dancing, she was just standing there. She was small and delicate and looked especially fine in a red pencil skirt with only a tiny row of kick pleats near the hem. Her dark brown hair had been twisted and primped into a thousand loosened pin curls. Her legs were not so long, but they were well-shaped and the calves tapered attractively to her ankles and the straps on her perilously high heels.

There was something so familiar about her. And I was really enjoying just watching her watch the dancers. When the music ended it was as if I were holding my breath. She applauded the band and then she turned in my direction.

From across a distance of a half dozen yards our eyes met instantly and I'm sure my jaw must have dropped open.

My rational mind made no decision to go to her, but my arms and legs acted upon instinct. A second later she leaped into my arms and I was pressing my face in her soft, sweet-smelling hair.

"Crazy Girl, my crazy girl!" I said over and over again.

"Bud, oh, Bud, I'm so glad to see you," she told me.

"Geri, I love you so much," I answered. "I know I haven't said that enough. But I've been so sorry that I didn't say it to you more."

She laughed. "I love you, too," she told me. "And as for your faults in the past, well now it seems you'll have eternity to make it up to me."

She was teasing me as she feigned toughness and raised that defiant chin I knew so well.

The musicians struck up another catchy tune.

"Dance with me," she said. "I've been waiting so long and I just don't want to dance with anybody but you."

I pulled her in my arms and we moved across the floor. We were as good together as we'd ever been and better than I even remembered. The sultry blond vocalist at the microphone sang the words that were in my heart. "You're the one who made my dreams come true. And when the angels ask me to recall the thrill of it all, I will tell them I remember you."

# ABOUT THE AUTHOR

Librarian **Pamela Morsi** once asked herself what she would do if she ever won the lottery. She decided, given the chance, that she would spend her time writing fiction. Now, years later, she is still waiting to win the lottery, but *Last Dance at Jitterbug Lounge* is her twentieth published novel. Pam lives in San Antonio, Texas, with her husband and daughter.